FISHING

"Leggo!" yelled Black Jack Finley, from the boat. *"Leggo the rod!"*

If the guide thought Bayles was going to give up the tarpon now, after fighting it for so long, he was very much mistaken.

The water around Bayles started to boil. The tarpon leaped from the spume not a yard from his face, blood streaming from its gills. Before it hit the water a much larger thing emerged from the white froth and seized the fish.

Cold, unblinking eyes. Alien eyes.

Shark a primitive corner of Bayles' mind screamed *shark*!

Trying to back up in the mud, he slipped and went under. He tried to claw his way to the surface, seeking air and light, his brain filled with the desire to live.

Something gripped him around the waist, an unbearable tightness, and then he was out of the water, being lifted into the thin blue sky, into the daylight.

He never knew what happened next.

WILLIAM R. DANTZ

HUNGER

TOR

A TOM DOHERTY ASSOCIATES BOOK
NEW YORK

**For Lynn,
dive buddy and mate.**

HUNGER

A Tor Book
Published by Tom Doherty Associates, Inc.
175 Fifth Avenue
New York, N.Y. 10010

Tor® is a registered trademark of Tom Doherty Associates, Inc.

ISBN: 0-812-51957-4

First edition: June 1992

Printed in the United States of America

0 9 8 7 6 5 4 3 2 1

Day One

1

Starry, Starry Night

THE TIDE CHANGES. Warm currents bring the scent of running shrimp from somewhere Outside. In the glistening dark the creatures stir, moving effortlessly through the shallow waters, heading for the chain-link barricade that encloses the lagoon.

Swimming as one, the beautiful, the six-partnered.

The creatures do not feed on shrimp. Shrimp are much too small, unworthy of the hunt. But sometimes a school of amberjack follow the shrimp, surging through small gaps in the barricade, and these succulent Others make a good kill.

It is not simple hunger that compels the response. The creatures fed earlier, snapping at the dead cut-fish dumped into the lagoon by the Others. Hunger is appeased, for now. But the amberjack, if they come, will make freshkill, and freshkill is always better.

Freshkill.

The creatures anticipate the jaw-feel, the shuddering fear-texture of freshkill. Stimulated by the rich, evocative scent of shrimp, they swim in precise formation, six together, riding their own slipstreams, surging to the barricades.

A chain-link net extends from the corral bottom to a height ten feet above sea level. Beyond the chain barricade is Outside—whatever it is that lies beyond the lagoon.

The creatures sense some of what is out there. Outside seems to be a kind of vast surge tide, a place from which the cool currents flow, bringing the mingled smells of many Others. Small Others, big Others. Others so distant and so smell-strange that the creatures cannot make a dream picture to go along with the scent.

Outside, the creatures sense, Outside there is unlimited freshkill—and unlimited fear. They sense fear as a pressure, a pulse-ripple in the water that moves like a low-voltage tickle along the lengths of their powerful bodies.

The fear is good. Fear is a stimulant, a flavor.

The creatures pause at the barricade, riding the tide change, soaking up the smell-picture. The shrimp are close, frantic in the shallow water, kicking up spumes of mud and sand and fear-stink as they are pursued by gorging predators.

The creatures begin to sing to each other. A song of shrimp and snapping amberjack. The high-pitched whistles that mark each creature as part of the Us.

Us, the six-partnered, the mighty, the powerful, the beautiful. Us, the lovers of freshkill.

Us.

An hour passes.

The creatures sing, rest, swim tight patterns at the barricade: all part of the waiting. At last an arm of the great shrimp migration breaks away from the main channel and the phosphorescent froth of tiny Others begins to pour through the chain link. Thousands of tiny facets of light, the red-point glow of the shrimp eyes.

The big creatures shiver. Their motions quicken.

Soon, they sing to each other. *It comes soon. Be wary. Be ready.* A school of amberjack, driven mad with feeding frenzy, crashes into the chain link. A number of jacks slip through narrow gaps in the coral bottom, enter the lagoon, and resume their frenzied, snapping pursuit of the shrimp.

Now, the creatures sing. *Now.*

They move as one, synchronized. Herding the formation of amberjack, cutting the prey away from the dim glow of the numberless shrimp. Singing, feeling, sensing. Working as one. Alive to each of the Us, and to the delicious fear now radiating from the amberjack.

The jacks, some fifty or so fish, huddle together. They too move as one, searching for an opening. Sensing the great dark shapes that gather, cutting off all horizons, narrowing the world. The danger-shapes seem to be everywhere, but the amberjack, who have been hunted before, know that only the weakest of them will be taken.

This is what ten million years of instinct tells them.

The jacks are mistaken. None will survive.

The danger-shapes, circling in perfect harmony, suddenly close in for the kill. And then the great jaws thrust open and the cold eyes are lidded and the pulse of water and death is as close as six hearts beating.

A moment later a few stray bits of bone and viscera drift to the coral bottom. The amberjack are gone, consumed.

Freshkill, the creatures sing as they glide through the tidewarmth of the night. *Freshkill is good.*

Just before dawn the Walking Others return. They stand on the floating pier, elongated in the dark surface reflection. Some of them hold hurtsticks. The Us are familiar with the pain of the hurtsticks, and therefore wary. They sense some other, greater danger—a danger that has been building for many days now, many nights. A subtle, troubling change in the routine of life in the lagoon.

It makes them uneasy, skittish.

Now the False Singing begins. This is an irritating noise the Walking Others put in the water. The noise of the False Singing means food will be dumped into the lagoon—more of the cutfish—but this time, their bellies bloated with amberjack, their instincts screaming *danger*, the Us creatures keep their distance.

Cutfish splash into the water. The Us react by circling out to the edges of the lagoon.

Ignore the noise, they sing to each other. *Ignore the cutfish.*

Another noise begins. The whir of a propeller as the white-bottomed chase boat pulls away from the floating pier.

The Walking Others are in the boat. The creatures see, through slightly blurred eyes, that the Others brandish hurtsticks.

Danger, the creatures sing. *Pain.*

The chase boat draws near.

Flee, the creatures sing. *Flee.*

Within the confines of the man-made lagoon, the chase boat cannot exceed twenty knots or so. The creatures are capable of almost twice that speed for short bursts. And it will require all of this power and speed to get a ton of muscle and teeth and cartilage airborne.

Fly, they sing. *Fly.*

And they do. They fly, all six of the Us, in great glistening arcs, clearing the chain link by perfect inches and slipping into the open sea beyond the barricade.

Free, they sing, tasting the song. *Free Free Free.*

Behind the barricade, a boat churns in aimless circles as the first pale streaks of sunrise illuminate the empty lagoon.

"Son of a bitch!" the Other curses, waving his hurtstick. "Son of a goddamn bitch!"

2

First Encounter

THE DIVE BOAT *Wild Child* dropped its hook in a patch of white sand a hundred yards from the reef. The water was so clear the boat's shadow was visible on the bottom, forty feet below. Sally, lithe and tanned in her lemon-yellow one-piece, threw a loop over the bow chock and held the line as Tom backed the boat down, setting the anchor flukes in the soft coral sand. He watched as she expertly released the line, leaving *Wild Child* with just enough scope to hold against the current and still be safely clear of the reef.

Looking good, Tom thought.

He meant the anchorage, the boat, and Sally herself. Squint a little and she didn't look a day older than the college girl he'd married, with that lean, compact swimmer's body and the thick, shoulder-length curls of sunbleached auburn hair sprouting from around her visor. That thin, french-cut swimsuit of hers made him want to reach out and . . .

Snap out of it, man, you're working here.

Tom rang down the diesel and in the sudden silence heard the bright chatter of his passengers.

"Hey! Manta ray!"

The charter was a party of five from a New Jersey dive club. One of them, a paunchy guy wearing a bikini swimsuit and a Key West salvage medallion around his fleshy, sunburned neck, was leaning over the side, pointing excitedly. "There's a manta down there," he said with an air of self-importance.

From his position in the wheelhouse Tom could see the characteristic puff of sand left by a small ray on the move. Disturbed by the thump of the anchor, it veered gracefully away, a strange and beautiful thing blending itself into a nearby formation of turtle grass.

Sally had come down off the forward deck to check out the sighting. Now she leaned over the rail and announced, "*Dasyatis americana.* Also known as the southern stingray. Very common in shallow water."

"Looked like a manta to me," the diver insisted.

Tom saw the way Sally's smile tightened and thought, *Be nice, Sal, these are paying customers. And customers are always right even when they're wrong.*

Sally glanced up at the wheelhouse, shook her head. *I'll be good*, her look implied. She turned to the diver. "Maybe you're right. Could have been a small manta."

"You said stingray. Do they sting?" The question came from a young, anorexically thin woman who was donning her dive gear, her slender fingers plucking nervously at her mask strap.

"No sting unless you step on the spiny spot," Sally assured her. "And you won't be walking barefoot on the bottom, so not to worry."

The man with the salvage medallion remained fo-

cused on Sally. "I don't see any coral heads," he
said stubbornly. "You promised coral heads."

Time to intercede, Tom decided.

He swooped down from the wheelhouse, clapped
the man on the back. Amiable but firm. "The reef is
over there," he said, gesturing. "More coral heads
than you can count. Elkhorn and fan coral, too. We
keep our promises, Ted."

"Theo. I prefer Theo."

"You got it, Theo. Okay, folks, let's check off the
equipment list, shall we? I know you're all certified,
but let's do it by the book."

A waste of time, the guy with the medallion complained. Time was money, he added, his tone ag-
grieved.

Tom gave him a big, reassuring grin. "You're
right, Theo. We'll check you out first, how about
that?"

"Okay, I guess."

Five minutes later Tom had the party in the water,
kicking toward the reef. He was not surprised to
discover that the know-it-all from New Jersey swam
like a ruptured duck.

Sally climbed up into the wheelhouse and took
the first watch, keeping track of five blaze-orange
buoyancy vests.

Six, counting Tom.

She adjusted her sun visor, applied zinc oxide to
her nose and lips, and smiled to herself. Look at
Thomas J. Hart, herding his little group of divers.
She's been married to the big lug for fifteen years—
since they were kids, really—and it never ceased to
amaze her how Tom managed to keep his good humor when dealing with obvious assholes like Mr.
Medallion.

They were full partners in the dive business—she
was a licensed charter-boat captain, just like her

husband—but it was easier to let Tom play skipper
while she crewed. Dive parties wanted a show, a
line of salty chatter, and Tom was best at that part.
Go with your strength. Sally's expertise was in finding and identifying the reef life, as the dive party
would discover in about thirty minutes, when Tom
took the second topside watch and Sally coaxed
Merlin out of his little cave.

It was routine now, if diving the last living reef in
the continental United States was ever routine. Certainly the customers had become routine. It was un-
fair, but she couldn't help seeing them as personality
types: the eager beavers, the macho posers, the neo-
phytes who gulped their air. Sometimes you got the
shy ones who marveled at the world beneath the
water and shared a sense of wonder—the shy ones
were fun. Like the girl who had been frightened of
stingrays. Get her under for a little while, let her feel
her way around, she'd be treating that little ray like
a pet poodle.

Sally stretched out on her canvas deck chair, made
herself comfortable. A quick head count, everybody
accounted for. Reaching into the waterproof bag she
kept in the wheelhouse, she withdrew her dog-eared
copy of Jackson's *Morphology of Aquatic Mammals*.
Glancing up now and then to keep an eye out for
blaze-orange buoyancy control vests, she began to
study the text, making notes in the margin.

What a way to make a living, she thought. Sunbathing at the reef with an interesting book and the
prospect of a cooling dive. Not to mention the gift
of having a partner who still looked at her with heat
in his sky-blue eyes. Life was perfect, she decided.

Well, almost perfect.

Tom knew right away that something was wrong.
With visibility as good as this, the reef should have
been swarming with fish. The schools of yellowtail,

parrotfish, angels, triggers, the resident posse of barracuda—they all seemed to have vanished. There were stray specimens here and there—a few grunts, a small Nassau grouper he'd never seen in the vicinity, a couple of skittish snapper who cruised uneasily along the fringes of the reef—but nothing like the abundance he'd come to expect.

His five charges were entering the coral formations. Shallow canyons cut by tide and weather, these areas were usually so rich with life that inexperienced divers sometimes complained about visibility being inhibited—too many fish. No problem with *that* today. Of course the coral shapes were as beautiful as ever, and those who had never before explored the Florida reef sanctuary might be too awed to notice the paucity of tropical fin life.

No such luck with call-me-Theo. He'd come up bitching, that one. Tom recognized him as a chronic complainer, the type who could ruin any kind of social gathering, from a cookout party to a fancy restaurant dinner. Nothing would ever be good enough for *that* guy.

Prepared for a barrage of complaints—you *promised* angelfish!—Tom decided to concentrate on locating Big Ben, the giant spotted grouper who never strayed more than a hundred yards from this section of the reef.

Show them Ben, at four hundred pounds or so, and maybe even Theo wouldn't have the nerve to demand his money back.

Orienting himself by a familiar formation of fan coral, Tom finned his way slowly along the bottom, breathing easily to conserve his air. He considered this section of reef to be his own backyard. The shallow canyon deepened here to a hole about sixty feet from the surface. This area of cooler water and shimmering shadows was Big Ben's "castle," so named by Sally because the surrounding coral cliffs were like storybook ramparts.

Ben frequently parked himself in one particular spot and waited with massive patience, ready to inhale any small prey that strayed too close. Never exerting himself because visiting humans often brought him chunks of freshly cut bait. Countless divers had had their pictures taken with the giant grouper.

If this section of the reef had a celebrity, Ben was it. You could *count* on the big guy.

Tom released buoyancy and drifted down into the hole, through the ramparts of the castle, aware of passing through the thermal incline as the cooler, deeper water came over his bare arms and legs. Get this deep for long, you'd want the full wet suit. Hands trailing at his sides, he descended at a steady rate, kicking smoothly, taking his time. Never rush a dive, never rush an ascension—two of his rules to live by.

Halfway down the ramparts he became aware that something was different. Was his mask fogging up? Nope. Clouds overhead, casting strange shadows? No again. The available light was just fine. The fog was on the sandy bottom. The area, normally free of currents because of the surrounding walls, was all stirred up.

Tom descended into the white smoke, expecting to find the giant grouper with some larger-than-usual prey. A prey that had led Ben a merry chase, kicking up the fine bottom sand.

Visibility was suddenly nil. He could make out his depth gauge, that was about it. Strange, indeed—it was hard to imagine Ben expending *this* much effort, no matter *what* the prey.

Can't see diddly.

Blinded by sand and refracted light, Tom pulled his knees up, decided to let himself settle all the way to the bottom. He expelled a little air from his buoyancy control vest, just to make sure he was still headed down. No way to tell, blind like this. Almost pretty, the way sunlight hit the sand particles. Like being caught in a strange, warm snowstorm.

Something large and dark passed inches from his faceplate.

His hands were still at his sides and instinct told him to keep them there. Don't touch. Don't make a sudden move.

He was aware of the pressure wave as something large and powerful displaced water, pushing him backwards. Aware of speed and strength and size. So close, right in his face, he could barely focus.

Then it was gone and he tumbled down until his tank rack hit the soft bottom. Dumped ass-over-teakettle.

Jesus freaking kee-rist!

Hang on, old son. Don't panic. Pros don't panic. They may get the piss scared out of them, but they don't panic. What was it you saw? Think. Something large and dark and fast? Hell, that was probably Big Ben himself, almost as sand-blinded as you.

You spooked him, he spooked you. No big deal, once your pulse stops trip-hammering. A spook show, old son.

And once again you've proved to yourself that there is nothing whatever wrong with your heart. Little stress test there, and you passed it.

No way, he decided, getting control of his breath. No way was that a giant grouper. It had passed within inches of his mask and he hadn't seen any scales. The skin tone was all wrong—not mottled with spots like the grouper. Darker. Besides, he *knew* Ben.

Not Ben, he decided, adding buoyancy to his vest, you just had an encounter with a Not-Ben.

Whatever the hell *that* is.

3

Chesty Says Search and Destroy

"WE BLEW IT," said Speke. "Makes you all feel better, then *I* blew it, okay? I approved the barricade design."

"Nobody ever thought they'd be able to leap that high, Dr. Speke. Nobody."

Speke shrugged. Assessing blame didn't matter right now, and in any event he himself would write up the report, answer to the directors. He could slant it any way he liked, blame whatever underling had recently displeased him.

The emergency staff meeting had been convened on the small, artificial beach of Sealife Key, a manufactured paradise that had been a private resort before its conversion to a marine research facility. Staff people lingered in the shade of the perfectly spaced coconut palms. Morning sunlight made the lagoon a rippling, white-hot sheet of metal. The air smelled of salt and the hot, rot-humid stench of mangroves rooting in the shallow water. Small gulls circled above, keening for bait fish.

Dr. Vernon Speke, the marine biologist who headed Special Projects for Sealife Research, Incorporated, was in Florida Keys formal dress, meaning that he wore long pants and a shirt with a collar. For the last few months he'd been combing his thin, colorless hair straight back in a short ponytail, which he kept in place with an elastic band. His small bright eyes, almond shaped and widely spaced, were concealed by dark, side-shaded sunglasses. Long limbs and an ectomorphic slenderness made him appear taller than his six feet.

A research assistant (since dismissed) had once described Vernon Speke as "E.T. with an attitude"—the resemblance to the skinny alien was an exaggeration, but not the bit about attitude. Special Projects was a pressure cooker, Dr. Speke made that clear before you signed on. Perform under stress or be gone.

As Dr. Speke paced the little beach his sandals scuffed up small explosions of pure white sand, shipped down from South Carolina when the lagoon area was being built. Natural beach sand was a rarity in islands protected from wave action by an offshore reef—you wanted a beach, you had to make one.

Quick, nervous gestures blurred Dr. Speke's hands as he spoke. "What are the options," he said. "Robby? Any thoughts?"

Roberto Mendez, the chief animal trainer, sat on his haunches in a slant of sunlight, running his fingers through the warm sand. A sky-blue Sealife Staff T-shirt clung damply to his skin. His thick black hair was matted down, uncombed. Mendez was in his mid-forties, a handful of years older than his boss; exhaustion made every year show today. He said, "I keep thinking the lagoon is imprinted. It's home to them. So I guess we keep the barricades open, hope they return."

Speke said, "Don't hold your breath. And don't assume we can predict behavior. Clearly we *don't* know how they think, since no one here ever predicted that a live-fish feeding frenzy would lead to an escape attempt. Anybody else?"

The next suggestion came from a young research assistant named Lucy Savrin, a leggy, Sarasota-born brunette whom Speke had been trying to bed for months, with no luck. "Locate them," she said. "Attempt recovery. I think we need to get them back before they really get hooked on live prey."

"Sure. Locate and recover would be nice." Speke responded without expression or emphasis, withholding his opinion. "Any specific suggestions on *how* we do that?"

Lucy stood up, hands in the back pockets of her lime-green shorts. Cut to show just a hint of tanned cheek, Speke noticed, not for the first time. "Sonar," she said. "Fish finders, whatever equipment we have on the chase boat."

"The chase boat is out there now," Speke said, "cruising the reef area. So far, no contact."

"We could get a pilot up for a visual sighting," Lucy suggested. "Have another boat standing by, ready to net them."

"You keep saying 'them,' " Speke said. "Is it your opinion, based on your studies, that our creatures will remain together? Swim as a pack? Hunt and feed together?"

Lucy nodded vigorously, dislodging a thick wave of sun-bleached hair. She said, "I'd stake my life on it."

Speke made his small mouth smile, an expression that seemed oddly disconnected from the rest of his face. He said, "Let's hope you don't have to. How about you, Chesty? Any brainstorms?"

Chesty was Speke's nickname for Dr. Chester Higgs, Sealife's genetic engineer. Higgs was a long-time associate of Speke's and had become, in the last year or so, something of a juicehead. Get near Chesty before he had his breakfast, what you smelled wasn't Bay Rum after-shave. On this particular morning, however, Dr. Higgs was cold sober. The funky smell he exuded was not booze but the flop-sweat of failure. Of fear.

"Dr. Higgs?" said Speke, snapping his fingers, pop-pop, like pistol shots.

"Huh?"

"Earth to Chesty. Any bright ideas?"

Dr. Higgs was slumped in a canvas recliner. His was a fleshy, pleasant face, his nearsighted eyes perpetually squinting behind untinted prescription lenses. He sat up, removed his glasses, rubbed his red eyes. He sighed. "I guess we should make an announcement."

Speke said, "What? What was that?"

"Issue a warning."

Speke paused for a moment, his hands still. Then he lifted his dark glasses and looked at Higgs as if he'd come upon a particularly gruesome road accident. "You're serious," he said. "You want us to hold a press conference?"

"Doesn't matter how we do it," Higgs said. "Inform the Coast Guard or the marine patrol or whatever."

"Call the Coast Guard?" Speke looked up at the sky, shook his head. Was the man crazy? Dr. Speke scuffed to the edge of the lagoon, kicked sand at the water. Facing the empty lagoon he said, "You better turn in, get some sleep, Chesty. You're off your head."

"They're out there now," Higgs said. "*Isurus maximus.* A highly intelligent, highly aggressive genetic mutation. We can't be sure they won't cross-breed with another species.''

''That's what worries you?'' Speke said. ''Progeny?''

''Among other things, yes.''

Speke turned, walked back to his little group. Legs and ankles heron-thin—you could see that even with the long pants. He said, ''Okay, suppose I have a complete mental collapse and do as you suggest: call the freaking Coast Guard. What could *they* do?''

Dr. Higgs was sitting up, staring down at his hands. Soft, white hands. ''Organize a hunt,'' he said at last. ''Search and destroy.''

Lucy Savrin made a small sound of distress. Clearly she thought Dr. Higgs was overreacting.

''I know you love them, Lucy,'' Higgs said, turning to her. ''I don't want to kill them, either. But it's the only way to be sure.''

Dr. Speke was grinning, his small white teeth on edge, as if he'd just bitten into something interesting. He said, ''He's right, Lucy. Not about notifying the Coast Guard. But the search-and-destroy part, old Chesty's right on about that.''

4

What Merlin Feared

SALLY RECOGNIZED TOM kicking at full speed, long legs pumping in smooth, powerful strokes. She got up from the deck chair, scanned the reef. Made a head count of all five charter divers in the shallow reef canyons. Nobody missing or in obvious distress.

Why the rush?

She hurried down to the boarding platform and got there just as Tom swarmed over the side.

He spit out his mouthpiece and said, "Lookout."

Sally reacted instantly, scrambling up the ladder to the wheelhouse, and from there up the rungs to the flying bridge.

"What am I looking for?" she called down. "Give me a hint."

Tom had dumped his tank, shed his fins. As he came up the ladder she could feel his weight shifting the boat slightly.

"Damned if I know," he said. He described his encounter in the giant grouper's castle.

"Shark?" Sally said. Her sunglasses were polarized, which helped cut down on the reflected glare— and it was understood between them that her eyes were the sharper when it came to reading through the water. A quick scan had revealed only human shapes on the reef, all of them wearing the brightly colored buoyancy vests.

Tom said, "All I know is, it was big."

Sally said, "We don't get really large sharks in water this shallow. They live in deep water."

"I know."

"Even if it *is* a big guy, we've never had a shark attack. Not once in ten years. We've had divers *chase* sharks and not get bitten."

Tom said, "I know."

"There has never, to my knowledge, been an unprovoked shark attack on a diver in this part of the Keys."

"I know," Tom said, shading his eyes. "I know."

"You want me to blow the horn, signal 'Return to Boat'?"

Tom shook his head.

"You look spooked, babe," Sally said, touching his shoulders, aware of the muscle tension under his skin.

"Must have been all that sand in the water," he said. "Magnified the encounter."

"You said it knocked you to the bottom."

"The pressure wave did. The thing never actually touched me."

Sally's hands moved, kneading his shoulders and neck. She said, "If that happened, knocking down a man of your size, it was big."

"Right." He sighed, dipping his head as she worked out the kinks. "Maybe it wasn't a shark. No scales, though. I'm almost positive the skin was smooth. Dark and smooth.''

"Like a shark,'' Sally said. "Or a mammal.''

"It happened so quick.''

"A dolphin?'' Sally said.

Tom shrugged. "That wasn't my impression. But like I say, it happened so quick. And it was bigger than a dolphin. Bigger than *your* dolphins, anyhow.''

"They're not my dolphins.''

Tom grinned. "Whatever you say.''

Sally was concentrating on the reef. "They're coming back in,'' she said.

This was a two-tank charter. The first of the divers, those who had used up the most air, were already heading back to the boat for their second tanks.

"You think we should cut it short?'' she asked.

"Tell you what,'' he said. "We'll let the customers decide.'' After Tom laid out the situation, described his encounter, Theo was the only member of the dive club to insist on the partial refund offered.

Theo said, "Half? You got a problem out here means I can't use up my other tank, I should get the whole amount back.''

"We don't have a problem out here,'' said Tom, keeping his smile intact. "I just thought everyone should know I had an unexplained encounter at sixty feet. Whatever it was, it's probably miles away by now—and too large to cruise in the shallows.''

Sally was pleased to see that the thin, nervous woman who'd been worried about stingrays was the first to don her new tank.

"I'm going back out there,'' the woman announced, her eyes flashing. "I wouldn't miss this for *anything*.'' She turned to Theo, who was adjusting the crawl of his bikini swimsuit and looking miserable. "Think about it, Ted—whatever it was, it didn't attack him, right? Came that close and he never got a scratch? I read where a shark will almost always turn away from a human diver. It's up on the surface where you get in trouble. Swimmers and surfers. Not divers."

"So you're an expert now?"

Go on, Sally silently urged. *Give 'im hell.*

"I didn't say that," the woman said. "All I'm saying, we came what, fifteen hundred miles? I want to go the last few hundred yards. It's *so* beautiful out there. It makes me feel . . . special, or something."

Theo said, "You go ahead. Feel special or something. I want my money back."

It was Sally's turn to play shepherd, with a promise to try and coax Merlin out of his cave for the divers. Tom would keep watch from the wheelhouse, and cut the anchor line if anything large was sighted. The plan was to bring *Wild Child* right up on the divers, if necessary, to get them back aboard quick.

Tom said, "Be careful out there. Theo and I will keep our eyes peeled."

The divers were already splashing in. Theo backed away from the rail and lifted his hands, like maybe the rail was dirty. He said, "What? Me work for you? Are you nuts?"

"Give me a hand up top, you'll get all of your money back."

"Not just half?"

"All of it," Tom said. "Come on, I could use the help."

"Deal," Theo said, looking pleased with himself.

The divers were all in now, all but Theo, and Sally was kicking along the surface, keeping them in sight. From the wheelhouse Tom spotted another boat off in the distance, maybe half a mile away and cruising at a sedate speed. He focused in with the binoculars and recognized the vessel, with its characteristic markings. White and blue stripes for the Sealife Research Institute.

Why was an institute boat steering a zigzag course over the reef at trolling speed? Curious, he tried to raise them on Channel 16, the VHF hailing channel.

"*Wild Child* to *Wahoo*, do you copy, over?"

He switched to several other marine band channels, but the chase boat did not respond. A few minutes later *Wahoo* changed course, picked up speed, and left the area.

"Friend of yours?" Theo asked, unable to restrain a smirk.

"Not hardly," Tom said.

The way Sally figured it, there was more danger in staying aboard with the black-bikinied creep from New Jersey. Out here on the reef no one could take advantage. She'd been among schooling sharks—big makos out in the Gulf Stream, feeding on king mackerel—and never been touched. Never felt herself to be in danger from attack. A submerged diver didn't look like prey, not even to a known aggressor like the mako or the more common hammerheads. Up on the surface, kicking away and making noises that might be confused with those from a distressed fish, *that's* what provoked an attack.

You had to believe you were immune or you didn't get in the water. Simple as that.

After ten minutes on the reef, any misgivings had faded. Sally felt reassured. There was nothing wrong out here, nothing to fear. True, there were far fewer species present than usual, but that could be explained by any number of factors. A slight temperature variation, the vagaries of the current, a temporary drop in the plankton that was the basis of the food chain—there were almost as many theories as there were fish in the sea.

Sally didn't really think there was anything seriously amiss until Merlin failed to emerge from his cave.

The big moray made its home in a coral fissure and had been taking bait from Sally's hand for almost five years. She never fed it enough to spoil its hunting instinct. That would have been contrary to everything she believed about keeping a balance between the reef, the species who lived there, and the divers like her, who were privileged visitors.

Don't mess with Mother Nature, that was her abiding philosophy.

But now Merlin wouldn't come out and play. Sally could see the eel, its slick mass nestled in the fissure. *Hey, Merlin, remember me? Your pal Sally? Come on out and get your snack, you beautiful, ugly brute.*

The eel stirred, but came no closer. Sally thumped her yellow-gloved hand softly against the coral—the signal Merlin had been responding to for years. She removed the pinfish from the net bag, dangled it temptingly at the fissure opening.

Come out of the cave and eat, Merlin. Please?

The moray clearly had no intention of leaving the hidey-hole. Sally could see its small, glittering eyes, the array of tiny, needle-sharp teeth in the partially opened jaws. That kind of aggressive display could mean only one thing: Merlin was frightened, prepared to defend itself.

What exactly did it have to fear? There was no evidence that any creatures had been menaced here in the shallows—at least nothing out of the ordinary feeding patterns.

Merlin, you schlub, you're making me look bad.

Sally backed away from the fissure, let the pinfish drift to the bottom, where it was immediately seized by an industrious spider crab who scurried for cover.

Sally made a shrugging signal—no moray today, sorry—to the woman who'd stood up to Theo. The woman nodded and signaled *OK*, then veered to the bottom, following the little crab.

Twisting around, Sally looked up, following the trail of bubbles jetting from her respirator. From here, barely twenty feet under, the surface was a bright shimmer of quicksilver, trembling as if alive. No matter which way you looked, you were confronted by breathtaking beauty. The formations of fan coral, elkhorn, the soft corals and anemones— was there an architect alive who would compete with "dumb" animals who built themselves such perfectly proportioned dwellings? A human artist who could create the luminous, ever-changing colors of your typical tropical fish?

You wanted great art, all you had to do was put on a mask and snorkel.

Despite the relative lack of reef dwellers and feeders, the charter crew seemed very pleased. Most of them looked either wistful or disappointed when Sally began to round them up, pointing at her watch and indicating that even the most careful breather would be getting low by now. Those already on or near reserve inflated their buoyancy control vests, swapped respirators for snorkels, and prepared to return on the surface.

Sally, bringing up the rear, cruised close to the bottom, where she could look up and see the line of silhouetted swimmers finning along. This was, she knew, the most vulnerable time for divers. But even if there *was* a big predator in the area, sharks had fairly predictable behavor patterns. Your larger *squali*, the hammers and makos and tigers, even the rare great whites, were wary, often cowardly hunters. Sharks almost always circled cautiously before a charge, checking out the prey. Plenty of time to get the ducks back aboard, provided the dive master was paying attention—and you could bet the ranch Tom was paying attention.

No need to worry, she decided. Might as well enjoy the last few minutes submerged.

Something there on the bottom.

At first she didn't know what she was looking at. It looked familiar, and yet out of place or somehow wrong.

Sally swerved, reaching out for what at first glance resembled a large, fan-shaped plant with a delicate, multi-striped membrane. She touched it and the plant tumbled over, kicking up a puff of bottom sand, and that was when it clicked: the ''plant'' was the tail of a giant spotted grouper.

The tail had been nipped clean off by something with a large, concave bite radius.

Sally shivered involuntarily. *Take a look,* she told herself. *Check out the area.* Using a corkscrew motion, she spun slowly through 360 degrees. Visibility was almost a hundred feet, and in that world there was nothing larger than a few curious needlefish.

The last thing she did, before heading up to the boat, was stuff the severed fish tail into her net bag. It was, she was quite certain, all that remained of Big Ben.

5

Fearless Fish Killers

VERNON SPEKE SMILED when he saw the *Squali* backing into her slip at Vaca Cut Boat Charters. There was a hammerhead lashed across the transom, had to be five hundred pounds—a big bloody thing and very, very dead.

This was a good sign. You wanted to hire a shark hunter, it was nice to see he knew his business.

"Cap'n Colson?" he said, shading his eyes against the slant of the late-afternoon sun.

"You Dr. Speke?"

He nodded. They'd spoken on the VHF earlier in the day, after the first flush of panic had subsided at the lagoon. After certain key decisions had been made.

Captain Colson said, "Lemme finish here, then I'll get right with you."

Git rhat weecha.

Speke knew from his hurried, computer-driven security inquiry that Wade R. Colson was a native

Floridian, had grown up poaching 'gator out of Everglades City before moving his charter business to the Keys a few years back. That was a good profile. Swamp cracker like Colson would likely take the money, do the job, and keep his mouth shut.

Exactly what was required, given the delicacy of the situation.

'' 'Kay, boys, unreel that hoist, we'll run this beauty up the pole,'' Colson was saying. That casual, good-old-boy drawl belied his quick, economical movements as he hooked a wire hoist around the tail fin of the shark.

An electric motor reeled in the line and Captain Colson had the hammerhead up and swaying over the stern of his charter boat in less than a minute.

Speke stood back out of the way, as one of the scrawny, sun-blasted mates aimed a Polaroid while the other used a video camera to record the grinning fool who'd landed the shark. Price of a day charter included the videocassette and a cheaply framed instant photograph.

Show it around back home, prove you were a fearless shark killer. Don't mention that the dim-witted beast was belly-hooked on unbreakable wire and then shot dead with a pistol before being hauled aboard. Prudent man like Cap'n Colson didn't want his charter customers getting all chewed up; that was ·bad for business.

"You want this baby mounted, we can fix that, too," Colson was saying. "Good man up in Tavernier, he does it just from the photograph. Unbreakable fiberglass. Put it up over your mantel, hang it in your den or whatever."

"I'd like that," the character customer said, already a little giddy from a congratulatory drink supplied by the mates. "Is it expensive?"

"Hey," Colson said, slapping the man's shoulder, "life is expensive. But worth it. Ain't she, boys?"

The mates agreed, handed the fearless shark killer another cocktail in a plastic go-cup. Eager, Speke supposed, to get the sucker drunk so they could take the carcass around the corner to the fish wholesaler, split the proceeds. Local restaurants would be serving shark steaks for the next few days. Maybe call it mako because mako was supposed to have a better taste.

Ten minutes later the potbellied shark killer was staggering toward the dockside tiki bar and Speke was aboard the *Squali*, making his pitch.

"You lookin' for a special guvmint rate?" the charter skipper said suspiciously. " 'Cause I'll tell you right off, I got bookings take me clear through Christmas." Colson was spraying down the cockpit, hosing the scuppers.

Speke stood out of range; no point in getting his new Top-Siders wet.

"We're not the Feds," Speke said. "We're an independent contractor. We'll pay your normal rate. Plus a bonus, you get the job done."

"Bonus, huh?"

Wade Colson turned off the hose, wiped his hands on a clean rag. He was of medium height and build, very neat and trim in khaki slacks and a long-sleeved cotton shirt that protected his arms from the sun. Like most of the charter skippers he wore shades and a long-billed cap; it was hard to see his expression. His white teeth didn't quite open when he talked.

"A substantial bonus," Speke said. "Listen, could we maybe duck inside, conduct our discussion quietly?"

Inside the *Squali*'s spare, businesslike cabin, Colson helped himself to a cold beer. Speke declined the offer. The captain dropped his shades, revealing pale, lead-colored eyes. That friendly white smile was all part of the package, Speke decided, turned on and off like the cabin lights.

"Best tell me what you mean by substantial," Colson said in his soft, high-pitched voice.

Speke named a figure. The smile looked real this time.

Colson said, "That's a generous sum." He perched on a berth, taking small, careful sips from the beer, as if he intended to make it last for a hundred years. He said, "Now tell me who exactly you workin' for."

"Like I said, the Sealife Research Institute."

Colson nodded thoughtfully. "The dolphin school."

Speke said, "We do dolphin research, yes. Less and less of it, lately." He frowned. "We had some . . . trouble recently."

"You mean those animal rights people, run that dive boat out of Tarpon Key. You got sued, right?"

Speke made a face. "Not exactly. There was a court injunction, means we can't recover a couple of dolphin who escaped during a training exercise."

Colson said, "Escaped, huh?" Used his white grin and said, "I guess you boys have a problem there, critters escaping."

Speke shrugged. "The dolphin were no big loss, really. That particular project was a failure."

The charter captain nodded thoughtfully, his eyes registering mild amusement. Like maybe he got a kick out of Speke's hard-edged, Yankee way of talking. "Back home we used to shoot them dolphin sometimes," Colson said, holding his gaze cool and steady. "We believed a school of dolphin would deplete the game fish, mess up the trap lines. 'Course, that was the old way of thinking."

"Yes."

"Different now. If a man was to go after dolphin

now, possibly even *injure* that dolphin, cause it undue stress or whatever, that man might get his ass sued like you did, maybe even lose his boat.''

Speke asked, ''That what you're worried about? Getting sued?''

Colson shrugged. ''Lose my boat, I'm out of bidness. Can't nobody afford liability these days.''

''This isn't a dolphin hunt,'' Speke said. ''Dolphin are not the subjects of this particular study.''

Colson nodded, waiting.

''All we want to do,'' Speke said, ''is recover what is ours. Legally ours. With as little fuss and as little publicity as possible. Which is why we want to hire a private charter, rather than use our own vessels.''

''Nothing illegal?''

Speke put his hand on his heart. ''Swear to God,'' he said. ''This is not a protected species. I know that for a fact.''

Captain Colson put down the beer bottle, studied his fingernails. He said, ''Tell me about the bonus again.''

6

The Enemy of Science

LOIS WAS WAITING at the dock. Showing off that dolphin grin, those rows of small razor-sharp teeth as she held her sleek gray and white head just above the water.

Sally leaned from the cockpit of the dive boat. Behind her was the snake-hiss of the hose as Tom washed down the decks, rinsed off their gear.

Sally said, "Hi, Lois. Glad to see me?"

The dolphin bobbed her head, making that high-pitched two-note squeal that Sally now recognized as a greeting. The dolphin seemed to be smiling. Its expression wasn't really a smile, of course; that was a human interpretation, a way of endowing another species with human characteristics. Anthropomorphism, the enemy of science. Because any scientist knows that animals don't have human smiles.

Try telling yourself that when Lois is right here in front of you, grinning like mad, Sally thought. So

call it a dolphin smile, not a human smile. Keep that
firmly in mind and you could still do good science.

"Where's your brother, Lois? Where's Clark?"

Lois came up higher out of the water, slapping her
fins. She wanted to play. This was a remarkable improvement over the stressed-out, neurotic behavior
of a year ago, following her escape from the dolphin
research project.

Too bad the male dolphin wasn't improving at the
same rate. Whatever had been done to the male at
Sealife, the scars were much deeper.

After discovering the two abused and frightened
mammals hiding in a murky canal area not far from
their Tarpon Key homestead, Sally and Tom had decided to take charge of the animals, help them recover if possible. With the help of expert testimony
on abuse of laboratory animals, Sally and Tom had
managed to secure a court injunction against Sealife
Research Institute, long notorious as a Department
of Defense contractor involved in the behavior modification of sea mammals, training dolphin to kill enemy divers or stand guard over submerged missile
silos. Although the matter had never been legally
resolved, Sealife had not responded to the injunction, apparently to avoid any further publicity.

Dr. Speke, the marine biologist representing Sealife, had shrugged off the loss: "You people want to
take responsibility for a couple of suicidal dolphin,
be my guest. Work with these animals as long as we
have, you'll learn the hard way that some animals
are just *born* crazy. And when that happens they *stay*
crazy."

Sally had decided then and there, on the Monroe
County court house steps, that Dr. Vernon Speke
was lying, trying to cover his scrawny ass.

Convinced that the abused dolphin had been *made*
crazy, Sally had thrown herself into the rigor of daily

therapy sessions. Her goal was simple enough. She wanted to build trust by gentle interaction and play, allowing the pair to relearn normal dolphin behavior. The long-term goal—a dream, really—was to help the captivity-bred mammals return to a life in the wild as "free swimmers," or at least have a life that didn't rely heavily on human contact.

Sally suspected that Sealife's dolphin program went beyond mere training. Especially disturbing was the small incision scar near the female's sex organs. Had the animal been rendered sterile for some reason, perhaps to alter her behavior or control her mating instincts? If so, Lois seemed unaware of any deficiency. Barring an occasional relapse into neurotic pattern swimming, the female was coming along beautifully. After months of gentle contact, Lois felt secure enough to frolic, showing herself above the surface and demanding playtime.

Clark, the adolescent male, was responding much more slowly. Although there was no sign of surgical alteration, he bore the marks of a Sealife training harness and still suffered from unpredictable mood swings. Sometimes fearful and skittish when humans were in the water, he did not yet fully trust Sally, and occasionally charged at her when she was interacting with Lois, as if he feared what she might do.

Where did the male go when he disappeared? Did he leave the canal and the shallow basin area to hunt or mate? Sally had no idea and as yet had made no attempt to track his movements. Establishing trust was the first order of business, and the way to Clark was through Lois, Sally was certain of that.

Tursiops truncatus, the species of dolphin commonly known as bottlenose, were favored by animal trainers because of their apparent desire to please human companions by learning tasks or performing tricks.

This playfulness was harmlessly exploited in places like Sea World, where the trainers clearly loved the animals. Military operations were another matter: the basic assumption was that dolphins, like men, could be conditioned to participate in war. The result was a couple of creatures who seemed to have been shell-shocked by Sealife's behavior modification program. Sally had no idea what Dr. Speke had been doing; she wasn't at all sure she *wanted* to know. What difference did it make?

The important thing was to heal the animals, help them get on with their lives.

Not that Sally didn't have her own agenda, her own needs.

She'd abandoned her doctoral studies at Woods Hole to come south with Tom and set up the charter business, and she didn't regret a minute of all those years. Still, there was something unfinished about her life, something not quite complete that in unguarded moments made her feel anxious and out of breath. It was more than the lack of an advanced degree (after all, she was doing doctoral-level work right here with Clark and Lois) or the fact that she was unable to have children. It had to do with wanting to leave something behind, make her mark in the world.

Tom jokingly called it the midlife syndrome, and his way of dealing with it was to try and finish the book project he'd abandoned when they made the move to the Keys. So far his efforts hadn't progressed beyond occasional columns for *Reef Life*, the monthly tabloid that billed itself as the ''alternative news source'' for the Keys.

Sally had responded, much to her surprise, by mothering Clark and Lois. There was, she admitted to herself, no other word to describe how she felt about the dolphins. It was unscientific, perhaps, but a very real interspecies bond had developed.

Healing the dolphins had become almost an obsession. Heal the dolphins and she herself would feel whole again.

Sally said, "Forget your silly brother. Let's try learning to catch a fish, shall we?"

Lois squeaked, plunged beneath the surface, and reemerged a moment later, impatient for Sally to don her mask, tank, and fins. That done, Sally slipped into the warm, salt-rich waters of the canal. Felt a swirl of pressure as Lois came up rapidly behind and nudged her in the butt.

Sally mouthed her respirator, deflated her buoyancy control vest, and sank into the cloudy waters of the canal. Visibility was less than twenty feet in here, where currents pouring between the Atlantic and the Gulf stirred up the muddy bottom. It was Sally's theory the two dolphins had chosen this sheltered area precisely *because* the visibility was poor—because it provided cover.

Lois circled and turned, presenting her belly and flukes. In the last few weeks she'd discovered the pleasures of having her tummy rubbed, and now she couldn't get enough of it. Spinning slowly, she writhed with pleasure, squeaking and blowing air bubbles.

At first Sally had taken the air-bubble display as a sign of distress. Then it became obvious that Lois was attempting to emulate the way Sally's own air bubbles streamed from her regulator.

It was Lois's way of saying, *We're alike. I can do that, too.* "Lois? Come here, girl. Let's try and catch a fish."

For months Sally had been trying the same live-fish experiment with the female. Free-swimming dolphin loved to feed on schools of mullet, but Lois, reared on dead fish presented by trainers, had never developed the necessary skills to catch a live fish.

Teaching Lois to pursue and catch her own food, that would be a real breakthrough. With that in mind, Sally now kept a few live mullet in a perforated plastic pail under the dock. At first Lois had been puzzled by the game of releasing a live fish in her vicinity. What was the point?

Lately Lois's behavior had changed. She seemed more interested in the mullet than before, had started chasing the live fish. One of these days, Sally hoped, the female would catch the fish and eat it.

"Ready, Lois? Watch me. Watch what I'm doing."

Sinking under the dock, Sally reached into the sealed barrel, managed to corner and grab a mullet.

This was tricky, getting the barrel closed again without letting any of the other fish escape. Lois nosed around, watching her. Everything was a game to the dolphin; you had to accept that fact and work with it.

Sally held out the struggling mullet, pulled her hand away when Lois made a move to take it in her jaws, as she would a dead fish.

Released, the mullet shot away, got clear by about ten feet, and then slowed down.

Lois flicked her powerful flukes, glided forward. Again the mullet shot away. Again the dolphin followed. After a few more passes at the fish the dolphin got bored, returned to where Sally waited, and presented her belly.

"Okay, girl. We'll try again tomorrow."

When the female had had her fill of being caressed, she began to circle in the murky waters, waggling her long head from side to side. A sign Sally recognized as *Follow me. I want to show you something.*

Sally signaled, *Go ahead*, and Lois instantly broke off and headed up the canal. Sally kicked gamely

after her. Several times the dolphin turned back to
keep her in sight, urging her along.

Hurry up, she seemed to be saying. *Why are you
humans so slow?*

The destination, when it finally came into view,
was the rotting remains of an old wooden pier, partially destroyed by Hurricane Donna in 1960. The
broken and twisted pilings had been part of the
property when Sally and Tom bought it. One of
these days they intended to clear out the debris, just
to tidy up. So far there had always been more pressing tasks, and as Tom was quick to point out, the
wreckage had become a home for numerous small
fish and a few sizable groupers.

Lois, excited by something, was swimming back
and forth in a tight pattern.

Here, she seemed to be saying. *Look in here.*

Sally looked. The mangroves had grown in overhead, beyond the bank of the man-made canal, and
the result was an area of dark shadows extending
all the way to the bottom. All she had with her was
the flashlight in her string bag—not powerful enough
to really cut through the gloom.

To please Lois she got out the flashlight, clicked
on the beam.

At first she saw nothing but the light itself, the
beam scattering in motes of mud, bits of debris from
the decaying pilings. And then the beam caught
something small and bright.

An eye.

Her first reaction was to back away. It was so
damn *eerie*. And then she recognized the eye and
swam forward. The beam of light played over the
sleek gray shape of Lois's male companion: Clark
was in there among the pilings, lying on the bottom
with both his eyes open.

For a brief, heart-stopping moment she thought

the dolphin was dead. Then she saw his eyes reacting to the light, his flukes trembling. He was alive.

What was he *doing* here? Hiding, obviously, but from what? Was he fearful of Sally, of the noise *Wild Child* had made entering the canal? Or was he reliving some terrifying experience he'd had at Sealife?

Show me, Sally urged, holding herself in a nonthreatening posture. *Show me what's wrong*.

Lois bumped her gently from behind: *Do something*.

Well, yes, Sally thought, I'd love to do something, but what? And how long can Clark stay down here without drowning? Even in periods of inactivity a dolphin couldn't stay submerged for more than thirty minutes or so. How long had Clark been on the bottom? Did he want to drown? Was he suicidal, as Dr. Speke had implied?

Sally checked her watch and her air reserve. Roughly twenty minutes left. She decided to stay with Clark until her own air was exhausted. Try to reassure him that he was safe, that he needn't hide. She reached inside the pilings, intending to stroke his flukes, but he backed away, kicking up a froth of mud and wood particles.

Either he'll surface for air or you'll watch him drown right before your eyes, Sally told herself.

Lois nudged again: *DO SOMETHING*.

As Sally twisted her way between the pilings, a loose spar moved with the current. She began to feel just a tiny bit claustrophobic, but she could more easily reach Clark from behind the nested pilings. Stretching out her arms, she slipped her hands under the dolphin's belly, urging him upward.

At first he did not react. She tried again.

This time he struck her right hand. He opened his jaws immediately, before she realized what had happened, but the damage was done. Already the salt was lacerating the wound—it hurt like hell.

Clark had bitten her. It did not seem possible.

Worse, in trying to back away, she'd come up against the loose spar, snagging her regulator hose. *Calm*, she told herself. *Easy does it. Think your way clear first, then act.*

Pressing her shoulder to the spar, she was able to shift it. Reaching behind her head, she found the hose, pulled it away from the snag. Aware of blood in the water, a dark cloud of it passing by her faceplate. She flexed her hand. All her fingers were still there and functioning, so the wound couldn't be too bad.

Crazy damn dolphin, why had he done that?

Because he's frightened, she decided. Animals sometimes lash out when they're scared. So do humans.

The air gauge told a sad story. She was already on reserve, having gulped air while getting free of the spar. Holding her wounded hand close to her side, she pulled herself along the bottom until she was free of the pilings.

Lois was circling overhead, a silhouette on a silver mirror.

Sally kicked, surfaced near the dolphin. She dropped her regulator, grabbed a lungful of sweet, sweet air. "Sorry, Lois," she said, panting. "There was nothing I could do."

Lois squeaked, thrashed her head, splashing with her flukes: *Look*, she seemed to be saying. *Look*.

Sally pushed up her mask, blinked the salty water from her eyes. There, among the pilings and the mangrove branches, she saw just the top of Clark's head, the dark depression of his air hole. He had surfaced, spouted, filled his lungs.

A moment later he was gone, returned to his hiding place on the bottom.

"What's he afraid of, girl?"

Lois shook her head. *Don't know.*

* * *

Tom had the grill smoking when Sally finally dragged herself out of the canal. He turned with the tongs in his hand, about to transfer lime-drenched yellowtail fillets from the platter to the grill, and saw the blood dripping down her wrist.

Without saying a word he put down the platter, leaped aboard *Wild Child*, and was at her side with the first-aid kit.

"It's not that deep," Sally said, struggling to keep her teeth from chattering. "For some reason it's bleeding like crazy."

After holding her hand under the dockside fresh-water nozzle, Tom dabbed it with sterile gauze. "Puncture wounds," he said. "A row of them right in the meat of your palm."

"Good," she said. "No need for stitches."

"No stitches," Tom agreed. "You going to tell me what happened?"

She held herself still as he poured peroxide directly over the wounds. Nothing at first; then a deep stinging sensation, hot under her skin.

"I did something stupid," she said.

"Those are bite marks."

"Very stupid," she said.

"Come on, Sal. What happened?"

"I need a beer first. Ice cold."

7

Queen of the Conchs

THERE WAS BEER in the boat cooler. Sally held the bottle against her bandaged palm and the hot stinging sensation decreased. She lay on a recliner, feeling her heartbeat return to normal. Tom was back at the grill, his large, burly form obscured by smoke and steam. His movements were quick, efficient, and reassuring. *Home.*

Behind the row of fan palms was the house they'd built together, a standard Old Florida design of white stuccoed block, with storm-shuttered windows and a couple of hot-air scuttles in the tin roof. Like almost all recent residential construction in the Keys, the house was suspended ten feet above sea level on poured concrete stilts—to ride out hurricane flood waters. The stilts had been partially enclosed with latticework and screening, making an open-air patio protected from rain and insects.

Another, smaller stuccoed building sat nearby at ground level, landscaped with crushed stone and a slat-wood walkway. This was the dive shop, with its compression pumps for refilling scuba tanks. The store's bins held piles of rental gear, from fins and snorkels to full dry suits for deep diving. A decade of scrimping and saving had gone into the shop and the gear and the dive boat. In another few years the mortgages and loans would be paid off and the charter business would begin to generate a profit beyond the meager salaries they drew.

For now they got by, and no complaints.

Tom served the grilled snapper fillets with a side of yellow rice and Cuban black beans. He pulled over a chair, sat down, cracked a beer of his own.

"Go on," he said. "Eat. You look starved. We'll talk after."

Sally was surprised to find that she was, as Tom had surmised, famished. Diving burns up a lot of calories, and she'd been down longer today than usual, and under considerably more stress. She ate slowly, savoring the fillet, wiped the plate clean with a chunk of Cuban bread, and then leaned back, the pain in her hand leveling off as a dull ache.

Tom, a quick eater, had long since finished. He strode along the edge of the canal, sandaled feet crunching the marlstone gravel. Hands plunged in the pockets of his khaki shorts, he turned to stare at the tangerine blaze of the sunset, bold streaks of magenta bleeding up from the direction of Key West, somewhere over the horizon.

"Was it Lois?" he said. "Is that why you don't want to tell me about it?"

Sally sighed, put down the half-empty bottle of beer. She longed, as she often did, for a cigarette. Just one postprandial puff. They'd both quit more than a year back: Sally had given up her filtered cigarettes and Tom his evening cigars. There would, alas, be no escape into the comforting fog of nicotine. "There's something wrong with Clark," she said finally. "He's acting very peculiar."

"Peculiar enough to turn on you?"

"He was frightened. Terrified, I think."

She described her encounter with the dolphin, and Tom's attitude seemed to soften. He said, "The poor bastard, he's always been neurotic."

"Not always," Sally corrected.

"We don't know that."

"I do," she said. "He's been traumatized."

Tom didn't argue with her diagnosis. His own encounters with Clark had not been entirely pleasant. The few times he'd been in the water with Lois, the male dolphin had put on belligerent displays, making charges and tail splashes until Tom retreated to the dock. Since then he'd left the dolphin therapy to Sally. He knew how much it meant to her and was loath to interfere unless he thought it affected her safety.

"Honest, I'll be fine," she said, waving her wounded hand. "If he'd wanted to really hurt me he could have taken it off at the wrist. One chomp."

"That's what worries me," Tom said. "We get complacent around dolphin because they seem so gentle. We forget they're carnivores. They kill for a living, that's their instinct. And God only knows what those Sealife bastards were up to."

"Tom, please."

He looked her in the eye. "You know what I'm getting at."

"Yes," she said. "I do."

Unspoken between them was the assumption that the male might have been trained to kill enemy divers, to go after human shapes. That would explain his fright and confusion, his spasms of aggressive or threatening behavior, particularly against Tom, who more closely fit the profile of an enemy diver.

If that was true—if the dolphin *had* been trained

to kill—was there a danger he'd revert to that learned behavior, as Tom feared?

Sally's gut feeling, not based on any scientific evidence, was that Clark had escaped from his Sealife trainers for a reason: because he did *not* want to kill. The male was neurotic but not, she believed in her heart, murderous.

"I've been thinking," Tom said. He plopped down on the edge of a chair, hands still thrust deep in his pockets, long legs straight out. "What if there's a connection?"

Sally raised her eyebrows.

"The reef," he explained, "and the canal."

Sally said, "I don't get it. What connection?"

"Okay, let's assume there was some kind of *intrusion* out at the reef. An unknown predator who killed Big Ben and who also managed to scare off most of the other fish. We both know that's unusual behavior. We've seen barracuda cleaning up a whole school of jacks—ten feet away none of the other species even move. Bigger fish are always feeding on smaller fish. They seem to accept the inevitable, right?"

"It seems that way sometimes."

"Not sometimes," Tom said. "All the time. A rogue shark cruises in, chomps on Big Ben, why should all the other fish leave the area? Why does your moray hide like it's scared to death? And why, for that matter, is your dolphin hiding under the pier and snapping at the only human who really gives a damn about it?"

"In the first place," Sally said, "it's not 'my moray' or 'my dolphin.' "

Twilight had settled quickly into night and Tom's expression was hard to read in the dimness. She assumed he was smiling because his voice registered amusement. He said, "You do see what I'm getting at?"

"No," she said, "not really. And you know I hate it when you make me play guessing games."

He said, "Sorry. I'm talking about our unidentified predator. Maybe it exudes some noise or smell that's scaring the hell out of everything in the area, including the dolphin."

"You really think Clark could smell another creature five miles away?"

Tom shrugged. "I don't know about smell, but we're almost sure he can hear Lois even further than that. Maybe he heard something out there, Sal. Think about it. Remember the Sealife chase boat that was in the area and then skedaddled as soon as I hailed it."

Sally shuddered. "I still think we may be making a big deal out of nothing."

"I hope so. I really do."

The outside bell rang. Tom went into the shop, returned with the cordless phone.

"It's Reggie," he said. "Queen of the Conchs."

Regina Rhodes was a native Key Wester, a Conch who had married rich and lived so much longer than her late husband that no one but Reggie seemed to actually remember him. When asked how he died, she inevitably replied, "Rum did it."

At the age of seventy, full of scorn for the tourist tabloids, she had founded *Reef Life* and brought it out on a monthly basis. The slant was keenly, sometimes rabidly, green, and after five years of deadlines, cost overruns, and a couple of lawsuits, she looked younger and more vital than she had when the first issue was distributed, via her old beach wagon, to Keys up and down the Overseas Highway.

The publication was, Reggie alleged, her Fountain of Youth, and she was quick to admit that any years she had gained were at the expense (often quite literally) of the developers and bureaucrats who had tangled with her.

Sally was convinced that her husband had a crush on the handsome, silver-haired woman, but oddly enough the idea never made her jealous, maybe because the typical Keys male was oriented toward nineteen-year-old beach bimbos. It was nice to be reminded that Tom was anything but typical.

Reggie, for her part, flirted like the southern belle she was, although there never seemed to be anything overtly sexual about it. She appeared on this particular evening in typical post-sundown regalia— a full-length cotton dress hand-printed with a warm, orange design that seemed to shift on the material as she moved. She wore huge hoop earrings, hammered bangles on both wrists, and displayed rings on most of her fingers. A massive gold brooch, an heirloom from the late Mr. Rhodes, clasped the flowing material over her breasts. Her toenails, exposed in Keno sandals, were painted dark orange to match the dress.

Sally couldn't have carried it off without looking gaudy, but Reggie, tall and slim, her posture erect, her thick silver hair loose at her bare shoulders, looked elegant.

As always, the old woman greeted Tom with a kiss and a full embrace, hugging his broad shoulders and winking at Sally. "Kin I borrow him someday?" she asked, her whole face smiling.

"Anytime," Sally said. "Just make sure he changes his socks."

"I don't recall this hunk of a man ever wearing socks," she said, "not to my recollection."

Tom caught Sally's look and shrugged, as if to say, What can a good hunk do?

"Drink?" he said to Reggie. He went to the outside bar and fashioned an iced vodka with a splash of fresh lime juice, what Reggie called a "fog cut-

ter." Before returning he switched on the outside
lights, illuminating the dockside area. Moths immediately appeared in the pale green halo of the sodium lights.

"Now," Reggie said, settling back into a lounge
chair with her drink in hand, "what's this about
your poor dolphin?"

Sally again described her encounter with Clark.
She found herself referring to the wound on her
hand as a "scratch" and was happy to find that Tom
didn't contradict her.

Reggie, eyeing the bandage, clearly knew better
but didn't press her on that point.

Tom said, "It's not only the dolphin. There was
something going on out at the reef today—an unknown predator in the area."

"Oh?" said Reggie sharply. "You see this thing,
did you?"

"I might have. Can't be sure. The visibility was
nil. Whatever it was, it killed Big Ben. Remember
the giant grouper I wrote about?"

Reggie said, " 'Course I remember. We ran that
photo on the cover, this time last year. Had to dis-
tribute extra copies. You know," she said, turning
pointedly to Sally, "the tush factor."

Tom laughed and Sally realized she was blushing.
The photograph that had accompanied Tom's article
showed Sally feeding Ben. She'd been wearing a
rather skimpy swimsuit at the time and hadn't actually seen what it looked like until her barely contained bottom was displayed on newsstands
throughout the Keys.

"That's so sweet," Reggie said. "I bet you blush
all over. Am I right, Tom?"

Tom didn't answer. He stood, saying, "Come on,
I want to show you guys something."

"Ooh-ee," Reggie said, "I can't wait."

Inside the house Tom opened the freezer, placed

a frost-covered plastic bag on the counter. Reggie sipped her drink, keeping her dark eyes focused on Tom as he unzipped the bag, shook out the contents.

"Ben's tail," he announced. "Sally found it on the way back to the boat."

Reggie frowned, shook her head. "Poor fish."

"See where the bite curves here?" he said, pointing. "That's typical of the way a shark gouges. Sort of a concave scoop, like you'd get spooning a melon."

"Pretty big spoon."

Tom nodded. "I measured the bite mark. According to Sally's textbooks, this was done by a shark of fifteen to eighteen feet. Might weigh as much as two thousand pounds. There were no teeth embedded, or else we might be able to identify the species."

Reggie peered at the mortal remains of Big Ben, wrinkled her nose in distaste. "Must be hundreds of sharks that size in these waters," she said.

"In deeper water," Tom said. "You want shark that big, you have to go out to the Gulf Stream. Not on the reef. They get to be that size, they usually won't cruise in shallow water."

"But this one did?"

"Had to, to get to Ben."

Reggie nodded slowly. She rattled her ice cubes. "Build me another, please," she said. "I've got something you better hear."

They went back to the patio, where Tom mixed another fog cutter. Reggie remained standing, staring off at the dock lights, where the air was thick with moths. "Got a strange phone call this evening," she said. "Why I dropped by, really."

"Who from?"

"Can't say. What they call an unnamed source. I can tell you it's the same source helped us out when you all went to court to keep those dolphin."

"Come on, Reggie. What did he say?"

"Did I say he?

"She, then."

"It's a he," she said. "Most definitely a he. And he was drunk, so we best take this with a grain of salt. But what he said, they had themselves a little accident at the Sealife Key last night."

"What kind of accident?"

"Another escape type of accident. Except this time it wasn't dolphin."

Sally said, "Are you sure of that?" Her mouth was dry and her stomach queasy.

Reggie put her glass down, leaned forward, her breath scented with lime juice, her voice as throaty and compelling as an alto saxophone. "All I know is what he said: 'They got away.' And I said, 'What got away?' and he said, 'The maneaters.' And then he hung up."

Hours later, after Reggie had gone home and Sally, full of aspirin, had lulled herself to sleep, Thomas J. Hart jerked himself awake.

His body was shivering, bathed in sweat. He'd had the dream again, about a darkness that sucked the air from his lungs. The nightmare of drowning, of his heart stopping.

Tom turned carefully so as not to wake Sally and realized that his heart was still pounding hard enough to make his ears ring. He fought the shivers as his dream-sweat quickly evaporated in the air-conditioned bedroom.

Was this breathless feeling an anxiety attack? Giving it a name didn't make it any better.

The nightmares had begun in earnest a few months ago. He could never quite remember the specifics of the dream, only the sense of foreboding, of not being able to breathe. And then, the wake-up part of the nightmare, he dreamed that his heart stopped beating.

Sitting up in bed now, hugging the pillow to his knees, Tom wiped his moist forehead and grinned into the dark. Sally, a blissfully sound sleeper, had no idea about his night sweats. Nor had he told her about his trip to the cardiologist.

That silly, panicky drive down to Key West, convinced he was on the verge of a heart attack, absolutely certain that his blood pressure was dangerously high. He could still see the look on the specialist's face as he checked Tom's electrocardiograms and said, "Mr. Hart, I don't know when you're going to die, but it won't be anytime soon and it certainly won't be because your heart is bad."

Tom had insisted on taking a stress test right then and there. Running on a stair-stepping machine with wires taped to his chest and a blood pressure cuff on his arm, like he was trying to prove the doctor wrong, drop dead right in his office, so *there*.

"Mr. Hart, I hate to disappoint you, but there is absolutely no indication of heart damage. What is it, thirty some-odd miles to Tarpon Key? Well, according to the test results you could run all the way home."

There had been a long, meaningful pause, a glance at the chart. "How old did you say you were, Mr. Hart?"

"I, um, just turned forty."

Another pause, and then: "Let me prescribe some Valium."

On the way home Tom had pulled the truck over in heavy traffic and laughed until he was really and truly out of breath. How old did you say you were? Old enough to have nightmares, Doc. Old enough to be afraid of something I cannot describe. Old enough to be no longer young. Old.

Tom slipped from the bed, padded into the bathroom, looked in the mirror, and saw that old familiar face. That slight, built-in smile that put creases in the corners of his mouth. It was a confident, happy, healthy-looking face.

Amazing how faces could lie.

No, there was nothing wrong with his heart, but that didn't mean everything was right. The nightmares meant something—*had* to mean something, if only he could figure out what.

He got carefully back into bed and comforted himself by watching his wife. Look at Sally sleeping flat on her back, splendidly naked. He did not envy her her untroubled dreams, he simply wanted to join her there.

As he watched, she turned on her side, threw her bandaged hand out, snuggled closer.

Tom closed his eyes, but it was no good. Reggie's strange, secondhand report of another escape at Sealife Key merely ratified his deep unease. He knew in his bones that something bad was going to happen.

Out-of-breath, nightmare bad.

8

Hand Lines

MAKING BARELY FIVE knots, *Squali* cruised the edge of Hawk Channel, just inside the reef. Her outriggers were not rigged, she trailed no baits or lures. A mate steered from the flying bridge while Captain Wade Colson remained inside the cabin, staring into the hood of the fish finder, watching the brightly colored graphics unfold on the video screen.

"See that?" he said. "That's a school of kingfish, sure as hell."

Dr. Vernon Speke, leaning against the console, grunted. He did not give a damn, the grunt said, for kingfish. Nor was he interested in a guided tour of the bottom of Hawk Channel.

Colson said, "Point is, they movin' real quick. No baitfish on the screen, so you figure they runnin' *from* somethin'."

Dr. Speke was suddenly attentive. He said, "What feeds on kingfish?"

Colson said, "Anything big enough and quick

enough to get 'em. Could be a beakfish—marlin or sail. Pretty rare to find a marlin in here. They favor the Gulf Stream. Tarpon will give chase, too, though they don't normally feed on kings."

"Shark?"

Wade Colson looked up from the scope. His lips twitched in a green-tinged smile. "Surely," he said. "Your typical shark will feed on just about anything. But this ain't a typical specimen, is it, Doc?"

Speke turned away. "We'll treat it like a typical specimen," he said. "That's our agreement."

"Our agreement is, we kill the damn things and I keep my mouth shut," Colson reminded him. "That don't mean you can't tell me what to expect. How these things behave."

"It doesn't matter how they behave," Speke said softly. "Not once they're dead."

A buzzer sounded and Colson ducked his head back to the scope.

"What is it?" Speke demanded.

"Hold your water," Colson said. "I got some sizable critters below. Four, five, could be six of 'em, I can't be sure, they keepin' pretty close together. Look to be bigger than tarpon, I can see that much."

"Stop the engines," Speke said instantly. "I'll lower the gear."

Colson killed the engines. The *Squali* drifted in silence. As Dr. Speke knelt in the cockpit, preparing his gear, the two mates appeared like bare-chested wraiths, dressed in grubby jeans and white rubber boots. A couple of vaguely related, swamp-bred boys who had accompanied Colson down from Everglades City. Cousins, the skipper had said, or was it nephews?

One mate wore an earring and the other had more tattoos—that was how Speke distinguished between them. "Give me a hand," he said to the earring.

"This wants to be eight feet down. Try to keep the wires from tangling."

"You gonna 'lectrocute 'em?" the mate asked, gripping the cable.

"This is an underwater broadcast device," Speke explained. "We've got more sophisticated gear on shore, but this is the best we can do on short notice. It should attract our, um, quarry to the vicinity of the boat. Then you can proceed in the usual fashion."

"Are you serious?" The mate grinned, his tongue exploring a gap in his front teeth. "This is a new one on me. Hey, Cap, this works, we gotta get us one. Call a shark like you hoot up a 'gator."

"Shut up, Cecil," Colson said without any particular emphasis. "Just do what Doc tells you. Mike, get the chum bag over and bait up the lines."

When the gear was secured beneath the boat, the cable cleated at the stern, Dr. Speke activated the cassette recorder. If the creatures were in the vicinity, they would hear the sound of themselves feeding and, it was hoped, come up to investigate. Speke was not a hundred percent confident of success—the creatures had not always responded to this stimulus in the lagoon—but it was worth a shot.

"Put the lines out," Colson was saying. "Let's see if these boys are hungry."

The mates had carved head-sized chunks from a semi-frozen beef carcass, cleverly threading monster-sized hooks into the bait. Six hooks to each leader, spaced ten feet apart. The wire leaders were attached to huge spools of five-hundred-pound-test monofilament set on pneumatic winches.

This was not, Captain Colson assured the doctor, sport fishing.

"We gon' catch and kill, the best way we know how."

"The quicker the better," Speke said, leaning on

the transom. The night was heavy with the stink of thawing chum, a trail of fragrant fish slime exuding from net bags tossed over the stern. The mate with the earring tipped in a gallon bucket of beef blood. It spread like an oil slick and smelled to high heaven.

The mate said, "Love that stink. They surely do love it."

Captain Colson got ready. He reached into a lazarette and removed a high-powered semiautomatic pistol. "Clip full of dumdums," he said in his high, expressionless voice. "Take the fight out of anything alive."

The chum was out, the bait was set, the underwater speakers were broadcasting; all they could do was wait. The mates settled down, tending the winch lines, adjusting the free play.

The idea, Colson explained, was to let the shark swallow the hook before setting it.

"Gut hooked, they die fast."

Dr. Speke looked into the dark water and saw nothing.

The creatures circle among the frenzied kingfish, hungering for the fear-texture of freshkill, when the False Singing begins.

As one they pause, adrift together: Us the beautiful, the terrible, the six-partnered. Listening, sensing, feeling the electrical flesh-crawl of the fleeing kingfish. Alive to everything the water brings, the messages it carries.

The False Singing comes from above. From that same direction comes the jaw-snap scent of cutfish. No, not cutfish exactly, the creatures decide. A new smell-picture, more pervasive.

A smell of rotting, of death.

The six wait, minds ticking together. The Us must decide. Shall they make freshkill with the fleeing kingfish or approach this new phenomenon? The

False Singing indicates the presence of Walking Others, with their hurtsticks and their strange demands.

Walking Others mean danger, fear, blood in the water.

Fear, the creatures sing, *fear is delicious.*

The mate with the earring sat by the starboard winch, smoking a cigarette, the glow of it a hot red dot in a dark corner of the night. Speke had settled into the fighting chair. The big rods and reels had been put away. This was not, as had been made abundantly clear, a normal fishing expedition. Killing weapons—pistol and gaff—were near to hand.

Colson came out of the cabin zipping up his fly. He reached over the side and gave the chum bag a tug, releasing a plume of ground-up fish into the current.

"How long?" Speke asked.

"You tell me, Doc."

Speke had bummed a Lucky Strike from the earring, was giving serious thought to lighting up. It would be his first in five years. But would it count, so far from shore? He dropped the cigarette into his shirt pocket. "Under controlled conditions," he said, "they often responded within minutes."

"This like a dinner-bell kind of thing?"

"More or less."

Colson rocked on his heels, studied the deck under his feet. "We'll give her another ten minutes, then we move on."

"Whatever you say."

"They off the scope now," the skipper said. "Either they out of range or they rising to the bait."

Speke looked at his watch, squinting to see the faintly luminous dial. He felt just a little queasy. No food to speak of and that awful stink from the chum and the blood. What was it Chesty called the feeling? The greasies, yes, that pretty much described it. And from the way he'd been drinking when Speke left Sealife Key, the good Dr. Higgs would be feeling the greasies by now without ever boarding a boat. The man had a problem with rum. Speke would have to do something about it just as soon as this situation was under control.

A cigarette, he decided, a lungful of sweet nicotine would settle his stomach. His fingers fished into his shirt pocket, withdrew the comforting stubble of tobacco and paper.

The earring jerked to attention. "Felt something," he said, easing out his line. "Little bump."

"You set the drag?" Colson demanded.

"Real light," the mate said, tapping the winch handle. "Won't feel a thing till we set the hook."

Speke slipped the cigarette back into his pocket. Maybe later, as a form of celebration.

" 'Nother bump," the mate said. He was excited, you could tell by the way his voice tightened.

Speke focused on the water lapping at the stern, concentrating: *Come on, you bastards. Go for it.*

The maxis had been free of the lagoon for a little less than twenty-four hours. The more time the new species had in the outside world, the wider they would range and the more they would learn about shark-hunting boats and the deception of baited hooks. Predicting their behavior was, as had been demonstrated last night, an iffy thing, but Speke did know this much: to stay ahead of the species' learning curve you had to move fast.

Bite, you bastards, bite.

"Look," the mate said.

Speke saw nothing.

"The line," Colson said. "He's taken it and he's moving off real slow."

Speke squinted, realized that line was running silently out of the winch reel.

"Count three and hit the drag," Colson ordered.

A few heartbeats later the mate jerked the winch handle and Speke saw the heavy monofilament line go tight. Humming tight, just for an instant. Then the line was slack again and loops of it poured from the reel, spooling on the deck.

"He broke off," Colson said. "Winch it up and check the leader."

The skipper leaned his thighs against the transom, the pistol held at his side. Calm and confident and grinning slightly. "You ever hooked into one of these things?" he asked softly, an aside.

Dr. Speke shook his head. "Our animal trainer sometimes used an electric prod, just to fend them off, but no, they've never been hooked. Never really been hurt."

"They do hit, you expect 'em to fight like a mako?"

Speke said, "I would think so. Like a very big mako. Last week we estimated body weight at almost two thousand pounds."

"Mako will sometimes jump," Colson said.

"Oh, these jump," Speke said. "We know that."

The mate at the winch raised his voice, "Don't feel nothing there. Just the bumps is all."

"Best get the line inboard," Colson said. "They ain't hit yet, they ain't going to. We'll rig different tackle, try to fool 'em."

The mate released the winch handle and leaned out to retrieve the last few yards of line by hand.

An instant later he shouted, "He's on, Cap! Jesus, look at this big son of a bitch!"

Speke came out of the chair. He saw a dark, glistening dorsal fin, the looming shape of the *Isurus maximus*. What Dr. Higgs called his "new and improved mako." There it was now, swimming tamely up behind the boat, struggling to keep up with the winched-in line. Smart enough to figure out how to minimize the pain of the hook.

Sleek, powerful. A beautiful creature.

Dr. Speke allowed himself one pang of sympathy and then thought: *No, kill this now, while we can.*

"Mike, bring out the gaff," Colson said. "The long one. Cecil, you bring his head up real slow, I'm gonna blow his brains out."

The mate continued to pull in the line by hand, coaxing the big creature up. It rolled behind the boat, exposing its silver underside, its mighty jaws. Speke had a glimpse of torn flesh where the hook protruded.

"Biggest mako I ever did see," said one of the mates.

"Roll him back the other way," Colson said, speaking from the side of his mouth as he steadied his sights.

The mate obliged by leaning out, tugging sharply upward on the line.

When it came, Speke was not ready. Lulled by the docility of the hooked shark, surprised and pleased at how easily this was going, he was not prepared to see another creature lift itself from the water, a blur of furious blue in his peripheral vision.

Isurus maximus, a living, killing ton of cartilage and teeth and muscle, airborne. Jaws unhinged, distended. Teeth as white as the mate's eyes. All of it crashing down on the man at the winch, tearing him out of the cockpit and over the side in an instant.

There was a small splash, then silence.

"Well, shit," Colson said.

Speke was stunned. Was it possible that a man could be there one moment and gone the next? No time even to cry out?

The tattooed mate, his whole body quaking, lashed out with the long-handled killing gaff, striking the water.

"Ease up," Colson murmured, holding his pistol at the ready. "The hooked one gone under the boat."

"They got Cecil!"

"I can see that," Colson said.

The mate responded by jabbing the gaff into the water, screaming incoherently. A frenzy of fear, rage, sudden loss.

Speke was trying to get hold of the man from behind, wrestle him away from the stern, when a row of white teeth opened below, seizing the gaff.

Knocked off balance, the panicked mate was reaching back to grab the transom, keep himself inboard, when Speke finally managed to catch him by the belt.

The second attack was executed with remarkable precision. Speke would reflect on this later. At that moment, as he pulled back on the mate's belt, he had no time to assimilate what happened next.

Another ton of teeth and muscle exploded from the black water. Suspended, for just that moment. Eyes, teeth, out-thrust fins, all eighteen feet of it looming high above the transom. Magnificent.

Then it fell, decapitating the mate in one furious snap of the jaws.

Colson fired the pistol, cursing when he missed.

Speke fell back to the deck with the hot corpse still twitching on top of him, drenched clean of blood by the explosion of water as the beast crashed back into the water.

Struggling to get free of the dead man, all Speke could think about was hiding under the fighting chair. Under the chair he would be safe. The desire filled his mind. Wedged against the cool steel of the pedestal, he saw another of the maxis arch over the stern, jaws snapping.

What terrible beauty, what killing grace.

Colson pivoted under the great body of the creature, falling back to the deck, the pistol flying out of his hands, skittering harmlessly across the deck.

There was a great splashing from the stern, another explosion of water. The hooked creature fighting to get free, inflaming the others.

Speke, clinging to the chair, was astonished to see the skipper on his knees, crouched under the overhang of the transom. Unharmed, apparently, and certainly unarmed. Or was he? The man seemed remarkably calm. Now he was reaching for something attached to his belt—Speke hoped it was another gun—and then another maxi lurched up from the black waters and Speke was drenched again, blinded by salt water.

He sputtered, wiping frantically at his eyes. Panic. The idea of dying blind.

When his vision cleared he saw Colson crawling to the winch with a pair of wire snippers in his hand. Reaching up, cutting the monofilament line.

Snip, as simple as that.

As soon as the line was severed the tail-smashing ceased and there was silence. The waves that had crashed over the cockpit washed quickly out the scuppers and Speke found that his hands were cut and raw from where he'd been holding on to the pedestal of the fighting chair.

Wade Colson was staring past him. Speke turned and saw the headless corpse washed up against the scuppers. Was that blood or sea froth? Hard to tell. The body did not look as if it had ever been alive. It was a dead thing thrown up from the sea.

"Give me a hand," Colson said as he crawled to the mate. "You son of a bitch, give me a hand here."

Speke realized the skipper was talking to him. Give him a hand? What did that mean?

"Help me get him over the side."

Speke shook his head. None of this made sense.

"Either he's going over or you are. Make up your mind."

Speke's mouth was dry and salty. "They'll eat him," he said.

Colson nodded. "That's the idea."

9

Eating the Fear

THE UNFISH THINGS die quickly, awkward in the water, and become food. Eating the fear. Great smooth chunks of flesh that shiver the teeth, filling the belly cavity.

Freshkill.

Unhinging the jaw to gulp. Tearing, ripping. Feeding, feeding.

In moments the unfish things are gone, devoured.

Only a few small morsels escape, drifting down into the darkness. Echoes of blood-smell cause jaws to snap instinctively, but nothing edible remains, the fear-thing is gone.

Us the beautiful resume swimming. All of the six-partnered finding a place in the precise formation as they accelerate. Aware of rushing water on their flanks, a familiar, reassuring pressure on the great lateral nerves. Feeling the power, the newness of the open sea. Nerves and sensors alive to a sea rich with blood-smells and fear-hungers and always, always, the jaw-snapping possibility of freshkill.

One of the Us is slightly injured, trailing a few inches of the hateful killing line from its lower jaw. A rawness where the hook tore away, where rows of teeth have been displaced. The small, sharp pain is shared by all of the Six.

Injure one of the Us and all of them are touched.

They learn by doing. Never again will they feed on mere chunks of flesh. Flesh that may hide a killing hook or pull them, unwilling, to the surface.

Never never never.

This lesson is imprinted, shared. They sing of it, pleased with themselves. Swimming in circles ever wider from the home-place, the lagoon. Us the beautiful, the six-partnered. Us the eaters of unfish. Exploring. Feeding. Learning.

Growing.

Day Two

1

Volunteers

THE DIVE BOAT *Wild Child* joined the search at dawn. The flotilla of volunteers, mostly charter captains and a few local fishermen, patrolled the perimeters of Hawk Channel, following the vagaries of tide and current.

Looking for snags.

"What are the chances?" Sally asked.

She'd come into the wheelhouse to tap hot coffee from the thermos and stayed, one arm draped casually over Tom's broad shoulder. Visibility was poor right now: at first light the molten glare of the rising sun painted the sea with streaks of impossible colors, making it hard to see.

Tom swiveled in the pilot's chair to face her. "Big ocean," he said. "They could be anywhere."

"The idea is, a body might snag on the reef."

"That's the idea."

"If there's anything left to snag."

"Right."

He turned back to the wheel and glanced at the fish finder, which had been set for human-sized sonar contact. So far they'd detected nothing other than schools of small fish, mostly yellowtail rising from the edges of the reef.

Sally sipped from the coffee cup, enjoying the physical promixity of her husband. He hadn't slept well, she knew; the tossing finally woke her for good just before the phone rang with the news that two of the *Squali*'s crew had been lost overboard.

Sally assumed Tom was worried about money— the mortgage was a tough monthly nut—or possibly about Clark biting her hand. Which was already healing nicely, so that was no problem. Although Tom did have a point about the danger of getting too close to a dolphin that had, they suspected, been trained to attack divers. Whatever the reasons for Tom's recent insomnia—odd that he didn't care to discuss it with her—they'd talk about it later; right now they had to concentrate on running the boat.

There was a slight chop in Hawk Channel, the long, mile-wide inner passage that ran between the string of islands and the reef. Her legs flexed automatically, anticipating the pitch of the deck under her feet. *Wild Child* was built for speed; doddling along at five knots made the boat feel heavy and sluggish. The diesel chugged and growled, as if impatient for higher revs. This was slow, numbing work. Sad work.

"I better go back up top," Sally said. "The light is getting better."

"Spell you in fifteen minutes," Tom responded. Grim and serious, dark circles under his eyes, he was hunched over the fish finder, checking out the bottom.

Outside the wheelhouse Sally steadied herself, then went up the ladder quickly, timing her ascent to the rhythmn of the hull motion. She'd taken a spill once, cracking three ribs against a stanchion. Now she was a little wiser, more cautious, more aware of how easy it was to get hurt on a moving vessel.

Settling into the high-riding conning tower seat, she clipped on the safety belt and scanned the sea.

On either side, illuminated by the pale light of dawn, loomed the tall skeletal structures of other flying bridges, other lookouts. A ragtag fleet of volunteers, with all the search boats moving at roughly the same speed. Everybody pitching in, aware that a couple of Coast Guard patrols couldn't cover much open water.

It was a big deal, losing two local crewmen from a charter boat. Almost unprecedented this close to shore. And from what little Captain Colson had said about the incident, there was not much chance of survivors.

Feeding frenzy.

That was the word from the tight-lipped skipper, who was by reputation a cautious, highly competent shark killer. Not a catch-and-release kind of guy, which made him, in Sally's view, something of a menace to the delicate reef ecology. Sharks, being slow breeders, were in serious decline, not yet protected by any regulation against overfishing, and professional shark killers were endangering several species.

Not that *Squali*'s crewmen deserved such a gruesome fate. Must have gotten awfully careless to be hanging off the transom with a couple of big sharks hooked under the stern. Careless enough to get themselves tangled in the line, dragged over the side, according to Wade Colson.

Maybe drunk or stoned, that was the rumor—had to be some reason why experienced crewmen would lose it like that. Must have been a party out there. The boys drunk or high, wanting to get bloody—all that macho "Old Man and the Sea" nonsense about killing sea monsters to prove their manhood. Had to be something dumb like that. No other reason, as Tom had pointed out, why such a notorious tightwad as Wade Colson would be night fishing, burning fuel without a paying charter on board.

That is, if the whole story hadn't been invented to cover the loss of two men. "Night fishing," after all, was local slang for drug smuggling. Who knew what had really happened out at sea, under cover of darkness? Sally didn't trust Colson. Never had. Didn't like the way he looked at her, or at Tom, for that matter. As if they were intruders in these parts, a couple of Yankee do-gooders interfering with the sacred hunting grounds of Old Florida.

The shout came from another boat. "There!"

Sally looked, saw a figure pointing almost in her direction. She stared down into the glistening water, squinting against the flicker of sunlight. Nothing, just the dull glare of twitching water.

Then she saw it, a kind of lumpish thing, rolling, almost completely submerged. Tom was already altering course.

The other boat got there first. A bare-chested, rubber-booted young crewman probed over the side with a long-handled gaff, grinning as he concentrated, fisting the handle.

Sally came down off her perch and stood with Tom, waiting.

Another gaff went over and then they could see it, pinned against the hull of the boat as it rolled free of the water: the partial remains of a small hammerhead, flesh splayed in such a way that it had looked, in the early light, almost human.

Tom's voice was low. "Makes you think," he said. "Maybe it's better if we *don't* find any remains. Cleaner that way."

"Maybe," Sally said.

She had no desire to see whatever gruesome thing the sharks had left, but Sally had her doubts about Colson's version of events. She didn't like it that his crewman had simply disappeared into the faceless mouth of the sea.

It was too neat, too terribly perfect.

Back at the Sealife compound Vernon Speke stayed in the shower until the water ran cold. He scrubbed himself raw, using soap and a hard brush, and he never did get clean of the feeling. That slick, stomach-turning sensation of freshly killed flesh quivering in his hands. Almost an electrical kind of sensation in his fingertips as he'd helped the captain heave the body over the transom.

Both of them diving back to the deck as the thing slapped into the water. Aware of a kind of gurgle-whooooosh noise as something big sucked it under. Jesus, what a cold noise *that* had been.

In his shower stall Dr. Speke scrubbed harder. The image, the feeling of the headless body still fresh in his mind.

He remembered how Colson, keeping low to the deck on his hands and knees, had got himself into the wheelhouse and started the engines. Speke had followed, his long, spidery legs skidding against the cant of the deck, and then looked down to find his shirt front soaked black with blood.

"I know what you're thinkin'," Colson had said. His face was expressionless, tinged green by the compass light. "Thinkin' you gon' double that bonus, make up for the loss of human life."

Speke had peeled the shirt off, gagging as the blood-slick fabric touched his mouth and nose. "Fair enough," he'd said. "Consider it doubled."

"Those things," Colson had said, looking straight ahead as he steered, "they ain't normal mako shark."

"No," Speke had agreed.

Silence for a time as *Squali* headed west. Getting a couple of miles down before Colson radioed his "man overboard" report to the Coast Guard. They'd already agreed that Dr. Speke would be put ashore before that happened, his presence not mentioned in the report. The longer Sealife was kept out of it, the better.

When Colson finally spoke, he had the tone of a man who'd been slowly working things out, getting it straight in his own head before putting his mouth in gear. "Most shark, one of 'em gets hooked, the others will turn on it," he said. "Shark tend to be loners."

Speke grunted. He wasn't sure how much Colson needed to know about *Isurus maximus*.

"These shark of yours," Colson had continued, "seems like they work together. Cooperate."

"We think they do, yes," Speke said. "They're identical, cloned from the same egg, so it makes sense they'd have similar reactions to external events."

"Don't bullshit me, mister."

Speke had shrugged. Right at that moment he didn't give a rat's ass *what* Colson thought as long as he kept his mouth shut.

Now, coming cold out of the shower, he felt the exhaustion begin to creep into his bones and he thought, yes, Colson would have to know more. Enough to catch the maxis. Enough to catch 'em and kill 'em dead before they ranged any farther, before they grew bigger or mated.

Before they learned any new tricks.

Speke's knees felt strangely weak as he padded into the small air-conditioned bedroom of the cabin. Shivering like crazy now—partly because of the air conditioning, partly from sheer exhaustion. He was drained, empty, so tired the bed seemed to shimmer

HUNGER

75

in the corners of his eyes. Took forever to find clean
trousers, a clean cotton shirt. Struggle to make his
fingers work the buttons.

More than anything he wanted to sleep for a week
or so.

Forget it. No rest for the weary.

Speke went to his bureau, opened the top drawer.
There, in the back, a small plastic vial saved for special occasions. Speke thumbed open the cap. Under
the tuft of white cotton lay a nest of small white
pills. His cache of wake-me-ups, medicinal Dexedrine. He had a prescription from a doctor friend in
Miami, made it all nice and legal.

He swallowed one of the tiny tablets, thought better and swallowed two more. Three for luck.

Fifteen minutes later the dexies made him sparkle.
Wide awake, alive with a fierce energy that made
his eyelids twitch, Speke left his cabin. Time to rouse
Higgs and Mendez and cute Lucy Savrin.

Time to kick some ass.

They didn't have, he decided, a hell of a lot of
time before the situation got seriously out of control.

At noon several of the search boats straggled into
Vaca Cut. Some would fuel up and return to Hawk
Channel. Others, like *Wild Child*, were ready to call
it quits.

"I can hardly focus," Tom said, rubbing his eyes.

They were waiting in line at the fuel dock, numbed
from the experience. Six hours had produced nothing but a series of false finds—flotsam and fish carcasses; a white rubber fisherman's boot that might
or might not have belonged to one of the missing
mates, there was no way to tell.

Sally put out bumpers, fending off one of the
charter boats that had joined the search. The skipper, a New Jersey native who'd come south for the
winter fishing and stayed on, was a talkative type,

pumped up on strong coffee and the morbid excitement of searching for body parts.

" 'Scuze the expression," he said, tipping his cap
at Sally, "but there's somethin' fishy about this
whole expedition."

"How so?"

The Jersey skipper pointed to *Squali's* vacant slip.
"I lose my men overboard, I'd sure as hell have a
lot more to say about it than Wade Colson. The man
acts like it's an everyday occurrence, a crew gets torn
apart by sharks. Which, you'll pardon me, that's a
lot of bullshit."

Tom had come down from the bridge, introduced
himself to the New Jersey skipper. Tom said, "Any
idea what Colson told the Coast Guard?"

"Same as he told the rest of us, I guess. Boys got
tangled up in their lines."

"And you don't believe that?"

A weary shrug. "Not sure what I believe. Except
I believe a rank amateur might get in trouble that
way. Not Colson. He's a sharp motherfuck— Excuse
me, ma'am, a sharp son of a gun. Might have one
man fall over, he was drunk enough. Not two at
once."

Tom was nodding. "It does strain credulity, I
guess."

"Huh?"

"Tough to believe it happened like he said."

"Absolutely," the skipper said. "Like this, um,
bullhockey about no charter on board."

"What?"

The skipper said, "This a small dock here. We all
in each other's pockets, you know? All in the same
business. Hustling customers. So a man keeps his
eyes peeled, you know what I mean?"

"Sure I do."

"He had a man on last night, I'm almost sure of
that. Tall, geeky-looking fella, he was slinking

around here earlier in the afternoon, making arrangements with Colson. Like he was arranging a charter. Right after he left, the *Squali* fueled up, loaded bait, like they intended to go out.''

Tom said, ''You know the man, this customer he had?''

''Not by name,'' the skipper said. ''But I'm pretty sure he's that strange bird runs the dolphin school.''

''Dolphin school?''

''I guess it *used* to be a dolphin school, that's what I heard. Sealife Key, you know the place?''

''Yeah,'' Tom said. ''We know the place.''

''The guy who runs it, he was on the *Squali* yesterday. I mentioned that to Colson this morning, he gives me that flinty look of his, tells me I'm mistaken.''

''But you're not mistaken.''

The skipper said, ''No way. Now, why do you suppose he'd lie about a thing like that?''

2

Snapshot

THE DIVE BOAT *Gold Bug* anchored in sixty feet of water, a half mile southwest of Sombrero Light, an unmanned beacon. The shoal area showed green under calm seas, with darker, deeper water all around. As the sun climbed in the sky the submerged reef would begin to glow, reflecting light upwards through the shallow water.

On certain days it looked like a huge lamp down there, a warm green lantern. Swarms of tropical fish were drawn like moths to the light.

Beyond the reef, strewn for miles, were the wrecks of ships torn open on the teeth of the coral shoal. Wrecked on stormy nights, in black weather, in the rare fog, or because of gross stupidity: napping captains, drunken navigators, sheer bad luck—it mattered not. The reef had no opinion, cast no blame, named no names; it simply disemboweled those vessels that chanced too close.

The *Gold Bug*, out of Marathon, was licensed for

twelve passengers. On this particular morning seven divers suited up, waiting for the boat to swing into the current and steady itself.

One of the divers was Ray Hurst, a twenty-six-year-old darkroom technician from Boston. Ray had done some wreck diving off Cape Cod, in water so black and cold it felt like an iron fist squeezing your skull. Visibility about from here to your elbow.

This was an entirely new and welcome experience, dropping into clear, eighty-degree water in the Florida Keys. "I can't believe it," he said to Pete, his dive buddy. "I bet you can see a hundred feet."

Pete said, "Sixty, they said. Sixty is average."

"Whatever."

Sixty, a hundred, Ray didn't care. He couldn't wait to get in the water. The dive master, a bleached-blond kid even younger than Ray and his buddy, unfurled a chart on the engine cover. The wrecks were marked with fluorescent orange Magic Marker.

"We should be almost over the *Henry Gore*," the dive master said. "For you first-timers, the *Gore* is a coastal steamer. Launched in 1937 and died the same year. It was salvaged almost immediately by the owners and stripped pretty clean—you'll notice the big bronze prop is missing, that's the first item got hauled up. The port side engine crashed through the hole in the hull. You'll see part of the boiler sticking above the sand right next to the wreck."

Ray studied the chart as the dive master gave his rote lecture. Ray liked to know exactly where he was underwater. It was easy to get disoriented, even with visibility this good, and with two knots of current sweeping the wreck, a miscalculation could be at the very least embarrassing.

Miss the towline streaming behind the *Gold Bug* and it was a long swim back, fighting that current. Ray had a new submersible Nikonos camera he wanted to try out, so he didn't want to waste a lot of time and energy on screwups.

"The entire port side is peeled open," the dive master was saying, "so access is easy. Plenty to see right there, no need to go deeper into the hull."

"What if we do?" Pete asked. "Go deeper."

The dive master sighed, started to roll up the chart. "Just be aware, okay? You get yourself lost in there, it'll be me has to find you. So be aware of your location, be aware of your air supply. Get inside that big hold, the storage area, remember you can find an exit on the port side, you don't have to go back into the superstructure to get out."

The divers began to line up along the rail, ready to enter the water. Roll back or just step out, it was their option.

Ray said, "What about the 'cuda?"

The dive master thumbed a splash of zinc on his nose and smiled. "What about them?"

"They bite?"

"Not unless you stick your hands in their mouths. Or try to corner them. Barracuda are curious, but they'll keep their distance. Just be respectful. We never had a smart diver bitten."

"How about dumb divers?" This was Pete again, being a wise guy.

The other divers laughed, just a little nervous.

"I can't help what happens to dumb divers," the dive master said. "So be smart, okay?

The amazing thing was, it looked exactly like a sunken ship. Ray had been planning this vacation for months, saving his money for the new underwater camera and the expensive strobe unit, and he'd made the dive in his imagination many, many times. He always pictured the wreck as blending into the reef, so well disguised you had to concentrate hard to make out the hull form where it melted into the white sea bottom.

For once the reality was an improvement on what he'd imagined.

At first sighting the *Henry Gore* looked recently painted. As he drew closer, following Pete's bright yellow Cressi fins into the cooler, deeper water, Ray realized that the "paint" was a thin layer of coral encrusting the iron skin of the ship.

The ship's funnel, dislodged as the vessel capsized, remained precariously attached to the superstructure, like a party hat worn at a rakish angle. The top of the huge boiler lay partially buried in the sand nearby, as the dive master had described, and you could see where the entire port side hull had been peeled open by the reef. Looked almost like the cutaway of a model—the deck beams visible, the empty cargo holds wide open to the sea.

It was beautiful, damn near perfect. The only disappointment was a distinct lack of fish. The dive master had promised the wreck would be swarming with fish—yellowtail and jacks and schoolmasters, angels and parrots—but the *Henry Gore* seemed devoid of life, eerily quiet. And according to the guidebooks—Ray was an avid reader—this particular wreck was home to a number of very large barracuda.

For an amateur photographer, 'cuda were a trophy fish. Ray wanted at least one good shot of that famous torpedo body, the underslung jaw with the row of bulldog teeth. Hence the new camera, the powerful strobe. The wreck was a lovely thing—better than he'd expected—but the dive was going to be less than satisfactory unless he captured a 'cuda on film.

Ray and Pete rendezvoused, as agreed, at the stern, where the huge rudder blade was partially buried in the sand. Pete, a casual friend who belonged to Ray's Boston dive club, used the empty nub of the propeller shaft as a point of balance, gripping it with his fins and applauding himself, clowning for the camera.

OK, OK, Ray signaled. He aimed the new Nikonos unit, snapped off a shot of Mr. Goofball. Who raised his hands to his mask, temporarily blinded by the strobe. Ray waited until his buddy had shaken it off—*serves you right for wasting my precious film*—and then they both began to swim the length of the *Henry Gore*. Amazing, come to think of it, that a ship as sturdy as this—it had lasted more than fifty years underwater—had been so easily pulled under by the harmless-looking reef.

Ahead of them other *Gold Bug* divers had already entered the superstructure, swimming in and out of openings in what had been the navigation bridge. Everything turned topsy-turvy here, canted almost ninety degrees from the vertical. It took a few moments to get it clear in your head, what was what.

Pete went inside first, kicking through the empty window openings, the glass long since shattered, or maybe broken out by other dive parties. Ray hung back, not wanting to tangle with the other divers, and saw Pete clutching at the ship's wheel. Clowning again. Through a stream of exhaust bubbles he indicated that this too would make a good picture. Ray obliged by triggering the strobe unit, and this time Pete kept his eyes averted.

Pete's offer to take the camera and get a shot of Ray at the wheel was declined; the truth was Ray had no interest in gag snapshots. He considered himself a serious photographer, had ambitions of giving up his tech job and going professional.

Through hand signals—a little rough, as they'd never really done all that much diving together—the two men agreed to rendezvous at the bridge in fifteen minutes, in time to make their ascent together. Meanwhile Ray would explore the exposed area of the cargo hold, hoping to locate the elusive barracuda, while Pete surveyed the exterior of the wreck.

Relieved to be free of his clowning buddy, Ray stopped and cleared his mask before proceeding into the cargo hold. Clearing the mask was a little scary at fifty feet—you had to tip the mask away from your face, blow the water out with a stream of respirator bubbles—but he was determined to improve his visibility, haunted by the thought that some great fish were lurking in the shadows, just out of range.

Satisfied with the improved condition of his faceplate, Ray powered ahead, relying on his fins to propel him over the edge, down into the darker, empty space of the cargo hold. The camera unit held at his chest, safety strap secure. A lot of money was invested here, so he didn't want to lose it.

Buoyancy was a problem, so Ray released a little air from his buoyancy control vest and then tucked into a sitting position, letting himself sink down through the thermal incline. Much cooler here, out of reach of the warming sun, insulated by sixty-foot-thick blanket of water.

As he sank, his eyes gradually adjusted to the spotty dimness of the interior. Light poured through the huge gap in the hull, making the shadow areas appear that much darker in contrast. Like entering a cave, floating down through shafts of milky light.

He landed fins first on the starboard side of the inner hull. This was now the bottom—looking up he could see other divers lazily swimming through the long, killing gash that had sunk the *Henry Gore*. The other divers seemed, from this vantage, a world away, although it was a distance of no more than forty feet, the width of the ship.

Inside, he thought, may be *that's* where the 'cuda were hiding. Keeping out of sight, away from the strangely human noise of clicking respirators and swishing fins.

Ray checked his gauges and his watch. Plenty of air left, but a mere twelve minutes before Pete expected him at the rendezvous. Not much time to explore the deep interior of the wreck.

Just give it a quick look, he decided, and try not to get too disappointed at the lack of fish.

Clutching the camera close to his chest, so as not to bump against the twisted bulkhead, Ray finned slowly out a shaft of light, kicking up clouds of rust with his flippers, pausing again while his eyes adjusted. Strange to be floating here in the dark, a visitor from another world. With his tanks and his weights and his demand-actuated respirator he was, he decided, more like an astronaut than a swimmer.

There.

Something moving just out of range.

Ray twisted, bumping the camera, and got a glimpse of what looked like part of a tail fin. Darting around the edge of the bulkhead, so slippery and quick he wasn't really sure. Maybe he wanted to see a 'cuda so bad he was imagining things.

He swam toward where it had been—where it *might* have been, he reminded himself—and was surprised to realize how far away that maybe-fin had been. He'd thought he could almost reach out and touch it. No way. Some sort of illusion maybe, a trick of water and scant light that had magnified whatever it was he had seen.

Now he was considerably deeper inside the hull, deeper than he'd intended to go, given his promised rendezvous.

Just a look, he decided. See if anything was really there, or if it was just his imagination running wild. Plenty of air left, that wasn't a problem.

Ray wormed his way around the ragged edge of the fractured bulkhead and found himself in a passageway between decks. A few ghostly shafts of light shimmering through from above, illuminating part of a stairway.

Something moved behind the stairs. A shifting of the shadows, difficult to focus on. An inky rippling effect, maybe a reflection of the light.

No, not a reflection, he decided. Something *large* moving, slipping away behind the stairs. A silvery, bluish color, contrasting against the black iron interior of the wreck.

Ray lifted the camera, aimed through the viewfinder, and then relaxed his finger on the trigger. It was gone, whatever it was. Slipped away deeper into the ship.

Decision time. Like that old rock-song lyric, should he go or should he stay?

Stay, he decided. Give it another try. An opportunity like this was too good to pass up. Might be a really huge barracuda back there, slipping away. A real trophy shot. *Denizen of the Wreck*, that's what he'd title the photograph. Or less dramatically, *Resident of the "Henry Gore"*: that sounded more artistic.

Holding the camera up, ready to shoot, Ray finned carefully around the stairway. Felt his tank rack bump gently against the stair rail. Behind the stairs, an open hatch or doorway. Dark inside.

Really dark.

A deep, perpetual darkness. He got a sense of space, though, as if this were the entrance to another, deeper cargo hold. Or possibly the engine room. Whatever, it was big in there. Big and black.

A perfect place, he decided, for a shy barracuda. If it *was* a 'cuda. Maybe he'd glimpsed a giant grouper, what the racist rednecks still called a jewfish. The guidebooks said the giant grouper, a docile creature not dangerous to divers, could get up to seven hundred pounds, and was known to inhabit wrecks. The dive master hadn't mentioned any big grouper, but then maybe he'd never actually gotten this deep inside the ship.

Ray checked the illuminated dial of his air supply gauge. More than enough, and that didn't count the reserve. He could get back to the surface on reserve from this depth, if need be. Pete would be worried, but what the heck, might do him good, make him take diving a little more seriously.

Be there, he thought, and kicked, propelling himself through the opening into the dark. Holding the camera unit with both hands, straight out ahead.

The camera nudged something. Not a solid part of the ship, but something that gave way, as if retreating. Instinctively his finger tightened on the trigger.

Ray pulled, activating the shutter, triggering the strobe.

In the flash of pure white light, he saw them.

Them.

The strobe light burning hot in their eyes. Beautiful, he thought. And then a thrum of panic convulsed his body.

Mistake. Mistake. Get away.

They move.

They have entered this quiet darkness to drift, to dream. To digest the fullness of their feeding.

When it—this alien, unfish thing—awkwardly enters their sanctuary, the maxis do not at first react. Do not, for several heartbeats, feel threatened. Until the cold explosion of light blinds them.

Hurts, they sing.

Danger thing, they sing.

Blinded, they sense the location of the unfish creature by the pressure it makes in the water. By the pitter-pat of its heart.

Destroy, they sing. *Feed and destroy.*

They attack. The unfish thing struggles, trying to

back away. Teeth seize it, tearing at the limbs. Jaws snap, severing the air hose, regulator. Its straps cut, the air tank falls away.

The unfish thing stops struggling. It seems to be waiting for the end. There is a moment, a heartbeat, and then an unhinged jaw rakes rows of diamond teeth through the soft abdomen, disemboweling the thing.

It stops moving.

The maxis tear the unfish thing to pieces and then devour the pieces, shuddering as they gulp, urgent in their need.

A few moments later the danger thing—the strobe unit that triggered the attack—drifts to the bottom and the blood-smell of freshkill permeates the water.

Jaws snap, but nothing sizable remains.

3

A Face in the Window

WHEN TOM CAME out of the dive shop Sally was sitting on the dock, her legs hanging in the water. Her hands were white with sunscreen and she was laughing as Lois sported in the canal, showing off the handprints of zinc oxide on the top of her glistening gray back.

"We're sunbathing?" Tom asked.

Sally nodded. "She seems to love this stuff."

"Not the stuff. She loves having you put it on her."

Sally said, "Whatever. She needs it this time of year."

Bottlenose dolphin tend to burn if they spend a lot of time exposing themselves to direct sunlight, as Lois did. One of several problems peculiar to domesticated dolphin. Clark, who spent much of his surface time under the shade of the dock, did not require sunscreen—a small compensation for his shyness.

Just as well the male was shy, in Tom's opinion. He didn't trust Clark, not with Sally, not with anyone. How much of Sealife's behavior modification lessons were still there in that mysterious dolphin mind, ready to take hold when you least expected it?

It was enough to give you pause. The female was clearly recovered, and not a danger to humans—if she ever *had* been—but the male—well, there were times when Tom regretted that the two dolphin came as a package deal. The male might be better off in another environment, out of human contact. If the animal didn't improve soon, he intended to raise the delicate subject of finding Clark a new home.

Not today, though. On this sun-drenched afternoon, with Sally obviously content to spend time with her animals, Tom didn't feel like playing the heavy. Sally knew the pair much better than he did; he simply had to trust her judgment. No need to spoil the rest of her day, not after a morning spent searching for human remains in Hawk Channel.

Tom said, "We're set. Reservations canceled through the weekend."

He ducked as Lois splashed her tail flukes, drenching the float.

Looking up at him, Sally said, "Any complaints?"

"Lots. I said, you know, give us a couple more days."

She said, "You explained about the insurance?"

"The lack of it? Yeah. People are still pissed off, they get their dives canceled at the last minute. They don't want to hear about how we can't afford to carry liability insurance."

Sally lifted one foot out of the water, let Lois nudge her. The animal was squeaking like crazy. Sally said, "Could be bad weather. Same thing would happen if a storm hit. We'd have to cancel for a few days."

"Yeah, well, a storm would be more convincing. I say shark problems, these crazy bastards *want* to dive."

"Are you serious?"

Tom crossed his heart. "One guy, this character down from Miami, he tells me he's always wanted to go one-on-one with a man-eater. He's got this big bowie knife he carries in a quick-release ankle holster. Wants to know if we can take movies of him killing a shark."

Sally said, "Unbelievable." She pulled her legs out of the water and stood up, wiping her hands on a towel. Lois was still by the float, splashing her flukes, making her familiar trills and squeaks. Clark was nowhere to be seen, maybe hiding in the old pier again.

Sally said, "We're in a crazy business."

"Stark raving mad."

"And that's what we like about it, right?"

"Sometimes I wonder."

Sally applied a damp hug, patted his backside. "Can we afford to cancel?" she asked.

Tom said, "Can't afford *not* to. I thought we agreed on that."

"We did. But I know how you worry about money."

Tom shrugged. He said, "That's my job. I'm a worrier."

He stepped into the cockpit of the dive boat, hopped up to the steering controls.

Sally said, "You could hang out with us. Log a little playtime."

Tom keyed the engine, heard it cough and catch.

"I want a word with Dr. Speke," he reminded her. "See if he can clear up that rumor we heard about him being on the *Squali* last night."

Sally tossed the dock lines into the cockpit. "Your old buddy, right?"

"Yeah, right."

Sally made a face. Dr. Vernon Speke was one of her least favorite people. As the current began to pull *Wild Child* clear, she stood on the dock, hands on her slim bikinied hips, her bright yellow T-shirt damp with dolphin splash.

"Give him my fond regards," she called out, raising her voice to be heard over the thump of the diesel. "And, babe? Watch your back!"

Tom eased *Wild Child* out of the basin, cleared the stakes that marked the channel, and then put the throttle down. The dive boat came up nicely on a plane, settled into cruising speed.

He had roughly three miles of open water to cover. Not a cloud in the sky and the sea as milky green as tarnished copper, darker where turtle grass grew in the shallows. High overhead, the fork-tailed silhouette of a frigate bird circled against the sun, looking to hijack a fish from some other less belligerent bird of prey.

Most days, just being out on the open water would calm him, erase any land-based anxiety. An at-ease feeling that flowed through his whole body, unknotting his muscles, slowing his heart.

Alone with just your thoughts, gliding along the string of mangrove islands that made up the Keys, you had to feel at peace with the world, with life. You got the feeling you might live forever.

Today was an exception. Something nagged at him, something he couldn't quite bring into focus.

Watch your back, Sally had said, and not in a kidding way. Tom didn't like Vernon Speke any more than Sally did, but he didn't consider him dangerous. After all, the man ran a research institute, depended on government contracts. However much of a threat he might have posed to the dolphin in his program, that didn't mean he was threatening on a person-to-person level.

Yet when it came time to turn toward the shoreline of Sealife Key, Tom almost hesitated. Why not
just glide on by, keep his peace of mind? But his
hands were already pulling at the wheel, altering
the boat's course.

Sealife Key, a fairly small island of less than fifty
acres, had at one time been used as a work camp for
the men who built Flagler's Folly, the railroad that
had connected Miami to Key West until a hurricane
wrecked it. Later, after the Overseas Highway replaced the railroad, the little island had been converted into a resort. The royal palms that soared over
the small, tin-roofed cottages dated from that time,
as did the artificial beach.

The lagoon itself was relatively new, dredged out
when the Sealife Research Institute took up resi-
dence, supplanting the bankrupt resort. The lagoon
was enclosed by stone jetties and a wire-mesh gate,
and had been home to Clark and Lois and a number
of other dolphin involved in the so-called Submarine
Defense Research Program. All of them gone now,
the surviving mammals shipped to other aquariums
or dolphin programs, at least according to Sealife.

*We're no longer engaged in the testing or training of
marine mammals or of any protected species.* That was
the company line.

Wild Child rocked on her own wake as Tom pulled
back on the throttle, steered directly for the big sign
that said: NO TRESPASSING, PRIVATE RESEARCH FACIL-
ITY.

There was activity at the Sealife pier. A Cigarette-
style chase boat and a big converted shrimp trawler,
repainted with the familiar Sealife colors—both vessels were alongside and in the process of loading
gear.

Busy, busy. So busy that nobody complained
when Tom laid the dive boat soft against the pilings.
He looped dock lines quickly over cleats and then

hit the pier on sneakered feet, moving very lightly for his size, sneaking up in plain sight. The crew of the chase boat looked up from the cockpit with expressions of mild surprise.

"Vernon around?" Tom said, making it sound like he was an old friend.

"Dr. Speke? Yeah, sure, he's around here somewhere."

Tom made a point of not staring and still managed to get a pretty good glimpse of what was being loaded into the chase boat. Electronic gear, what looked to be sophisticated sonar equipment—not your typical fish-finding gear, that was for sure.

A few yards farther on, the converted shrimp trawler, riding high in the water, was being fitted with new heavy-duty net winches.

Tom ambled along the pier, wearing his best smile like a disguise. Just a good old boy, friendly as a puppy dog. He came upon a couple of kids trudging toward the boats, arms loaded with gear. "How do," Tom said, executing a mock salute. "Vernon this way, that old rascal?"

"Try the lagoon."

"Thank you kindly."

Tom walked on for a hundred yards, skirting the beach in the shade of the royal palms, and paused to check out the lagoon. The surface was quiet. No dorsal fins; no sign of any resident dolphin or of anything else, for that matter.

Behind him a voice said, "Excuse me?"

He turned and glanced down into the wary blue eyes of a young, yellow-haired woman. Challenging him.

"Tom Hart," he said, extending his hand.

The young woman rather reluctantly offered her hand. "Lucy," she said. "Lucy Savrin. We're, um, closed to visitors right now."

Tom stood his ground and said, "So I understand. Where's Vernon at?"

Ms. Savrin stared at him uneasily. "Is Dr. Speke expecting you?"

"I expect he is," Tom said with a grin. Tone down the good-old-boy act with this one, she wasn't buying.

"Wait here, please."

He watched her march off toward the research buildings on fine, sturdy legs and was reminded of the day when, two thousand miles and almost twenty years from here, he'd met another young research assistant and determined then and there to make her part of his life.

A tingling sensation on the back of his neck made Tom turn around. He saw a fishnet spread out on the ground. Crouching next to it was a man. The man was staring intently at him.

"Hey," Tom said, ambling forward, hands harmless in the pockets of his shorts. "How's it goin'? I know you—Roberto Mendez, right?"

Mendez stood up from the net, glanced uneasily in the direction of the research buildings.

Tom said. "I'm Tom Hart. We met in court once. Couple of your dolphin played hooky, ended up in our canal?"

Mendez said, "Ah, yes. The dive-boat people."

"You're the animal trainer, right? I heard you're very good. No hard feelings about us getting custody of your animals, I hope?"

Mendez shrugged. He said, "That program was concluded. We had no objection to you taking charge of the dolphin. Although technically, I think, they still belong to us."

"Technically, yeah."

As Tom moved closer, Mendez shifted to the side, standing with his arms folded, staring off into the middle distance, avoiding eye contact. Fidgeting, clearly anxious for Dr. Speke to come to the rescue, handle the situation.

"The male," Mendez said, making conversation. "How's he doing?"

"Much better," Tom said. "Sally's done wonders with them both."

"So I heard."

Tom said. "Is that right? What did you hear exactly?"

Mendez took off his long-billed cap and sighed. A glint of gray showed in his dark, close-cropped hair. He wore a polo-style shirt with a Sealife logo, denim cutoffs, and boat shoes. Although fit and trim, he had the hangdog expression of a man who hadn't been getting enough sleep.

Mendez said, "Look, I worked with dolphin for almost twenty years, I love the animals, okay? Lois was always a sweetheart. Clark, he had some problems."

"You remember their names," Tom said, impressed.

Mendez said, "I *gave* them their names. Of course I remember."

A standoff. Tom found that he believed Mendez; despite his involvement with the train-to-kill program, the man really did care about the dolphin.

Tom said, "I had the impression, there in court, that you weren't quite as enthusiastic as Dr. Speke. About what you were doing with the dolphin. Training them to attack enemy divers or whatever."

Mendez looked miserable. "I can't talk about that," he said. "The whole project was classified. You know that."

Tom dropped into a crouch, fingered the mesh of the spread-out fishnet. He said, "Hey, Bob? What the hell are you fishing for, you need a wire mesh?"

There was a shout. Tom let go of the net and stood up.

"Dr. Speke! Just the man I want to see."

Vernon Speke hurried across the grass, a gangle of long thin arms and legs, almost at a run. His bony, angular face was contorted into a deep scowl. Not a happy camper.

"You're trespassing," he said, confronting Tom. "You'll have to leave immediately."

Speke looked twitchy as hell, in Tom's opinion. An ants-in-his-pants attitude. A pace or two behind him, young Lucy hurried to keep up, an expression of bright confusion on her fresh and pretty face— she'd just tumbled to the fact that Tom did not have an appointment with her boss.

Tom said, "Sure, I'll leave. Anything you say, doc. Walk me to my boat?"

"Look, we're very busy—"

"That's the deal," Tom said, hardening his grin. "Walk me to my boat, we'll discuss it on the way."

Grabbing Dr. Speke firmly by the elbow, he steered him back to the gravel path. The institute director, an inch or so taller but forty pounds lighter, struggled to jerk his arm free.

"How dare you," he said, pouting as he rubbed his elbow. "What's this all about?"

Tom said, "Take it easy, doc. Just a couple questions."

"I could have you arrested."

Reluctantly Dr. Speke had fallen in beside Tom, keeping pace. His skinny, nervous fingers fiddled with his ponytail; on him it looked affected, girlish.

Tom said, "You could do that. Have me arrested. Might be better all 'round if you put my mind at ease, though. You acquainted with Captain Wade Colson, runs the *Squali* out of Vaca Cut?"

The way he reacted, Tom knew he had at least part of his answer. Speke definitely knew Colson.

Tom said, "Reason I ask, the *Squali* lost a couple of men last night. Bodies are still missing, believed to be killed by shark. A feeding frenzy, that's what Colson told the Coast Guard. You know anything about that?"

Dr. Speke seemed to be suffering from dry mouth. He almost stammered, then spit it out. "Why should I know anything about that?"

Tom smiled, scratched the side of his nose. "Scuttlebutt," he said. "Word on the waterfront is that you were aboard when it happened. That you chartered the *Squali* last night."

Dr. Speke stopped moving, got very still. "I don't respond to rumors," he said. "And anyhow, what business is it of yours?"

"No business at all," Tom said. "Except you have to wonder, why would a guy from Sealife be hiring a shark killer?"

Speke said, "You're out of line, mister. Way out of line."

Tom grinned, acknowledged that he was indeed out of line, that he made a habit of being out of line, so far as the Sealife operation was concerned. He said, "The other question I have—if you people are no longer training dolphin, then what *are* you training?"

That one seemed to hit Dr. Speke right between the eyes. He stood there blinking in the sunlight, his skinny hands twitching at his sides, on the verge of bolting, maybe—anyhow, making some kind of move.

Go for it, Tom decided, see how he reacts. "Steel-mesh nets, super-duper sonar gear. What exactly are you trying to catch? Hey, doc? You people suddenly in the shark-fishing business or what?"

Dr. Speke turned away, coughing into his fist, averting his eyes. "Three minutes," he said, jerking his thumb at the pier. "In three minutes I call the sheriff, and I swear to you, this time I'll prefer charges.''

Tom said, ''On my way, doc. Color me gone.''

As he pulled away from the pier he happened to glance back at the row of tin-roofed staff cottages. A motion in one of the windows attracted his attention.

Tom squinted, saw someone move out of the shadows, into a slant of light. A sad-eyed man staring right at him.

The man raised a hand as if he intended to wave goodbye, and then the hand dropped as if it were too much effort, and the man simply stared until Tom got *Wild Child* under way and left Sealife Key in his wake.

4

What Lois Wants

SALLY PACED THE dock, wet from the waist down.
Lois was acting up, slapping the water with her tail:
a hard, demanding bang that sent spray flying.

"Easy, girl," she said. Fighting that helpless feeling that overcame her whenever one of the animals
started behaving in ways she didn't understand.

Usually it was Clark acting out, but right now it
was the normally placid female who was slapping
the hell out of the water and speeding frantically
around the canal. Lifting up her curved beak and
spewing shrill gibberish at Sally as if she expected,
demanded to be understood.

The try at live feeding had not gone well. Sally
had released several mullet and Lois had ignored
them, had made no attempt at pursuit. Instead, determined to act on her own mysterious agenda, the
dolphin had been raising a commotion, creating a
storm of wavelets in the canal.

Again and again she showed her teeth and chattered at Sally: a wild, elliptical twittering that was almost birdlike.

"Easy, now," Sally said, using a tone that usually calmed the animals. "Take it easy, please? Hear him out there? Tom's coming back."

The dive boat's familiar engine could be heard in the distance long before the flying bridge appeared over the tops of the palm trees. A few minutes later Tom had cleared the narrow entry into the canal.

As *Wild Child* approached the dock Lois came half out of the water, shivering her flukes, squealing frantically. Tom shut down the engine and said, "What's with her?"

Sally answered by leaping into the cockpit. "I think Clark has run off," she said. "Lois is going berserk. She wants to follow him."

"So what's stopping her?"

The canal area was open to the Atlantic on one side, the Gulf on the other. As always, the dolphin were free to come and go, although they rarely took advantage of that freedom.

Sally said, "She wants us to follow her, I think."

Tom gave her a look. "Are you serious?"

"She keeps making runs, as if she's headed outside. Then she comes back to the dock and splashes me."

Tom grinned, shook his head. "And you translate that as 'follow me'?"

"Yeah," Sally said, adamant. "I do."

"What the hell, it's been a crazy day, why not?"

He hit the button, cranked the diesel back to life.

Sally went to the bow of the boat and leaned out over the safety rail. Lois was circling ahead of them, weaving back and forth in the canal as Tom steered between the channel markers.

"Okay, girl? Is this what you want? You want to find Clark? Go ahead, go find him. Go!"

Sally was aware of the fact that you couldn't have

a conversation with a dolphin, any more than you could really talk with a dog or a domesticated ape. An animal as intelligent as Lois might respond to an emotional resonance or to simple sign language—*go fetch*—but it could not actually communicate abstract concepts. The reverse was also true: if dolphins used their incredibly sophisticated echo location system to communicate with each other, as some suspected, human science had not yet been able to detect or quantify dolphin speech. Distress cries, mating calls, yes—but not an actual language.

So it was probably just coincidence when Lois seemed to shake her beak in acknowledgment to the words "find Clark." Coincidence that she accelerated away from the bow with torpedo-like speed, aiming in the direction of the reef. Keeping herself easily in sight, no more than a foot or two below the surface of the water, her sleek form perfectly adapted for maximum speed with minimum effort.

"Go, girl, go!"

Sally gripped the safety rail and held on as Tom opened the throttle. This was the first time she'd ever been out on the open water with Lois, and she was thrilled to see the dolphin swimming at full speed. It was all *Wild Child* could do to keep up. Clearly the animal hadn't lost any of her natural ability.

Sally jumped when the boat horn blasted. Hair streaming, she glanced over her shoulder and saw her husband grinning at her from the wheelhouse, giving her the thumbs up. He seemed to be as thrilled as she was to see the dolphin streaking like a missile for the heart of the reef.

"Beautiful!" he shouted, shaping the word against the wind.

In that instant Sally knew he meant both of them: the animal speeding through the water and the woman at the bow of the boat.

* * *

Dr. Speke was acting weird, Lucy decided. Totally uncool. He'd always been a little odd, had a kind of strange, geeky-macho way of doing things, but this was different. This was off-the-wall behavior. Speke had been ranting about the security problem for more than an hour, first raking poor Robby Mendez over the coals, and then her, and none of it made any sense.

It wasn't as if Mendez had given away any secrets. And *she* certainly hadn't told the dive-boat captain anything about the maxi project.

"Walked in here like it was a summer camp," Speke was saying, his lips cracked with sunburn, his small eyes blinking furiously. "Like a goddamn summer camp! And what do you two do, you make him welcome! You make *conversation!*"

They were in the main research lab with the doors locked and the air conditioning on high—another "security precaution." Speke seemed to be paranoid about being bugged, about leaks, and he was filling the sealed room with his anger.

Lucy and Rob just had to sit there and take it; you couldn't argue with the man when he was in a state like this.

"Lest you've forgotten," Speke said, his voice thick with sarcasm, "just in case you let it slip your little minds, you've both signed security documents with the Department of Defense. Absolutely *nothing* can be disclosed about this project without clearance from the DOD. Right? I mean, correct me if I'm wrong."

Mendez stirred, cleared his throat. "You're right, Vern."

"Damn right I'm right." As Speke's head twitched, his ponytail moved, jumping around on his narrow, sloping shoulders as if it had a life of its own. He said, "That didn't stop you from running off at the mouth with Thomas fucking Hart, did it? Here's the guy, he and that bitchy animal-rights wife of his screwed up about six years of research, the last contract we had, and you *talk* with him, you ask about the research animals they practically *stole* from us?''

Mendez sighed, gave Lucy a sidelong glance. He said, ''They're not really animal-rights people, Vern. I mean, they're not fanatics. Sally Hart is a marine biologist—she was in graduate school at Woods Hole, remember? And the dolphin project, we were ready to drop it anyway. You said so yourself. It was a dead end, we couldn't control the animals. You wanted to concentrate on shark modification.''

Speke, who had been pacing the lab like a rat in a maze, seemed to freeze suddenly. His expressions stiffened and his long fingers clenched.

Lucy crouched a little on her stool, ready to duck if he picked up a beaker and hurled it—that was the reaction she expected.

Instead he surprised her by becoming outwardly calm. Almost, if you didn't know him, serene. ''And that's what we did,'' he said, nodding thoughtfully. ''We activated the shark modification program. We brought Chesty and his bag of tricks down from Sarasota. We negotiated a new contract with the DOD. And the new contract, Rob, the new contract made it very clear: in light of the public relations problems we had in the past, the maxi project would be conducted in absolute secrecy.''

Mendez was nodding right along with the boss, convinced he'd finally gotten through. ''Right, Vern. And we did. We kept the lid on. But nobody anticipated that we'd lose the experiment. That it would leap a goddamn ten-foot barbed-wire fence for no apparent reason.''

Lucy interrupted. ''They were stimulated by live fish,'' she said. ''The amberjack that got in under the net. That's what made them want to get outside the lagoon—the scent of live prey.''

"But we didn't anticipate that reaction," Mendez continued. "We *couldn't* know they could leap that high. Even dolphin have to be trained to jump, and I sure as hell didn't teach the maxis *that* trick."

Speke said, "What's your point, Rob?" Now the man was fiddling with his ponytail, running it through his fingers like a worry bead. Seemingly calm, except for the nervous hands.

"My point is, now that they're out there, we *have* to make some kind of statement," Mendez said ernestly, wanting to sell the idea. "Maybe not the actual truth, okay, but some kind of statement or warning. That's the way I see it, anyhow."

"That's the way *you* see it, Rob?"

Mendez shrugged. By nature he was self-effacing; he did his job and let Dr. Speke run the show. This, speaking his mind on an important decision, was new ground.

Dr. Speke's response was so quiet that Lucy Savrin found herself leaning forward to hear him. He said, "I'll tell you the way I see it, Rob. I see an animal that comes out of the water without warning and takes a man's head off as easy as you'd snap your fingers. An animal *we* created. Oh I know Chesty did all the genetic engineering, but he was working to our specifications. Enhance the intelligence. Increase heartbeat, circulation. Heat up the metabolism until it could support a larger brain mass. Improve and maximize the old reliable, easily killed mako until it's as smart as a dolphin. Make it so we can *train* the damn things."

Mendez said, "Vern, you've got to understand that nobody—"

Speke said, "Shut the fuck up," and Mendez did, he shut up. Speke said, "Where was I? Oh, yeah. Training. The training program, that was your specialty, Rob. Conditioned response. The Navy wants to secure sub bases against enemy divers? We provide the underwater attack dogs. The Dobermans. And you trained 'em, Robby.''

Mendez looked at his hands, did not respond. He flinched when Speke raised his fist, and then looked sick and a little stunned when the fist opened and patted him warmly on the back.

Speke said, "And you *did* it." With his spindly spider arms he gave Robby Mendez an awkward hug. "It was beautiful. I mean, you had to have *been* there. *Isurus maximus* versus a professional shark killer and boom, the maxis win in a heartbeat."

Mendez said, "Jesus, Vern, a couple of innocent guys got killed out there."

"Yes. Terrible tragedy. But also, by coincidence, an opportunity to test the product. And the product *works*. It functions. It performs. Our contract calls for testing under controlled conditions, correct? Okay, so this was uncontrolled. It was *real*. And the DOD, they're going to love it. Provided we regain control of the experiment."

Speke made the phrase roll on his tongue like something cold and delicious: *regain control of the experiment*.

Mendez glanced at Lucy and shook his head. Speke was grinning at the both of them, looking for approval. "Huh?" he said. "What do you think? Can we do it?"

Lucy cleared her throat. There was something about watching Dr. Speke act so jittery that made her mouth dry. She said, "You, um, mean get them back alive?"

Speke nodded vigorously, his small eyes gleaming like chips of ice. "Good girl," he said. "Alive. We need to keep at least one of them alive."

* * *

Sally wanted to suit up, get in the water with the dolphin, but Tom exercised his veto as co-captain and partner.

"Absolutely no way. Not until we know it's safe to dive again."

"Come on, babe. Lois will protect me. No shark will come near, not with a dolphin in the area."

Tom looked out at where Lois was aimlessly circling the boat, making chirping noises that sounded, to his less-than-expert ears, like cries of distress or confusion. "Lois doesn't know what the hell she wants," he said. "Plus, we agreed on a safety system: either of us vetoes a dive, it stays vetoed.

Sally said, "Yeah, but I think she wants to show me something." She had it fixed in her mind: she wanted to swim with Lois out here in the open sea, and she wasn't going to give up without an argument. She said, "She dragged us all the way out here to show us something."

"Yeah? I thought she was looking for Clark."

Sally shrugged. "That was a guess. I just guessed wrong."

Tom said, "Exactly my point." He attempted to slip his arm around her waist, felt her stiffen. He said, "We're guessing it would be safe to get in the water with a dolphin to protect you. But we don't *know* that. Just like it should have been safe hooking shark from the *Squali*. Except it wasn't."

Sally twisted away, out of his reach. She didn't want to be touched when he was being so stubborn, bringing up that old veto business. She said, "We could flip a coin."

"Sal? How about you keep watch, I'll dive?"

She said, "Forget it. Not today."

"What, it might be dangerous?" Tom was giving her that cockeyed grin, trying to charm her.

"Maybe," she said. "For you."

He said, "But you're immune? Come on, be reasonable. If it's not safe for me, it's not safe for you. Besides, the sun is so low that visibility stinks."

This was true. The clear, vapor-thin blue of the sky had thickened and the Keys themselves had become mere bumps on the horizon. Distance was hard to judge now, edges seemed to soften, blending into the vague area between sea and sky—it was getting hard to tell where one ended and the other began.

Tom said, "Clark could be hiding down there, you'd never see him. Or anything else, for that matter."

Sally made a face. "We don't even know if there really was a shark attack. Wade Colson is lying, you said so yourself. And we *both* know you can't trust anything that Sealife creep says."

Tom said, "You're forgetting something."

Sally waited, let him make his point—if he had a point to make.

"Big Ben," Tom reminded her. "You found his tail. And the tooth marks." He spread his hands apart, indicating the width of the jaws that had severed the giant grouper's tail.

Sally sighed, let her hands slip from the safety rail. "Poor old Ben," she said.

In the end it was Lois who made the decision to return home. After circling the boat and submerging for several short dives, she took a soaring leap out of the water and crashed loudly, a dolphin belly flop that indicated boredom, a desire for change.

Moments later Lois was streaking for shore.

Wild Child followed, steering into a sundown that made the sea a shimmering orange mirror streaked with blood.

5

Palm Trees in the Mind

RON MATUSALEM. GOOD name for an old and trusted friend. *Hey, Ron. Hey, amigo. Can you help me out here? Can you make the world a little better, a little easier to take?*

Dr. Chester Higgs, known to his Sealife colleagues by the affectionate nickname "Chesty" because he'd never really felt himself to be a Chester type, studied the liter bottle of rum as if it might impart some secret message. And so it did, if you kept an open mind.

Ron Matusalem Golden Dry. Winner, according to the small print on the label, of a gold medal awarded in Havana in 1911. Keep reading the label, you could suss out that Ron used to live in Cuba, he'd made the big move to Puerto Rico about the time Castro came to power. Chasing the cheap sugarcane, that was our boy Ron, something of an international figure now, a debonair expatriate.

Drink me, amigo, Ron said wordlessly. *I'll make the world new again.*

Chesty cracked the seal, fingered the twist-off top. This much was allowed. He made the rules here, this was his own little game of spin the bottle. Vernon Speke liked to joke about "Ron Chesty's rum"—his way of maintaining an edge, exerting his authority—but for Dr. Higgs the rum was a way of life. Resisting the impulse for days, weeks, for as long as a month before slipping back into the amber pool of comfort and ease. Palm trees in the mind, that's what the rum did for him.

His hands trembled ever so slightly as he put the bottle down. Señor Matusalem had his own space, there on the wicker table within easy reach of his bunk. A special place, an easy-to-reach-in-the-middle-of-the-night kind of place.

Dr. Higgs knew he was an alcoholic. He'd accepted this as a given while he was still young. The need was imprinted so deeply that he would *always* be an alcoholic, whether or not he drank—this he knew, and knowing it, had paid the price, entering into a kind of contract with himself, finding a way to do his work and still dive into the private world of drinking whenever the need was great. Which meant, inevitably, a series of positions lost, opportunities squandered in a long career slide down the Eastern Seaboard. Last stop the Florida Keys. Had he not been an alcoholic—had he not been, in essence, Chester Higgs—he might still be doing genetics research at Johns Hopkins. Would have, by now, his own labs, his own program, research assistants by the dozen, patents that would make him wealthy beyond imagining. Not to mention a wife, the two point two kids or whatever. That was the only part he really missed, a family.

Of course he had his own little family of colleagues at Sealife Key. *We're just like family here,* isn't that what Vernon had said? Vern the tempter, luring Higgs away from a perfectly adequate if rather dull position with the Florida State University System at Sarasota. Engineering the genetic modification of a species of tropical fish "invaders" that were upsetting the fragile ecological balance of the Everglades. An important project, but not, as Vern had pointed out, exactly exciting.

"So big deal, you're cloning a garfish that will eat goldfish, isn't that what it amounts to? Come on, you can do better. And if you work for me you won't have to answer to any board of regents. No paperwork, no requests for funds—I'll handle all the details."

Higgs had not bothered to defend his life at the university. It *was* boring, and most of the tedious lab work was handled by graduate students. Vernon Speke, with his slightly mysterious connections to the much-rumored-about Sealife Research, Incorporated, was himself a kind of exotic invader. For Higgs the spiel was irresistibly seductive. He would be engaged in a top secret project, developing what amounted to a new species of shark.

Vern had promised there would be no oversight board cramping Higgs's style, asking pesky questions about the dangers of genetic engineering—nobody to answer to but Dr. Speke himself, who would handle liaison with the DOD.

The way Vern dropped the Department of Defense acronym so carelessly, "the dee-oh-dee," that's what convinced Higgs to make the move. That and visions of a tropical isle. Clear green water, palm fronds rustling like rain in the gulf breezes. Tanned girls in tight shorts . . . Well, to be brutally honest the tanned girls didn't really matter, because sex was no longer a major drive with Chesty Higgs. He slept with Ron Matusalem now, and his occasional bouts

with 80-proof rum gave him all the pleasure he
needed.

Like a lover he took one last look at the rum before
leaving the cottage.

Maybe later, the bottle said.

Right now he had work to do, promises to keep.

Higgs found Lucy Savrin in the cafeteria, filling a
tray with go-cups of coffee. She was wearing a loose
cotton pullover and safari shorts, beige-colored boat
shoes without socks, showing off elegant, perfect
ankles. Leggy Lucy, with her sweet smile and innocent eyes and, Higgs suspected, the tightfisted
heart of a highly ambitious scientist. Still, she was
young enough and new enough not to have irrevo-
cably linked her career to the current project.

Lucy could do the right thing, Higgs thought. She
could still get out while the getting was good.

"Hi, Dr. Higgs," she said. Her smile was discreet,
distancing.

"Chesty," he said. "Please."

"Sure, of course. You, ah, feeling better?"

Higgs poured coffee, added three sugars; he
needed the energy, the spark. "If you mean, am I
sober, yes, I'm sober."

"That's not what—"

"No problem, Lucy, okay? Naturally you're concerned. Old Chesty goes on the juice, you want to
know about it."

She said, "Hey, I never said—"

"It's okay. Really. I know who I am. What I am.
I know—and this is what's really important—I know
what I did. What we *all* did."

Lucy tried to ease her way around him. Higgs
countered her move, placing himself in her path. He
said, "Just a minute of your time, dear. Please? Now
put down the tray and listen to your old pal
Chesty."

Lucy smiled grimly, put the tray down as requested.

Higgs said, "We fucked up big-time. You know that?"

Lucy said, "Dr. Higgs—I mean Chesty—we discussed this already, okay? Nobody suspected they'd jump that barricade. Like Robby said, even dolphins have to be trained to jump."

Higgs sipped the coffee. It was lukewarm but he felt a hot sweat beading on his forehead. He said, "I'm not talking about that part."

"Then I don't understand."

He said, "I think you do. The fuck-up is not about letting the maxis escape. The fuck-up was letting them exist. Creating them."

Lucy looked surprised. She said, "But you *made* them, Dr. Higgs. That's what you do. You engineer new forms of life."

He shook his head violently, took a deep breath. "Not large predators. I never did large predators before. Vern made it so . . . exciting. And it was. Indeed, it was. Still is, I suppose, if you don't think about it too closely. About what might happen."

Lucy's hands reached for the tray. Her eyes were already focused in the middle distance, cutting him off. "It's been nice talking to you, but I really have to go."

Higgs held his ground, blocking her. "I know," he said. "Vern has a plan in mind. But of course he *always* has a plan. That's why he's the project director. He's going to destroy the evidence, right? Clean up the problem. Make it all go away."

"Right," Lucy said, a little too quickly. "Isn't that what you wanted? Destroy the maxis before they mate?"

He said, "That's part of what I want, Lucy. It's essential they be destroyed. But the other thing we have to do, we have to come clean. We have to tell the world what we've been doing here.''

Lucy said, ''But the DOD. The DOD says—''

''Fuck the DOD,'' Higgs said. ''You think they'll take responsibility if a new species gets into the gene pool? The hell they will. They'll hang us out to dry. And they've got the perfect fall guy.''

''Oh, come on.''

Higgs said, ''Me, Lucy. Good old Chesty. It'll go down like this: Dr. Chester Higgs, an unstable alcoholic, took it upon himself to violate established laboratory safeguards for purposes of unauthorized genetic experimentation.''

''That's crazy.''

He said, ''Blame it on Chesty. That'll be the plan. But we can stop it now, Lucy. Tell Vern to go public. He listens to you.''

Lucy picked up the tray, handed it to him. She seemed to have arrived at a decision. ''Here,'' she said. ''Follow me.''

''Where are we going?''

She said, ''The chase boat. You're going squirrelly, hiding out in that little cabin.''

''The chase boat?''

He was having trouble balancing the tray, keeping up with her quick young legs.

''You're so worried about the maxis,'' she said, looking back over her shoulder, ''you can help us catch them.''

6

Out of the Blue Twilight

THIS TIME IT was Clark who was waiting at the dock. Waiting with a fish in his mouth, proudly displaying his catch.

Sally was off *Wild Child* before it hit the bumpers. Amazed, she knelt and reached her hand out to the male dolphin.

Clark backed playfully away. The fish in his mouth was still alive, gills working.

Sally said, "I can't believe it. Clark? You've been right here all along, haven't you? Chasing that little mullet. Are you going to eat it, Clark, now that you've shown it to me?"

The dolphin chattered, flipped his jaws up, and gulped the fish down.

Sally gaped, shook her head. This was simply . . . amazing.

"What's going on here?" Tom wanted to know.

He looped the dock lines over the cleats and then knelt next to Sally. Lois stuck her head out of the water and squealed. The sudden appearance of the older female seemed to startle the male dolphin, who slipped under the water but remained nearby, circling under the dock.

"Wild stuff," Sally said, drawing a breath. "I've been trying to get Lois to do that for months—catch a live fish and eat it—and now Clark does it on his own, out of the blue."

"So you haven't been working on that with him?"

Sally shook her head. "He seemed too skittish. Lois was the one who liked to play with her food."

Tom stood up, looked into the darkness offshore. "Strange," he said. "They're acting strange, the both of 'em. All of a sudden."

"This isn't strange," Sally insisted. "This is wonderful. I can hardly believe he did that on his own. You know how unusual that is, a domesticated dolphin teaching itself to hunt?"

As if on cue, Clark came up from under the dock and flicked his tail, wetting Sally's feet. He was clearly excited and impressed with himself.

Tom said, "The boy is smarter than you thought. He's been watching you and Lois, and he's learned."

Sally stood up, crossed her arms. Her expression was puzzled. "We knew he was smart, that wasn't the problem. Why *now*? Why is he showing off now? What's different about today?"

Tom thought about it. "Well, Lois was gone. That was different."

"Huh?"

"Big sister was out of the picture, leading us a merry chase out to the reef. Maybe that's what he was waiting for. Maybe she didn't *want* him catching prey on his own." Tom shrugged. "Hey, what the hell do I know."

"No," Sally said, catching his hands and giving him a squeeze. "No, that's brilliant! That could be

it. We already know that certain mature females figure out ways to control male adolescent behavior.
Especially *aggressive* behavior. Maybe this is Lois's
way of keeping him in line.''

''She doesn't want him to kill?''

Sally nodded eagerly. ''It's only a theory, but it's
a *good* theory. And the really great thing is, I can set
up an experiment right here in the canal, see how
they both respond.''

Tom chuckled, shook his head. ''You're thinking
doctoral thesis.''

Sally said, ''You bet I am. This is great. Look at
me, I'm shaking.''

Tom went to the dive shed, returned with a blanket. ''You're wet and cold,'' he said, draping the
blanket over her shoulders. ''I better get us something to eat.''

Sally shook her head. ''I'm not hungry. Maybe I
should do something tonight. Strike while the iron
is hot, you know? Before Clark forgets.''

Tom put his arm around her waist, walked her
toward the house. ''Food first,'' he said. ''Give it a
rest. He won't forget.''

''This is a breakthrough,'' Sally said, her teeth
chattering. ''A real breakthrough. I've got to write
it down. I've got to take notes.''

But she did not resist as Tom helped her up the
stairs, into their home. Behind them, under the glow
of the sodium dock lights, the singing dolphin
moved like quicksilver in the night.

''Dramamine, anybody? Last call for Dramamine.''

Dr. Vernon Speke was in a buoyant mood as the
chase boat pulled away from Sealife Key. The refitted trawler was already out in Hawk Channel,
awaiting instructions. Rob Mendez was aboard the
big trawler; he'd handle the special hydrophones,

newly installed. Lucy and Higgs and Speke would crew the smaller and faster chase boat, with Speke himself in charge of identical hydrophones.

Organized, everything was organized down to the last detail.

"You want a hit, Chesty?" Speke jiggled the bottle of seasickness pills.

Higgs shook his head. He was still a little confused. He wasn't a boat person, how had he let Lucy talk him into this? It was not like he had any romantic ideas about wanting to experience danger or to push the edge. Far from it. And he, as much as anyone involved in the *Isurus* project, knew the potential danger of an encounter with *Isurus maximus*. Cracking and rearranging the genetic code gave one a certain . . . intimacy. Even before the escape from the lagoon, Higgs had been wary of the maxis, content to monitor their progress from the relative safety of the lab.

"You sure?" Speke grinned, snapping his teeth, click-click. "You look a little green around the gills."

Higgs said, "I'm fine." He waved away the bottle.

Speke said, "Cheer up. We've got it licked, man. We've got it under control."

Higgs shrugged. Vern thought he had everything figured out, but then he'd been convinced of that *last* night, when two experienced shark killers got yanked out of the boat. The problem with a new species, you didn't really have a baseline for behavior comparison. For instance, the jumping. The old mako, *Isurus glaucus*, who would sometimes jump when hooked, was considered a prime fighting fish for that reason. The normal mako did not, however, leap to defend other makos. No way.

Every shark for itself, that was the rule of the sea, of nature.

A rule that had been broken now, with mortal

consequence. You had to wonder what other rules of nature might be in jeopardy, the results of a little genetic recoding.

Higgs said, "What makes you think the maxis are staying in the area? Have there been other sightings?"

"There was an, er, possible sighting southwest of Sombrero Light." Speke turned away, coughed lightly into his fist.

"That's on the reef?"

Speke said, "Right, the reef. The wrecks nearby make good cover. And Lucy's got a theory that the maxis won't stray too far from shallow water. Not for a while. The lagoon was shallow and that's all they've ever known until now. Take 'em a while to adjust to the feeling of deeper water."

Higgs said, "They learn fast. We already know that."

"Hey, Chesty. You just relax, okay? Enjoy the ride."

Lucy was driving the chase boat, monitoring an autopilot course to a prearranged rendezvous with the trawler in Hawk Channel. "I think they're circling," she said, swinging around in the pilot seat. "Swimming in wider and wider patterns, with the lagoon as dead center. Getting to know their new environment. They're fairly cautious, we've already seen that."

"Yeah," Higgs said. "Cautious. Until something triggers a feeding frenzy."

Speke frowned, poked him in the ribs with a blunt finger. "There something you want to share with us, Chesty? Some pearl of wisdom?"

Speke's eyes looked small and hard in the harsh underlight of the steering console. The slant made him look older, more drawn, as if the bones were pushing through from beneath his skin.

Higgs decided to go easy, not press his luck here,

already a mile or more from shore. He said, "I guess not. No."

" 'Cause we sure could use some pearls of wisdom from the Great White Father of the lab-or-atory," Speke said in a mocking tone, enunciating every syllable. "The best we could do on our own was come up with this plan, go with sonar location."

"That might work," Higgs conceded uneasily.

Speke said, "What I tried last night, the simulation of feeding sounds? I don't think that would work twice, do you?"

"I don't know," Higgs said. "Probably not."

" 'Cause like you say, they learn fast." Speke grinned, clicked his teeth again. "So we have to keep ahead of the curve. Surprise them like they surprised us."

"Good idea," Higgs said. "Excellent idea."

Dinner was a strip steak, quickly marinated and then blasted on the gas barbecue, with butter-drenched garlic bread, pan-fried potatoes, and a Caesar salad, no anchovies.

While in his teens Tom had worked summers as a short-order cook, and he still retained the ability to get out a quick, basic meal in about the time it took Sally to unload the refrigerator and open her gourmet recipe books. Sally hadn't been eating much red meat lately—neither had Tom—but the steak-and-taters hit the spot, made her feel warm inside. The shivering stopped.

"I needed that," she said, pushing her chair back from the table and wiping her lips with a linen napkin.

Tom, as quick an eater as he was a cook, was already out in the kitchen alcove. "Room for dessert?" he called.

Sally laughed. "Depends. What do you have in mind?"

He came around the corner carrying a frozen ice cream cake. "Imagine a big candle," he said. "I couldn't find the damn candles."

She said, "Is it somebody's birthday?"

He said, "We're celebrating your breakthrough." Mighty pleased with himself, he dished out the cake.

"You mean Clark's breakthrough."

He said, "Right, of course. Maybe you'd prefer a little raw mullet?"

"The cake's fine. Really. And thanks."

Sally had a sweet tooth, she couldn't resist, and she found room for the dessert. She'd burn it off tomorrow, since she planned to be in the water most of the day, rigging the canal for the live-fish experiment. First she'd have to physically separate the two dolphin, and that meant erecting some sort of barricade. A net, perhaps, with the mesh small enough so there was no danger of the animals getting entangled. Release live fish in the vicinity of Clark, monitor his behavior, and at the same time monitor the behavior of Lois. Would Lois try to distract the younger male? Discourage his attempt to catch and kill? Anything was possible. The thing was, you had to go into it with an open mind, not draw any conclusions, just let the results speak for themselves, then try to interpret the data.

After a few moments she became aware that Tom was trying to attract her attention.

"Sal? Earth to Sally."

"Excuse me?"

Tom was grinning, shaking his head. "You didn't hear it, did you?"

"Hear what?"

"The phone. Reggie called."

"Reggie?"

He said, "You remember Reggie. Close friend?

Stopped by for a drink last night? She's got some pictures she wants us to see."

"That's nice," Sally said. The conversation was distracting. In her mind she was getting back into the canal, conducting the live-fish experiment.

Tom said, "Doesn't sound nice at all, I'm afraid." He took both of her hands in his own, urged her up from the table. "I hate to eat and run," he said, "but we're needed."

"What's this all about?"

"Sharks," he said. "Man-eating sharks."

7

Sharing the Hammer

THE SCHOOL OF African pompano feeds on small baitfish, darting like small bolts of liquid lightning in the thin water covering the reef. Feeding is good here, and easy, and the pompano swarm, now moving as one entity, now splitting into a hundred separate parts, each driven by need, sensitive to the tiny, fluttering twitches of the baitfish. Now coming together again into the security of the swarm, the *us-ness* that is their most basic survival instinct.

The pompano, intent on the ease of snatching food from the reef, have no awareness of the much larger creatures circling on the periphery, vague shadows in this world of night, no more troubling than thunderheads on a distant horizon.

The pompano are fat and lazy. Life has been too easy here.

Us the beautiful, the six-partnered, sense the weakness of the pompano swarm. They move together, gradually tightening the circle; the sweep of their elegant curved tail fins make fading, phosphorescent swirls in the water.

They sing, using the sound to locate their prey. The song returns as a series of echoes and is instinctively processed, forming an image of the pompano swarm. The six-partnered share the mind-vision of the prey, see it as distinctly as if daylight was illuminating the shallow waters of the reef.

Now, they sing. *Attack!*

The fat pompano are doomed. As the looming circle of the six-partnered suddenly collapses inward, the pompano try to explode outward. There is nowhere to go. Nowhere, in the shallow water, to escape the gaping jaws. The six-partnered move as one, cutting away escape, anticipating each furtive, futile move of the panicked freshkill.

Only a few stunned fish remain, drifting belly up in the dark water, when another predator approaches swiftly. Moving in a darting, zigzag pattern through the dark water.

Danger, the Us sing. *Danger thing.*

Drawn by the irresistible scent of the freshkill, stimulated by the vibration of dying prey, a mature hammerhead shark races from the outer edges of the reef, hungering after each molecule of blood in the water.

It hungers for prey.

Us the beautiful react by giving the hammer room to move. Aware, as they shape it with their echosong, of the terrible danger of its extruded jaws.

The big hammer, equal in size to any one of the six-partnered, at first ignores them. It twists and snaps over the killing ground, searching for prey, driven nearly mad with the rich smell of the freshkill. Behaving as if the six-partnered do not exist, as if nothing exists but the need to feed.

The six-partnered move warily, tolerant of this huge intruder. Curious, watchful. How awkwardly it hunts, this massive fear-thing. Jerking around as if blind, jaws gaping and snapping.

Now the big hammer makes a fatal mistake. It veers suddenly at one of the six-partnered and attempts to snatch away a morsel of pompano.

Instantly, and together, the six-partnered react.

Together they turn, all six acting in concert to seize the hammer by the bony head, by the tail, imprisoning the dorsal fins. Clamping down.

In an instant the hammer is disemboweled. It writhes instinctively as the small brain fades, unaware that it is already dead. The six-partnered release the savaged body. It begins to settle to the coral bottom, nearly a ton of flesh bleeding from a thousand killing wounds.

Freshkill, one of the Us sings.

And so the Us makes this discovery: larger prey are better, easier. Less work, more efficient. They feed, dividing the big hammerhead equally among them, feeding on this rich prey until their bellies are full, singing, *Freshkill. Freshkill is good.*

Sated for the moment, unable to continue feeding, still they want more. They always want more.

8

Casting Nets upon the Water

THE CHARTER BOAT *Squali* joined the hunt in Hawk
Channel. Skipper Wade Colson came up neatly beside the chase boat, tipped a bumper over the side,
and took a line. The water was glassy and flat inside
the protective barrier of the reef. Night made the sea
seem small, enclosed; to the undiscerning eye no
more dangerous than a pond.

Colson was alone; he hadn't taken on a new crew.
"Ain't anything we're gonna do out here I can't do
myself," he announced. End of discussion.

Speke grunted his approval. Best to keep this in
the family.

"Chesty? Go up forward, get Captain Colson one
of those new hand-held radio units."

Higgs found himself obeying without hesitation.
Something about the way Speke handled himself
made you react that way. The small forward compartment was outfitted with a sleek V berth, a head-
and-shower unit, and a galley that had never been

used for anything but dispensing drinks—looked more like a gleaming bachelor pad than a damn boat, Higgs decided. Close your eyes and you could see young Lucy, or another girl much like her, frolicking down here. Body as sleek and tan and firm as the soft leather upholstery. Was Vernon getting any of that? No, Higgs decided, he wasn't picking up anything but normal sexual tension between the two. Poor Vern—he obviously wanted her. You could tell by his attitude, the way he carried himself around her, the forceful, confident image he was trying to project. How much of the maxi project was conceived to impress Lucy Savrin? An interesting topic of speculation—you'd never get a straight answer out of Vernon Speke, that was for sure.

"Higgs! Hurry it up!"

Higgs managed to locate one of the new radios. When he returned topside, there was a moment of awkward silence. He got the impression the others had been discussing him in his absence. Poor rum-soaked Chesty.

"This has a scrambled frequency," Speke said, presenting the unit to the charter skipper. "You need to say anything important, use it."

Colson clipped the unit to his belt. "You all know enough to keep inside the boat?" he asked softly, swiveling his gaze to include Higgs.

Speke said, "They know. We'll be ready this time."

Colson said, "I stand by to assist the trawler?"

"That's the idea," Speke said. "We've rigged hydrophones that can pick up the maxis. If we can range in on the source from two boats, we can calculate their location. Home in on the bastards."

Colson let the *Squali* drift a short distance away and then restarted his engines. He called out, "How's that work, that hydrophone? What the hell you pickin' up? These critters fitted with a signal location device?''

Speke said, "Something like that." His tone indicated he wanted no further discussion on the subject of how the maxis would be detected. "Just keep us on monitor, you'll know what to do."

"Oh, I already *know* what to do, doc! You bet I do!"

Reaching down, Colson lifted up a high-powered semiautomatic rifle and held it shoulder-high. His smile was white and thin in the light from his wheelhouse.

The two boats separated, and a few moments later *Squali* melted into the darkness, detectable only by the distinctive sound of its high-speed gasoline engines.

Higgs said, "Charming guy."

Speke said, "He's a good man, Chesty. And he knows how to keep his mouth shut. Unlike some of us," he added darkly.

Higgs wanted to ask what that meant, exactly, and then thought better of it. This was Vern's show; he was simply along for the ride. Very determined to keep his head down. *Very* determined.

When the chase boat was roughly a few miles miles down-channel from the trawler, Speke ordered that the engine be shut down. To Higgs the sudden silence was both a blessing and a curse. The big Cigarette mill made a hell of a racket, but the feel of it, the vibration, made the boat seem alive, capable of defending itself. Dead in the water the high-speed hull seemed lifeless, an overpriced chunk of flotsam bobbing in the splash of its own wake.

Speke unclipped the scrambled radio unit. "Robby, do you copy?"

Mendez's reply, when it came, made him sound like a man trapped in a tin box: *"Copy. We're getting signal here."*

"Got a range?"

"*We have a general direction, not a range. They seem to be moving around. How about you?*"

"Give us a couple minutes."

Speke clicked off the radio, clipped it to his belt. "Lucy?"

Lucy had already slipped on the headphones. She crouched over the hastily installed detector, fine-tuning the frequency. "Pretty damn noisy out here," she said. "We're picking up lots of stuff."

"Get the program up," Speke said. "Exclude everything but the maxi signature."

"I'm trying, Vern."

Higgs watched as she slipped a diskette into the onboard computer. The small screen filled with color bars. A sonic wave pattern danced through the bars, identifying and eliminating those that lacked the "signature" of the maxis. Dr. Higgs was impressed: he'd heard talk about the program, modified from submarine detection software, but hadn't actually seen it functioning. The technology had been there for a few years, originally developed to identify certain types of whales that were a danger to shipping—each species had its own distinctive voice, or "signature." The talkative dolphins were particularly easy to identify. Never before, however, had the system been used to track sharks—mostly because normal shark species were virtually silent.

Unlike *Isurus maximus*.

"There it is," Lucy announced, tapping the screen.

The color bar writhed like a skinny, luminous snake, disintegrating and re-forming. Almost hypnotic, if you stared too hard.

"They seem to be pretty far away," Lucy said. "That would explain why the bar keeps breaking up."

"Can we get a direction?"

Lucy manipulated the receivers. Under the chase boat the hydrophones turned, electronically focusing in on the signal.

"We're in a fairly narrow band," Lucy said, "but it's not exactly loran-type location. Somewhere between forty-five and sixty degrees. That's the best I can do."

"It'll narrow as we get closer," Speke said confidently. He punched the coordinates into the navigation computer, established a rough area where the maxis seemed to be located. "Somewhere between Bahia Honda and the Harbor Keys," he said, consulting a chart.

Lucy said, "The reef sanctuary is right in there." She was looking over his shoulder, being careful not to let her breasts brush against his back. "Maybe they like to feed in shallow water."

Speke said, "Any thoughts on that, Chesty?"

Higgs said, "Makes sense. If they're using their echo soundings to locate prey, it might be easier in shallow water." He cleared his throat, squinted nervously as he stared out into the fog of darkness beyond the bow. "Easier at first," he added. "Eventually they'll discover they can thrive in deep water."

"Relax. There's not going to be an 'eventually.'"

Speke radioed the rough coordinates to Mendez and Colson, using the scrambled channel. All three boats would narrow the search, taking up positions on opposite ends of the ten-square-mile reef sanctuary area. The *Squali* was not outfitted with the detection gear, but Colson had highly accurate fish finders; put him in the right area, he could locate maxi-sized sharks.

And this time there would be no foolishness about trying to hand-line the creatures. This time the job would be left to nets and winches and high-powered rifles.

"Unless you think bullets won't kill 'em," Speke said. He reached out, placed a finger over Higgs's heart. "Is that what you think, hey, Chesty?"

Higgs backed away, almost lost his footing as Lucy restarted the engines, pushed the throttle down. "Bullets are good," he said. "Unless, of course, you'd rather use high explosives. Depth-charge the bastards."

Speke ignored the remark about using explosives. Lucy, after a nervous glance at her boss, also refrained from commenting.

"Have a seat, Chesty," Speke said, turning to face the helm. "Be pretty embarrassing, we lost another man overboard."

Reef Life was published from an office complex on Big Pine Key. Cinder block modern, with a jagged, Spanish tile roof, the complex was set back fifty yards from the more or less endless traffic of the Overseas Highway. Inside it was air-conditioned cool and quiet, except for a rhythmic clicking noise.

"Reggie?" Tom called out, feeling air move as the door swung shut behind them. "Is that you?"

Regina Rhodes was in the lobby, leaning against a glass partition, tapping the heels of her Keno sandals against the floor tiles. Tap-tappa-tap-tap, a waltz rhythm, dancing in place as she waited. Wearing a white half-sleeved cotton blouse and knee-length safari shorts that showed off her remarkably firm, septuagenarian legs. She fiddled with a braided-gold necklace, looping it through her fingers, and did not bother with the usual southern protocols of making her guests welcome, offering refreshments, and so on. This time it was down to business immediately.

"I don't like this," she said, leading Tom and Sally into the room where her glossy, color-drenched monthly was put together. "We've got a great picture that will make one hell of a cover, but I *still* don't like it.''

"There's a diver missing?" Sally asked.

Reggie said, "That's putting it mildly, I'm afraid, but the body hasn't been recovered, so he's officially 'missing.' One of the wreck diving boats out of Marathon. Tourist named, let me see, Ray Hurst. First dive in the Keys, don't that beat all?''

Reggie was shuffling through notes on the paste-up table, amid photostats of ads and restaurant menus. "Young gentleman from Boston. Down here with a friend from a dive club. The friend's name is Peter Scalia, he's the one brought in the photographs.''

Tom pulled up a stool for Sally, another for himself. "Hey, Reg? Take us through this, okay? What photographs?''

"Sorry, honey. This has got my liver in an uproar." Reggie shook her head, earrings jangling lightly, her own personal wind chimes. "You know how I hate it when a tourist gets himself killed down here. 'Specially a dumb type of accident, it gives us all a bad name. These dive boats, they supposed to make sure the divers buddy up, right? I mean, isn't that the way *you* do it?''

Tom spread his hands. "That's what we *try* to do, Reg. You can't force it. Some of these divers take crazy risks.''

Reggie made a face, shook her head. "Let me put it another way. Everybody in the business knew about what happened to those boys on Wade Colson's boat, right?''

"Right. Sure.''

"And how many of the charter boats canceled today's dives?''

Tom shrugged. "We did. Never checked with the others.''

"None of 'em, that's how many. Except you.''

Reggie snorted, tapped her notes with a glossy painted fingernail. "I just called 'round, real polite. You know what? Even with this tourist missing, presumed killed by shark, nobody else has canceled. They're issuing a 'shark alert,' and that's it."

"Wait a sec, Reg," Tom said. "Was this attack witnessed? Does anybody *know* it was a shark?"

Reggie gave him a look. "Oh, it was witnessed. By a camera."

She explained that the missing diver had been an amateur photographer, with new high-performance underwater photographic gear. "What apparently happened," she said, "is he got separated from his dive buddy. This guy Pete? Pretty casual about the fact his buddy got killed, if you ask me. *Very* interested in how much I'd pay for the photograph. Anyhow, they apparently split up and Ray went pretty deep inside the wreck. The other divers, including Pete, return to the dive boat. No Ray. The dive master starts a search. At first, nothing, and then later in the day they found his tank and one of his flippers deep inside the wreck. Also his camera."

"He'd taken pictures?"

"Right." Reggie started pawing through the piles of paper on the layout table. "Pictures of the wreck," she said, "pictures of his idiot buddy, Mr. How-much-will-you-pay-me Peter Scalia. I remember his name 'cause I wrote him a big fat check. Anyhow, Pete got his buddy's camera back and took the roll of film to an instant process shop in Marathon. Then he came to me with the picture."

Sally stood up from her stool. "Come on, Reggie. Quit teasing."

Reggie said, "I'm looking, honest. Where the hell did I put the damn thing? It's slide film, so I was able to blow it up on the Xerox."

The enlarged photocopy was finally located under a seafood menu.

"Take a gander at *these* critters," Reggie said, smoothing out the copy.

Three of the sharks were brightly illuminated by the strobe. Three other virtually identical creatures were in the background, slightly blurred. Looming into the picture.

Sally said, "Look like mako." A moment later, after closer examination, she wasn't so sure. "The coloring is mako, and so are the fins. But there's something about the gill slits and the eyes . . . I'm not sure. They look *different* somehow."

"Could it be the strobe?" Tom asked. "The way the shadows hit?"

Sally said, "Maybe. You'd need to have a shark expert check these out. To make sure we've got the right species. I know someone in Key West who could do it."

"Mako dangerous to divers?" Reggie asked, tapping the photocopy.

Sally said, "Not usually. But every shark can be dangerous if provoked."

Tom said, "And the theory is, this shot was taken just before the sharks attacked the diver?"

"More than a theory," Reggie said. "I got this from the dive master, it didn't cost me a thing."

The handsome old woman reached in her blouse pocket and withdrew a large shark tooth. She held it up by the flat part, avoiding the razor-sharp edges.

"This was embedded in the poor man's tank harness," she said. "The tank itself was pretty well chewed up. Like these critters were mighty pissed off. Or mighty hungry."

"Or both," Tom said.

Sally shivered. Air conditioning on too high, she decided. What *was* it about that photograph?

9

The Singing

Us THE BEAUTIFUL drift slowly. Thin water covers the reef, maximum depth twenty-five feet or so. Just above them faint points of light shimmer on the surface. The six-partnered respond to this canopy of stars, locating themselves in the world. An ancient inner geometry, untouched in their genetic code, continually readjusts to the great clock of the stars, wheeling through the night.

Bellies full, the hunger is briefly, very briefly, appeased. The need to feed has increased, is increasing as each hour passes. The confines of the lagoon limited their hunger, their size. Now, with horizons ever expanding, the Us respond to the surge of increased metabolism. Growth hormones flood muscles, viscera, resonating in the brain. Hunger and need keep increasing, and the stimulating smell of freshkill lingers in each particle of water as it washes over their gill slits.

They drift, singing softly to each other, using the

song to locate more freshkill. Nothing sizable remains in this area of the reef. The prey have fled.
The current and tide will change that, bring new
possibilities for the hunt. The sea is rich, life-forms
are abundant.

The feeding has been especially rich in the last few
tide changes. First the bright-flashing fear-thing in
the wreck. Then the school of fat, easily confused
pompano. Just recently the delicious, fat-shuddering
gluttony of the big hammerhead. The satisfying size
of the hammer resonates. Big is good.

Drifting, singing. Their song, a series of high-
pitched squeals and clicks, serves a dual purpose: it
locates each of the Six and the returning echoes help
shape the darkness, providing an inner map of the
bottom, the reef, and any prey that strays within
echo range.

All at once the Us cease singing. They listen intently, using the entire length of their bodies to
shape the sound. It is a danger-sound, growing
steadily louder. Engines, props frothing the water.

Danger. Danger. Danger.

The Us circle quickly, draw close to one another,
taking comfort in proximity. Reveling in their
strength, their beauty.

Danger, they sing. *Eat the fear.*

"It's working," Speke said, staring at the fish
finder. "They're falling for it."

The plan was clean and simple. Locate the maxis
with the hydrophone gear, then pinpoint them with
conventional fish finders and drive them into the
nets deployed by the trawler. The location part had
been easier than expected: the maxis were noisy as
hell, didn't seem aware that their almost continuous
babble of clicks and squeaks gave them away.

Which demonstrated that *Isurus maximus* didn't
have a human level of awareness. See them in ac-

tion, exploding out of the night, a man started to imagine all sorts of possibilities. Fear made you endow the fear-making thing with godlike power and intelligence—that was a normal human reaction, Speke knew. You had to fight it. You had to keep in mind that for all their genetic improvements, the maxis were just another species of shark. Smart, exceedingly aggressive sharks, to be sure, possibly as intelligent as marine mammals, but so what? Humans had achieved complete dominion over the marine mammals. Whales, dolphins, seals, hundreds of species had been forced to submit to human cunning and control—submit or face extinction.

The maxis would be no exception.

"I'll bet they can distinguish between boats," Lucy said, raising her voice over the muffled roar of the engines. "We've got a 'signature,' just like they do!"

"You may be right," Speke conceded. "But that should help. They already know Colson's boat is dangerous. They'll run from it."

The *Squali* was a half mile closer to shore, keeping pace with the chase boat. It was Colson who'd first detected the maxis on his fish finders. Six large signals moving close together, veering away from the sound of his prop. Now both boats were driving north across the shallow waters of the submerged reef, forming a battering ram of prop noise, driving the maxis forward.

The trawler, with Mendez aboard, had already set out more than a thousand yards of steel-reinforced net. The nearly invisible net was weighted and buoyed, forming a movable barricade in water no more than twenty-five feet deep.

Thin water. Shark-killing water.

"It's going to work," Speke announced. "Look at 'em run, Chesty. We strike the nets, it'll be like shooting fish in a barrel."

Not even wily, intelligent dolphin could escape such nets. Millions drowned in similar gear each year. Surely the maxis would share the same fate. And it might be possible, Speke hoped, to take one of the creatures alive. Slaughter five and keep one. Build a bigger barricade in the lagoon and keep one beautiful maxi as proof of what had been accomplished at Sealife Key. Living proof would be very helpful when it came time to negotiate a new contract.

Best not to tell Chesty Higgs about the plan to save one, Speke had already decided. The man seemed intent on destroying everything he'd helped create.

"Depth-charge the bastards," Higgs kept muttering, staring blindly into the night. "Blow 'em to kingdom come. That's what we ought to do."

Speke looked up from the fish finder, his skinny face liver green in the dim light of the scope. "Give it a rest, Chesty. We'll handle it."

Higgs said, "To shoot 'em you have to see 'em. Explosives, you just have to be in the vicinity. You can drop it over the side."

Speke said, "Do me a favor? Shut the fuck up."

"But if we just—"

"I said zip it, Chesty. That's an order."

Higgs slumped into one of the upholstered deck chairs, swung around and looked into the night-glow of the wake, a rooster tail of foam kicked up by the high-speed props. The chase boat had been picked up at a DEA auction—owned briefly by some high-flying coke dealer, Higgs supposed, who hadn't balked at abandoning a hundred-thousand-dollar craft on a moonless night, the Coast Guard in hot pursuit. Might have been a full moon, or even daylight. Smugglers were bold, made daring by the prospect of easy wealth. Higgs had thought it silly when Speke acquired the expensive, gas-guzzling chase boat for Sealife's small flotilla. Now he realized it had been a wise choice—not even the fleet-finned maxis could outrun it. Had Speke foreseen such an eventuality, the possibility of the maxis escaping from the lagoon? Had he *planned* it somehow, just to test the species in the wild, under uncontrolled conditions?

Crazy idea, Higgs told himself. Not even a risk junkie like Vernon Speke would take such a chance. Vern had to be aware that if the maxis mated with a closely related species—true mako, for instance—fertile offspring might survive. Such offspring would, if Higgs's calculations were correct, tend toward gigantism. Unrestricted growth. Size limited only by the food supply. A new, dominant species genetically programed to wipe out all other species.

Sharks, mammals, nothing prey-sized would stand a chance against wolf packs of *Isurus maximus*. Pods of killer whales were mildly aggressive by comparison, and confined their feeding to a few vulnerable species. How long would the maxis take to wreck the ecology of the reef? A few years? A decade? Long enough to make the name of Higgs a curse. A word like spit on the tongue. Because Dr. Chester Higgs of all people should have known better. As a genetic engineer, he was responsible for making certain an experimental species could not reproduce. That was basic to the science. Irradiate them, surgically neuter them if necessary. Instead, he'd let it go, left all precautionary measures to Speke, the project director. Surrendered control.

If he'd ever *had* control. Oh, Vernon had given Higgs the run of the lab, never interfered during the long, grueling process of genetic culling and fetal implants. Hadn't bitched about the many early failures. Speke was a master at that, letting a man think he was in charge. But as soon as the first proto-maxi fetus survived, as soon as six successful clones had been implanted in the host mother, Speke had swooped down and seized control. The maxi project became Speke's baby, as it really always had been.

No surprise, then, that the man had his own agenda. What exactly that was, Higgs had no way of knowing, but it was pretty obvious that Speke didn't want all of the maxis destroyed. Speke the risk taker was willing to take another chance here, playing it cozy with creatures so new and powerful and unpredictable that no human could anticipate their behavior.

Higgs, holding tight to his upholstered seat as the chase boat plowed through the night, decided then and there that given the opportunity, he would take matters into his own hands. Kill 'em all. Be ruthless. That was the only option that made sense.

He was aware of the chase boat slowing, altering course.

"They've stopped," Speke said. "Son of a bitch."

Higgs stood up. He could make out the navigation lights of the big trawler up ahead, the faint silhouette of Colson's charter boat drifting a few hundred yards away. It was muggy, the air heavy with moisture and the sea smell of ozone.

"They can't see the net," Speke said. "If dolphin can't see the net, then the maxis sure as hell can't. Isn't that right, Chesty?"

Higgs shrugged. He didn't know what the maxis could sense. He didn't know their limits. That was the biggest problem, not knowing what the limits were.

"Something to keep in mind," Higgs said, having to grab hold as the wake suddenly caught up with the drifting chase boat. "They're not the only fish in the sea."

"What the hell does *that* mean?"

"Exactly what I said. They're not alone down there. We're driving them forward, right? Which means every other fish in the area is running ahead of *them*."

Lucy caught on right away. "He's right, Vern. They may sense other fish entangled in the net."

"Well, shit," Speke said. "We'll just have to close the circle. Leave 'em with no place to go."

The Us feel the proximity of death like a soft caress, a tingling in the water. Up ahead, well beyond the limits of what their eyes perceive, the Us sense the panicked dying of other, smaller fish.

Danger behind, from the noise of the chasing propellers, and danger ahead. The Us stop moving. Adrift in the black water, they are alive to every sensation. Their great lateral nerves detect the tiniest vibration, nerves as sensitive to motion as a dog's nose is to scent. The vibrations paint a mind image of many fish dead or dying, drenched with fear-panic.

Are the fish being killed by another predator, coming from the opposite direction? The Us are momentarily confused by their sensory receptors. But the prey are not fleeing, they form a wall of suffering, an invisible area of death that seems to extend from the surface to the shallow bottom.

Avoid, the Us sing to each other. *Avoid, avoid.*

Now there are choices to be made. Behind and to either side are the idling propellers that represent surface danger. Ahead is the invisible wall of death.

Wait, the Us sing.

Wait.

"What are we doing?" Higgs wanted to know.

Speke was impatient now, acting even more hyper than usual. Walking a tight circle in the small cockpit of the chase boat, his long, skinny legs flickering in the glow of the deck lights. The radio unit was glued to his ear as he traded terse communications with the other two boats.

"You've got the buoy in tow? Good. Rob, you copy? Just keep the floats clear. Let Wade do it."

Higgs approached Lucy Savrin, who remained seated at the steering station. The chase-boat engines made deep glugging noises; to Higgs's untutored ears the idling motors sounded ready to stall at any moment. He said, "What's going on?"

Lucy glanced up. "Colson is bringing one end of the net around. Sort of like a purse seine."

"I'm not a commercial fisherman," Higgs said. "I don't know a damn thing about this stuff. What exactly does that mean, 'sort of like a purse seine'?"

Lucy said, "Means we're doing the best we can with these gill nets." Her voice had acquired an edge that made her sound older. Blunt and to the point, no kidding around, no games. She said, "Basically we're trying to loop it around, cut off any means of escape. If we get both ends of the net together, then we can keep tightening it up until the maxis panic and run into the net."

"*If* they panic," Higgs said.

"Everything panics, you scare it bad it enough."

Speke snapped off the radio. "What's this about panic?"

His manner was gruff but not, surprisingly, impatient. He seemed to be savoring the excitement of working the nets, outmaneuvering the maxis. "Just keep to the center of the boat, Chesty, you'll be okay. Things get hot, go hide below, get yourself out from underfoot."

Higgs said, "Oh, I intend to. I suggest you both do the same."

Speke said, "We'll be fine. Just keep your ass in the boat, don't reach over the side."

"Rules to live by?"

"Goddamn right." Speke clicked on the radio unit. "Wade? You copy, Wade? Come back to me."

The radio crackled loudly. Speke jerked it away from his ear, cursed. At the same time a soft glow began to light the horizon, making the clouds luminous.

"Make it quick," Speke said urgently, stabbing the broadcast switch. "Looks like it might blow up out there."

Higgs jerked involuntarily, his legs gone liquid at the knees. He said to Lucy, "Jesus Christ, what does he mean, blow up?"

Lucy chuckled, a musical, two-note laugh. "Take it easy. He means thunderstorms. The weather is going to blow up. It's just a phrase."

"Oh," Higgs said, sinking into a seat. "I thought . . ."

Lucy said, "Do us a favor, Chesty? Break out the slickers. It may get a little wet."

By the time Higgs returned with the rain gear the air had changed. Maybe ten degrees cooler, a steady breeze coming from the southeast, ruffling the surface of the water. You could just barely hear the distant rumble of thunder above the throb of the boat engines. Overhead the sky seemed very close; the darkness was moving, swirling. The weather had become angry, as if a temper tantrum was in the making.

Lucy said, "Should we set an anchor?" Her voice was higher now, bright with anxiety.

"Hell no," Speke said. "Just keep us into the wind."

A spattering of rain hit the windshield hard. Sounded to Higgs like nails rattling in a tin bucket. In his little cottage he sometimes was comforted by rain pounding on the tin roof, felt safe and cozy. Out here on the open water it had the opposite effect: Higgs had never felt more uncomfortable in his life.

"We got 'em," Speke announced with satisfaction. "Wade brought the net around. They can't get away now."

"What do I do?" Lucy asked. She'd put up her hood, looked gnomish in her fluorescent orange parka.

"Hold this position," Speke instructed. "We don't want to cross the buoy line or we might foul the net in our props."

Higgs didn't know what the hell they were talking about, but he was beginning to think it was a very bad idea to be out in this huge open space when bolts of electricity were jumping from cloud to cloud like Christmas tree lights gone berserk. Although he had no phobias about thunderstorms, this was clearly a dangerous place and he wanted to be elsewhere fast.

He toyed with the idea of hiding in the small cabin area, but when it came right down to it, he didn't care to display cowardice in front of Lucy Savrin. Dumb, he thought, you're being dumb, but he remained in his seat, hood up, rain wetting his glasses, dripping down his nose. What he wouldn't give for a good stiff belt of rum.

"Back it down!" Speke was crouched in the cockpit, trying to work his long arms into the parka as he shouted into the radio. "We need to tighten up. Wade, do you copy?"

More crackles from the radio. Higgs wiped his glasses. An incandescent flash seemed to linger, and as he waited for the crack of thunder to follow, he saw the blurry image of Wade Colson's charter boat passing close behind the trawler.

This was "backing down," he assumed, drawing the huge net tighter. Would the maxis surface? Or would they hide on the shallow bottom until they were entangled in the nets?

The delayed concussion of thunder cracked and roared. The chase boat seemed to sink deeper into the water under the weight of the noise. You could feel it deep in your chest, as if the storm was trying to snatch the air from your lungs.

All at once the sky emptied.

The sea flattened under the downpour, a dark mirror punctured by a continuous explosion of hard-driving rain. Higgs could see that Speke was screaming into the radio. You couldn't hear him. You couldn't hear anything but the rolling thunder of a sky alive with jagged electricity.

Then the lightning stopped as suddenly as if a switch had been pulled. The cloud-glow faded. It was black night again, and raining harder than ever.

Speke screamed, "Hang on!"

Turned the wrong way, Higgs hadn't seen it coming: a squall preceded by a line of white froth. As it struck, the chase boat skidded sideways.

Lucy hit the throttle and tried to steer into the blast of wind. The boat would not respond, continued to skid.

"More!" Speke screamed. "Give it more!"

The deck bucked as the props bit into the water, lurching the boat forward, kicking up a wind-blown spume at the stern.

Moments later Lucy had regained control and the chase boat powered directly into the wind.

Higgs heard a series of muffled explosions—rifle shots, he realized.

"Shit!" Speke was shouting, stamping his foot in frustration. "Shit! Shit! Shit!"

Another voice shouted in the distance. More rifle shots followed.

It took Higgs several minutes to suss out what had happened. The trawler, blown backward by the sudden squall, had tangled up the net.

With one end of the net fouled, a gap of fifty yards had opened. In frustration Wade Colson had begun firing into the gap. Standing atop the *Squali* and shooting like a wild man, emptying his gun into the sea. Not seeing or hitting a damn thing.

"Come on up, you bastards! Come and get it!"

The maxis were gone.

They feel it, the wall of dying fish opening to the sea beyond. Overhead the night-shimmering surface of the water is now opaque with the wind and the downpour. There are no stars to guide them now, and none needed.

The Us run for their lives, shooting through the gap into the open sea. Keeping close to the bottom, they are unaware of the rifle fire that dies a few yards from the surface, made harmless by the insulating blanket of water.

The Us run, keeping close together, streaking away from that part of the reef. Away from the noise of the threatening boats. Away from the invisible walls of death.

Danger, they sing. *Run. Run.*

10

When the Wind Blows

THE STORM DOES not awaken Tom for the simple reason that he has not slept. He lies on his back, eyes firmly closed, the backs of his fingers brushing his wife's warm flank.

He can hear the wind tearing fronds from the palm trees. The scratching noise of the brittle fronds windblown across the gravel. There will be a mess to clean up after, and for the hundredth time he tries to remember exactly how he tethered *Wild Child*.

Did he make sure the bumpers were properly rigged?

Are the dock lines tight?

Night worries. In a few heartbeats he will get up and look out the window and *Wild Child* will be there at the dock, exactly as he left it. Tom knows that neither anxiety about the dive boat nor the noisy, flashy thunderstorms breaking over the island are what is keeping him awake. The boat has weathered a hundred storms like this. What worries him, what clenches like a fist in his belly, what makes his heart thud heavily . . . is fear.

Plain and simple fear. The image of the strange killer sharks is thumbtacked to a bulletin board in his brain. The photograph scares the sleep out of him.

What if he has to dive in the same water as those sharks?

What if his courage fails?

What if—and this is what he's *really* scared of—what if his heart stops?

Wide awake, Sally lies on her stomach, arm tucked under her pillow, feigning sleep. She is smiling in the dark. Her mind is racing. The idea of killer sharks should trouble her, she knows, but all she can think about is her dolphin. Clark catching his fish and holding it up so proud, like a kid who'd just hit a home run.

Look at the ball, Ma! Look at me!

Domesticated dolphin couldn't learn to hunt, couldn't fend for themselves in the wild. That was the conventional wisdom. And now she had proof that the conventional wisdom was wrong, at least the fish-catching part of it. Living proof, right out there in the canal. Plus there was something complex and mysterious going on between the mature female and the adolescent male, a type of behavior that didn't fit into any of the current behavior models.

She had a chance, as a virtually unknown in the field, to make a major breakthrough in dolphin research. All the more reason to get it right, make sure she followed standard scientific procedure, make certain the documentation was solid. First thing tomorrow she would go over her notes. Make sure everything was down on paper, entered into her computer files.

As to the actual experiment, releasing live fish and observing how the dolphin reacted, she had to find a simple, methodical procedure and stick to it.

Tom shifted, sat up. He was trying to be quiet about it, but the big lug couldn't be quiet to save his life. The bed lightened as he stood up.

Sally shifted, saw him go to the window. Checking on the boat. "Babe?" she said.

His head turned in silhouette. "It's okay," he said. "Just a squall. Go back to sleep."

"I wasn't asleep." Her voice changed, pitched lower. "I need my back rubbed."

He padded back to the bed, slipped in beside her, his hands tracing down to her hips. "Is that what you need?" he whispered. "A back rub?"

Sally turned and welcomed him.

Day Three

1

Wet Offerings

Bahia Honda State Park, at mile marker 37 on the
Overseas Highway. The locals call it "Bayah Honda"
and know it as a convenient point of departure for
fishing trips into the "back country"—the world of
shallow mangrove islands on the gulf side of the
Florida Keys. Others venture out into the Atlantic,
to the fish-drenched reef or beyond, into the deep,
marlin-blue Gulf Stream.

A mile or so of white Bahia Honda beach holds
back the ever-encroaching mangroves and the co-
coplums. Palm trees function as primitive beach um-
brellas. Campsites face the Atlantic, a few sandy
yards from the water. On certain tides bonefish feed
on nearby flats, in water so thin and clear their eager
tails are exposed to the air.

The park marina is in a protected cove, with an
easy-access trailer launch. The launch is open to the
public, used by both local fishing guides and trailer-
towing visitors vacationing in the Keys.

On this particular morning, paradise has been washed clean by overnight thunderstorms, and wet palm fronds litter the marina parking lot. The air smells of salt and seaweed and heat. Inhale deeply and you will encounter a wake-up whiff of gasoline.

At the busy launch site a local fishing guide decides to cut in front of an obvious, pink-skinned tourist. '' 'Scuze us,'' the guide says. ''We gotta make a tide at Horseshoe Key.''

The guide is Black Jack Finley, renowned for his fly-fishing expertise, champion of many a tournament. Finley is broad-shouldered, big-armed, black-bearded, well-muscled, a six-foot plug of a man. He is not asking permission to cut in line; he is announcing his intention to do so, regardless.

''Excuse me? You want to do what?'' The tourist, preparing to launch a rented Boston Whaler loaded with dive gear, is accompanied by his ten-year-old son. The tourist's name is Roger Craig and he is an insurance salesman from Des Moines, Iowa. He is nervous about backing a rented car and boat down the slippery ramp, and he hasn't been paying attention to the bearded fishing guide or to anyone else in the line behind him.

''Locals first,'' Finley announces. He jerks his thumb at the Boston Whaler. ''Go on and move it.''

The boy says, ''Um, Dad? Dad?''

''Just a minute, son.'' Roger Craig scratches his noses, smiles uneasily. ''We been waiting half an hour, mister. We're next, won't take ten minutes.''

Finley nods, moves a step closer. His chest is massive. His hands look capable of crushing baby skulls, and his eyes are bloodshot with last night's tiki-bar vodka. ''Won't take you ten seconds to move outta line,'' he says. His voice is pitched higher than you might expect, given his size. ''I guess maybe you didn't hear me the first time.''

''Um, Jack? Mr. Finley?'' The query comes from

Finley's customer, who made reservations with the famous guide six months ago to ensure his availability on this particular date. The customer is Leonard Bayles, a software engineer from Macon, Georgia, and he is embarrassed by Finley's rude behavior. He has been dreaming about fishing the tidal flats for months and did not envision the day starting off like this, with an air of menace.

No need to embarrass a man and his son, Bayles thinks, no need at all. He says, ''Mr. Finley, we miss the tide at, um, Horseshoe Key, it's okay by me.''

He smiles nervously at the Craigs, wanting them to know this intimidation is not his idea.

Black Jack gives Bayles a dark look. A cold, withering look, and it is obvious that Finley does not care to have his rudeness interrupted or excused by a computer geek from Macon, Georgia, or by anyone from anywhere.

The boy says, ''Dad, I gotta go to the bathroom.'' He tugs at his father's shirt. He does not really have to go to the bathroom, but the bearded man's belligerence disturbs him and the boy wants to give his father an excuse to back down. Give him the room. ''Dad?''

''Go ahead, son,'' Roger says without looking at his son.

The boy stays right where he is, backing up his dad. Holds his ground, and now he really *does* have to use the bathroom, although he'd sooner die than admit it.

The queasy standoff ends when a park ranger ambles over, clipboard in hand. The ranger knows Jack Finley by reputation, has dealt with him on a couple of other occasions, has overheard the exchange, and has read the signs of trouble brewing.

''Problem here?'' the ranger says.

No one says a word. The slight cracking sound is Finley clenching his jaw muscles.

"I believe you're next," the ranger says to Roger Craig, and stands there smiling firmly while the rented Boston Whaler is backed into the water and launched.

Fifteen minutes later Roger Craig and his son are in the Whaler at the dock, going over their dive gear. They do not speak of the incident with Black Jack Finley, who is already a mile into the back country, punishing his client Leonard Bayles with a tooth-rattling fifty-mile-an-hour ride against the chop.

When Bayles loses his hat and it is instantly eaten by the curling wake, Finley grins and pushes the throttle down another notch.

What fun.

Black Jack and Mr. Bayles, Roger Craig and his son—all four have this much in common: none of them knows that *Isurus maximus* exist and are hunting in these waters.

And the maxis are hungry.

Sally and Tom hit the road an hour after dawn, edging themselves into the fast-moving stream of early-morning commuters headed for Key West. The Overseas Highway, also known as U.S. 1, is for most of its length two fairly narrow lanes, with equally narrow bridges spanning from key to key, a crazy-gorgeous roadway linking islands from Homestead to Key West. The hundred-and-ten-mile run makes it one of the longest overseas highways in the world. At times the roadway seems to be no more substantial than a thin ribbon of sun-bleached asphalt heading straight out to sea. Passing a slowpoke means facing off against big diesel trailer trucks screaming east to Miami in the opposite lane.

Tom's rule, after years of day trips on the Overseas, was to simply take his place in line, not push his luck. The forty-mile run from Tarpon Key down to Key West might take thirty minutes, it might take an hour. You lived here, drove this wild-ass high-way, you developed the patience of a conch inching along a coral bottom, now and then swept along by the unforgiving tide.

They stopped at a Circle K on Big Pine for go-cups of coffee. Sally took it black; Tom was a one-cream, no-sugar kind of guy. Out of habit Sally bought a *Miami Herald* from a vending machine, didn't bother to unfold it. Coffee first.

On the seat between them was a manila envelope containing prints of the slide film Reggie Rhodes had bought from the wreck diver's buddy.

"You're sure you want to do this?" Tom asked, not for the first time. He was driving the Ford pickup, one hand on the wheel, elbow out the window.

"Of course I do," Sally said.

" 'Cause I know you wanted to get right to work."

"Tom? It's okay. The dolphin can wait. I want to show Monty that picture, see what he makes of it."

"Because I could, you know, do it myself. See your old pal Monty."

"Stop. You're being a pest."

"Am I?" he said, grinning, as if being a pest were his greatest ambition.

Sally said, "Just drive."

The bed of the Ford was rusty from hauling wet dive gear, the fenders flapped, and the side mirrors were cracked and bent. When the business debts were paid off, Tom wanted to buy a good used Mercedes-Benz 240D sedan, air conditioning a standard feature, and be able to drive all the way up to Miami with the windows sealed. He'd had enough of conch cruisers. What a treat it would be to own a proper automobile that would never ever be used to transport anything that had ever touched salt water—a luxury getaway car for weekend shopping sprees.

Until that day came, they drove rust buckets.

Tom thought about that someday-Mercedes as the pickup shimmied over the bridges, the bad front end making the steering wheel vibrate under his hand. Which reminded him that the last time he'd driven to Key West he'd gone alone, on that anxious, secret visit to the cardiologist, and his hands had been trembling even *without* the front-end shimmy. This morning was better—no pre-exam jitters—and he was actually very glad that Sally was along for the ride. He'd managed a couple of hours of sleep, had not dreamed, surprisingly enough, but he still preferred not to make this particular trip alone.

Having Sally at his side made things seem right. *Alone* reminded him of his recurring nightmare: the suffocating sensation of a great weight on his chest, the dream of dying underwater, unable to move.

And it was a stupid goddamn dream, because he intended to live forever. Or as near as he could make it.

Roger Craig had a chart unfurled on his knees. His son leaned over his shoulder, looking very serious indeed as his father tapped a spot on the chart.

"What we do, we'll stay along here, pretty close to shore. Make our first dive in shallow water. Fifteen feet max. Can you handle that?"

The boy said, "Dad, I went down thirty feet in the quarry. You know that."

"That was holding a rope, with a dive instructor right nearby."

"Yeah, but you couldn't *see* anything. It was dark. Fifteen feet, you'll be able to see me right from the boat."

Roger nodded. The boy had given this a lot of thought, obviously. Of course if his mother—

Roger's ex-wife—ever knew that he was going to let her precious boy dive in the *ocean*, my God, she'd have a conniption fit. Go back to court, claim he was endangering the boy's life. Because she had no idea how safe it was down here, diving in warm, reef-protected shallows. Water clear enough to see a dime glinting on the bottom, that's what the guidebooks said. And that's how it looked, too: water as clear as bottle glass.

The boy said, "Why's it called Spanish Harbor Keys, Dad?"

Dad consulted the chart, found the reference in the guidebook. "Right around the corner there, under the bridge? That's Spanish Harbor. Some Spanish galleons took refuge there and the name stuck."

"Is there treasure?" the boy asked. He was serious.

Roger made sure he didn't smile at the word "treasure." He said, "You never know. Stranger things have happened."

" 'Cause I saw this guy on *National Geographic*, they found millions of gold coins from a treasure ship. What do you call them?"

"Doubloons," Roger said, "pieces of eight."

" 'Cause they cut 'em up in eight pieces, right?"

"So they say."

"What happens, Dad, if we find a doubloon?"

Roger thought about it. "We'll give it to your mother," he said. "Tell her we found it on the beach."

A pause. Then: "You mean lie to Mom?"

Trust the boy to pick up on that. What a radar screen the kid had, he spotted adult hypocrisy at long range. Roger cleared his throat and said, "What I mean is, it's like a beach down there, in water this shallow. We just won't mention you were wearing a scuba tank and fins, okay? Deal?"

"Deal." The boy paused, glanced at the dive gear

stowed between the seats. "This is just so excellent, you know, Dad? Like we're on a real adventure."

Roger said, "We are."

He pushed the start button and was relieved when the outboard motor perked instantly to life. Observing the NO WAKE sign, Roger powered slowly out of the marina basin, cleared the channel marker, and then turned to the right.

You're heading east, he reminded himself. Stay oriented. Just keep within a few hundred yards of the shore—the remains of Flagler's old railroad bridge casting a skeletal shadow in the shallow water—and you can't miss the dive site off Spanish Harbor Keys. First set of islands east of the state park. Hell, you could see the highway from there, yell for help, if anything went wrong with the boat.

Roger's major concern was that the outboard would fail. The rental boat was equipped with a paddle, but if the wind and the current were against you, how effective could it be? Paddles were for canoes, not dive boats.

After they had run parallel to the beach area for a few minutes, his anxiety began to subside. The motor sounded smooth and flawless and the water was so transparent that he could easily avoid any submerged rocks or dangerously shallow areas. The weather—well, there was hardly a cloud in the sky, and with this much sunshine illuminating the bottom, diving should be spectacular.

The boy was in for a real treat. Hell, maybe they *would* uncover a few pieces of eight. Why not?

Ten minutes later Roger Craig was circling the dive site a quarter mile off Spanish Harbor Keys, looking for a good place to drop anchor and set out the dive buoy.

A song was running through Roger's head, a song that made him feel like a kid again, not a day older than his ten-year-old son.

Sixteen men on a dead man's chest, yo-ho-ho and a bottle of rum.

Leonard Bayles was simply amazed. A fifteen-minute, tooth-jarring ride on the guide boat had brought him to a world so far removed from civilization that he seemed to have bounced through a time warp. As far as the eye could see there were dozens of low mangrove islands floating on a mirror of luminous green water—and that was *all* that the eye could see. Aside from a few primordial, white-winged ibises wheeling under the ancient sky, no other living things—and certainly no human beings—broke the spell.

By some miracle the razzle-dazzle of Florida's building boom had left the backcountry untouched—the mangrove islands were breeders of insects, devoid of freshwater, not suitable for housing—and the area was now a protected wilderness. Although renowned for fishing and bird-watching, the waters were so shallow, the narrow channels so meandering and treacherous, that relatively few recreational boaters risked a visit.

You almost expected to see a brontosaurus looming over the mangroves, that's how primitive, how perfect it looked.

"Careful how you step on the deck," the guide said sternly. "Every fish for a mile can hear you thumping around."

"Sorry."

Jack Finley was up on his perch above the tipped-up motor, pushing the boat with a long fiberglass pole. The boat seemed to skim effortlessly over water no more than two feet deep. Patches of turtle grass tickled the bottom of the boat, sounded like a whisper. The last echo of the screaming outboard had finally faded, and now Bayles began to pick up on the backcountry silence. You could hear water lapping against the hull. You could hear leaves hushing in the mangroves. You could hear the whoosh of an ibis taking flight—and under it all was an immense and natural silence.

So quiet you could almost hear yourself think.

" 'Cuda at two o'clock," Finley announced. "Thirty yards."

Leonard Bayles wasn't sure how he was supposed to react. Finley had supplied him with a light spinning rod rigged with a rubbery, wormlike lure. By the time he'd gotten the bail open and tried to make a cast—where the hell was two o'clock?—Finley told him to forget it.

"Saw you waving that thing around like a baseball bat, them 'cuda took off."

"Sorry," Bayles said.

"Don't be sorry for me, them was *your* 'cuda."

"I, um, never saw 'em."

"That's my job," Finley said evenly. "I'll spot the fish. You just cast where I say."

"Could you explain this clock stuff again?"

Finley stopped pushing the pole and sighed. "Twelve o'clock is straight ahead. Nine o'clock is directly to the left side of the boat, three to the right. Rest fits in like a clock face. Mostly you'll cast between ten and two."

"I got it."

"I *hope* you got it. Ain't much time for conversation, I spot a bone or permit."

"I'll do better next time," Bayles said. And hated himself for feeling like a kid in school, wanting to please a stern teacher. He left the bail open, his finger resting on the six-pound-test line. Ready to rock and roll with a bonefish, that would be something to tell the folks back home. Or even a barracuda—he'd heard you got a good fight from a fifteen-pound 'cuda.

Bayles paused to clear the polarized sunglasses

that made it easier to see through the glinting surface of the water, look into that secret world. So strange and beautiful.

Hell, even if he didn't catch anything it was worth it, coming to this place. Worth the money, worth putting up with a boorish guide. Just to hear the awesome silence, smell the ancient air.

''Get yourself ready,'' said Black Jack Finley, grunting as he shoved at the push pole.

I'm ready, Leonard Bayles thought. *Ready as I'll ever be*.

The tarpon are feeding in Spanish Channel, chasing school of mullet and pinfish. Hundred-pound silver-bellied tarpon gorging on the crazed baitfish. The tarpon devour their prey in the deep channel and then rise to the surface and roll, slapping their big tails in the sheer, insolent thrill of feeding.

Us the Beautiful watch. The maxis are poised like sleek-finned torpedoes against the running tide, holding close to one another. Smelling the fear of the baitfish, the dumb joy of the tarpon.

The tarpon are big enough to be interesting. Quick and strong and fearless, they ignore the hovering maxis. In the dimness of the tarpon brain, instinct tells them that shark-shaped creatures are rather skittish hunters who select wounded or dying prey. Therefore not dangerous to a large, healthy tarpon.

So the tarpon keep surfacing in a flash of sunlit silver, returning to the bottom to feed, as they have for eons. Quick and strong, and only slightly more intelligent than the addlepated baitfish.

The maxis wait patiently, hard blue snouts poised in the current. Instinct tells them they must kill soon to feed the heat of their enhanced metabolism.

Eat to live. Eat to grow. Eat to make the fear delicious.

If not tarpon, then whatever presents itself.

2

What Monty Saw

THE GERMANS HAD landed. You could see the gleaming white hulk of a cruise ship from blocks away, looming over the Mallory Square Dock like a floating condo scheme. Troops of tourists, each with a group leader, reconnoitered Duval Street.

One of the tour leaders was a young woman with glossy corn-yellow hair, a crisply ironed white blouse and matching knee-length walking shorts. She halted a foot or two from Sally and said, "Ernst Hemway?"

"Excuse me?"

"The noveler Ernst Hemway. We seek his domicile."

"That way," Sally said, pointing. "Whitehead Street. You can't miss it."

Tom watched the group march briskly off. He said, "You've done your good deed for the day."

"Poor Ernst." Sally had an edge to her voice. "The last of the great white fish killers."

"Not by a long shot. Are you kidding?"

"I thought you liked his style," she said, frowning. "All that blood-soaked, macho posturing."

Tom handed his wife the fresh cup of coffee he'd just picked up at Shorty's. Sally hadn't wanted to stop at the breakfast counter even for a minute—this wasn't a leisurely visit to the Old Key West. "Have another dose," he said. "Hemingway's been dead a long time—give the poor man a break. He was killing game fish when it was cool to kill game fish."

Sally said. "Cool? Please."

Tom said, "Times change. If old Hem were alive today maybe he'd be a catch-and-release kind of guy."

"Yeah, sure," Sally said, sipping from the cup and giving him a dark look. "And he'd be writing about life in the suburbs, right?"

Tom wanted to reply—he really *did* admire Hemingway the writer, if not the trophy-obsessed hunter—but thought better of it. Sally had very strong opinions about the propriety of recreational slaughter—no patience with the man-getting-in-touch-with-his-nature argument—and it would be pointless to argue. Moody as hell this morning. She'd been uncharacteristically silent for the duration of the drive; preoccupied, he assumed, with concerns about her dolphin. Aware, as he was, that something was seriously out of kilter in the reef environment.

"Sorry," she said, touching his hand, her eyes gone soft and moist. "Not enough sleep makes old Sal a grouch."

Tom said, "Onward," leading the way into Mallory Square, the tourist hub of Key West, primary location for stalls and vendors and shell hawkers.

Montgomery's Shark Aquarium was located on the waterfront in a sprawling, gulf-blue building with a stuccoed facade. The propane-powered Conch

Train originated not far from the aquarium entrance, the little open-air cars awaiting the first load of passengers. On good days a whole trainload of eager money spenders would disembark and head directly into the aquarium. On bad days—and bad days happened, even in Key West—the proprietor sometimes hung out his *gone snorkeling* sign and locked the door.

On this particular morning the small clock sign was in place, set for 9:00 A.M., meaning either that the owner intended to open in forty-five minutes or—and this was a distinct possibility—that he'd forgotten to change the clock hands.

"What are the odds?" Tom said, his finger over a small unlabeled buzzer. "That he'll actually open on time, I mean."

"He didn't answer his phone at home," Sally said, feigning a confidence she did not feel. "That usually means he's here. Probably out back tinkering with that old pump of his."

Tom pressed the buzzer, *dit-dit-dit*. They waited.

"We could try the museum number again," Sally suggested.

After the telephone proved futile, Tom went around to the public pier, stood on the bumper of a parked rental car to look over the fence, and spotted the scrawny, bald-headed shape of Stewart Montgomery asleep in a lawn chair behind the aquarium building.

"Asleep or maybe dead," he reported to Sally, who waited by the fence. "Got a pipe wrench in his hand."

"A pipe wrench?"

"Must have been working on that old saltwater pump, like you said."

When roused by Tom's two-fingered, fog-cutting whistle, Monty sat up abruptly and gestured with his big red pipe wrench—whether in threat or greeting it was hard to tell.

Tom stood tiptoe on the car bumper, waving his hat over the fence, and eventually the aquarium owner staggered to his feet, unbolted the back gate, and let them in.

"You caught me," he said, not bothering to stifle a yawn.

"You spent the night in a lawn chair?" Sally asked, incredulous.

Monty grimaced, examined his bone-thin, sun-blasted limbs. He was not much taller than Sally, probably didn't outweigh her by more than a few pounds. "Must have," he said. "I'm covered with dew."

Sally rolled her eyes, shook her head. In her opinion Monty didn't look after himself—didn't, for instance, eat regular meals or use the proper sunscreen.

"I know, I know," Monty said sheepishly. "So this time the pump won. I'll get her next time, promise."

The saltwater aquarium pump, a bronze-clad monster as big as a compact car, had been an antique when acquired by Monty's mother, who had founded the place as an open-air shark pool shortly after World War II. Monty had periodically rebuilt the thing many times since he was a boy, and refused to replace it. He sometimes struggled with the burden of keeping up the family business, preferring repairs and specimen acquisition to interaction with the paying customers. In Monty's ideal world, as Sally had once pointed out, the aquarium would be stocked with only the rarest specimens of reef life and would never, ever, be open to the public. Friends only—and that included most everybody who had been in Key West for more than ten minutes. Monty had inherited his mother's affable, easygoing nature, if not her business acumen.

"You look worried," he said to Sally, rubbing a hand over his brown, egg-bald skull. "What's wrong?"

Sally hesitated, looked at Tom, then took a deep breath before speaking. "We're not sure," she said. "We may have intruders on the reef. Man-eaters."

Monty looked like he was about to laugh—had they awakened him out of a sound sleep to pull his leg?—but a glance at their expressions convinced him they were serious.

"Better come into the temple," he said.

He led them into the main gallery, through the eye-level rows of plate-glass aquaria that contained the smaller specimens, mostly reef dwellers like Florida lobster, spiky crabs, moray eels, dozens of strange and colorful tropical fish species. Most of the floor space was taken up by several large, tiled pools. Nurse sharks, dogfish, Florida rays, an adolescent lemon shark, and a few small, perky bonnet sharks that looked like miniature hammerheads, all circling endlessly in the bubbling waist-deep water.

The deepest pool was outside, surrounded by a viewing platform, and it was home to the larger specimens: Biscuit, a nine-hundred-pound hammerhead, was the star of the show—not that he did any tricks. Sharks, unlike sea mammals, had never been successfully trained, which was not, as marine biologists often pointed out, necessarily an indication of low intelligence. It was simply that shark intelligence, the cunning that had enabled them to thrive for millions of years unchanged, seemed alien or even repugnant to human observers. Tom had been observing reef shark behavior for years and never stopped marveling at how *mechanical* they looked.

Their herky-jerky, machine-like swimming motion made sharks seem like marvelous, dangerous toys wound up by some prankster god and let loose to rule the sea.

Monty's office, located in a funky corner of the building that overlooked the old navy pier, was part workshop, part memorial to his late mother. Thumbtacked to the wall were yellowed newspaper clippings and publicity photographs: a young and vital Bev Montgomery in a shiny black one-piece, dive goggles up on her forehead, posing with a live tiger shark just after the first pool was built. Bev laying the cinder-block cornerstone of the present building. A more mature Bev at the wheel of *Monty*, the dive boat she'd fitted with live wells. In the picture the nine-year-old namesake of the boat stood right beside her, looking very serious and very freckled.

No photos, quite significantly, of Monty's father, a mythical figure whose identity and occupation had changed at Bev's whim: at one time or another he had been a navy pilot she seduced on a wild weekend, a handsome French submariner, a movie star, or a cowboy from Montana. The suspicion, shared by the adult Monty and others, was the Bev died not entirely certain *who* had fathered her only child.

Might have been that tiger shark, Monty liked to boast, tapping the old photograph.

This morning, a little bleary-eyed from a night of fighting the old pump, he fetched a bottle of seltzer from a small, decrepit-looking refrigerator and hungrily drank the fizzing water. Then he said, "Ahhh. Dehydration makes me light-headed. I actually thought I heard you use the word 'man-eater.'"

When neither of them disputed the term, Monty plopped down on a saggy canvas deck. He said, "You'd better tell me what's going on."

Tom said, "Night before last a couple of mates fell overboard while they had a shark on the line."

"Fell?"

"That was the story. Missing, presumed dead. The captain's lying, but we don't think he's lying about that part."

Monty leaned back, wiped his mouth. "What part *is* he lying about?"

Tom shrugged. "Not sure. What brought us down here was the snapshot."

Sally handed Monty the manila envelope. "Yesterday a wreck diver went missing. They found his chewed-up dive harness and his camera. This was in the camera. We're assuming he snapped the picture just before he was attacked."

Monty thumbed open the envelope and drew out the print and a couple of color photocopy enlargements.

"Mako," he started to say, and then the word died on his lips. He got up from the canvas chair and went over to the window, where the light was better. "You know your species," he said to Sally. "What do *you* think?"

"Like you, my first reaction was mako. But then I wasn't sure. My specialty is marine mammals, you're the shark expert."

"Mmmm."

Placing the pictures on a worktable, Monty went to the bookshelf and located a large bound volume. He put the volume on the workbench, licked his thumb, and opened to facing pages of colored illustrations.

"*Isurus glaucus*," he said. "He might be anywhere, but he likes deep water. A Gulf Streamer. Likes to feed on schools of kingfish. Typical size of a mature specimen is three to five hundred pounds. Gets as big as half a ton if he lives long enough.

Sleek, elegant animal. Very fast and aggressive—he has to be, if he wants to eat kingfish." Monty tapped his finger on the edge of the photograph, pursed his lips. He said. "There's something off about this picture. Help me."

Sally moved closer. "The dorsal fins look right. You can see that little notch. Lateral fins have that downward swoop, like stubby wings."

"Yeah, the fins are mako. No doubt about that. And that high-peaked tail, the way it rakes back."

"Color is typical," Sally said.

"Yep. That's your mako blue. How deep was this, the wreck?"

"Fairly shallow. Fifty or sixty feet. Just beyond the reef."

Monty leaned on his elbows, getting a closer look at the original photo and the enlargements. He squinted, peered, finally fished in a drawer for a magnifying glass, which he polished on his T-shirt.

Sally said, "Oh, I almost forgot. This was found embedded in the tank harness."

She opened her purse, shook a triangular shark tooth from an envelope.

"Could be a mako tooth," Monty said, holding it up to the light. "A big mako. Tooth this large, it would have to go fifteen hundred, maybe even two thousand pounds."

Sally had been studying the photo. "It's the eyes," she said suddenly. "Damn it, the eyes are wrong."

"The head," Monty said. "It's the head area, the skull casing makes the eyes look different. Rounder than normal," he added, tapping the photograph. "More massive."

"Bigger brain cavity?"

"Bigger something. And if you count 'em, I think we've got a couple extra gill slits."

Sally counted. "Right! I should have noticed."

"You noticed they weren't typical mako," Monty said. "That takes a very sharp eye, from just this one photograph. Now what's the other thing that's wrong with this picture?"

Sally shrugged, aware of Tom's hands on her shoulders, the warm weight of him standing behind her. She said, "Just the head shape is different. And the eyes."

Monty said, "Too many makos. And too close together. You'll sometimes find quite a few hunting a big school of kingfish, but they don't hang out together. Independent buggers, usually. They don't hunt in packs or fraternize, except to mate."

Tom gently squeezed Sally's shoulders, making himself known. He said, "Extra gill slits? That's pretty unusual, right?"

Monty chuckled. His eyes crinkled in a smile. "Unusual? You might say that. Unheard of is more like it." He paused, seemed to shake the cobwebs from his head. "Okay, you maybe get the occasional shark born with the wrong number of gill slits or a messed-up tail or whatever. But not *six* of the damn things with extra gills."

"So we're talking a subspecies?"

Monty said, "I don't know. Can't make a call like that, just from one picture. But yes, that's what it looks like. A subspecies that's never been identified. Never been *rumored* even. A bigger version of *Isurus glaucus*. And if the larger skull cavity and the extra gills means a bigger brain, then it may be smarter than your average mako. Which already has a fairly high shark IQ."

"A new subspecies," Sally said reverently. "Is that really possible? If it's this aggressive—three kills in two days—then why hasn't it been seen before?"

Monty stood up from the workbench, sipped from the seltzer bottle, his eyes gleaming. Wide awake now for sure. "Could be lots of reasons. Could have been seen or even caught and mistaken for a plain vanilla mako. *We* almost mistook it, and we know better. Who the hell counts gill slits?"

"There's always old coelacanth," Tom said, putting in his two cents' worth. "Supposed to be extinct for a million years and it was out there all the time."

Monty nodded. "Good point."

Sally said, "Come on, Tom. This can't be an accidental discovery, not if Sealife is really involved."

"Sealife?" Monty said. "You don't mean your old friend Dr. Speke?"

"Afraid so," Sally said. "He was on board the charter boat when the mates were killed. And yesterday he gave Tom the bum's rush."

Tom gave a thumbnail sketch of his visit to Sealife Key and Speke's reaction.

Monty nodded thoughtfully. "Okay, Sealife may be involved somehow. That might make sense, considering the other thing I just noticed."

Sally said, "What's that?"

"Look at the picture again. What do you see?"

Sally said, "Come on, Monty. I studied this until my eyes were crossed. That's why we brought it to you, for a fresh look."

Monty said, "They're all the same."

Sally said, "Sure, I agree. Same species, whatever it is."

"More than that." He paused. "They're the same, Sal. Identical. Exactly the same size, same markings. *Exactly the same.*"

Tom bent down, had another good look at the picture, and nodded in agreement. "Like twins," he said. "I mean, what do they call it—sextuplets? Can sharks do that? Give birth to six divided from the same egg?"

He looked up from the picture, found both Sally and Monty staring at him, as if he were a kid who'd uttered something profound, beyond a child's understanding.

Monty said, ''Not in nature it can't.''

3

Three Chances

BLACK JACK FINLEY pointed and said, "See that swirl in the water?"

Leonard Bayles shaded his eyes. The glare was pretty bad, even with the brown-tinted polarized sunglasses that were recommended for shallow water conditions. He studied the glinty, sun-dancing surface and sighed. He said, "Can't say I do."

"Tarpon over that way. Sometimes they come up out of the channel, feed at the edge of this flat, the tide is rising. Which it is. Your smaller tarpon will chase a baitfish in shallow water, he don't know no better."

"Tarpon?"

"What I said, yes. Won't be no trophy winner, that size, but he'll give you a fight. You interested?"

Bayles said, "Hell, yes. Sure. How do you catch a tarpon?"

The guide grunted, came down from his perch above the outboard motor. Very light on his feet, didn't make a sound as his boat shoes touched deck. Working deftly, quickly, Finley rigged a medium-action rod with a heavy, transparent leader and a flexible plastic lure that mimicked the herky-jerky movements of a fleeing pinfish.

He handed Bayles the new gear and said, ''There are some will only fish tarpon with live bait.'' He made a noise in his throat, dismissing the idea. ''I had me some good hits on these lures. The idea, don't try to cast directly at the fish. What you want to do, draw the lure past him, come at him sideways. Then you reel it in quick. Don't worry about being *too* quick, the tarpon is quicker than you.''

Bayles said, ''Draw it past the fish.''

''Only way to learn it is do it.''

Finley got back on the elevated platform, hefted the fiberglass pole. ''Good luck,'' he said. He thought a moment, then added: ''You always need luck with tarpon.''

The boat skimmed over patches of turtle grass and Leonard Bayles could see where the water deepened, the color changing slightly, although he could still see every detail of the bottom if he looked straight down. At a distance the glare made it hard to discern anything except a kind of quivering molten glow on the surface of the water.

He tried adjusting the bill of his hat and that helped some, or possibly he was learning how to look. The next time Black Jack Finley said, ''See that swirl in the water?'' Bayles surprised himself by agreeing that yes, he *did* see that swirl in the water.

A moment later he made his first excellent cast.

''Reel,'' the guide urged. ''*Reel.*''

Bayles reeled in, letting the tip of the rod do the work of making the lure dance, approximate the action of a fleeing pinfish. A couple of times the lure broke the water, then slipped back under, just like a real pinfish.

Black Jack Finley said, "Good. That was good. Try it again, a few yards to the left."

Now Bayles could see the dark shape of the tarpon zooming along the edge of the flat. Several tarpon, not just one. He made his cast, not quite where it was supposed to go but not bad, either, and this time when he reeled in he saw a dark shape react, darting toward the lure.

"Come on," Black Jack Finley urged. "Come on, you goddamned thickheaded fish. *Strike.*"

But the tarpon did not strike on that cast or the next. Too many other baitfish in the water, too much to choose from. Bayles had the thrill, and it was an actual *physical* thrill, like knuckles running up his spine, of seeing a tarpon come right out of the water with a fish in its mouth, slamming its big tail on the way back down. A "take that!" from the tarpon that energized Leonard Bayles, software engineer, and convinced him to keep on casting, keep on until his damn *arms* fell off, if that's what it took.

Twenty minutes after sighting his first tarpon Bayles got his first hit. Bang! He'd been reeling in when suddenly the line was moving out again, the drag making a weird kind of noise, like a high-pitched hum. Instinctively he raised the rod above his head and yanked back, setting the hook, and then *holy shit*, this great big beautiful silver creature stood up in the water. Stood up in the water right on its tail before falling, *wham!*, no more than thirty yards from the boat.

"Bow to him!" Finley urged. "Drop the tip of your rod."

Bayles did exactly as he was told, bowing to the mighty king tarpon, who responded by peeling off fifty yards of line in about the time it took to draw a breath, *zoom*, it was that fast. Bayles hanging on for dear life, so excited he could feel his knees shaking and so what, he didn't care: *he had a tarpon on the line.* No way to reel *this* in.

Touch the reel and the line would snap, sure as hell. It felt hot, that line, as it was stripped from the reel.

"Lift the rod a little," Finley suggested. He was pushing the fiberglass pole, shoving the boat along after the fleeing tarpon. "Let it feel the hook again."

Bayles did as he was told, and sure enough, the tarpon came up out of the water again, not quite so spectacular on the second rise, but impressive, oh yes.

Leonard Bayles couldn't help it; he asked, "How big is it, do you think?"

"Small," Finley said, huffing quietly as he shoved at the pole. "Forty, fifty pound."

Fifty pounds of fighting game fish and that was *small.* What was it like to get a really big tarpon on a rig this light? Leonard Bayles kept a little pressure on the fish now, and he decided what the hell Lenny boy, quit the software job, move down to the Keys and fish tarpon for the rest of your life.

That's how good it felt.

The guide said, "He wants to find deep water."

Bayles said, "Yeah."

"Deep water makes him strong. Keep him out of the deep water, you'll win."

The idea was to get the tarpon to the side of the boat, take a scale, and then release the fish. Pushing it along until it revived, if that's what it took. The fish scale was to prove you'd caught one, and to get an idea of the tarpon's weight, which could be estimated by the size of the scale. Then you could order a "mount" of your catch, cast from fiberglass, if you really wanted something to hang on the wall.

Bayles was actually thinking about that, whether

or not he should order a wall plaque, when the boat bumped against the bottom and came to a stop.

The reel started screaming again as the tarpon continued on up the channel, searching for deeper water.

"What happened?"

"Ran out of water," Finley said, calm as could be.

"What do I do!"

"Get out and run, you want to get that fish. I'll push off this sandbar, try to catch up to you."

Bayles said, "Holy shit! He's stripping off all the line."

Holding the rod in both hands, Bayles hopped over the edge of the boat, felt his boat shoes sink an inch or so into the soft white mud. The water was warm as air around his ankles.

The line screamed.

He began to jog over the mud flat, splat-splat-splat, lifting the rod to keep the line from rubbing. Thirty yards to his left his tarpon was racing like a speedboat up the channel, trying to peel off the last few feet of line.

Leonard Bayles knew he looked like a fool, waddling as he tried to run through the clinging mud. And he knew that Black Jack Finley was getting a kick out of this, probably laughing like hell, but he didn't give a damn.

He wanted his fish.

The boy took to the water like he had gills, he was that natural. The Craigs, father and son, were anchored in water fifteen feet deep, over the partial remains of a small turtle sloop that had sunk about the time of the Civil War. Probably driven near the shore and abandoned, the guidebook said, when the hull seams opened. Lot of older, poorly maintained boats used in the turtle trade, not unusual to have one sink this close to shore. The years and the storms

and thousands of previous dive expeditions had
taken their toll. All that remained now was part of
the keel and a few ribs encrusted with coral. Just
enough so you could see the shape of a boat there,
lying just under the water.

The boy, raised on the dry prairie, trained in chlo-
rinated swimming pools and algae-darkened quar-
ries, had been so excited his eyes were like thin blue
puddles ready to spill out of his face. Hurrying to
put on the scuba tank harness, as if the wreck might
disappear before he got into the water.

"Take it easy," Roger Craig had said. "We've got
all day. As long as it takes us to go through two
tanks each."

The boy simply nodding. A look that said, *Please,
let's stop talking about it and just do it.*

"You go first," Roger had said. "I'll be right behind you."

They had gone into the water quietly, with a minimum of fuss, clutching their masks, and settled
languidly toward the bottom, stirring up puffs of
pale sand as they touched down. No problem, no
panic, a day at the beach for sure.

Now, after a thorough examination of the wreck,
the boy had become interested in the small fish feeding in and around the coral. Look at him floating
there, patient as can be, keeping himself carefully
balanced so as not to touch the coral itself. Following the rules. Every minute or so the boy would
check his dive gauges, see how much air he had left.
As careful as any adult diver, more careful than
most.

Roger Craig kept a discreet distance, maybe ten
yards to one side, not wanting to crowd the kid. Let
him have this experience, a young man all alone at
the bottom of the sea as a whole new world slowly
revealed itself.

It was Roger who jerked involuntarily when a

good-sized ray suddenly freed itself from the bottom and jetted off. Hadn't even seen the damn thing, the camouflage was that good. The boy merely looked up from the coral, studied the fleeing ray, then pointed and signaled AOK to his father.

See that? No problem, Dad.

The temperature and visibility were such that you were barely aware of the water, except where it slowed you down or made you feel buoyant. With the nice little wreck and the abundant sealife it was hard to imagine better first-time dive conditions for a ten-year old, or for anybody. The way Roger figured, if they were lucky, a father and son shared maybe two or three experiences like this in a lifetime. Most *never* had a day like this.

Roger felt something tap his tank from behind. Where the hell was the boy? He turned, feeling suddenly ill coordinated in the water, discombobulated, and his son was right there behind him. Excited, you could see his eyes grinning behind his faceplate. Pointing over his shoulder, trying to get his father's attention.

A shark was whipsawing along the bottom. Hard to say how big it was, maybe five or six feet, Roger decided. A nurse shark; he recognized the catfish-like whiskers around the mouth. Which meant it was a bottom feeder, not dangerous to humans unless you did something really dumb like put your fingers in its mouth. The boy knew this, too, because he was interested, not the least bit afraid. And it was true, there was no sense of menace when you saw a shark of this size in the wild, only curiosity. Weird, how unreal it looked. Like a fake shark at Disney World.

Perfectly harmless.

But when the boy started to swim off after the

shark, Roger reached out and grabbed one of his
bright yellow power fins. Made the NO, BAD IDEA
sign by shaking his finger and then pointed to his
dive gauge.

It was time to surface, change their tanks.

Leonard Bayles was in knee-deep water, his shoes
sinking into the puffy white mud, when the tarpon
finally turned. The steady, unrelenting pressure on
the line finally loosened and he was able to reel in
twenty or so feet of line.

Guessing, from the feel of it, that the tarpon was
swimming in his direction. Tired of fighting the
hook, giving up.

Bayles said, "Baby! Oh, yes, come to Papa."

He glanced to the side, saw where Black Jack Finley was maneuvering the guide boat around the
sandbar, mud bar, whatever. The tide was rising,
that would help. And for the first time since dawn
Bayles felt like he could handle the situation on his
own.

What the hell, it was only a baby tarpon. Okay, a
teenage tarpon, half the size of a mature specimen.
If Finley was right about its weighing no more than
fifty pounds. Goddamn big fish by any other standard. Guys flew to Canada to catch fifteen-pound
salmon, thought it was a really big deal.

Sudden pressure on the line now. The fish had
changed its mind, wanted to turn and run. Bayles
raised the rod high overhead, letting the drag do the
work. The line no longer screaming out, just the tick-
tick of the drag.

Lost maybe ten of the twenty feet he'd cranked in
when he felt the line go slack. Jesus, had it broken
off? Spit the hook?

He cranked hard, retrieved maybe fifty more feet
of line when he felt it there again, a jerking pressure. He couldn't see the fish—it was down there

somewhere, hugging the channel bottom, probably scared shitless—but the way the line reacted he could picture the little tarpon shaking its head: *Son of a bitch, won't this guy ever let me go?*

The answer to that was no. The way Bayles felt, he'd be willing to swim a mile for this one; he wanted to see it, look the beast in the eye before he released it.

You're mine, he wanted to say. *I'll set you free, but you'll always be mine.*

"He still there?"

Finley's voice was so close it was like he was whispering in his ear. Bayles jerked around, saw the guide boat about twenty feet away. Black Jack Finley, big and confident, grinning inside his beard, leaning on his push pole.

Bayles nodded.

Finley said, "You doin' real good."

"Thanks."

"What I propose to do is come up behind you real gentle, get you back aboard. Then we ease on out to the deeper water, see if we can get your tarpon alongside before he worries himself to death."

Bayles was able to reel in another ten feet of line before he felt resistance. He said, "Fine, let's do it."

A moment later the rod was almost jerked from his hands. He went down on one knee, the splash wetting his face, warm salt water blinding him for a second, but he didn't let go of the rod.

Shit. Plenty of fight left in that little tarpon.

It yanked again, a strong, steady tugging. Line stripped from the reel again, the drag shrieking.

Son of a bitch, it was getting away from him.

Bayles lowered the rod and ran toward the channel. Up to his waist in water now and the mud sloping soft underfoot. He put on the brakes when the water got up to his armpits, and that was when he heard Black Jack Finley screaming.

"Leggo!" Finely yelled. "Leggo the rod!"

Bayles couldn't see where the boat was—somewhere behind him, he assumed—and if that bastard Finley thought he was going to give up this fish now, after fighting it for so long, the guide was very much mistaken.

"Drop it, you son of a bitch! Leggo!"

Something in Finley's tone of voice, some desperate quality, made Bayles think twice. Maybe he *should* let go of the rod.

Screw it, he thought, no. I lose any more ground, *then* I'll let go. Finley probably was worried he'd drown, unaware that Leonard Bayles was an expert swimmer, had a couple of lifesaving badges stowed away in a drawer somewhere.

Then the water around him started to boil and he was no longer thinking about Black Jack Finley or the tarpon. Something cut into his bare leg. The line. Son of a bitch, that hurt. And then the line broke and the pressure stopped and suddenly it came out of the boiling spume not a yard from his face.

His tarpon. Leaping in terror. Blood jetting from its gills. Before the tarpon hit the water a much larger thing emerged from the white froth and seized it.

Cold, unblinking eyes. Alien eyes.

Bayles heard the crunch of bones, the brittle gnashing of teeth, saw the tarpon halved. Glistening fins, the pressure of rushing water.

Shark, a primitive corner of his mind screamed. *Shark!*

Trying to back up in the mud, he slipped and went under. Eyes open, he could see nothing but the froth of white mud. And something darker, like a trace of red juice whirling in the bottom of a blender. He began to gag as water filled his throat and he had the presence of mind to try and claw his way to the surface. Seeking the air and the light, his brain filled with the desire to live.

Something seized him around the waist, an unbearable tightness, and then he was out of the water, being lifted into the thin blue sky, into the daylight.

He never knew what happened next.

4

A View from the Bridge

BLACK JACK FINLEY was close enough that the blood hit him, and still it all went down so quickly he could barely comprehend what had happened. He'd seen the dark fins breaking the water and that's when he'd started yelling at the client, trying to get him to drop the rod. Up to your waist on slippery mud was no way to fight a shark, it happened to get on your hook.

His first thought, seeing the way the water had started to boil, was that the big old hammerhead who lived under the Bahia Honda Bridge had come up the Spanish Channel chasing tarpon. Something that lazy old hammer never did—he mostly ate hooked-up tarpon right under the bridge—but there was always a first time.

A heartbeat later Finley changed his mind, seeing more than one large, triangular fin break the surface—hell, there were *several* sharks there, makos from the look of those fins, and big ones, too. Much bigger than any shark he'd ever seen in the back-country shallows. Hell, the channel wasn't much more than ten feet deep, this far up. Shark of this size preferred deep water, out beyond the reef, everybody knew that.

That was when he started screaming at his client to leggo the goddamn rod and get in the boat, but by then it was already too late. There was so much splashing you couldn't really see what had happened.

All he knew was that the client went under and then a moment later a body was being lifted into the air. Several big makos coming right out of the water, tearing the body into pieces and devouring it so quickly that Finley dropped his push pole and fell to the bottom of his boat, stunned.

Jesus freaking christ.

He got to his knees feeling woozy and wobbly and wondering if he had maybe been hallucinating—too much cheap vodka at the tiki last night. What had he been drinking at the end, kamikazis? Maybe this was all part of a killer hangover. That was when he noticed the spatter of blood on his white T-shirt. Touched his face and felt a thick wetness in his beard, saw the slime of red on his fingertips.

So it really *had* happened.

Finley, a cautious man who understood the dangers of the sea, lifted his head, peered over the shallow sides of his little guide boat. The boat was rocking from the wake of a passing vessel. No, he decided, glancing around at the empty waters, the wake of a passing shark. *Several* passing sharks.

The turbulence of the kill had pushed the guide boat away from the channel area, back over the flats, into water barely a foot deep. Which meant he was safe here. Unless the freaking things could get up and walk.

What a thought.

Finley shivered like a sick dog in the hot sun and crawled to his marine radio. Snapped the switch and heard the comforting crackle of static and chattering voices on Channel 16. Charter skippers and gabby fishermen using the Coast Guard emergency frequency as a hailing channel or for gossip about hot fishing spots.

He pressed the send button on the microphone and growled: "Get off the air you rat-ass bastards! This is Captain Finley on the guide boat *Skimmer*. There's been a shark attack off Little Spanish Key."

He let go of the send button, thought better of it, and pushed it down again. "Man-eaters," he said into the microphone. "You copy that? Man-eaters."

The air in the second tank was cool and sweet. Funny how compressed air in a scuba tank sometimes had a particular flavor. This flavor, you had to put a name to it, you might say mint. Or really it was the taste of palm trees, a little spicy and fragrant. Key lime air, was that it?

Odd thoughts.

Roger Craig grinned around his mouthpiece and wondered if he was getting just a little bit wiggy after more than an hour in the water. Air that tasted of mint and palm trees and Key limes, his imagination must be running wild. Couldn't be the bends, since they were in less than fifteen feet of water, hardly any pressure on a dive this shallow.

Was the boy having similar thoughts? Tasting his air? Look at him there, searching for treasure. After changing over to the new tank, the kid, looking very serious and sober, had put on rubber diver's mitts and announced he was going to rake through the sand around the buried keel. Not saying anything about gold or treasure, but Roger knew.

No point reminding the boy that hundreds of divers had combed over this wreck. That it was just an old, leaky turtle sloop, there never *had* been gold aboard; even the turtle shells had been salvaged long ago.

What harm could it do? Let the kid have his dreams.

Roger was so relaxed that he was content to simply float weightless a few yards from the wreck, keeping an eye on the boy. Aware of soft corals undulating in the slight current. So peaceful it was like a drug experience, a really clean drug that didn't mess you up or make you feel anxious.

Prescription for peace of mind: Take one scuba tank, add warm water.

He was feeling so dreamy that he didn't at first register the discovery. All of a sudden his son was kicking away from the keel area, holding out his gloved hand.

Coming quickly to show his father something.

Something small and dark cupped in the bright yellow gloves. The boy's hands opened and Roger instinctively caught the thing as it drifted down.

Glass. Dullish green.

A bottle, yes, it was a small, intact bottle. Made opaque by more than a century under the soft coral sands.

Roger held up one hand, made the AOK sign. From the expression in his son's eyes he knew that this was the treasure the boy had been seeking. Not impossible gold, but an artifact from the wreck. A rather splendid reminder of the young man's first real dive.

A bottle this small, it had probably contained medicine. Some elixir carried by a turtle hunter.

Snake oil, maybe, to cure what ailed you. Touch it, you felt the history, somehow it made the wreck seem like it had once been a real boat, not just a collection of coral-encrusted timbers.

Reverently Roger handed the bottle back to his son, who transferred it to the net bag hanging at his waist. The boy signaled, COME ALONG, FOLLOW ME, and he did, Roger following his son to the base of the wreck, where the ruined remains of the keel emerged from the coral sand.

They both began to sift through the sand, looking for buried treasure.

Crossing onto Big Pine Key, Tom had the nagging, back-of-the-neck feeling that he was forgetting something important. The ride back from Key West had been pretty quiet so far—both Harts digesting what Monty had said about the mako, or the not-quite-mako, or whatever the hell they were.

Not found in nature.

One man's opinion, maybe, but for a lifetime of hands-on, out-on-the-reef experience it was hard to beat Stewart Montgomery, who had been consulted by marine biologists and shark experts the world over. If Monty said six totally identical specimens of an unknown species were not found in nature, then they weren't natural.

Which left a pretty disturbing alternative, that Sealife had developed a new species, altered a normal mako somehow. The puzzler was why would Speke and his staff be messing around with sharks? They'd been a dolphin outfit for years, living off U.S. Navy contracts, experimenting with sea mammals trained to defend submarine bases and attack enemy divers.

Sharks were untrainable, everybody knew that.

"My God," Tom said.

"What?" Sally had been examining the photographs, consulting a book on shark morphology scored from Monty.

"Just had a thought," Tom said.

He pulled over at the Big Pine lights, into the drive-in liquor-store parking lot, left the motor idling. Fingers drumming nervously on the wheel.

"You look like you've seen a ghost," Sally said.

"Six ghosts. You and Monty think this new species may have larger-than-normal brains, right?"

"Can't be sure."

"Yeah, but that's what you *think*, right?"

Sally allowed as to how it was a theory, or more accurately a supposition. Not wanting to commit herself without more evidence, more study.

"Look," Tom said, exasperated. "I'm not some editor of a professional journal, I just want to know if you think these particular sharks might be smarter than average."

"It's possible," Sally conceded. "All we've seen is a photograph. You really want to get an idea of the brain capacity, you'd have to do a dissection. Even then you can't be sure that brain size relates to intelligence."

Tom shook his head. Even at a time like this, and with her own husband, Sally was cautious about postulating from photographic evidence. Scientific caution, never go out on a limb unless you'd carefully surveyed the tree.

"My question is this," Tom said. "Would a more intelligent shark be easier to train?"

Sally shrugged. "You can't train sharks at all. Not in any meaningful way. I'm not sure that enhancing shark intelligence would help, if your goal is programing behavior."

Tom thought about that. He hadn't shut off the truck and he could smell the fumes from a hole in the exhaust pipe. That and the dead-rot stink of Big

Pine mangroves, you couldn't get away from the smell, it was everywhere in the Keys if you paid attention.

"Okay, forget training," he said. "Would a more intelligent species of shark be more dangerous than your average mako?"

Sally nodded thoughtfully. "I think it might, yes. More intelligent species are more adaptable. They tend to dominate similar, less intelligent species. Or wipe them out."

"I'm talking about dangerous to humans, not to other sharks."

"Oh."

"We don't know that they've been preying on other sharks, Sal. We're pretty sure they've killed at least three people."

Sally shook her head. "Most animals will attack when threatened. You can't blame an animal for protecting itself."

Tom snorted, put the truck in gear. "Look, we're not debating motive here. All I'm saying, these creatures, whatever they are, are smart and dangerous. And if Sealife really is involved, they're *supposed* to be smart and dangerous."

Sally gave him a lingering look, then said, "What's on your mind, babe?"

He got the truck back on the Overseas Highway, melded into the stream of traffic before replying. "What I propose to do is have another talk with Wade Colson. Find out what *really* happened that night. Are you game? Can Clark and Lois wait?"

Sally thought about it. "I'm game," she said. "And yeah, the dolphins can wait. Hell, maybe they'll teach themselves a couple of new tricks before we get back."

They were just clearing Big Pine, heading for the bridge, when a siren came up behind them. Traffic veered into the narrow slot that served as a breakdown lane. Moments later an ambulance went careening by.

Probably another traffic accident, they decided, fate colliding on U.S. 1.

"Crazy snowbirds," Tom said.

"Crazier locals," Sally responded.

When they got to the Bahia Honda Bridge, traffic came to a standstill. Only the ambulance was able to weave around, get down to the state park entrance.

"Must be a boat accident," Tom said. He shut off the truck. "Look at all those rubberneckers on the bridge."

Several dozen onlookers lined the bridge, facing the gulf and the distant backcountry islands. Tom and Sally got out of the truck, ambled over to the rail. Below, the clear green waters of the channel looked placid enough. No wrecked or burning boats in evidence, nothing to explain the call for an ambulance or all the gawkers on the bridge.

A friendly truck driver told them what all the fuss was about. "Heard it on the CB. Some poor fool got et by a shark."

Tom elbowed his way to the rail, made room for Sally. "You sure about this?" Tom asked the driver. "They said an actual shark attack? Not just a sighting or a scare?"

The driver tugged at his Miami Dolphins cap, paused to spit over the rail. "Ain't sure about nothing, mister. That's what it said on the CB, is all. Don't see nothing out there, but if he really *was* et, there'd be nothin' to see, right?"

There was no arguing with the truck driver's logic. From this high up on the bridge you could see fairly far into the backcountry. There were several guide boats staked out over the flats, widely spaced—they didn't crowd each other, these professional guides. There was one boat way up in Spanish Channel, coming south toward Bahia Honda, moving right along, too, but no obvious signs of panic. No flares or smoke. No sign of anyone in the water.

"Could be a prank," Tom said to Sally. "Some jerk messing around on the marine bands. They get false reports all the time."

Sally nudged him and pointed. "Out there, in the channel. I see something moving."

Toms squinted, adjusted his Polaroids. His eyes weren't as sharp as Sally's—she could identify a bird in flight from miles away, or so it seemed—and it was a few moments before he was able to discern the dark shapes of large fish streaking along in the clear waters of the channel. Hard to get a head count, the way the sun glinted, but it might be as many as half a dozen creatures.

"Can't tell if they're shark," Tom said. "Could be really large tarpon, I suppose. Or dolphin."

"Not dolphin," Sally said, shaking her head. "No way."

Other sharp-eyed observers picked up on it, reported the sighting, and now everyone was pointing, the buzz of the crowd getting louder and louder.

"That deep in the channel, you'd never see 'em from the water," Tom said. "Not unless you were right on top of 'em."

"I think they must be running," Sally said, never taking her eyes from the streaking shapes. "Headed out to sea. They're going to pass right under this bridge."

"Come on," Tom said, taking her hand. "Let's see which way they go."

They crossed through stalled traffic to the other side of the bridge, facing out to sea, out to the reef, and close by, the entrance to Bahia Honda State Park.

Tom was the first to spot the anchored dive boat,

and the dive buoy marker, a few hundred yards off-shore.

"Hell," he said. "Somebody's down on that old turtle sloop."

Just then the dark shapes streaked under the bridge, heading straight for the dive boat.

5

What a Father Does

THE WATER WAS a warm, translucent blanket, insulating them from the surface world. Look up and you did not see the sky, you saw a rippling silver mirror. Piercing this silver membrane was the bottom of the Whaler, the outboard motor prop, and the anchor line—items intruding from another world.

Roger Craig stopped pawing through the sand—he'd come up with precisely nothing—and watched the dive boat swing around over the wreck site, responding to the current or the surface winds, it was hard to tell.

In five minutes they would have to pass through that silver membrane, return again to the surface world. There were reserves in the scuba tanks that would give them a little more time, if you wanted to push it, but Roger was a cautious diver and this was his boy down here, his son, and he didn't want to take any chances.

He'd already decided to rent the Whaler for another day. There were dozens of wreck sites and reef areas to explore, why stop here? The boy had proved himself quite capable of a sustained dive. Tomorrow they'd range a little farther, out to the reef sanctuary. More fish out there, more varieties of coral. With any luck they'd sight something really awesome, like a manta ray.

You could swim right along with a manta, which looked like a Stealth bomber gliding on a flight path; sometimes they'd leap from the water, make a hell of a splash. Roger had seen it on a dive video and had always wanted to swim with a giant manta or something really large, like a whale or a harmless basking shark.

Couple more minutes, they really *would* have to surface. His son was still methodically sifting through the sand at the base of the keel. Hadn't found any other bottles or artifacts, just a few small chunks of petrified wood, the remains of the planking or whatever. The boy didn't seem particularly disappointed, it was like he was doing a job and wanted to finish it up.

Roger didn't plan to tell his son that technically they weren't supposed to remove any artifacts from a dive site. The state of Florida had rules and regulations. But the turtle sloop wasn't registered, nobody owned it, so he planned to stretch the law, let the kid keep his bottle. What the hell, the next diver who found it would be sure to take it—the site had been picked over, you could tell.

Time to go. Roger dropped his gauge, tapped his son on the shoulder, pointed to the surface. As the boy looked up, something caught his attention. Roger could see the blue eyes squinting behind the faceplate, an expression of puzzlement or wonder as the boy looked into the middle distance.

Roger turned, expecting to see some fish or other.

He had manta ray on the mind. What he saw made him freeze, the regulator heavy in his mouth.

Shark.

Big shark.

Big and powerful, with a sleek, pointed snout, streamlined fins, and a long, curved-back tail. The tail fin was twitching back and forth, sort of like a cat tail except the fins made the shark move with incredible speed, back and forth on the other side of the wreck. Swimming in kind of an inverted S-pattern. Dark blue on top, milky white underneath, really a beautiful creature, except that Roger Craig wasn't in a mood to contemplate beauty.

He was scared. So scared his anus had contracted to the size of a pencil point. So scared he forgot to breathe, forgot that the regulator delivered air on demand. You had to suck in, get the valve to open.

He breathed again when his son tugged at his wrist.

Pointing. Roger looked, too frightened to be startled at the fact that the shark had suddenly transported itself to the *other* side of the wreck. And then he realized there were not one but *two* sharks exactly the same size and shape and coloring, and in the next heartbeat he saw that they were *surrounded* by sharks, two, four, six, too many to count, you couldn't keep track of all of them at once, it was impossible. All of them huge, longer from snout to tail than their sixteen-foot Boston Whaler. All swimming in that tight S-pattern, so powerful Roger could feel the thrust of their tails stirring the water.

Roger took his son by the hand, pulled him close to the keel. Close and down low, Jesus, make a smaller target. The boy did not resist, but he did keep pointing to the surface. When Roger didn't respond, the boy pointed to his dive gauges.

Right, air was low. They didn't have a lot of time down here. But there was no way Roger wanted to

give up the relative safety of the wreck, risk exposing himself in the open water for even a few yards.

Not that the wreck was safe, exactly. Just a partial
keel, a few ribs, some tall fan coral. Nothing to *really*
keep out these things if they decided to attack.

And an attack was very much on Roger Craig's
mind. He'd read enough about shark behavior to
know that this was extremely rare, all of these huge
creatures in shallow water, getting this close to a
couple of divers. Sharks were supposed to be shy.
Rarely bothered divers unless there was blood in the
water, and even then, plenty of crazy divers had
gotten out of their protective cages, swum among
feeding sharks and never been touched.

Not sharks *this* large, though. No way.

From the bridge you could see where the sharks
had arrayed themselves under the dive boat, as if
coordinating an attack.

"Amazing," Tom said. "I've never seen sharks
behave like that. Almost like a wolf pack. Usually
they just swarm in, fight over their prey."

Sally was tugging at him, wanted to get off the
bridge, down to the rocky shore. "We've got to do
something," she said.

Tom sighed, pulled her close. "Sal? There's been
half a dozen guys on the CB, okay? The Coast Guard
is on the way."

Sally shook free of his arms, looked scornful.
"Give me a break—the Coast Guard? They're too
busy chasing drug runners."

"They're not that bad," Tom said, although he
had his doubts about a quick response this close in-
shore. Sally was right about the Coast Guard's emphasis on offshore smugglers; most of the patrol
boats worked the reef or the Gulf Stream. "Any
case, there's nothing we can do. Not from here,
without a boat."

"I feel terrible. Helpless."

Tom said, "You're the scientist. Observe and take notes. Maybe we'll learn something useful."

Behind them a car horn began to bleat, as steady as a pulse.

They were closing in, circling the wreck.

Glancing down, Roger noticed the sheath knife strapped to his ankle. It was there strictly as a safety device, to cut yourself free from a tangle of line or whatever. Probably useless against one of these creatures, certainly of no use with this many.

Roger knew with an absolute certainty that a man wouldn't last three seconds in the midst of these creatures. God, look at the way they swam! Jaw muscles flexing, showing their teeth. Sleek, powerful bodies whipping around with such pinpoint precision, such perfect coordination that they never bumped into each other. Radiating menace and cunning and intelligence.

Forget three seconds. You'd be dead in a heartbeat.

Roger hugged his son, then released the boy. It was hard to communicate, hard to concentrate on signaling, but the boy seemed to understand what his father was trying to say. They had to conserve air. They had to try and breathe shallowly. Very important.

Before starting the dive they had discussed what to do if air suddenly ran out. Drop the weight belt and tank harness, then head straight for the surface. They'd both had to practice the procedure before becoming certified divers. But that was under supervision, in a pool. Trying to keep a level head under these conditions was another matter.

Could he trust the boy not to panic? Could he trust himself?

Roger slipped off the weight belt, kept it in his

hands. Let go of the weights and he'd start rising, make himself a tempting target. So hang on for now, and if they got the chance he could just let go of the weights and race for the surface.

The next thing Roger did was unsnap his tank harness. He didn't shed the tanks, he simply wanted to be ready to do so at a moment's notice. It would be a hell of a lot easier to scramble up over the sides of the Whaler without a tank or weight belt.

Sharks snapping at your feet, or worse.

Keep calm, he urged himself. A panicked diver is a dead diver.

He watched his son take off his weight belt and place it over his flippers, holding him right to the bottom. Good move. Roger did likewise, draping the heavy weights over his fins. The boy loosened his tank harness, just as his father had done. Getting himself ready. He looked expectant, there behind the mask, and trusting, as if confident that his father would know exactly what to do.

Roger wished *he* were that confident.

A sudden rush of water made him teeter backwards. He saw the dark curve of a tail pass inches away from his faceplate and his guts turned icy.

Had the attack begun?

He wanted to close his eyes—he really, really didn't want to know—but the trust of his son forced him to look.

An eye, looking right at him. A silver, iris-slitted eye beaming with cold, alien intelligence as the creature glided by, just on the other side of the keel. Checking them out.

You could reach out and touch the things, they were that close. Not that he *did* reach out. If anything he wanted to make like a turtle, pull all his limbs inside his body. Shrink himself to the size of a rock and play dead, hope the things would lose interest and go away.

They said with a bear you should curl up and not resist. Would that work with a shark? Jesus, there was so much he didn't know, so much the dive manuals had never explained.

His respirator valve clanged shut. No air.

Panic.

For just a moment Roger forgot that he still had his reserve. Damn near kicked off the weights, and then he remembered and reached for the reserve valve, pulled it.

Sweet, cool air flooded into the respirator.

He reached for his son's reserve valve, but the boy stopped him. Tank not quite empty yet; he was smaller, possibly less frightened, he'd used up less air. *Don't worry, Dad*, the kid's eyes seemed to say, *I'll handle the reserve valve. You just figure a way to get us out of here.*

If only he could. The reserve gave them only a few precious minutes, and then they would *have* to surface, sharks or no sharks. Surface or drown, no other alternatives presented themselves.

Something had changed in the way the creatures were behaving. No more S-patterns. They seemed poised now, as if ready to strike. All of the creatures facing the wreck—everywhere you turned you saw the same damn shark, like mirrors in a funhouse.

If only he had a way to distract them, draw them away from the wreck. The boy was quick, he could get himself into the Whaler pretty damn fast, given half a chance.

There *was* a way, of course. Had been all the time, except he hadn't really wanted to think about it. Now, with only a minute or two left, it seemed perfectly logical.

He would swim away from the wreck, make himself the target. Swim fast and hard, attracting that animal-quick attention. And who knows, maybe the creatures would not attack, maybe they'd simply follow him out of curiosity.

Best to think of it that way. Just being followed. Pied piper of the shark world.

Roger could feel his reserve shrinking. Could almost count the lungfuls left before the tank went hollow.

Looking directly into his son's eyes, Roger poked himself in the chest, then pointed away from the wreck. I GO THAT WAY. Pointed at the boy, then at the surface. YOU GO THAT WAY. UP.

The message was very clear; they both understood what he was saying, what it meant if he did this thing.

The boy shook his head. BOTH GO UP, he signaled. BOTH.

Stop looking at your son and just do it, Roger told himself. Do what a father does.

He tore himself away and turned. Kick. Kick. Kick.

Roger Craig, Sr., was clear of the the wreck, exposed, out in the open. He did not feel courageous or noble. He was terrified.

Kick. Kick. Kick.

He couldn't help it, he found himself counting. How many kicks before it happened? How many before he was crushed by those terrible, jutting jaws?

The water moved around him. They were coming.

From the bridge you could see where the swimming patterns had changed. The sharks were veering away from the wreck site, tightening the circle, several of the dark shapes blending as they closed in.

Somebody is about to die, Tom thought, but he couldn't look away; there was something hypnotic about the way the six shapes moved, almost as if they were one creature.

Then Sally was stirring next to him, her body tense

with excitement. She said, "Look! Under the bridge!"

Tom looked straight down, saw a backcountry guide boat explode outward from under the bridge, and he said, "Hey! That's Jack Finley, see the beard?" and he glanced out to the anchored dive boat and saw an amazing sight.

Six huge makos leaping straight up out of the water. Leaping like goddamned *dolphins* except there was nothing playful about this coordinated leap. It was menacing, as if they wanted to *see* what all the noise was about. Rising together.

And then suddenly they were down again, under the water, the black shapes racing away as Finley steered his little skimmer in a crazy circle around the anchored dive boat. Sending up a rooster tail and wake that was going to swamp him if he wasn't careful.

"It's working!" Sally shouted. "They're running away!"

They were running. Hard to see because they moved so fast, dark ripples shooting like torpedoes just under the surface. Gathering together, as if seeking each other's slipstreams.

Heading for the horizon, gone.

A cheer went up from the bridge. Horns began to honk.

Black Jack Finley couldn't hear the reaction, he was still circling the dive boat at full speed, driving his shallow-water skimmer like a madman. Creating a wake that spread out behind the fleeing sharks and was just now reaching the shore, boiling white against the rocks and the bridge abutments.

"I never thought I'd be glad to see Jack Finley," Sally said.

Another cheer went up as a diver emerged from the water and scrambled into the anchored dive boat.

A boy, you could tell that much. He looked worried, frantic.

Some yards away from the dive boat another diver surfaced. Clawing and splashing but very much alive.

The crowd on the bridge watched as Finley immediately slowed his skimmer, headed for the struggling diver. Got to him quickly. Reached down into the water and yanked the diver straight into his boat, a feat of strength and nerve that got an admiring *oooooohhh* from the crowd of observers on the bridge.

"Scream of the prop," Tom said.

"What?" Sally didn't quite hear him, she was watching as Finley carried the rescued diver over to the dive boat. The boy looked very excited, very relieved.

Tom said, "The damn things have learned that boat engines and propellers mean danger. So how they hell do you catch them if they run from boats?"

6

Getting Buzzed

VERNON SPEKE KNEW it was going to be a bad day when his ponytail got caught in the fan belt. He's crouching in the engine compartment of the converted trawler, helping Robby Mendez and the diesel mechanic rig up another pneumatic pump for the new gear, try the fucker out, see if it works, when bang! his head is yanked back and zip! his ponytail is sheared off by the belt. Burned right through in about two seconds flat. Stink of roasted hair making them all gag and everybody on the boat is saying hey, you're lucky, could have been worse, and then regaling him with some horror story about this guy they knew, cut off his fingers or lost his hand or whatever.

As if Speke gave a shit what happened to some other guy.

"Just fix it," he said to Robby. "Jesus, what else can go wrong?"

"We're on it," Mendez said, cleaning his hands

with a rag. "I can't promise this new rig will work, but we'll get the gear on board, no problem."

Speke turned back, fixed Mendez with a hard look. "Robby? It better work. Okay? That fucking admiral from the DOD, he's giving me a lot of shit over the phone. He's got the contract up on his screen and he's quoting from some clause about 'unauthorized divulgence of privileged information.' I go, 'Come on, nobody divulged anything, we've been very discreet about this little problem we're having,' and he goes, 'Losing the product is a form of divulgence.' "

Mendez grimaced and said, "What? Are you serious?"

Speke with his hands on his hips, chin up as he talked. The big lump of his Adam's apple reminded Mendez of a snake swallowing a rat.

Speke said, "Bottom line, Robby, this kind of resource development deal, they can cancel the program anytime they want, without giving a reason. They don't need to find some goddamn clause."

Mendez said, "I didn't know that."

"Well, now you do." Speke stalked off down the dock, really and truly pissed about losing most of his ponytail. Six months of letting it grow and now it looked like some geek barber with a blowtorch had hacked off his hair. Plus the smell.

Another worry, the Sealife parent company. The directors were all money men, of course, no real scientific training. Just a deep, deep reverence for Defense Department contracts. The result was, they let him run his own show. The Pentagon checks came in regular, his books balanced, that's all the Sealife execs really cared about. Get a buzz from some paper-pushing Pentagon admiral, that would change everything. There'd be consultants, evaluators, legal opinions, lengthy reports. What a nightmare, really ruin the nice thing they had going down here, being left pretty much to themselves.

Also they might decide to fire the project director, and *then* where would he be? Racking test tubes in some giant bio-gen company, that's where. Another cog in the machine. No more tropical perks like Cigarette boats or morning conferences on the beach or young research assistants who wore bikinis to work.

If he could even *get* another job, after a screwup like this.

"Excuse me, Vern? Dr. Speke?"

Scuffing along the dock, he hadn't seen Lucy Savrin running along the footpath. And here she was all shiny with sweat, a look of concern clouding her otherwise clear and pretty features. Lucy had been trying out his first name lately; that was a good sign, might mean she was preparing herself for a deeper intimacy.

Speke threw back his narrow shoulders and said, "Yes, Lucy, what is it?"

"You know you said to monitor Channel 16?"

He nodded, wondered if she could smell the burned hair. Get himself into a shower, double up on the shampoo, that might do the trick.

"There's been another attack," Lucy said. She seemed out of breath, very nervous.

Speke said, "Ah, shit."

"One confirmed dead. And, Dr. Speke? It sounds like there were a bunch of people around, all these witnesses, right? Down at Bahia Honda, they could see it from the bridge."

Speke said, "Shit, shit, shit." Then he was jogging off to the radio shack, forgot all about his hair.

The two dolphin were loafing around under the shade of the old pier. Sally forced herself to slow down to a walk, be sensible in the heat of noon, telling herself, See? See? Tom said they'd be fine, and sure enough, they were.

As soon as her feet touched the floating dock, both dolphin came shooting over to greet her. Clark was hanging back just a little, not squeaking much, but lifting his head out of the water to look her directly in the eye.

"Clark? How you doin', guy? Catch any more mullet, huh? Huh?"

Not reacting but keeping eye contact. Sally became aware of that strange, shivery-warm sensation that happened whenever she made real emotional contact with one of the animals. So far it had mostly been Lois. Clark had been too nervous, too hyper to bond with a human. In that respect he'd improved rather suddenly. Was it because he'd caught the live fish, picked up on her approval? Or was something else going on, some kind of dolphin interaction that was beyond human understanding? Something to do—and the idea really disturbed her—with the shark attacks?

The dock shifted and Tom was behind her. Clark broke off eye contact, dipped under, as if to say, *Later, we'll try this again later.*

Tom said, "Everything is copacetic, I see."

"They're fine."

"Look, I'm going to rig those barricades. You want to explain to these guys, or will they just figure it out?"

Sally stood up, faced her husband. "They've been confined before," she said. "In the Sealife lagoon. I'm not sure how they'll react here, where they've always been free to come and go." She paused. "I really hate to do this."

Tom brushed her bare shoulders, his voice low. "You're the one worried they'll go out to the reef," he reminded her, "mix it up with those sharks."

She said, "I know. Go ahead, set up the gates.

I'll get in the water, try and make them understand it's for their own protection."

Tom grinned. "Hey, Sal? I don't know about Clark, but Lois understands every word you say."

Sally shook her head, very firm. "We don't know that."

"Maybe you don't," he said, "since you require scientific proof. But an ignorant savage like myself can pick up on these things. Don't worry, it'll be fine."

Tom was right, it was fine.

Sally got into the canal in just her swimsuit and flippers, no need to submerge for any length of time. Couldn't help thinking about what she'd seen from the Bahia Honda Bridge, those two divers lucky to get out of the water alive, unscathed. Telling herself that if this new species got spooked that easily by boat noises, they'd never come into the restricted area of a canal. Too much human activity and motor sounds, with Tom out there in *Wild Child*, engines thumping as he set up some makeshift barricades to close off the canal.

Nothing to fear but fear itself.

Sally kept telling herself that as she slipped into the water. Which meant, of course, that nothing was as scary as what the mind invented. What reassured her, however, was the certain knowledge that the dolphins would know if there were intruders in the area. They showed no excitement or anticipation, beyond their usual playful urgency.

For instance, Lois was very interested in having her belly rubbed. Sally obliged, aware, as she always was, of the surgical scar on the female's abdomen. She'd asked Dr. Speke about that outside the courtroom, wanting to know exactly what had been done to Lois, and had gotten nothing more than a cold look and a smug remark: *You wouldn't understand.*

He had a point, Sally conceded—no way did she understand the necessity of surgically altering a domesticated dolphin. Not with the bottlenose population in serious decline worldwide. Why not let them mate, increase their progeny?

She was rubbing the female on the belly when Clark tried to push between them. As if he, too, wanted to be rubbed. A much trickier proposition with an adolescent male, although Clark had thus far showed no signs of sexual excitement when Sally was in the water. Had always, until now, been very shy of physical contact.

"Clark?" she said, stroking his beak, trusting him enough to let her fingers stray close to his teeth. "Is this what you want, boy, you starved for affection? Huh?"

When he rolled over, presenting his belly, there it was, big as life. Bigger.

Tom, drifting up behind her in *Wild Child*, hooted. "Hey, Sal? He's in love. I'm jealous."

Sally knew she shouldn't be embarrassed by what was a perfectly normal display of dolphin sexual arousal, but she couldn't help it. Hauling herself up onto the dock, Sally pulled off her fins, got under the dockside shower, and rinsed herself off.

Lois popped up near the float, chattering loudly.

"I know just what you mean," Sally said. "But he's *your* problem now, not mine."

The core staff would have lunch in Dr. Speke's cottage, brainstorm about the problem. Lucy Savrin had suggested the brainstorm part, and Speke came up with the location.

He liked the idea of Lucy in his place, not far from his bedroom. Who knows, maybe she'd linger behind when the others left. Work off some of that youthful energy, offer him a special dessert or whatever. Fun to think about.

"I got a bag of crab claws out of the freezer," she said, easing the screen door shut. "Also, some Dijonaise sauce. Robby's bringing bread and butter and fruit salad."

He was about to say, here, let me show you around; yeah, that *is* a waterbed, you ever tried one out? Say it like he was making a little joke. Keep cool, give her time to think about it. But here was Roberto coming right along behind her, carrying Cuban bread in white paper wrappers and a green Tupperware bowl of his goddamn salad, saying, "Hey, Vern? You got a hammer for the crab claws?"

"In the top drawer," Speke said.

Now the screen door slammed again and there was Chester Higgs with a rack of beer dangling from a hooked finger. "Hi, guys," he said. "Am I invited?"

"Of course."

This was from Lucy. After saying it she glanced at Speke for confirmation and he nodded. Sure, why not?

"All I had," Chesty said, holding up the rack like he had a finger hooked in the gills of a fish. "I tried driving over to Big Pine to pick up something non-alcoholic, but the traffic is still backed up. You can see where they got a TV van up there now, shooting from the bridge."

Roberto popped the Tupperware lid and said, "What do you expect? I'm almost afraid to turn on the tube."

Chesty Higgs pulled a can from the rack, very casual, and popped it open. "They're gonna love it, the TV people. Oh yes."

Speke opened the cabinet drawer, fished around for the wooden crab mallet, and banged it on the counter. *Wham.* Silence, except for the sound of Chester Higgs downing his beer.

Speke said, "Let's call this meeting to order, shall we?"

Higgs wiped his mouth with the back of his hand. "I heard you got a buzz from the big boys," he said.

"I did get a call, yes," Speke said. "This fucking admiral wants to know if we can solve this problem within the next twenty-four hours, I had to tell him yes, we could."

"Dynamite," Higgs said. He'd made his first beer go away and he was feeling very relaxed, better than he had in a long, long time. "Or we could try depth charges. Spot 'em from the air. I heard they could see 'em real good from the bridge."

Speke tapped the wooden mallet against the palm of his hand, slap, slap. "Chester? Just shut up about explosives."

"The point is, Vern, it would work."

Speke said, "Yeah, and we'd kill all the sealife for miles around. Fish, mammals, whatever's down there. Not to mention damage to the reef."

Higgs popped open another beer, making no attempt at discretion here; it was nobody's business what he had for lunch. "Vern? So far four people have been killed in the last couple days. Four that we know of. We use a little dynamite, nobody is going to object."

Speke stared at his hands, smiling. He shook his head, put the mallet down. "Chesty, shit, you haven't got a clue, have you? First place, we can't acknowledge the maxis. That's first. This admiral, he's checking out our contract, monitoring the situation; he made that very clear. No divulgence of information. None. Zip. *Nada.* So if we go out there with spotter planes in broad daylight and bomb the shit out of these creatures, that's as good as holding a press conference, announcing that we're responsible, okay? So no daylight activities. We have to handle this discreetly. Does that make sense to you, Dr. Higgs? Do you get it?''

Higgs shrugged. "Sure, I get it.''

"Then shut up about this dynamite, you've been obsessing on the idea since last night.''

"Fucking right I get it," Higgs said. "You want to take them alive. Or at least one or two. Am I right? Isn't that the plan? And if you screw up, you can always blame it on me, 'cause I occasionally take a drink to relax.''

Speke shook his head. "Rob? Lucy? Help me here. Get it through his thick head.''

Higgs said, "This admiral, he ever come down here for the fishing? Maybe we could fix him up with Jack Finley. Let him try his luck.''

Lucy had set the table with paper plates and napkins, put the stone-crab claws in one big bowl, with an empty bowl for the shells. "Let's eat," she said. "We can argue about this after. Or maybe we can discuss the plan of action for tonight, which is, I believe, what we're supposed to be doing.''

"You go ahead," Higgs said. "I had a late breakfast.''

He cracked another beer. Two down and he was feeling exactly right, perfectly even. All he had to do was maintain this level. Just maintain.

Speke pulled out his chair, situated himself where he could feel the glow of Lucy Savrin's bare legs.

"I don't know why I let him get to me," he said, indicating Higgs. "It's like he presses a button, I respond.''

Chester Higgs muffled a burp. "Hey, what's different about you, Vern? Let me guess. Oh, wait, I know, you just had your hair cut.''

7

Blue Light Special

THE *SQUALI* WAS right there at her slip, washed down and ready to go, but the skipper was not around.

"Try him at home," the ticket agent suggested. "I believe he's got a trailer up on Grassy Key."

"I called," Tom said. "No answer. You happen to know who hired him, the last few nights?"

The ticket agent examined her nails, avoiding eye contact. "No, sir, I sure don't. Cap'n Colson, he's his own man, keeps his business real private, you know what I mean?"

Tom nodded. "I do, yes," he said.

Sally was waiting out on the charter dock, wearing a long-billed cap and sunglasses, a pale yellow canvas bag slung over her shoulder. Cool green cotton blouse, soft khaki shorts. Her slender, athletic build made her look like a typical Keys girl, nineteen or twenty, until you got up real close and saw the crinkles at the sides of her eyes, and knew she was too good for twenty.

"He's under a rock," she said. "That's where guys like Wade Colson go when they hide."

"He's just a working stiff," Tom said, uneasy with her vehemence. "A genuine Everglades cracker. Part of a vanishing breed."

Sally snorted. "Can't vanish soon enough to suit me," she said darkly.

"Let me have a talk with the guy before you make him disappear, okay? What have you got against the man, anyhow, aside from the fact he's a professional shark killer?"

Sally said, "Isn't that reason enough?"

"No," Tom said. "He wants to kill those things we saw today, I for one have no objection. With you it sounds more personal."

"You'd have to be a woman."

Tom grinned. "Oh, it's that sort of thing, is it? What'd he do, make a pass at you?"

Sally wrinkled her nose. "Not even close. It's just a feeling you get about certain men. I can't explain it."

Tom said, "You got that right. You *can't* explain it. Come on, we'll check out the bars and bait shops, see if we can run him down."

The Marathon strip had an air-conditioned saloon or open-air tiki bar every fifty yards or so, and that didn't count the ones away from the highway. Tom knew Colson's pickup truck—a white Chevy with the guide's gold-lettered name on the tailgate—but didn't see it at any of the local watering holes, marinas, or bait shops favored by charter skippers.

"Maybe he's out on a different boat," Sally suggested.

"Could be," Tom said. "In that case I'd expect to see his truck at a marina. Somewhere, you know?"

They were about to give up, get back to Tarpon Key and check on the dolphin, when Tom spotted the truck in the K Mart parking lot.

Sally said, "What's he after, a blue light special?"

"Could be," Tom said. "You coming?"

"I think I'll stay right here, thanks. Have fun."

"I'll have a blast," Tom said.

Wade Colson was in back, beyond the racks of fishing tackle, leaning on the gun display. He had a charge card out, tapping the edge on the glass countertop, ready to hand it over. Pretty fair selection of firearms at most Florida department stores, K Mart no exception. The clerk, an eager-looking kid with straw-yellow hair and a gap in his teeth, was busy stacking ammo boxes on the counter, talking aloud as he tried to keep count.

"Seven . . . eight . . . nine . . . and ten makes a thousand rounds."

Colson grunted. The normally meticulous skipper was wearing wrinkled slacks and a sweat-stained *Squali Charters* T-shirt with a ripped sleeve. Looked like he'd slept in the bilge, or maybe not slept at all, his normally erect posture sagging, taking the weight on his elbows as he leaned forward to check out the ammunition boxes.

Tom, moving softly over the squeaking floor tiles, came up right behind him. "Hmmmm," Tom said. "Seven-six millimeter, that's for a semiauto, right?"

Startled, Colson raised his arm as if to fend off an attack. "What the fuck is this?" he said, backing away.

Tom moved in closer, wanting the wiry Colson to be aware of his mass and bulk, to keep the man a little off balance. "Sorry," he said, offering his hand. "Tom Hart. We've met once or twice. The wife and I run a dive boat out of Tarpon Key?"

Colson blinked. Deep circles under rabbit-pink eyes, and his breath smelling sharp and rank. Also, his teeth needed brushing.

"Yeah?" he said. "That right?" He tried to back away, get some distance.

Tom adjusted, stayed right with him. "We were out there with the search party yesterday," Tom said, "looking for your mates."

Colson nodded, did not react when the clerk adroitly removed the charge card from his fingers and rang up the sale.

"You know what surprised me?" Tom said. "You weren't out there with us."

Colson had recovered his balance and eased giving up ground. He stood up straighter, seemed wide awake now that he'd placed Tom Hart. "Engine trouble," he said. "Not that it's any of your business what I do or don't do."

Tom raised his hands, palms open. "Whoa! Did I say it was my business? Just making conversation here, Cap, while you load up on ammo. What I saw from the Bahia Honda Bridge this morning, you might want bigger bullets. I dunno, bazookas maybe."

No response from Colson, who signed the slip, snatched back his charge card, and gathered up the cartons of ammunition.

He marched off through the store with Tom dogging his tracks.

"Hey, Wade? Could we talk? All I want to know is, what the hell does Sealife have to do with this? What's their angle?"

Colson kicked through the exit out into the muggy air of the parking lot, making straight for his truck.

Tom said, "We already know they're not normal mako. They're bigger and smarter and they hunt together."

Colson put the cartons in the back of his truck. Without looking at Tom he said, "What makes you say they're smarter than normal mako? You a shark expert?"

Tom leaned against the door on the driver's side, folded his arms. "We had an expert check out some photographic evidence. He concluded they might be a new species. A man-made species.''

Colson nodded as if that confirmed his own suspicions. ''I can't talk about it,'' he said. ''That's just the way it is.''

''You're working for Sealife?''

Colson got out his keys, said, ''I don't work for nobody but me. Now you gonna let me get in my own truck or what?''

Tom moved aside. ''They run from the sound of a boat,'' he said. ''How do you plan to hunt them, they know enough to run from a boat?''

Colson pulled open the door. He'd put on his shades, covered his bleary eyes. ''What makes you think I'm huntin' those critters?''

Tom glanced at the ammo cartons in the back of the truck. ''Just a wild guess.''

Colson slipped behind the wheel, started the motor. ''One thing I *can* tell you,'' he said.

''What's that?''

''Keep guessin', you Yankee dickhead.''

If Tom hadn't moved quickly, the front tire would have gone right over his feet.

The Faro Blanco Marine Resort, on the Gulf side of Marathon, is a prime feeding ground for charter skippers and their customers. The Angler's bar is upstairs, overlooking the marina and an Olympic-sized swimming pool, and as you enter from the stairway below you pass dozens of framed photographs. Pictures of men posing with big dead fish, photographs dating back forty years. Everything about the place reeks of fish and fishing—not the smell, mind you, but the resonance of a million lies and a million liars who have passed through, buying or cadging drinks, selling fantasies of leaping tarpon and other dreams that got away.

On this particular afternoon Jack Finley was holding forth, seated at the corner where he could watch the barmaid bending over for ice and also keep good sight lines on the pool; you never knew when a keeper might appear wearing one of those thong bikinis, show off her well-tanned butt.

Day like today, he might get lucky.

"You sayin' there weren't a *thang* left of him?"

This was Cindy Lee, the new barmaid, had a sweet Georgia peach way of speaking; it gave Finley a tingle just to hear her talk.

"They et him up, Cindy Lee, what can I say? He never had a chance."

Cindy Lee said, "The poor man."

Some good old boys from the half-day tarpon boats came in, headed right for Jack at the bar, made it a party.

"Hell you doin', Jack, hidin' here in broad daylight?"

"I ain't hidin', boys."

"Any truth to all this horseshit we been hearin'? We heard you took on five, six big shark single-handed."

Finley stroked his beard and winked. "I cannot tell a lie, boys. It's all true, every word."

"Well, shit. I ain't never had no client got took by a shark. The one I threw over that time? Got hisself back to shore in one piece and then sued my ass for assault. Cindy Lee, honey? This man needs a drink and I'm buyin'."

The ritual lies were just beginning to get interesting when a woman came up the inside stairs from the restaurant below. Standing there with one slim hand on the rail, the other clutching a bright orange clipboard. Striking a pose and she didn't care who knew it.

On an island chock full of pretty, leggy blonds, this particular specimen was remarkable enough to stun five Florida charter skippers into silence. Look at all that silky hair and those smart, sassy blue eyes taking them in, hunched at the bar like they were, and not the least bit intimidated by what she saw there.

"Excuse me, gentlemen, is one of you Captain Finley?"

Every man at the bar raised his hand.

The blond got a laugh out of that. A real laugh, not a giggle.

She walked over, all business in a silky blouse and skintight designer jeans. Perched on a stool and said, "Kathy Kruze from KTV, Miami. When we're through playing 'I've Got a Secret,' I'd like to see about interviewing Captain Finley for the five o'clock news."

8

Dueling Air Horns

ON THE WAY out of Marathon they stopped at the 7-Mile Grille for a late lunch, Tom going with the conch fritters and Sally digging into the house special, a sloppy joe that threatened to spill off the oval plate. Sally, drinking a tall iced tea in the shade of the counter area, stared out at a nearby trap yard, where stacks of creosoted crawfish traps baked in the sun. Take away the tourist scams and the hype, this was the real Florida Keys, crawfish traps in the sun.

She said, "I still think we should report the son of a bitch to the Coast Guard."

Tom dipped the last conch fritter into a paper cup of hot sauce and said, "If I could think of something to report, I would."

Sally shook her head and grimaced. "He practically admitted that Sealife is after those sharks. Which implies they are somehow responsible for what happened."

Tom wiped his hands on a paper napkin. "*Implies* is the operative word here, Sal. So what if Sealife hired Wade Colson to kill a few sharks? There's no violation of any law or regulation. You and I may disagree with current policy, but as of right now there's an open season on sharks. No restrictions at all on recreational shark fishing."

Sally shook her head. "That's not what I mean. I mean Sealife did something to those creatures, programed or trained them somehow. That's why they're attacking humans."

Tom nodded. "Okay, that's what I think, too. But how do we prove it? Report an unsubstantiated theory to the Coast Guard? Come on, you know how those guys are. We tried reporting Dr. Speke for dolphin abuse. They gave us the brush-off, remember? Sealife has a defense contract, and that makes them practically invulnerable to another government agency."

"But this isn't about dolphin," Sally insisted. "These sharks are killing people. That should make a difference."

Tom sat at the counter with his hands folded, debating whether or not to order a slice of Key lime pie, the only dessert on the menu. Keeping his voice low because it was amazing the scuttlebutt that got started at the grill. It would be all over the waterfront in minutes.

"Look, big sharks have *always* been dangerous," he said. "We're almost positive that something strange is going on, but we have absolutely no proof that Sealife is involved."

"Four dead so far." Sally said. "That's proof enough for me."

"Yes, but that doesn't mean that Dr. Speke is using sharks to target humans. All we know for sure is that they've hired a professional who is trying to *kill* these things, and believe me, that's gotta be a very popular strategy right about now.''

Their quiet debate about whether they should make a formal complaint to the Coast Guard was interrupted by a sudden blast of air horns from the marina behind the grill. Loud enough so everyone at the counter reacted. The horns sounded angry, impatient.

Tom got off his stool, went around to the marina docks. Sally was right behind him, carrying her go-cup of iced tea.

''Uh-oh,'' she said. ''Dueling assholes.''

Several large sportfishing boats were attempting to gain access to the narrow channel at the same time. Backing down their big diesels and laying on the horns. Skippers pointing fingers, waving fists. Mates exchanging threats.

''Men,'' Sally said.

Tom, who had a lot more tolerance for loutish male behavior, was disturbed for another reason. ''Look at how they're rigged,'' he said. ''Pulpits, harpoons—and they're sure as hell not going after swordfish down here, this time of year.''

He went out on the dock, took a line from the first of the big boats as it maneuvered into a slip. The boat was the *High Flyer* out of Key West, fully rigged and crewed and iced down for serious game fishing. The mates were standing around the cockpit bare-chested, swigging from beer cans in insulated holders, talking in loud, excited voices.

''Get that hose over here,'' the one with the biggest beer gut said. ''We gotta fuel up fast, get back out there.''

Tom grinned. ''The dock attendant is on his way.''

''Sorry, man, thought you worked here.''

''No problem,'' Tom said. ''What are you fishing for, mind my asking?''

The question produced gales of laughter from the

cockpit. "Ain't you heard mister? You all got a school of man-eaters up here, feeding on your tourists."

"That right?" Tom said, playing dumb.

"Must be a hundred boats on the way here. Every shark-killing machine from Key Largo to the Dry Tortugas. Hell, they'll be in from the Bahamas, this time tomorrow."

The Us hover close together near the bottom of Hawk Channel, in thirty feet of water. The danger noise is everywhere. The sea has become mad with the whirring of propellers, the high-pitched squeal of fish-finding sonar systems, even the occasional flat thump of a bullet skidding harmlessly over the surface of the water.

The Us remain nearly motionless, uncertain of what to do, where to go. They have tried running within the channel, out to the shallow waters of the reef, but the danger noise comes from all around.

Wait, they sing. *Wait*.

And yet another instinct speaks from deep within, driven by a metabolic rate that is increasing day by day, hour by hour.

Hunger, the instinct says. *We must feed. We must eat. We must grow*.

9

Rum Talking

THE BICYCLE LYING in the driveway was an old one-speed Schwinn with fat tires. It had been converted into a Conch cruiser by the addition of raised handlebars and a big front basket, a popular mode of transportation on the dead-flat roads of the Keys.

Tom got out of the truck, moved the bike to one side, then drove on.

"Must be a kid," he said to Sally, "leave it lying out in the road like that."

It wasn't a kid, though. They found him asleep on a patio chair, a big guy wearing a flowered shirt and old cutoff dungaree shorts and dirty tennis shoes. Forty or so, with a thinning, gray-streaked crew cut and a fleshy, sunburned nose.

He was snoring; Tom could smell the booze from several yards away.

"Somebody had a party," Sally suggested. "He took a wrong turn on Big Pine, ended up here."

"I dunno," Tom said. "He looks sorta familiar."

"You *know* this man?"

Sally, hands on her hips, was eager to get back in the water with her dolphin, forget all those blood-crazed shark hunters wracking havoc on the reef.

"I said he looks familiar," Tom said. "I didn't say I know him."

"Well, I've never seen him before in my life."

Tom patted the man's face, tried to rouse him. In response the unconscious stranger stirred and then managed to fall out of the chair, thumping wetly to the gravel. Didn't wake up, though, not even for an instant. The snoring resumed almost immediately.

Tom said, "Well, shit." He turned to Sally, who had backed away with a look of undisguised distaste. "You think it'll be okay if I go through his pockets, see if I can find out who he is?"

Sally said, "You're going to *touch* him?"

"Find out who he is, maybe I can call home, they'll come get him."

"Just be, um, careful."

Tom lifted the flowered shirt, discovered the empty liter bottle of Ron Matusalem rum tucked in the waistband of the dungaree shorts. Gingerly he reached into the man's pockets, found nothing but a small wad of bills, a pack of unfiltered Lucky Strikes, and a piece of yellow paper.

"What's that?" Sally asked.

Tom unfolded the paper. "Our ad in the Yellow Pages. 'Reef Diving Aboard the *Wild Child*.' "

Sally made a face. "Okay, so he came here to see us," she said. "I hope he doesn't think we'd let him on the boat in *that* condition."

"The guy is drunk out of his mind," Tom said. "I doubt he was thinking at all. Come on, give me a hand here."

Making an effort not to breathe through her nose—the man smelled like he'd been washed up in the mangroves for the past few days—Sally helped shift the fragrant, unconscious bulk while Tom shoved a couple of chair cushions under his shoulders and head.

"Let's get him over on his side so he doesn't choke on his tongue," Tom said, heaving. "Damn, it's like moving the dead."

The drunk made a gargling sound, then babbled. "Shamashi," he seemed to say, mumbling in his sleep. "Shamashi."

Sally said, "Shamashi? What the hell is shamashi?"

"Sounds like a sushi bar," Tom said. "Hey, mister? Come on, wake up."

"In the old days, a situation like this, they used smelling salts," Sally said.

"Great idea," Tom said.

He went to the dock, dipped a white plastic bucket in the canal, and emptied it over the drunk's head.

That worked.

The drunk woke up screaming, pawing and kicking at the gravel. "God! No! Get 'em away from me! No!"

The fear in the man's voice was so vivid, so chilling, that Sally shuddered.

Tom responded by grabbing the thrashing hands, holding him still. "Hey, it's okay! It's okay!"

"Not okay," said the drunk. His eyes had begun to focus, taking in Sally and Tom, and he immediately calmed down, although his hands continued to tremble. "That's the pro'lem, not okay."

"Coffee?" Sally suggested.

Tom shrugged. "Can't hurt. Better make it strong."

The man groaned, tried to stand up, and toppled over.

"Take it easy, mister," Tom said. "Just rest easy."

"Can't. Shamashi."

"What the hell is shamashi?"

The drunk seemed to be concentrating on getting his pronunciation right. "Not shamashi," he said thickly, fighting his booze-thickened tongue. " 'Sa maxi.''

Tom said, "The maxi? I still don't get it. What is the maxi? Is that a place? Is that where you're staying? You got a name, a number I can call?"

Vigorous head shake. "No, don't call. Came here to warn you."

Tom pulled over another patio chair and sat down. "I saw you over at Sealife Key, didn't I? Was that you in the cabin, watching me pull away from the dock?"

This time the response was a vigorous nod in the affirmative. The man was making a mighty effort to keep his eyes focused, breathing heavily through his nose as he concentrated on speaking clearly. "*Is-u-rus max-i-mus,*" he said, enunciating each syllable. "The maxis. Like mako shark, okay? Only different."

"Oh, my God," Tom said, jumping to his feet. "Sally! He's here about the sharks."

Sally was already on her way back from the kitchen with a coffee. "This is instant, just nuked. I hope that's okay." She put the tray down on a patio table and turned to Tom. "So he was up there on the bridge, is that it? He saw the attack?"

Tom explained that their visitor was from Sealife Research.

The drunk nodded vigorously, pointed at himself. "Higgs," he said. "Dr. Higgs. My fault, all my fault."

Lucy Savrin found them at the dock, refitting the trawler with the new equipment.

"Chesty's gone," she said. "Can't find him anywhere."

Vernon Speke stood up, reached for a rag. His

hands and forearms were black with grease and the hair on the back of his head, where his ponytail had been, was sticking up. Physically he looked exhausted, but his eyes were bright, almost too bright. Feverish.

"You seen him, Robby?" Speke said.

"Not lately," Mendez said. He was sitting at the edge of the engine hatch, his legs hanging over, sweat glistening in droplets from his hair. Dark circles under his eyes, he looked in desperate need of sleep. "He was at the staff meeting and then he cut out early."

"Rum," Speke said. "Chester fell off the wagon again." He was trying not to stare at Lucy's chest, where her damp T-shirt clung to the nipple area. Had to be the size of sand dollars, but you weren't supposed to notice. Like you weren't supposed to notice a little cheek, those hiking shorts she sometimes wore.

"Don't worry about old Chesty," he said. "He'll sleep it off. Probably on the beach right now, passed out under a palm tree."

Lucy said, "I already checked the beach. And the lab. And the rec hall—all his usual hangouts. There's a bike missing from the rack. I really think he's taken off somewhere."

Speke paused. He was picking up on something in her tone of voice. "You think there's a problem with Dr. Higgs?"

She shifted uneasily. "It's just I happened to notice how he was reacting, at the meeting. He seemed very disturbed."

"Oh?" Speke dropped the oily rag, stepped onto the dock. "In what way disturbed?"

"It's just . . . he was shaking his head and muttering. You know the way he does? And I had the impression he, um, profoundly disagreed with the new strategy for, um, recovering the maxis."

Speke drifted closer, wished he had his sunglasses on so he could stare at those pretty little breasts. Well, not so little. He'd taken a few wake-up pills and he felt wide awake all over. "And what, you think he's going to pedal his bike into Marathon, denounce us to the press? Something like that?"

"I'm not sure. If he was, um, drinking, he might do something foolish."

Speke nodded. "She's right. Chester's been off the beam the last couple of days. Robby? We'll finish up here, you go see if you can locate Dr. Higgs."

Mendez crawled to his feet. "Shit," he said.

"Robby? Just do it, please." He paused, shifted into casual. "Lucy will help us here, won't you, Lucy?"

The coffee helped some. Tom got about three cups into their guest, who refused a sandwich as if the idea of solid food was revolting, and the caffeine seemed to straighten out his tongue, made him semi-intelligible even if it didn't really sober him up.

Dr. Higgs sipped the coffee and said, "What happened, Vern heard about this project of mine, altering a garfish to make it more aggressive, able to hold its own against all these tropical fish that are taking over the swamps. The trick is we built in this genetic flaw so the 'improved' garfish wipes itself out in a few generations, doesn't get to be a bigger problem. Brilliant, really."

Dr. Higgs was sitting up now, holding the cup in both hands, the trembling under control.

"This is for the Everglades?" Sally said. "Trying to control exotic species?"

"Exactly," he said, nodding eagerly. "People don't understand, you throw a couple goldfish out the back door in Homestead, ten years later they've taken over from the original species. Wiping them out, changing the ecology.''

Tom said, ''I don't get it. What do goldfish have to do with these big makos? What you called the maxis.''

Higgs took a deep breath and closed his eyes. You got the impression he was dizzy inside, his personal gyroscope messed up somehow. *''Isurus maximus,''* he said, as if the phrase had a power all its own. ''Maxis for short.''

Sally said, ''So it *is* a new species.''

''Brand spankin' new,'' Dr. Higgs said. ''Miracle of genetic engineering. Cloned from a single egg.''

The coffee cup fell from his hands and just like that he unfolded, passed out, the back of his head thumping against the patio chair. An instant later he was snoring.

Sally looked at him, shook her head. ''Get the bucket,'' she said.

''He needs to sleep it off.''

Sally gave him a look. ''Tom? He sleeps it off, he may change his mind about telling us.''

''You really think we should take advantage of a man when the rum's talking?''

''Yes,'' she said, ''I do.''

This time Tom simply flicked a little water on Dr. Higgs and he came around.

''Stupid,'' he mumbled, struggling to sit up.

''Sorry,'' Tom said.

''No, no. *I'm* the stupid one, okay?'' He rubbed his hands over his face, shook his head, trying to sober himself up. ''Stuck to my little garfish, none of this would have happened. Never did a large predator before. Seduced. Visions of palm trees, dancing girls.''

Sally skidded her chair closer. ''Dr. Higgs, we've examined a photograph of the maxis. They seem to have extra gill slits. Is that to improve the flow of oxygen to the brain?''

Higgs stared at her, blinked, then rubbed his eyes. He was fading again. ''Oxygen. Little O_2. That might help me think.''

Tom said, ''Sorry, doc. All we have is compressed air, scuba tank stuff. No pure oxygen. Try a little more coffee.''

Sally said, ''Dr. Higgs? Look at me. If you can't talk straight, at least respond to my questions. Can you do that?''

He tried to nod, spilled the latest cup of coffee.

''Increased oxygen to the brain. Does that mean the maxis have a larger brain capacity?''

''Smart as whips,'' he said. ''Anyhow, smart as dogs.''

''Smart as dogs so they can be trained like dogs, was that the idea?''

He nodded vigorously. '' 'Zactly,'' he said. '' 'Cept I should say dolphin, not dog. Smart as dolphin, that's what I mean.''

Sally glanced at Tom, her eyes saying she was stunned and amazed by this confession. Trying to act normal, to keep Higgs talking, she said, ''So you genetically altered a mako egg, cloned it, and made the offspring as intelligent as a dolphin? Is that what you're saying?''

Dr. Higg's eyelids fluttered. ''More complicated,'' he muttered. ''Much more complicated.''

''I'm sure it was very complex,'' Sally said. ''But was that the result? A new species of mako that is smart enough to train like you'd train a dolphin?''

''Plan,'' he said, struggling to keep his eyes open. ''That was the plan. The best laid plans, right? Never supposed to leave the lagoon.''

Sally reached out, tugged at his shirt collar, trying to get his attention. ''Okay, we know they escaped. We've seen them in action, Dr. Higgs. So far your maxis have killed at least four people. Were they trained to attack divers, is that it?''

Higgs's head lolled, his cheek resting against Sally's hand. ''Ofttimes go astray,'' he muttered. ''Ofttimes.''

He passed out sitting up and started snoring again.

''Tom!'' Sally said. ''Do something.''

''Short of giving the guy a transfusion, I don't know what we *can* do, Sal. He's got about a liter of booze in him. I'm amazed he can talk at all.''

''The bastards did it,'' she said. ''They couldn't train dolphin to kill divers, so they came up with a new species that preys on divers.''

''You know what?'' Tom said. ''I'll bet this guy is the same one who was calling Reggie late at night. Her source with the warning about man-eaters? She said he sounded under the influence, remember?''

Sally eased the unconscious Dr. Higgs down into the chair. ''So why didn't he go to her?'' she said. ''I mean, why come to us?''

''We're closer, you happen to be on a bicycle.''

''I dunno,'' Sally said. ''Drunk as he is, I think he has a reason for seeking us out.''

''Let him sleep it off for a few hours,'' Tom suggested.

Just then the doctor's legs kicked and he came full awake briefly, his eyes wild with a dream. ''Big!'' he said. ''Getting bigger!''

''Dr. Higgs?''

''*Maximus*,'' he sputtered. ''*Maximus! Isurus maximus!* Growth gene, hormones . . . getting bigger.''

A moment later he was snoring again, so deep under he didn't respond to being shaken or having water splashed in his face.

''I give up,'' Sally said.

''You know what?'' Tom said, pouring himself a

cup of coffee. "That last bit? I think he said the damn things aren't full grown yet."

Sally nodded. "It's possible he found a way to alter the genetic material that controls growth. Maybe that's what the *maximus* refers to. Potential size."

"Bigger," Tom said. "I wonder. How big is bigger?"

10

Man-eaters, U.S.A.

ABOARD THE SPORT-FISHING machine *High Flyer*, the bilge pump was jetting blood over the side, pumping it warm and red into the chum-filled waters of the Florida Reef. The pump barely kept up with the inflow as mates in rubber boots waded through the slaughter, gutting small makos and removing the fins.

"Be sure you cut them fins off clean," the skipper bellowed from his perch high atop the conning tower. "Ice 'em down good, there's a shark-fin buyer flying into Key West tomorrow, give us a good price."

What had started as a lark—hunting the man-eaters—had quickly developed into a financial bonanza for boats working the reef. The makos had come in from deeper water, driven mad by the scent of hundreds of gallons of beef blood dumped into the outgoing current. The tons of chum dropped by scores of serious fishing machines, a fleet that had turned the reef into a rich, killing soup, drew bait-fish and feeding sharks from miles around.

Makos were money. The *High Flyer* had set a mile or more of winch-reeled hand lines, trailing a baited "monster" hook every ten feet. With this many sharks in the water, almost every hook had a customer. And not only makos—hammers, lemons, blacktips, grays, you never knew what was on there until the winch hauled it up to the transom, where one of the mates administered a 9mm killing shot before flipping the carcass into the cockpit.

"Gut the hammers and cut 'em loose," the skipper ordered. "Ain't no market for hammerhead, not when we're taking this many mako."

"Wanna keep these lemons, Cap?"

"Nah. By the time we get back to the fish house, they won't even offer cat-food prices for them lemons or blacktips. Just fin 'em and throw 'em back."

Only the makos were keepers, mostly juveniles in the hundred-pound range who could not tear themselves loose from the monster hooks. As each carcass came aboard it was hurriedly gutted and finned. The hollowed-out mako husks were stacked like canoes, iced down in the hold.

"Hey, Cap! We gettin' full up here!"

The skipper leaned from the conning tower and surveyed the blood-stained cockpit with the grin of a man who knows he is pulling money from the sea. "You all just keep haulin' on that winch line, hear? I'll say when we're full up," he said. "And keep checkin' those bellies. We get ourselves a man-eater, *then* we'll head back to the dock, get ourselves on the TV."

Kathy Kruze did her *Five Alive* stand-up at the Faro Blanco marina. The palm trees and the fuel docks and the circling fishing machines made good background, but what decided her was the life-sized plastic shark hanging from the bait-shop hoist. Cast from fiberglass and convincingly air-brushed, the beast looked like it might come to life at any moment.

The giant plastic shark was a hell of a lot more impressive than the small specimens slung from the transoms and ginpoles of the returning boats. *Those* sharks weren't big enough, or mean enough, and would look puny on television screens throughout South Florida.

"Time?" she asked after glancing in a compact mirror and brushing a speck of stray makeup from her eyebrows.

"Twenty seconds," said the voice in her earphone. "We'll give you a five count."

A sizable audience had gathered to watch the live broadcast. Most were marina customers or residents, relatively quiet and well-behaved despite the free flow of beverages from the bar, the plastic go-cups of vodka and gin and sour mash and fruity blender drinks.

One or two of the good old boys attempted to whistle their appreciation as the camera's red light winked on, but a warning glance from the formidable Ms. Kruze stopped them cold.

Kathy looked right into the eye of the lens and said, "That's right, Hal, earlier today a tourist was killed and devoured by several sharks, tentatively identified as large mako sharks. This is the fourth confirmed shark-attack fatality in the last forty-eight hours, and here on Key Marathon the mood is, well, maybe the best thing is to let you see for yourself."

The camera zoomed over Kathy's right shoulder to the marina basin, where a number of boat crews were celebrating, hooting and hollering as they hauled shark carcasses up by the tail.

The shot drew quickly back to the reporter, who glanced up from her notes and said, "Several hundred fishing boats have descended on the Keys, turning the fragile reef area into a killing zone. Although hundreds of sharks have been slaughtered in the last few hours, the pack of large, man-eating makos seems to have eluded capture thus far. There is speculation that the killer sharks have headed out to the Gulf Stream and are no longer in the area. That remains to be seen." She paused, implying that the story was far from over. "Joining me now is local fishing guide Jack Finley, who chased the killers away from a dive party earlier today. Jack?"

One of his buddies had to shove Black Jack Finley forward. Whatever courage he'd exhibited on the water had vanished. He was quite plainly stricken with terror at the prospect of facing the camera.

"Captain Finley? Don't be shy, come on over and tell us what it was like, battling those man-eaters." Kathy kept smiling as she reached out of camera range and grabbed the back of Finley's belt, pulling him closer.

Jack Finley gave her a sick-puppy smile and stammered, "Well, um, I didn't exactly, ah, battle 'em, okay? All I did was give chase and they, ah, took off."

Kathy shook her head and grinned intimately into the camera. "Take my word for it, folks, Captain Finley is a real live hero. Bear in mind he'd just seen his client ripped to pieces by sea monsters and then, knowing that a father and son were in danger at a nearby dive site, he got in his *tiny* little boat and took off after half a dozen killer sharks. And each of those sharks was bigger than your boat, isn't that correct, Captain?"

Jack had gathered up a little courage by now, although he still had the look of a man who'd swallowed spoiled meat. "I guess that's right. They were big buggers. Excuse me, big mako. Least I *think* they were mako."

"And you distracted the sharks until the two divers could escape?"

Finley nodded. It was hard to tell whether he was embarrassed or simply suffering from nausea.

Kathy Kruze grinned again and shook her pretty head. "Getting this gentleman to admit he's a hero is like pulling shark teeth, folks. But everybody who works this waterfront knows what courage is all about, and a lot of them are out there right now, trying to hunt down these killer sharks. Any advice for them, Captain Finley?"

Finley started as if he'd been poked with a sharp instrument. "What? Oh, yeah. Don't lean over the side, you want to keep your head. That's my advice."

Kathy shivered, as if thrilled by the idea. "Thanks, Captain. And one more thing, folks. For years this island has been known as Marathon, but as of today this sleepy little fishing village is going by a new name."

The camera panned to the side of the bait shack, where a banner had been displayed. In bold, blood-red letters, it said:

WELCOME TO MAN-EATERS, U.S.A.

In the *Reef Life* newsroom Reggie Rhodes had the television on with the sound down, and she watched the camera pan over the banner as she listened to Tom Hart on the line, calling from Tarpon Key.

"Dr. Chester Higgs," Tom was saying. "Claims he's been with Sealife for the last couple of years. We need to know if the guy's for real."

"I know they have a Dr. Higgs on the staff," Reggie said. "I've never met him, at least not face-to-face. Hang on there, I'll see what we've got."

Reggie hadn't skimped on the *Reef Life* computer system. Through it she was able to access numerous data banks with a few key strokes. It didn't take her long to confirm that Dr. Chester Higgs, formerly affiliated with a marine research program at the state university system at Sarasota, was presently employed by Sealife Research.

"The man has a pretty impressive résumé," she said, staring at the computer screen. "And you say he's passed out on your patio?"

Tom said, "Dead to the world. Drunk as the proverbial skunk."

Reggie said, "If I could hear his voice, I'd know if he was the one called me night before last."

Tom said, "Got to be him, Reg. Doesn't really matter if he's the original whistle-blower, though, 'cause he's sure as hell blowing the whistle now. Or he was until he passed out again. Is he on the level? Is it possible he messed with mako genes and created a new species, like he said he did?"

The computer was dredging up more data on Dr. Chester Higgs, matching his name with periodical and news listings. Reggie hit a key, activating the printer. "I'm getting hard copy of this stuff," she told Tom. "One of the data files lists all of his scientific publications. There's one entitled 'Practical Cloning Techniques' that was published in something called *The Journal of Experimental Genetics*. And three years ago the *Miami Herald* quoted Dr. Higgs in an article about a project to reduce tropical fish populations."

"That's him," Tom said.

"Well, way it looks, the science journals tend to list Dr. Higgs as a biogeneticist. The *Herald* article calls him a genetic engineer, which I guess is pretty much the same thing. I haven't got hard copy of the original article, but the computer synopsis says the Sarasota lab created a 'super' garfish, supposed to eat up all the exotic species that have taken over the food chain in the Everglades."

"Right. That's what he said."

"And this is the same guy is taking credit for these killer shark?"

She could hear wind in the phone, the lapping of water from the canal, and she picked up as well a sense of Tom Hart's excitement, the energy he was bringing to the conversation.

He said, "Reg, this is the guy. I think he *made* these things, or at least tinkered with normal mako until he got a super-aggressive strain. He's a real mess right at the moment—Sal is keeping an eye on him, to make sure he doesn't choke to death in his sleep—but he seems to have something pretty heavy on his conscience, made him inhale about a liter of high-octane rum. You want to get over here and see if he's still willing to talk when he wakes up?"

Reggie said, "Hell yes, honey bun. You tie him to that patio chair, hear?"

The *Reef Life* office on Big Pine was less than three miles from Tom and Sally's homestead on Tarpon Key. The backcountry road linking the islands was narrow, curving through a wilderness of mangroves and the remains of a private airstrip, since abandoned. Reggie kept the high beams on, riding the brake because you never knew when a Key deer might appear in the headlights. The miniature deer were the last of a vanishing species, protected by state and federal laws, but no statute or regulation could save a delicate creature from a fast-moving car on a backcountry road at twilight.

As she drove, Reggie smiled to herself. Tom Hart was finally coming around. His first forays into writing articles for *Reef Life* had been tentative, self-effacing narratives of dive experiences that revealed his profound respect for the sea and all the creatures who lived in it. Lately, with her encouragement, he'd begun to find a voice for his monthly column, which was no longer restricted to simple accounts of dive experiences. Tom's viewpoint had expanded to life in the reef environment, the continuing struggle as humans found new ways to intrude on the natural world.

Of the "amateur" journalists who contributed to her publication—all of them paid a pittance, and she was the first to admit it—Thomas J. Hart had the most talent. He was still hesitant about making a total commitment to the craft, did not yet think of himself primarily as a writer, seemed afraid to make that final leap of faith that was required before the *real* voice of a writer emerged. But Reggie had high hopes for him, was convinced that he had a chance to do for the Florida Reef what Marjory Stoneman Douglas had done for the Everglades with her book *The Everglades: River of Grass*.

Reggie knew that writers often took a long time to develop the necessary confidence, not to mention the skills required, and although Tom was something of a late bloomer, he was still relatively young as a writer. Marjory Stoneman Douglas had been in her fifties when she wrote that first, important book that changed the way people thought about the Everglades, so there was plenty of time for Thomas Hart to make his place in the world—maybe even to change the world, just a little.

Now he had a big, book-length story in his strong and gentle hands, and if he didn't quite know it yet, he soon would; Reggie would see to that. Although she loved to flirt and it tickled her to make a beauty like Sally just a little bit jealous, the biggest kick she got lately was to act as Muse. Being there when Tom emerged as a real, honest-to-himself Writer had to be a greater thrill than taking the big hunk to bed. Although that would surely be fun, too, you could tell by the way Sally's eyes followed him around.

Reggie hit the brakes, steered around a family of raccoons who had staked out a curve in the road like gang of masked bandits, bold as brass. Which reminded her of the piece Tom had written about watching raccoons from underwater as they used their eerily human hands to wash food and pluck at mangrove oysters. . . . *hands as delicate as those belonging to a race of leprechauns living secretly in plain sight of the rational world,* he'd written.

Bring that kind of observation and sensibility to a story about the arrogance of men who played God, making new and "improved" creatures, and Tom would have himself one hell of a good book.

When she reached the Harts', Dr. Higgs was regaining consciousness, attempting to sit up.

Reggie hurried over, digging through her purse for the little microcassette recorder she always carried; it worked better than a notebook because she had trouble reading her own handwriting.

"Coming!" Higgs was shouting. His trembling hands batted at invisible objects. "They're coming!"

Tom nodded a greeting at Reggie and said, "Dr. Higgs?" He attempted to grab the man's flailing hands. "Wake up, you're having a bad dream."

"They're coming! You've got to believe me! They're coming!"

Now that she could hear the stranger's voice Reggie had no doubt about his identity. This was the same man who had called her, intoxicated, muttering about man-eaters that had escaped from the Sealife lagoon.

"Dr. Higgs," she said, crouching next to his chair. "Dr. Higgs, it's Regina Rhodes. I publish *Reef Life.* You called me the other night."

Higgs's eyes were wide open, staring, but she had the unsettling sensation that he didn't see her at all, that he was seeing some other, terrifying nightmare vision.

"They're coming!" he cried hoarsely. "They're coming . . ."

He lapsed into indistinct mutterings and fell back in the chair.

"I think he's got the D.T.'s," Tom said. "He seems to be hallucinating. We better get him up to Fisherman's Hospital."

Sally was ready with a blanket. The night was warm and muggy, but Dr. Higgs was shivering like a man lost in a winter storm.

"Sorry, Reg," Tom said, turning to her. "I don't think we'll get anything more out of him tonight."

"You tried pouring strong coffee into him?"

"Yeah. The poor devil's beyond coffee. I want a doctor to check him out."

They were attempting to lift Higgs from the chair when a pair of headlights swung into the yard, illuminating the patio.

Sally said, "What now?"

Squinting, Reggie was able to discern that the vehicle was a van. Doors slammed and several figures emerged, their feet crunching on the gravel path.

The van remained idling, the headlights on. "Hello?" came a voice. "Is Dr. Higgs here? We saw his bicycle out by the gate."

When the visitors came into range, Reggie recognized Roberto Mendez, the Sealife animal trainer.

"Chesty's been drinking all day," Mendez said, coming forward. "We thought he might be headed into Marathon, trying to find a liquor store that would serve him."

Mendez was accompanied by a couple of young, athletic-looking staff members from Sealife Key, and they moved toward Dr. Higgs.

"Now hold on," Tom said, intervening. "I'm not sure he wants to go with you. I think he should go to the hospital, myself."

"We'll take him to the emergency room," Mendez assured them. "Just as a precaution. Chesty's an old friend, I've seen him like this many times. He'll be okay by this time tomorrow.''

Tom said, ''Maybe so. But unless he *wants* to go back with you, I suggest we wait for the sheriff.''

Sally, thinking along similar lines, had already started dialing the Monroe County Sheriff's Department.

Mendez made an instinctive move toward the phone, and then seeing how Tom reacted, changed his mind. ''Tell you what,'' he said. ''Let's wake up Dr. Higgs, see what *he* has to say.''

The glare of the headlights seemed to be bringing Chester Higgs around again. This time he did not flail or shout, but sat up of his own accord, breathing heavily through his nose. ''Robby,'' he said groggily. ''Is that you?''

''At your service. Looks like you've been bothering these good people, Chester.''

''No bother,'' Sally interjected. She'd aborted the call to the sheriff, held her thumb ready over the redial button.

''We've been worried about you, man,'' Mendez said, offering his hand to Dr. Higgs. ''You want a ride back home?''

Higgs looked around at the little crowd gathered on the patio. His eyes skidded right by Reggie, who detected just a trace of cunning showing through all the booze.

''Yeah, I'd like that,'' Higgs said, attempting to stand. He leaned on Mendez, obviously at ease in his company. ''Thanks for being so nice,'' he said to Sally. ''Sorry we didn't get a chance to talk. You're the people who take care of the dolphins, isn't that right? Clark and Lois?''

''That's right,'' Sally said. ''Listen, Dr. Higgs, you're perfectly welcome to stay here. You could spend the night. We could, um, talk about the dolphins in the morning, when you're feeling better.''

Higgs looked from Mendez and his assistants to the van, and then to the canal. "Better not," he said. "I better let Robby take me back. Better for all concerned."

"If you're sure."

Higgs hesitated. "I'm sure," he finally said. "This is for the best."

When the van had loaded up Dr. Higgs and his bicycle and backed out of the driveway, Reggie turned to Tom and Sally and said, "Well, my goodness, *that* was interesting. I don't mean to sound blasphemous, considering, but could you spare an old lady a drink, by any chance? Anything but rum."

11

Buzzards on the Wind

JACK FINLEY WAS feeling no pain. He couldn't *buy* a drink at the Angler or Locals or any of the tiki bars.

"I don't care about no fifteen minutes of fame," he'd announced to the jubilant crowd at the Hurricane. "Just give me my fifteen drinks' worth."

He'd gotten all of that and more, if you counted Cindy Lee getting friendly and a couple of other offers he hadn't been able to take advantage of because with this much free vodka on board he couldn't find his sea legs—or that was the excuse he'd used when he couldn't get it together with Cindy Lee.

"Rain check, honey?" he'd said, fighting to keep his balance on an isolated picnic table out behind the tiki bar.

The little redhead had pulled up her hot pants, put the gum back in her mouth. "Use it or lose it, Jack honey, that's the rule. We'll just have to see about a next time."

"Anything you say, sweet thang. Only doan mention this to the boys, huh?"

"Are you kidding? Anyhow, they always blame the woman, and this time it ain't my fault." Cindy Lee gave him a quick, indifferent kiss on the cheek and hurried back to the action at the tiki bar.

Jack was trying to follow her, unsure of his inner compass, when a firm hand gripped him on the shoulder. A familiar voice said, "Finley, you're drunk."

" 'Course I'm drunk." Finley spun around, tripped over his own feet. "Hey, Wade, Buy me a drink?"

"Well, shit," said Wade Colson. "You ain't no use to me like this. How long it take you to sober up, you have to?"

Finley thought about it. Thinking required great concentration, and concentration made him dizzy. "Couple hours, I guess."

Colson was leading Finley away from the lights of the tiki bar, out to the parking lot. "That might do,' he said. "Won't be nothing happening until later tonight, early this morning. You can sleep it off on the *Squali*."

Mention of the *Squali* made Finley straighten up. "Hold on now," he said, pulling himself free of Colson's grip. "What you got in mind, Wade, huh?" He leaned back against Colson's pickup truck, tried to focus his mind. A glittery tiki bar beckoned, and he didn't much like Colson's tone of irreverence.

"Got in mind a little night fishin'," Colson said, leaning close, his eyes like cold wet stones in dark water. "Money's good," he added.

"Well, shit, Wade, you know I don't run no dope," Finley said, indignant. "Not lately, anyhow."

Colson's laughter was soft and high-pitched, had that swampy, Everglades drawl that always made

Jack Finley feel like he'd stepped in deep mud that wanted to suck him down real slow.

"I mean *real* night fishin'," Colson said. "Got a charter tonight, I could use a hand. Somebody who knows what the hell is going on."

The vodka haze cleared a little, and Finley said, "Hell, you still chasin' them things? That what you're on about?"

"You give 'em chase yourself this morning, out Bahia Honda way, ain't that right?"

Finley snorted, straightened himself up. "Lemme tell you about that, Wade old buddy. Them fuckers *devoured* my client, wallet and all. So I never got paid, which *really* pissed me off. Also this was in broad daylight, I could *see* the sons of bitches, meant I could get myself to high ground if they turned on me."

He slumped back against the truck, having made his point.

Getting crafty and low, Colson said, "You turning chicken on me, Jack? A tough hombre like you?"

That made Finley giggle. "Chicken?" he said, cackling. "Chicken?" He made a rooster sound. "Chicken? Hell, I got more brains than a chicken. And no *way* am I goin' after those fuckers at night, in *your* boat. Shit, you already lost two mates. What'd you do to those boys, call 'em chicken? Huh? Finger-lickin' good, is that what happened?"

Exasperated, Colson slammed the side of his truck. "Take a look at this, Jack, you think you're so funny." He lifted the lid of a toolbox. "Go on, take a look."

Finley grinned through his beard. "It's *dark*, Wade, didn't you notice? Happens I can't see in the dark."

Colson clicked on a flashlight. "Just look, you son of a bitch."

Finley looked, tried to whistle but could not make

his lips work. "That what I think it is?" he said. "Where the hell'd you get that?"

"Five hundred bucks," Colson said, lifting the machine gun from the toolbox. "This greaser up in Key Largo, deals out of his trailer. Put a hundred rounds in the water in about fifteen seconds, you hold the trigger down."

Finley was shaking his head and laughing silently. "You're nuts," he said. "Loony tunes."

"This is just for insurance," Colson said, ignoring the insult. "For peace of mind. What's going to kill 'em is this."

He reached into the toolbox, held up a grenade. "Navy Seal tactical explosive," he said. "Good to a hundred fathoms."

Finley shook his head. "You are," he said. "You really are nuts. You want the truth, Wade? You crazy, swamp-stinking son of a bitch? The truth is, I'd rather have my dick pecked off by buzzards than go out in a boat with you."

He staggered away, set a wobbly course for the tiki bar, and didn't look back.

Reggie stayed for less than an hour, sipping on a single drink, and laying out the way she intended to cover the man-eater story in *Reef Life*'s next issue.

"This has the makings of a tragedy," she said, lifting her glass and pointing it out to sea, toward the unseen reef. "An ecological disaster, any way you slice it. Right now we have every shark-happy fishermen in the Keys out there killing everything that moves. That's one part of the disaster. If nobody manages to kill these things before they start reproducing, we've got *another* kind of disaster."

The sea breeze had died away, leaving the air with an eerie stillness that distorted sound. The thump of distant engines was clearly audible, a constant undertone, and now and then the tin-flat sound of gunfire carried into the canal area. Oddly enough the nearby sounds of the human voice seemed muffled or cloaked, so that you had to lean forward and cock an ear.

Tom was saying, "Yeah, but the point is, what do we do about it?"

"Make the facts known," Reggie said. She stood up, picked up her purse, ready to leave. "That's all we *can* do. Of course, first we have to determine what the facts *are*, and then we have to get corroboration. Anything less, we'll be vulnerable to a lawsuit. We've got to keep that in mind."

"You mean Higgs isn't good enough?" Tom said. "What he told us?"

"Sure, if he'll repeat himself in public. If he won't, we have to find a way to confirm what he told you—that Sealife is engaged in the genetic engineering of marine predators. What did he call them, maxis?"

"From *Isurus maximus*," Sally said.

"*Maximus*," Reggie echoed. "So how big are these things supposed to get?"

"He didn't say. I'm not sure he even knows."

"Something to think about," Reggie said.

"Not if you want to sleep tonight," Tom said.

After Reggie left, Sally went into the house. Tom busied himself picking up the patio area, and when he looked up Sally was back, wearing a swimsuit.

He said. "Whoa. You're going in the water?"

"I need to do this," Sally said. "I need to be sure they're okay."

Tom put down the empty drink glasses, followed her to the dock. "They're fine. Lois is over there rubbing her back against that piling and Clark has been chasing a fish around, he's probably got it by now. Hear his tail slap?"

"That's not what I mean," she said. "I can't explain it."

She donned her flippers and mask.

Tom hooked a finger in the back of her suit. "Come on, Sal, let's go to bed. We'll get an early start in the morning."

Sally wiggled away and plunged into the canal. She came up by the side of the dock, cleared her mask, and grinned. "What are you worried about?" she said. "You've got barricades at each end of the canal, right? Even if you didn't, they'd never come in here. Not with Clark and Lois around."

"We don't *know* that," Tom said. "These aren't ordinary makos, we *do* know that."

Lois, drawn by the familiar noise of a human entering the water, came up from under the dock and began to squeak and chatter, splashing with her flukes.

"Lois knows," Sally said. "I'm safe here, babe. Honest."

Tom stepped aboard the dive boat, retrieved a carbine from the lazarette. Sally spotted him from the water and said, "That won't be necessary, babe. Put it away, please?"

He shrugged but kept the carbine, and stood watch on the dock, where he had a good view of the canal. He'd never actually used the rifle from the dive boat—there'd never been a need—and he wasn't entirely sure that the ammunition was still good, after a couple of years in a damp storage compartment. But what the hell, it was better than nothing.

He knew it was useless to argue with Sally about night dives with her dolphin. She had absolute faith in Lois, was convinced the female would protect her. And the canal *was* blocked off from both ends; only the smallest fish could get through the mesh grill. It was almost as safe as diving in a swimming pool, so why did he feel so damned nervous, this icy chunk of anxiety in his gut?

Tom took a deep breath, forced himself to relax.

Aware of his heart thumping in his chest. Aware also of the joyful noise the two dolphins made, playing splash and chase games with Sally.

"Come on, Clark, can you catch a fish at night? Can you? Can you teach Lois how to do it? Huh?"

It was safe in here, barricaded in their own private canal, safe as churches, and yet he couldn't shake the image of the maxis, sleek and strong and purposeful, streaking under the Bahia Honda Bridge, headed straight for the nearest divers.

Tom made sure the carbine safety was engaged, returned it to the dive boat. Sally and the dolphins were right under the stern, in the full illumination of the dock lights. Rolling and diving, it was amazing how Sally handled herself in the water; there were moments when you could confuse her with the dolphins. Either she was mimicking their moves or they were mimicking hers.

The next time she came up for air he said, "Sal, honey. Please? Humor me on this."

He reached down, felt her wet hand grip his own, and in one move he pulled her clear of the water and up onto the transom of the dive boat.

"Clark won't eat cutfish now," she said, gasping for breath. "He wants to catch his own. Isn't that amazing?"

"Yes," he said. "You are."

12

Dead Meat

THERE WAS A spare bottle in the bottom drawer of his office filing cabinet. Prescription Dexedrine, he'd gone through quite a lot of it in the last few days, keeping the edge.

Dr. Vernon Speke got down on his knees, searched the back of the drawer, finally located the bottle. He stood up, cracked open the cap, and tipped three—no, make it four of the little pills into the palm of his hand.

Big night, he wanted to be wide awake, on top of things. He added a couple more dexies, just for luck, and raised the beaker to his lips.

Damn, no water in here, nothing to wash it down.

The pills were already starting to melt on his tongue, a bitter taste, as he exited his office and walked quickly to the lab. Tap water in there, he could drink from a nice clean beaker.

He opened the door, headed right for the sink. A

moment before he noticed that the lights were already on.

Higgs was in the lab. Startled, a rabbit caught in the headlights. Speke waved hello, poured himself a drink, and washed the pills down. Higgs waited, not sure how to react.

"Hey, Chesty, I thought you were passed out in your cabin. Robby told me all about your little adventure."

Dr. Higgs was damp from a shower, dressed in fresh clothing, obviously doing his best. The bloodshot eyes gave him away, though, and he was moving like a man walking on eggs, uncertain of his footing. You knew him, you could see the booze at work, even if he didn't appear to be staggering drunk, had sobered up considerably over the last few hours.

"You can't go ahead with this," Higgs said, gripping the edge of a lab table and leaning his bulk against it. Breathing heavily through his nose.

"You're supposed to be in bed," Speke said, putting down the beaker. "Sleeping it off. So what are you doing in here at this time of night, huh, Chesty?"

Higgs ignored the question. "Vern? You can't *do* this to those people. It's not right."

Speke patted his lips with a brown paper lab towel and stared at Chester Higgs. The man was in his early forties, looked about a hundred years old tonight, the way his flesh sagged. Clearly he was keeping himself vertical by sheer force of will. "So," Speke said, "what did you tell them? Those people who stole our dolphin."

"Never mind that," Higgs said. He took a deep breath. "The point is, you've got to stop right now. Tell Robby and Lucy you've changed your mind about tonight. Cancel the plans."

"Chesty?" Speke came up close, not quite touching Higgs. "If you discussed this project with civilians, there could be real trouble with the DOD. So tell me, what exactly did you say to that idiot diver and his wife?"

Higgs closed his eyes. "I don't recall."

"Because I haven't got time for this right now," Speke said. "We can discuss it in the morning."

"Sure, sure, *after* you've done this terrible thing, *then* we'll talk."

Dr. Speke opened his mouth to respond, then shook his head. This was really too much. Unbelievable that he should be getting this ration of crap from a drunk who not three hours ago was pedaling around the keys on a goddamn bicycle, shooting off his mouth. "Hey, Chester? You're out of line. Way, way out of line. What I'm doing is correcting a problem that if it doesn't get corrected, you can forget the good life at Sealife Key. Hell, you can forget ever getting another job. So what we're doing later tonight is absolutely necessary. It's our only shot. We all agreed."

Higgs said, "Like hell we did. You came up with this crazy scheme and the others went along."

Speke was aware of a pulse of pressure behind his eyes, made everything blurry for a moment. The dexies kicking in, he could feel the familiar tingle, the bitter taste of the drug lingering in his teeth. "What do you want from me, Chester? Huh? This morning you were raving about how we had to blow the bastards up, and that's exactly what's going to happen if this goes according to plan."

Higgs sighed and said, "I wish I could believe you, Vernon."

"Ask Robby, he rigged the charge himself."

Higgs pushed himself away from the lab table, threw back his shoulders, and headed purposefully for the lab's walk-in freezer.

"What's on your mind?" Speke said, following him.

"Just taking precautions."

"What the hell are you talking about, Chester?"

"You say you're going to blow up all the maxis? Fine. I just want to make sure you can't make any more of them."

Speke reached out, grabbed a fistful of Higgs's shirt.

He said, "Hold it right there, mister. You stay out of that freezer, hear?"

Higgs, the larger man, wrenched himself free, kept on going.

Speke hurried after him, got to the freezer door first. "The genetic material belongs to Sealife research," Speke said. "The board will decide what to do with it."

"The hell they will," said Higgs. He began to pry Speke's fingers from the door handle.

"Chester, I'm warning you."

Higgs yanked on the door handle. The seal opened and cold air wafted suddenly into the lab. "It's over," he said to Speke. "Find a new project."

"I forbid you to touch those embryos! I'll call the security guards, have you arrested."

"Go ahead," Higgs said, stepping through the freezer door, his sandals slipping a little on the thin layer of frost.

"Chester, goddamn it, no!"

Higgs was reaching for the frozen embryo compartment when Speke grabbed Higgs's shirt collar with both hands and yanked back with all his might.

The shirt ripped. Higgs's feet skidded out from under him and for a fraction of a second he seemed suspended in midair, his head thrown back and his eyes wild with surprise.

A moment later the back of his head struck the protruding handle of a steel freezer compartment and then he lay on the floor, staring up at Vernon Speke. His expression was reproachful and a little sad.

"Chesty? Look, I'm sorry. But damn it, you can't . . ."

Speke knelt beside Higgs. Glasses slightly askew. Funny, he didn't seem to be blinking behind his thick eyeglasses. Eyes wide open, looking right at him. An expression that now seemed to be saying, oops, look what you did.

Speke reached out tentatively, touched the side of Higgs's neck. No discernible pulse, but that didn't mean anything, did it? He picked up a limp wrist, pressed first with his thumb, then with two fingers. Not even a flutter.

"Chester? Come on."

Finally he removed Higgs's glasses, held the lenses close to his mouth and nose. Figuring the glass would mist up if Chester was breathing.

The glass did not fog.

Right about then Speke noticed a thickening pool of blood oozing from under the back of Higgs's head. He made the mistake of trying to lift Higgs's head, and then *clots* of the stuff emptied into his hands.

The intercom phone rang out in the lab.

Speke ran to the sink, quickly rinsed the blood from his hands, and picked up the receiver.

It was Lucy. "Dr. Speke? Vernon? Robby said to tell you we're all set. Ready to cast off."

"I'll be right there."

He disconnected and went back into the walk-in freezer. "You're fucking me up," he said to the staring eyes. "You think I'm going to stay here and explain this right now? The hell I am."

What he did was back out of there and close the door. All he had to do was walk back in here tomorrow morning and discover that Dr. Higgs, in a state of advanced inebriation witnessed earlier by beaucoup staff members, had managed to slip and fall and break his rum-soaked skull.

Right now, Speke decided, hurrying away from the lab, right now the important thing was to take care of the maxi problem. Higgs would just have to wait his turn.

Us the Beautiful sing quietly. The danger noises— the whir-cries of the propellers—are not so numerous now, or so near. A comforting darkness has seeped through the water and the darkness makes the Us feel safer, less vulnerable.

Hungry, they sing to each other. *Hunt. Feed.*

The hunger is a terrible need. Given time, that need will overcome any fear or caution. Hunger burns in their metabolism, flooding their brains with need. Flooding each muscle and nerve ending. Hunger makes their jaws ache, their rows of teeth tingle with desire.

Eat, they sing. *Eat the fear.*

Now, they sing. *Eat now.*

The Us begin to circle, rising from the bottom of the channel.

The Us swim away from the danger, away from the whir-noise of the reef. Faster, gaining confidence with each flick of the tail, they swim into the shallow waters of the Keys, looking for prey. Shaping the darkness with their song.

Eat the fear, they sing. *Eat eat eat.*

They look for large, easy-to-hunt prey.

Day Four

1

After Midnight

It is one heartbeat after midnight, and in Tom's dream his heart has stopped beating. It is dark, black dark, and he is on his back underwater with a great weight pressing down on him and he can't find his respirator mouthpiece.

His lungs hurt and his heart has stopped beating and he can't find his mouthpiece. His hands flail weakly in the water. He is so weak that even if he finds his respirator, his fingers won't be strong enough to hold on to it.

His ears are ringing. Chimes underwater. He knows what *that* means.

It means he is dying, his mind is fading. His heart—well, his heart is already dead and now the rest of him is dying. He opens his mouth to breathe the water but there is no water. There is nothing, only the heavy darkness pressing him down, down. He can't move now, not even to squeeze his fingers together, can't even feel his fingers; his whole body is shutting down, all his sensations replaced by a tingling numbness. The numbness spreads.

All he feels now, all he is aware of, is his stopped heart, his empty lungs.

And then, as if from a great distance, the ringing in his ears begins to focus, sharpening, until he realizes that the ringing is a voice and the voice is calling—can this be, is this possible?—the voice is calling his name.

"Tom! Tom! Tom, wake up!"

And he does, he wakes up and finds that he is able to open his mouth and gulp in a lungful of air, and he feels, or thinks he feels, his heart begin beating again, thump thump, and Sally is with him in the darkness, her hands on his sweat-slick body, urging him to wake up because something is wrong, something is *very* wrong.

"My God, babe, you were so deep asleep. It was like you weren't breathing. Like you were made of stone."

"What is it?" he said, getting his breath. The heat in his lungs felt good; it hurt, but it felt so good. "What's wrong?"

"I heard something," Sally said.

She was up on her knees in the bed, naked in the dark, trying to get a look out the window. Very little illumination here, just the glow of the single dock light he'd left on for the night.

Sally said, "There was a boat in the canal. I heard it, caught a glimpse. A big boat, like a fishing boat. A trawler."

"Oh, shit," he said.

Tom tried to sit up, but his left foot was still asleep, the circulation cut off and just now coming back to life as the blood jetted in, hurtful but good, the same with his hand where it had been under the weight of his body, the prickly numbness of the nightmare. Was it a nightmare? Could a dream be *that* powerful, powerful enough to actually stop his heart?

But his heart *couldn't* have stopped.

"Tom, can you hear me?" Sally again, tugging at him. "Are you really awake? Something's wrong, babe. I've got a *really* bad feeling."

She sounded on the verge of tears and that helped him wake up some more, struggling to clear the suffocating fog from his head, it wasn't real, hadn't happened; his heart didn't stop, it was all a dream. Wake up, you silly son of a bitch. *Sally needs you.* "What," he said. "A boat in the canal. But—"

"I know, there *can't* be a boat in the canal because you blocked it off. But there *was*, Tom, it woke me up. Can't you hear it?"

He managed to sit up, tried to concentrate on listening. Might be the thump of a diesel out there, but not in the canal. More distant, and going away.

"I know," Sally said. She was up now, going to the window, reaching for her kimono. "It's gone now, but it was very close. Right down there in the canal."

"Okay," he said. He stood up, hopped on the pins-and-needles foot, forcing blood to flow. "I'll go down, take a look."

"I'm coming with you."

Tom didn't argue. The fact was, he wanted the company. He found a pair of shorts and yanked them on, his mind beginning to clear, and Sally was right behind him as he stumbled through the bedroom door into the familiar hallway, turned right at the kitchen, and then out the front door and into the warm night, a flashlight in his hand somehow, he must have grabbed it from the kitchen counter on the way out, it was a comfort to have something solid and heavy in his right hand.

He ran down the steps, didn't realize he was barefoot until he hit the gravel, but even *that* didn't hurt, it felt so good to be alive again.

Behind him Sally had switched on the rest of the dock lights. Kimono flying open, thin legs pumping, she ran to the canal, calling her dolphins. "*Lois! Loooo-is!* CLARK! CLAAAA-AAARK!"

Sally stomped around on the float so the dolphins would know she was there.

"They're not here!" she cried. "Something happened!"

"Try again," Tom suggested. "Keep calling."

He was running alongside the canal, down to the curve where it intersected with the ocean, and even before he got there he could see that the barricade was down, pushed aside.

Relieved, very relieved to find her still on the float, looking forlorn in that sexy silk kimono, and as he got closer he could see the tear lines glistening on her face, he could read the despair in her eyes.

"Barricade's down," he announced, giving her a quick hug, and then he was leaping into the dive-boat cockpit and firing up the engine.

He swung *Wild Child* around, almost but not quite bumping the canal wall, and gunned it, hitting the spotlights as he steered almost blind for the Gulf end of the canal. Where he found that the *other* barricade was down. Using the spotlight he could see part of the wire mesh twisted and bent where it had been shoved to one side by an entering vessel.

By the time he got back to the float he thought he knew what had happened.

"Dr. Higgs tried to warn us and I didn't listen," he told Sally.

She stood unspeaking on the dock, her arms clasped tight over her chest, crying, crying.

"They're coming," he kept saying. "That's what he kept saying: 'They're coming.' I thought he meant the sharks. He meant the Sealife people. They busted in here and they took back the dolphins, Sal. That's what must have happened."

Sally nodded shakily. "I heard the b-b-boat."

Tom left the engine idling, took her in her arms. He said, "We'll get them back, I promise. On my life, I promise."

Robby Mendez needed stitches, but the stitches would have to wait. For the moment he made do with a bandage, Lucy doing the honors as she wrapped gauze tightly around his left forearm, the blood continuing to soak through where the male dolphin had managed to take a chunk out of him.

The male was still thrashing in the net even though the net had been winched onto the deck. Insane thrashing, really; the thing seemed to be driven mad by the cries of the female, who was being transferred to a mesh cage at the stern.

"I don't know," Mendez said, shaky from the surprise of the wound. "He's gone berserk."

The three boats were a couple of miles offshore now, rafted together, idling in the flat, moonless waters. Showing no running lights at all. The trawler, which had towed the nets through the Tarpon Key canal, snagging the dolphin. The charter boat *Squali*, Wade Colson alone aboard, acting moody and strange. The chase boat, crewed by Lucy Savrin and Dr. Speke—and *he* was acting moody and strange, too, hadn't reacted with much sympathy when Mendez got bitten.

"Berserk is just fine," Speke said. He was standing on the rear deck of the chase boat as the female's cage was lowered by winch from the trawler. "Berserk is just what we need."

Mendez decided to get himself together, deal with this. It was just a wound—deep and nasty, but just a wound. His fingers still moved, so that was a good sign. "If the animal really is insane, this will never work," he pointed out.

Speke settled the cage on the stern. He said, "Hey, Robby? You a dolphin shrink?"

Mendez didn't like the tone, didn't like it at all. "I'm an animal trainer," he said, mustering his dignity. "A good one."

"Hell, I know that. This was partly your idea, right? To use the dolphin?"

Mendez shrugged. He wasn't sure how much credit he wanted to take for this, after seeing the animals react. They were both out of their minds with terror, the male was just much more violent about it than the female.

He knew their names, of course, but at the moment, considering what Speke had planned, it was better to think of them as animal objects, male and female.

Help keep it straight in his head what had to be done.

"Hey, Robby?" Speke was saying. "Can you handle it? Just tell me, one way or the other."

"I can handle it," he said. Gritting his teeth as a thrum of pain resonated in his wound.

"Because what I've got to do," Speke said, "I've got to get the female back to the lagoon right now. We've got what, a little more than five hours until daylight."

"Go ahead," Mendez said. "Just be sure to keep her wet."

"I *know* how to transport a goddamn bottlenose," Speke said. "I get back, drop off the cage, and then we'll take up our positions, is that understood?"

Mendez said, "Sure, of course."

"Captain Colson? Wade, did you hear me? We'll be taking our positions in thirty minutes or less."

Colson muttered, "I heard you." Made it sound like he was clearing his throat. He was visible to the others in silhouette, pacing the cockpit of his charter boat, just the red tip of a cigarette glowing to illuminate his chin, the tip of his nose. His voice sounded small, choked off. He said, "Got the dynamite rigged, Vern? You sure about it?"

Speke's laughter sounded like a bag of broken glass. "Affirmative on the explosives," he said. "The charge is set to detonate on my signal."

Colson said, "You all give me that signal box, I'll do the honors."

There was not a chance, no way, that Vernon Speke would relinquish control of the detonator, certainly not to Wade Colson.

"There's nothing to blow up yet, Wade," Speke said.

He lashed down the dolphin cage. The frantic spew of clicks and anguished squeaks had ceased and the female lay unmoving, eyes wide open, barely breathing. "Won't be anything to blow up until we get the maxis back to the lagoon. Take your boat over to your position, I'll contact you when we're ready, is that understood?"

No response from the *Squali*.

Speke sounded like a man exerting all of his rapidly dwindling patience: "Wade, you hear what I said?"

Colson shouted, "Them fuckers is dead meat! Dead!"

In the gleaming darkness of dead calm waters, the three boats separated.

2

The Cage

WHEN THE TEARS stopped Sally looked like her face was carved from hard white stone. Her lack of expression frightened Tom because he had never seen it before, not in all their years together. Like part of her was dead.

"They must want them for something," Tom said, trying to assure her. "So they won't kill them."

"Maybe not right away," Sally said. "Later, though, so they can deny they took them from us."

"We don't know that."

Without turning her head, she said, "Yes we do. Think about it. We know what the son of a bitch is capable of doing. Four people have been killed so far. Do you really think they'd hesitate to kill a couple of dolphins if it suits their purpose?"

They were loading dive gear into *Wild Child*, tanks and regulators and sheath knives and a couple of old spear guns, anything in the shop that looked useful.

Not that they had a plan. They'd called Reggie, who was still at her office, and she promised to get on the horn, raise hell with the marine patrol, try to instigate an investigation. Tom called the Coast Guard station in Marathon, was told rather briskly that he could file a complaint in the morning, any time after 8:00 A.M., sir, although it sure sounds like a civil case, sir, sounds almost like a custody case, sir, and can you prove ownership of the dolphins, sir, if it comes to that?

"Bastards," he'd said, slamming down the phone. There had been no need to explain to Sally, who'd overheard his end of things, and who from previous experience had very little faith in any government agency when it came to protecting dolphins from Pentagon-financed experiments.

"We're on our own," she'd said. "I think we always knew that."

So the choice was wait until daylight and begin the process of going through legal channels, or do something now and risk the consequences.

A glance at Sally meant there was no choice, none, and all Tom could think to do was confront the Sealife staff, locate the dolphins, and use whatever force was necessary to free them. Which sounded, even as he made the suggestion, like a mighty tall order.

Sally's response: "We'll do what we have to do."

And so they loaded gear aboard *Wild Child*, fired up the engine, and at a little before one in the morning released the dock lines and left Tarpon Key in their wake.

The dolphin cage was too heavy to slip off the stern by hand, so they had to position the chase boat under the dock hoist in the lagoon and lift it clear that way. Lucy was aware of a flutter in her belly, it might be anxiety or fear or even a vague sympathy for the animal in the cage. Those big eyes staring at her—it was silly and unprofessional, but she had to look away as she hooked the lifting straps up to the hoist. She said, "Hang in there, you'll be back in the water in a minute."

Vernon Speke, working the hoist controls, said, "Lucy? Don't waste your breath. That particular animal has no comprehension of human speech."

She said, "Oh," and let it go at that. No point in debating the subject with Dr. Speke, he was acting particularly spooky tonight. Stressed out, she assumed, hyper from high levels of caffeine and adrenaline in that long, scrawny body of his. He had an insect look about him she'd never noticed before, kind of praying mantis thing—the way he held himself, the way he swiveled his head.

Dr. Speke had been coming on to her lately, more than usual, and Lucy had come to the conclusion that after tonight, after this situation with the maxis was concluded, she would have to find a way to politely tell him to forget it. Get together with the bug man? No way.

Poor Vern was too egocentric to respond to the usual signals of noninterest, signals she'd been flashing from the very beginning, when he'd first interviewed her for the research position. He just didn't get it, had no idea that on a physical level she found him repulsive.

Kiss those thin, rubber-slick lips? Gag me, please.

Not that she didn't respect the man as a scientist, an innovator. *Isurus maximus* had been created because of his vision, his determination to apply state-of-the-art genetic technology to a specific problem: the Navy's long-stated requirement for an attack animal to guard undersea missile installations from enemy divers. Or enemy dolphins, if it came to that. The maxi project filled a very specific need, yes, but by doing so they had engineered a virtual new species and—here was the important part—the patented offspring were the property of Sealife Research, Inc. The applications of the maxi experiment were much wider and more important than the solution of any particular Defense Department problem.

The use of live animals, the lifeblood of scientific research, was under attack everywhere, with fanatical groups insisting that all animals had "natural" rights just like humans, or even superior to the rights of humans. The activists were making headway, too, getting new laws passed, lobbying oversight committees and picketing labs. But the rights argument could not be sustained with the maxis because there was nothing natural about them—they would not exist in any form if Sealife hadn't *created* them, in the same way that patent drugs were synthesized from compounds found in nature.

Isurus maximus was, in a legal sense at least, a synthesized species. True, the first experiment had failed and the progeny now had to be destroyed, but so what? Failure was part of the scientific process, a necessary step, really. The Sealife team would learn from their mistakes, and by the time the next generation of progeny came out of the embryo freezer, the team would be ready with an improved containment facility and a new behavior modification program that would ensure absolute control of the maxis.

"Lucy?"

"Sorry, what was that, Dr. Speke?"

"Push the cage to the left so it clears the stern."

"Got it," she said, shoving against the weight of the cage. It swung clear. The hoist motor hummed, unreeling a few yards of cable as the cage slipped into the dark water.

"How about the flotation pontoons?" he said. "Can you see if the level is correct?"

Lucy knelt by the stern and used a flashlight to check the pontoons that kept the top of the cage above water level. The dolphin need a few inches of air space, room to surface and breathe through its blowhole, or it would quickly drown.

It was important to keep the animal alive, for now. The male would not react as they desired it to if the female wasn't alive, according to Mendez, and he *knew* these two animals, had a well-informed notion of how they would respond in a given situation.

Speke landed with a light thump on the deck behind her. "Okay," he said, looming over her shoulders, his breath sour and damp. "Tie the short lines off to the cleats, we'll move the cage into place."

"She—I mean the animal is bumping the sides of the cage."

Speke said. "Good. That means the animal is active. Don't worry, there's no way it can escape. I padlocked the cage door just to make sure the release lever doesn't pop loose."

Lucy stood up, turning her back to the caged animal, and said, "Dr. Speke? Is it really necessary that we put the cage right here in the lagoon? I mean, wouldn't it still work if we anchored her *outside* the lagoon?"

The dock lights made Speke look more elongated than ever, his features shifting like pale molten plastic. Hard to tell whether he was smiling or frowning, the way his mouth twisted. "I thought you knew better than that, Lucy."

"I do. It's just that—"

"You're feeling sympathy for the animal." He paused, then stroked the back of his head, his hands running over the stub of his lost ponytail. "I want you to know it's okay to feel sympathy. That's a human reaction. But that doesn't mean we let sympathetic feelings endanger the experiment."

"No," Lucy said. "Of course not."

"Especially, and I know you understand this, especially when this experiment is our last shot at rounding up the maxis. Our *best* shot.''

"I understand.''

"We can't settle for half measures.''

"I was thinking out loud," Lucy said. "Forget it.''

Speke moved closer, his awkwardness making him rigid, and he did it, he embraced her, patted her back. That sour breath and a peculiar, yeasty smell coming off his body.

Lucy pretended to lose her footing and slipped out of his arms. "Oops," she said. "These deck shoes.''

They towed the cage into the middle of the lagoon, to a prearranged location, where it was anchored in place with a set of heavy galvanized mooring chains.

When Lucy released the towlines she could feel the vibration of the female bumping herself against the sides of the cage. A frenetic activity that might well continue right up to the end.

Don't think about it, Lucy decided.

A minute later the chase boat had cleared the lagoon entrance and Speke was jamming the throttle down. They ran without lights, a dark wedge skidding over the surface of the black water. Lucy watched the loran numbers unreel on the navigation screen and thought: *It will all be over soon, they'll never know what hit them.*

A mile or so from Sealife Key, Tom suddenly cut the engine. *Wild Child* bucked forward, buffeted by her own wake, and he said, "Did you hear that?''

Sally stepped away from the bridge, cocked an ear. "Another motor," she said. "There are tons of boats out there, babe.''

"Yeah, but that's a Cigarette engine, you can tell by the way it roars. The pitch.''

"I can't see a thing," Sally said.

"I'm going to head in there, see what I can find out," he said. "No point in chasing noises in the dark."

Sally didn't respond. She was staring out there, concentrating with all her might, but there was no way to see anything beyond a range of a few hundred yards. And even at close range you could be fooled by your own imagination. See things that weren't there. Not see things that were.

In her cage the exhausted female gave up. There was no way out, no escape. She knew where she was now—this lagoon had once been home—and the knowledge terrified her almost as much as being snatched from the canal and forcibly separated from the male.

For the last ten minutes she had been calling him ceaselessly as she banged from side to side in the cage, a call that he had never failed to answer. The song of his name, a joyful whistle that he always answered with his own short burst of song.

Singing her name as he came to her, appearing playfully or sometimes concerned and frightened for her safety. But always answering. Always coming when she called.

If he did not answer, if he did not come, that meant only one thing: the young male was dead. The people of the nets had killed him.

After her lungs filled again, restoring some of her strength, the female resumed her frenetic activity, smashing herself against the bars of the cage. This was not hysterical behavior. She knew exactly what she was doing. Punishing herself, exhausting herself until she was weak enough to overcome her instincts. Her intention was to drown.

If the male was dead, then she too would die.

3

The Prospect of Redemption

WADE COLSON SAT on the engine hatch cover, in the absolute center of his boat, as far from the sides of the boat as a man could get. Staying in the boat—well, that was the first and only rule.

Let yourself look over the side, check out the ink-black water, you never knew what might rise up in a heartbeat. Rows of glistening teeth, the jaw unhinged in that creepy way all sharks had. To swallow their prey.

Snap, snap, off with your head.

No, thank you, Mr. Mako, I'll just stay here in the middle of the boat and await further instructions from these eggheads, who seem to think they know what you'll do before *you* know what you'll do.

Colson had his doubts about the geniuses at Sealife Key. Hence the black-market machine gun and the Navy Seal grenades, the crate containing both items close at hand. The grenades were packed in loose Styrofoam peanuts so they wouldn't roll around when the boat moved, set each other off.

On a holster at his waist, a 9mm semiauto handgun. In his pockets, two spare clips. Also a KA-Bar knife in a sheath on his belt.

Sitting there adrift in the Gulf on a moonless night, miles away from the mayhem and slaughter on the reef, Colson couldn't help but remember what it had been like, that first attack. Come up out of *nowhere*, as if he and his mates were the ones being lured to their deaths and not the reverse. Who was fishing for whom, that was the point. It was unnatural and that made him afraid, and being afraid—a brand-new sensation for the adult Wade Colson—made him angry.

Fuck that bastard Jack Finley, he didn't want to help.

Wade had been raised on a squatter's homestead in the village of Everglades City. Not a proper homestead, just several wretched old house trailers shoved together at the edge of the waterway. Hell, the shacks were underwater if a drop of rain fell from the sky, and oh, did it fall. Wade the runt of ten kids, his mother run off to avoid regular beatings, the old man locked up on a regular basis for assault or poaching or raising hell with the wealthy hunters and sportsmen drawn to the area, looking to bag a record fish or maybe shoot a Florida panther.

When sober and out of jail—occasions rare enough to be memorable—the old man had hired out to the sportsmen, guiding them to 'gator holes, shining the critters with spotlights so the rich sportsmen could shoot between the little red eyes and say they'd killed a genuine Florida alligator. Not a legal kill, no, but the sportsmen were paying for old man Colson to take the risk, go to jail if they got caught. Which they did, and which *he* did, leaving that leaky pile of trailers at the edge of the rising water, and ten kids to fend for themselves while the old man ate hot meals in jail and told lies to the Collier County deputies.

At fifteen Wade had his own boat, a flat-bottom skiff with a pole and an ancient ten-horse motor, and he made a business of jacking illegal 'gator. Kept himself sober and straight and saved his money like his old man had never been able to, so that at eighteen he had a bigger boat and a proper hull with an inboard, and he was clean enough and straight enough and smart enough to find work as a *real* guide, not a 'gator thief, taking parties down into the Ten Thousand Islands. Fishing tarpon and snook, whatever was hot with the monied anglers who came to Everglades City by chartered automobile or private aircraft, gentlemen who annually spent more on their fishing tackle than old man Colson had ever spent on his barefoot family of ten.

As soon as he had the right boat and enough money saved, Wade got the hell out of the Everglades, took himself across the bay to the Florida Keys, where nobody knew about those wretched leaky trailers set out on swamp that never even belonged to the family. Got himself into the charter business and *ran* it like a business, and never looked back. Shit, he hated to think about the old days, and here he was remembering because he was afraid for the first time since he'd had shoes to wear.

Oh, yes, screw that grinning bastard Finley if he was too cowardly to lend a hand. Who the hell did he think he was, rejecting a request from a fellow waterman? Wade had killed more shark than Finley had ever *seen*, that was no lie, and getting his big hairy kisser on the TV news show didn't make it right that Black Jack was suddenly an accidental hero and Wade Colson was that coldhearted bastard who'd let his mates down.

Wade did not think in biblical terms—he hated Bible thumpers almost as much as he hated carpet-baggers—but in his own way he did believe in personal redemption. What would redeem him, what would get him back to even with the world, was to kill these terrible creatures himself. Kill his own fear with the same blow—with the same grenade or machine gun or whatever, so long as it happened, so long as he was right in there for the kill.

His radio squawked and Wade couldn't help it, he jumped inside.

"Calling the *Squali*, over. You monitoring, *Squali*?"

Wade found the hand-held unit, pressed the coded send button: "Mendez, that you?"

"We're ready to proceed. Keep your engine shut down until I relay the signal, is that clear?"

Wade said, "Hell, yes." They'd gone over all this, Mendez was just repeating it to please Dr. Speke, that was his way.

This was good though. He felt better, knowing it was about to happen.

Tom cut the engine, let the dive boat drift. They could see lights on Sealife Key from here. Just a few lights, no signs of activity, and the silence hit them both the same way—it was a bad sign, an indication that the dolphins had not, as they had hoped, been returned to the lagoon.

"I'll set an anchor," Tom said. "You have to move fast, just cut the line and go."

"But I'm coming ashore with you."

Tom took Sally by the shoulders and persuaded her to sit down on the swivel seat behind the wheel. "I need you here on the boat," he said. "I need you to call for help or rescue my ass if I get in trouble. Now doesn't that make sense?"

"I suppose so."

He went forward, set the small anchor. Straining

to listen as he crouched on the bow. All that came off Sealife Key was the sleepy whisper of palm fronds, sounding like distant rain. Not a damn thing happening in there, and no boats visible at the dock. From here the little island had the air of a place deserted, left behind in haste.

When he came back into the cabin Sally was perched on the swivel seat where he'd left her. He said, "Help me tank up?"

Tom didn't need help getting on his tank or his weight belt, he could do that in his sleep or blindfolded, but he wanted her hands on him, a reminder that she was still there—it was disturbing how distant she seemed, as if a fundamental part of her was out there somewhere, with her dolphins.

"I'll take a flare gun," he said. "You see it go off, get on the radio and then bring the boat in close to shore, if you think it's safe."

Despite Sally's obvious distraction, when Tom was ready to tip back, enter the water, she touched his face and said, "What are you going to do, babe?"

He took the respirator from his mouth. "I wish I knew."

"This is crazy," she said.

"If there's anyone left behind, I'll get him to talk. I can be very persuasive."

"Babe? Be careful."

He didn't let himself think about the sharks until he was in the water, kicking away from the boat. Funny, the tricks you played in your head. Think too much about those sharks, the way they hunted together, and getting into the water would be like jumping from a plane without a parachute. What were the chances, though, that the maxis would be back here, the very place they'd fled from?

Nah, they were miles away. *Miles.*

He kicked harder, his powerful legs flexing the big power fins. Keeping just under the surface, making a near-invisible approach to the islands. Just the bubbles to give him away, and bubbles were almost impossible to spot on a moonless night. Clutching an old sling-style spear gun in his right hand and thinking how much good could it do, the whole pack came after him?

Dark as hell, even a foot or two under the surface, so he had to come up a few times to get a sighting on the Sealife lights. Through the blurred faceplate he could just make out the row of small cabins, a couple of lights left on; the place had the look of a party long over, but he hoped he was wrong about that.

Tom had dropped back under for the last hundred feet or so, powering his way through water no more than waist-high, when something hit his left foot hard.

A bang of something alive, something with razor-sharp teeth that tore loose the fin strap and cut open the back of his ankle.

Flooded with a white, blinding panic, he reacted stupidly, standing up in the shallows. Gasping for breath as he exploded from the water. Heart trip-hammering, waving his puny spear gun.

Was that a glistening dark fin cutting up through the water? Were the maxis there, ready to strike from all sides?

Nothing touched him.

He staggered out of the water backwards—the imagined mako fin was just a wavelet produced by his own panic. Thinking: a full-sized shark would have taken, at the very least, his whole foot.

So what had hit him?

Tom collapsed on the shore, gulping air—his heart was still beating wildly—and he gingerly removed the damaged fin, checked out his ankle. A small, scalpel-sharp gouge that had opened the flesh almost to the bone, it was just starting to hurt. Must have disturbed a sleeping barracuda; a 'cuda had teeth about that size and would sometimes strike if frightened or suddenly disturbed in murky water.

Years of night diving and he'd never been bitten or injured, so why did this have to happen now? Had he brought it upon himself somehow?

With trembling fingers he tore a sleeve from his wet T-shirt, tied it around his foot. Bleeding like a stuck pig here, and to make it worse he was exposed in a circle of light spilling from one of the cottages. Why not just come ashore with a foghorn, announce his arrival?

Get it together, Thomas J. Hart. Don't screw this up, not with Sally waiting on the boat, trusting you to make things right.

He unhooked his weight belt, slipped out of his tank harness, and stood up. Shaky, his knees strangely numb and weak. The aftereffects of the adrenaline that had surged through his body when the 'cuda bit him. He'd be fine in a few minutes, once he caught his breath, brought his heartbeat under control.

No time, do it now.

Working quickly, keeping a nervous eye on the blank windows of the nearest cottage, he picked up his dive gear, piled it neatly in a cluster of palm trees.

There. First step done. So what was the next step?

Check the place out. Find a Sealife employee, make him talk. Make *her* talk. Make *somebody* talk.

He scanned the dock area. Day before yesterday there had been all kinds of activity there, a couple of boats being rigged. A big trawler and a hot chase boat. Nothing there now, the dock was deserted.

He crept up to the lighted cottage, crouched to one side of the window, and peered in. Wicker furniture, an overhead fan, an old brass bed, neatly made. All the light coming from a single, paper-shaded lamp. The normalcy of the cottage interior calmed him, he was able to breath normally. These were just people here and he knew how to handle people, in most situations, so why get himself worked up over this? Just do it, make himself known.

Having arrived at that simple decision, his heart seemed to slow to something like a reasonable rate. He got up from his peeper's crouch and limped to the cottage door, not bothering to muffle his approach. The inner door was open and the screen door had been latched from the outside.

That's right, Sherlock, Tom told himself, nobody home.

He unlatched the screen door, stepped inside. Decided immediately that this was a woman's place, the way it had been arranged. Not just the neatness, but the scent and tone of the interior. His supposition was confirmed when he entered the tiny bathroom—cosmetics and hair things and a pink plastic comb. He caught a glimpse of himself in the sink mirror and damn near scared himself again—God, he'd hate to come upon himself on a dark night, looking like that. Wet and mean and massive, a killer or at the very least a rapist invading a woman's bedroom.

Scary. That was good, he would use it. *Be* scary if that's what it took.

Tom found rolls of gauze and adhesive tape and made a neat job of taping up his ankle wound. Might need a stitch or two to make it heal correctly, but he'd worry about that later.

As he left the cottage he eased the screen door closed. No need to be *too* loud about this.

But stealth did not, he soon discovered, matter. None of the cottages was occupied. The residential area of the island was deserted.

He took a deep breath, steeling himself for he

knew not what, and headed for the other set of lights he'd seen from the water. The cluster of low, interconnected buildings not far from the lagoon.

What looked, he recalled from his daylight visit, like a science building or a laboratory.

Stare into the dark for long enough and you will start to see things. The mind, confronted with nothingness, begins to manufacture images. Sally knew this, but she couldn't help it, she kept staring through the binoculars, straining her eyes as she scanned the dimly illuminated shoreline. Thought for just an instant that she saw a figure moving resolutely through the palm trees.

Could that be Tom?

No, he wouldn't just walk through an open area like that, letting himself be seen. Must have been a shadow, a flicker of hanging plam fronds, and her mind had supplied the rest.

This was useless, trying to see. Sally put down the binoculars, closed her eyes, and concentrated on listening. Picked up, from miles away, the low insect buzz of boat engines. The reef. She didn't want to think about that, the senseless slaughter going on out there. She wanted to hear Lois slipping through the water, announcing herself with that characteristic tail slap. Or Clark, coming up beside the familiar dive boat with a freshly caught fish in his mouth.

Impossible hopes. If the dolphins had been taken, for whatever purpose, it was unlikely they would be released. She knew this. Her initial reaction—to charge ahead, to do *something*—had given way to a feeling of numbness.

It was too late. Tom was in there risking arrest, at the very least, and it was all for nothing. The dolphins were gone forever, she had to try and get used to the idea, painful as it was.

What was that?

A series of small, quick splashes. Coming from hundreds of yards away, out there in the bay. No chance of seeing, you just had to listen.

There it was again, a shivery wet sound, flip-flip-flip. Closer this time.

Coming this way.

Sally went to the lazarette and took out the rifle. Tom always called it "the carbine" and she didn't even know what that meant, she'd fired the thing only a few times when he'd first bought it, a little target shooting so she'd know how to use it. They'd been concerned about having their boat hijacked or stolen for the drug trade; there'd been a rash of hijackings at one time, fewer in recent years.

Now here she was in the dark with a gun in her hands, all because of a few slapping noises. What the hell was wrong with her?

She kept hold of the rifle, though, remembering now that you had to click off the safety—that lever there you used to eject a spent shell, get to the next. You're no Annie Oakley, girl, but you can make do in a pinch; just try not to shoot yourself in the foot.

The noise of wet splashing increased, multiplied, until it was like heavy rain striking the water: spat-spat-spat-spat-spat. Sally crouched, duck-walked to the stern of the dive boat, lifted her eyes above the level of the transom.

Something out there making the water ripple and splash. Little vapor trails of white froth where things were moving very rapidly, throwing up a fine mist of spray that looked like a thin layer of fog upon the water.

What the hell was going on out there?

All at once silvery *things* emerged, slipping quickly back under, and Sally, her hands slick with nervous sweat, almost laughed out loud. It was fish. Fish running. Thousands of fish thick in the water and swarming, making a spattering noise as they neared the surface.

Not swarming, she realized, watching the silvery tails break the surface. Running. Fleeing for their lives. Now a swarm of larger fish broke the surface—maybe amberjack, it was hard to tell. A couple of them thumped wetly against the side of the boat, sounded like birds hitting a windowpane.

The splashing became intense as the fish surged through the bay, creating small waves that lapped against the boat. Waves of panicked, fleeing fish, trying to get airborne in their fear.

Something was chasing them, inducing terror, Sally decided. Something large.

4

The Signature of Fear

THE US ARE feeding. The fear is still there—they are aware of the constant prop whir from the distant reef—but the hunger is stronger than any other instinct now.

The maxis have not as yet found large prey in these relatively shallow waters. What they do find is an immense school of amberjack chasing smaller baitfish. The maxis drive into the amberjacks, twisting and turning, snatching a jack or two with each snap of their jaws.

Gulping hungrily. The need for food is like heat, burning in the blood. *Feed, feed.* The maxis coordinate the attack with their song, a song that keeps each of the Us in position, cutting away at the panicked swarm of amberjacks. Driving the jacks into water so shallow there can be no escape. Wave upon wave of fleeing jack, a wall of quivering flesh.

Cutting, snatching, gulping.

Feed the heat. Eat the fear.

The Us shoot forward, pursuing the school of amberjacks, dimly aware that they are entering familiar territory.

The truth was, Robby Mendez felt like hell. He denied it to the others, made light of the wounded arm, but the shock of it was making him dizzy with pain. In one savage bite, the animal had torn at muscle and nerve. Serious damage in there, even if he *could* wiggle his fingers.

Mendez, an marine animal trainer for all of his adult life, found it impossible to hate the dolphin. His own casual bravado was at fault: after months of working with the maxis he'd forgotten that the male dolphin was similarly aggressive when threatened, that its teeth, though small, could do terrible damage.

Fortunately his duties on the trawler were limited. Aside from monitoring the radio, all he had to do was see that the male was released when Speke gave the order. Either the dolphin would respond as anticipated or it would not—whatever happened, it was no longer his responsibility. This was Dr. Speke's show. If it worked, he got the credit; and if it failed, Sealife would have no choice but to go public, destroy the things in broad daylight, by whatever means was necessary, even if it meant massive depth-charge attacks from military aircraft.

Personally, Mendez didn't give a damn. He was up to here with Vernon Speke and the maxi project. When this ugly business was concluded, he intended to look around, find another position. Put out the word, get into some nice, safe civilian program teaching dolphin to jump through hoops or whatever. He'd take a cut in pay, but so what. Trade the big paycheck for peace of mind, not to mention personal safety.

These thoughts kept running through his head like

a fever-pain as the radio speaker crackled with Lucy Savrin's voice: *"We have signature. We have signature."*

Signature. She meant the computer program that tracked and identified the maxis, turning their echo location noises into color bars on the screen. Once the sonar gear focused on the maxi "signature," their direction and distance could be extrapolated. With two boats picking up the signature, the maxis' precise location could be accurately determined, as had been demonstrated the night before last, when that sudden unlucky squall had ruined their opportunity to net the creatures.

"We have signature, too," Mendez replied, pressing the microphone button with his good hand. From his position in the wheelhouse he could see the glowing screen, the young technician giving him a thumbs-up sign. "It appears to be a strong signal," Mendez said, speaking carefully because he still felt light-headed. "The directional readouts keep breaking up," he added. "The source appears to be somewhere southwest of here."

"Confirm on that, Robby. Very strong signal here. They're moving real quick out there, changing direction. We show the source in a northwest quadrant."

You could hear the tension in Lucy's voice even through the static. A glance at the charts showed why. Even with the directional readouts breaking up it was obvious that the maxis were on the Gulf side of the Keys, within a few square miles of the Sealife lagoon.

Exactly as Speke had anticipated, working on the assumption that in times of stress—the noise of numerous pursuit boats on the reef—the maxis would gravitate to the familiar shallow bay territory where they'd been born and nurtured.

All that remained was to nail down their location and then position the trawler for the male dolphin's release. Mendez was starting to believe that the scheme might actually work as planned.

Now Speke's voice was booming over the radio: *"We'll stay in this position, Robby. You move a half mile or so to the southwest. Keep it at slow speed, the less prop noise the better."* There was a pause, then a crackle of static as Speke came back on. *"How's the arm, partner? Any better?"*

Mendez smiled grimly to himself and replied, "I'll live."

He meant it, too. He intended to stay right there in the wheelhouse once the male was released. Why take chances?

Tom expected to find the doors locked. He was fully prepared to break in, bust the glass with the butt of his flare gun if need be. No problem, though. Turn the handle and he was in like Flynn. The cool air of the laboratory complex made him shiver as the flop-sweat evaporated.

It was quiet in here, *too* quiet. Tom had expected to find, at the very least, a security guard in place. Maybe a research assistant or two who might, with a little persuasion, tell him where the dolphins had been taken and for what purpose.

What he found was an empty reception desk, a pale cinder-block corridor leading into the building. Somebody had forgotten to turn out the lights, or maybe they were routinely left on all night, the low-watt fluorescent tubes giving off, if you listened real hard, a barely audible hum. The whole place had the air of a building exited in haste.

His bare feet made squeaky noises on the linoleum floor. Tom tried to recall if he'd actually seen any armed security guards the last time he visited Sealife Key. No images came to mind, but then security types tended to blend in, right? Wasn't that the idea? And here he was looking damp and demented and carrying a weapon—the flare pistol. A sensible guard might shoot first, take his chances with Monroe County law, which tended to favor the use of lethal force against obvious intruders.

The corridor made a ninety-degree turn to the left, ended with a steel-jacketed door. This one is *sure* to be locked, Tom told himself, but the thumb-latch clicked down when he tried it and the door opened easily and silently on well-oiled hinges.

Bubbling water. That was the first thing he heard. And then under that the drone of an electric motor or compressor, somewhere out of sight.

The lab itself seemed vaguely familiar. Reminded him, he decided, of the marine biology lab where Sally had been assigned when they first met. Shiny and neat and solid, with a lot of cool Formica surfaces. While some of the equipment was familiar to him—various microscopes, sterilizing autoclaves, a centrifuge—other, more high-tech stuff was a puzzle. They hadn't been messing with genetics when Sally was at Woods Hole. It was amazing how much had changed in those relatively few years; even a former English major could appreciate the rapid pace of scientific innovation.

The bubbling noise came from a row of thick-glassed aquarium tanks. No specimens in the tanks, at least none that he could see. The liquid being circulated by the pumps had a slightly milky look and Tom decided that it was not, as he'd first assumed, salt water. Some other, richer solution, perhaps? Had *Isurus maximus* been bred in those tanks, the genetically altered embryos nurtured right here in the lab?

Tom went to the computer console, checked out the terminals. Although he used a word processor and understood a little basic programing, this stuff was beyond him—or so he thought until he spotted the Mac and mousepad nestled in among the more exotic terminals.

A Mac he could handle; in fact this particular model was similar to the one he used at home. Not that he expected to find a file marked "Dolphin Abduction," with their location neatly entered into the memory. Still, it was worth a quick look. He reached behind the Mac, turned it on, and waited as it booted itself up. The monitor came on and the screen filled with the icons that represented various files and software stored on the internal hard disk.

One of the icons was labeled "Chesty's Notes." "Chesty," wasn't that what Mendez had called Dr. Chester Higgs when he came to take him away? Using the mouse, Tom clicked the icon and watched the screen images dissolve and re-form as the "Chesty's Notes" file was dredged up from the hard disk memory.

The on-screen files were listed by date and time, as entered. Tom clicked one at random, brought up a profusion of jottings, mostly in scientific shorthand jargon, *chain nucleotides undamaged in postinfusion process* and so on, and then one phrase leaped out and claimed his attention: *Tursiops files deleted, copied to diskette*.

Tursiops was the genus name for the bottlenose dolphin.

Tom found the plastic box of diskettes stored on a shelf just above the computer. Maybe a hundred or so diskettes in more or less alphabetical order. He found one labeled "Tursiops, Xenografting Procedures," slipped the diskette into the Mac, and clicked the new icon as it appeared on the screen. The *Tursiops* files were listed in order of time and date entered, sometimes with a few words or phrases to describe the entry. Again a particular entry jumped out: *Dolphin L., recovery from surgery*.

Dolphin L.? He clicked the file, waited impatiently

as it was extracted from the memory, and then his impatience was replaced by a cold, sinking sensation that spread through his belly as he scanned Dr. Higgs's notes:

. . . *dolphin L., a mature female, successfully sedated. Ovarian probe used to remove several eggs. Emerged from sedation after approx. two hours, transferred to care of R. Mendez, who appears satisfied that heart and respiration are normal . . . eggs to be frozen for eventual extraction of genetic material [see xenograft files].*

The xenograft files were stored on a separate diskette. Tom booted it up, went directly to the index, looking for references to "Dolphin L." Found instead numerous references to "*Tursiops*, central nervous system" and "*Tursiops*, echo location ability," and finally, "*Tursiops*, xenografting procedures." He called up *that* file and found that his hands felt almost too weak to manipulate the mouse.

. . . *isolation of Tursiops echo location genes complete. Embedding procedure in the Isurus maximus embryo appears successful—actual success can't be quantified or tested until new species reaches maturity. Cloning should produce twelve identical embryos for further study, pending freezer storage.*

Tom found himself standing, unaware that he had leaped up. It was incredible, but it made perfect sense. The "improved" makos had been implanted with genetic material from "Dolphin L."—that had to be Lois, who bore a surgical scar near her reproductive organs—and the new genetic coding had resulted in a dolphin level of intelligence, as well as a dolphin-style echo location system, something no other shark possessed.

If the maxis, like dolphins, could locate prey by echo location, might they not also communicate with each other using the same echo sounds, as dolphins did? That would explain the eerie "wolf pack" behavior, their tendency to hunt together and to protect each other.

The maxis were not just as intelligent as dolphin, they were *part* dolphin. Lois was, on the genetic level, a kind of mother to these beasts. Was *that* why she had been kidnapped, to be used as a donor again if the maxis were destroyed?

It was a horrifying thought, but if it was true, then Lois was undoubtedly being kept alive. As for Clark, maybe the male just had the bad luck to be around when the abduction took place.

Tom had turned off the computer and was headed for the door when a particular phrase stopped him: . . . *pending freezer storage.*

According to Dr. Higgs's notes, he'd made twelve clones of the original embryo and stored them, frozen, for further study. There were six *Isurus maximus* out there right now; did that mean another six remained in a freezer somewhere?

The hum of a compressor, he'd noticed that right off. A freezer unit required a compressor. And once he was actually looking for it, the door to the walk-in freezer was fairly obvious.

Tom opened the freezer door.

On the floor, his head bent backwards and his open eyes glazed with a layer of white frost, was the body of the man who had come to warn them, Dr. Chester Higgs.

5

Maxi Logic

ROBBY MENDEZ WATCHED from the wheelhouse as the cage containing the male was lowered into the water alongside the trawler. To release him, all they had to do was pull on the cable that tripped the spring-loaded door latch.

"Just make sure there's enough clearance so it can breathe," Mendez instructed the crew. "It drowns, we're *all* in trouble."

"It's making a hell of a racket," a mate reported.

"Let him," Mendez said. "That's the idea."

Mendez sat down by the helm, weary and unsteady. He closed his eyes for a few moments and tried to concentrate on not feeling the pain. He had the portable radio unit clipped to his belt, the gain up high, awaiting orders from Dr. Speke, ready to release the goddamn dolphin and get done with this wretched business.

What the dolphin would do, and Mendez was *almost* sure of this, the male would streak for the female in distress. A normal enough reaction, particularly for *this* male. The maxis—whose echo location signature was almost identical to the female's "song"—would pick up on the flurry of communication between the two mammals.

How the sharks would respond was anybody's guess. Dr. Speke was convinced the maxis would seek out the female, home in on her voice, follow *that* voice and the chattering male right back into the lagoon. Mendez wasn't so sure—would natural curiosity overcome their apparent fear of the lagoon? And how would they react when they discovered that the dolphins who shared their voice were a different species?

All very interesting, but he was too exhausted to really give a damn about the outcome. And in a way it didn't matter, because as soon as the maxis entered the lagoon Speke was going to detonate the explosives.

Concluding, as he liked to say, this particular phase of the experiment. Like this disaster had somehow been anticipated by the brilliant Dr. Speke, the lying son of a bitch.

Mendez settled back in his seat, keeping an eye on the computer monitor. The sonar color bars were looking solid and the directional readouts were beginning to steady. The maxis were not that far away, at most a few miles from the lagoon.

"Come on, Vern," Mendez said aloud. "Let's get this over with."

The bruised and exhausted female did not at first believe her senses. Having convinced herself that the male was dead, she did not trust the song she was hearing, distinctive and clear, although coming from a considerable distance. Was it some other free-swimming dolphin whose song resembled the male's? Was she already drowning, was this part of her death-dream?

The female gathered her strength and called out.

After a slight interval the male answered her.

The female called again, and he answered again, and the answer filled her with joy, and hope. She soared to the top of her cage and shouted her joy into the open air, rattling the cage with newly revived strength.

The male was alive, the male was alive, the male was alive.

A reason to live.

The swarms of fleeing baitfish had come through in waves, sometimes followed by a few leaping amberjack, sometimes not. Whatever was chasing them out there, it was keeping its distance from the boat, from the lagoon area. Might be the maxi, might be some other predator, she had no way of knowing.

Sally crouched in the cockpit of the dive boat, Tom's rifle slick and warm in her hands, trying to concentrate on any sounds from the island. Keeping an eye on the dark sky overhead, in case Tom fired off his flare gun. Getting on toward three in the morning; in a couple more hours dawn would break, and they'd have to be gone from this place, dolphins or no dolphins.

Now that she'd had time to soberly review the situation, she had come to the firm conclusion that their expedition to Sealife Key was a wasted effort. Two ordinary people up against a well-financed Defense Department contractor? Forget it. Tom was in there doing God knows what, risking prosecution and maybe even his life because his wife, who should have known better, had allowed herself to become emotionally and irrationally attached to a couple of animals.

Animals.

Not, as she had allowed herself to feel, children. Certainly not *her* children. Pet owners succumbed to the same emotional bond, you saw it all the time, and she for sure hadn't wanted to treat the dolphins as pets; no creatures with that much intelligence should ever be thought of as pets.

Sally couldn't help but think, there in the dark with an alien-feeling weapon in her hands, that if she had put more effort into releasing the two dolphins, into helping them become free swimmers, they wouldn't be in the hands of the Sealife people right now. Allowing them to stay in the canal, keeping them dependent on humans, had made them vulnerable to the very people who had abused them in the first place.

Her fault. Bad enough that the dolphins had been put in jeopardy. Much worse that she'd allowed, hell, *encouraged* Tom to put himself at risk. Get him back aboard, they'd go home where they belonged and fight Sealife in the courts, by whatever legal means was available.

The first shrill chattering brought her head up. Hope crashed back into her with such unexpected intensity that her first response was fear. Could this be real?

Again she heard the high-pitched chatter and squeak and she knew, somewhere deep in the core of her being, that Lois was alive.

Alive and nearby.

Sally couldn't help it, she stood up and shouted: "Lois! Lois!"

Now the chattering was directed back to her, a response. Lois knew she was here.

The lagoon, dark and deserted as it now appeared, was *not* empty. Sally, heart beating wildly, put the rifle back in the lazarette and with trembling hands started the dive-boat engine.

So far, so good. Tom always left a boat knife

hanging from a hook near the helm. She slipped it off the hook and went around to the bow to cut the anchor line—no way she could raise it by herself without anyone to bring the boat forward—and noticed that the water was quiet for the moment. No leaping baitfish being chased by God knows what—that had to be a good sign, right? Maybe whatever it was had been frightened away by the noise of the diesel. She didn't give a damn about the maxis now, all that mattered were the dolphins.

Sally reached under the taut anchor line, severed it with the blade. No time to rig a buoy, mark the spot. Not with Lois trapped in that damn lagoon and Tom prowling the beach.

With the boat knife between her teeth, Sally scampered up the ladder to the conning tower. She would steer the boat from here—high up, the visibility was that much better. That's how Tom did it, navigating unknown waters with great caution, and he'd never put *Wild Child* aground, not once in the eight years they'd owned the boat.

All you have to do, she told herself, is think like Tom. Think like Tom. Think like Tom. That was the mantra, that was the way.

Your mind is racing, she warned herself. Slow down, take a breath. She forced herself to do that, take a few moments to let her heartbeat return to something like normal before she put the engine in gear and steered for the narrow entrance to the lagoon.

She took a deep breath, eased it out. Slipped the lever forward, engaging forward gear. Now easy, easy on the throttle.

The dive boat gathered speed and began to swing around until the bow pointed in the general direction of the lagoon. There were channel markers out there somewhere if only she could find them. She *had* to find them. Stray from the channel and she'd risk putting a hole in *Wild Child*.

Sink the boat and they'd all be in *real* trouble.

Speke stroked the computer screen with his index finger, the color bars reflecting on his gaunt face. Trick of the light made it seem like you could see the skull beneath the skin. He needed a shower. He smelled unclean.

Lucy stood behind him, hanging on to a strap because the chase boat was rocking now, ever so slightly. Not from the wind; the air was so still it was eerie. You didn't want to think too much about where the ripple in the water was coming from. Creatures that strong and powerful, they could make themselves felt from a distance of several miles.

He said, "Look. See that? They seem to be hesitating, all of a sudden. Maybe they're finally picking up on the female. That's her bar right there, see how it almost matches the maxi signature?"

Lucy said, "Yes, I see."

"Remarkable, huh?" He stroked a long thin finger across the screen, a caress. His voice was intimate, a lover's croon. "Run to Mommy, boys. Come on. Do it."

He tapped the screen, waited. The directional readouts shifted slightly, the luminous digits ticking over.

"Tell Robby to go ahead and release the male," he said. "It's now or never."

Lucy reached for the radio unit and gave the order. There was a thirty-second interval before Mendez acknowledged: *"Roger that. He's out, took off like a rocket."*

Speke entwined his fingers, propped his chin on his hands, and stared at the readouts. If the computer was correctly interpreting the sonar data, the maxis did not seem to be reacting.

"Maybe the male is just running away," Lucy said. "Out to sea."

Speke snapped, "Not a chance. He'll run to her. I guarantee it."

"I'm sure you're right," Lucy said, picking up on the brittle edge to his voice. This was a time to just go along, agree with anything the boss said.

Tap, tap. That skinny finger touching the luminous screen again, it was starting to look obscene. "They hear him," he said. "See? They're shifting, confused. He's coming right at them now, heading for the female, you can bet your sweet little ass on that."

He turned from the screen, leered at her. Probably intended it to be a charming smile, she decided. The man just didn't have a clue.

The readouts were starting to click over.

"I think they're moving," she said.

Speke's head snapped back to the screen. "Oh, yes," he said. "Look at that. They're fanning out. They don't know *what* to make of this."

"Is that good?"

"Hell, yes. We need them confused. We need to have them react on instinct. None of that cunning maxi logic, thank you very much."

He stood up from the computer console, moved to the helm. "We'll follow them in," he said. "Believe me, we don't want to miss this little reunion."

The Us scatter, confused by this new singing. A voice like their own but inexplicably different. And now *two* voices, two songs coming from opposite directions, converging.

Can there be more of the Us? More than the Six Who Are Beautiful?

The concept is new, wonderful, and frightening.

It makes the Us hungry. *Everything* makes them hungry.

6

The Great Meltdown

TOM STOOD OVER the body for what seemed like a long time. His mind ticking over, trying to grasp what had happened here. Had Dr. Higgs slipped, fallen accidently? Or had he been struck from behind while messing with the frozen embryos?

They're coming, Higgs had warned them. *They're coming*.

However it had happened, whatever had come for him, he was sure as hell dead. It required only one touch on the frozen flesh to be absolutely certain of that.

You were supposed to call the cops in a situation like this. Get on the horn to the sheriff, wait here and follow the cop instructions. Could be hours, with the distinct possibility that an eager deputy might try to detain him even longer.

No time for that. Not with Sally waiting for him, anchored offshore. And how would he explain his presence here? *Well, Mr. Deputy, I was*

*trespassing, entering the staff housing and the lab, and
breaking into the computer system, and I just happened
to open the freezer door and* voilà, *discovered a human
Popsicle.*

Tom couldn't help it, he giggled. Nerves, he told
himself. No wonder cops always joked around at a
murder scene, relieving the tension. Violent death
was simply too horrifying to comprehend all at once.
You had to absorb the enormity of it a little bit at a
time.

Fine, he thought, but you still have to do *something.* What? Drag the body from the walk-in freezer?
Bad idea, don't touch a thing here, leave it exactly
as it is for the proper authorities.

His eyes drifted up to the shelves above the body.
Racks of sealed glass tubes, all with neat little num-
bered labels. Might be able to figure out what was
what, cull out the remaining maxi embryos if he
went back into the computer system, but that
seemed crazy now, too lengthy a process.

The solution he came up with was simple and took
less than a minute to execute. He found the circuit
breaker for the freezer unit and snapped it off. The
compressor cut out instantly.

Let the whole thing thaw in the tropical heat.

And now get the hell out of here, Tommy boy,
before your luck runs out.

He left the freezer door open, to speed up the
thawing process, and exited the room. Jogged down
the empty corridor, back to the reception desk. No
doubt his fingerprints were everywhere, but he decided that trying to wipe every surface he'd touched
would make matters worse, possibly obscure important evidence if it turned out that Higgs was mur-
dered. He'd just have to take his chances, confess
to his presence in the lab if that seemed like the right
thing to do.

* * *

When Tom came out of the lab door the first thing he noticed was the familiar sound of a diesel engine. That was *Wild Child*, he'd know her anywhere.

Sally must be coming in. But he hadn't fired the flare gun, so why was she doing that? Was the Sea-life fleet returning, or had she panicked?

Easy, he told himself. Sally is not the panic type. You're the one who almost panicked in there, freaked out at the sight of dead eyes all frosty from the artificial cold.

Sally was bringing the boat in, therefore she must have a good reason. He couldn't wait to tell her about the maxis, their ability to communicate like dolphin, possibly *with* dolphin. Tell her about Higgs, too, and the great meltdown.

Tom ran for the waterfront, cursing his own stupidity at not bringing along sandals or shoes. Running barefoot on this damn gravel, all two hundred pounds of him coming down hard on his tender feet.

It was a relief to get to the wooden dock—better splinters than the sharp points of stone underfoot—and he looked out to the Basin, expecting to see *Wild Child* ghosting in. He could hear the diesel getting closer, but it wasn't there; the basin area was empty.

So where the hell *was* the boat? Were his ears playing tricks? He spun around, eyes searching the darkness, and then spotted the dive boat's conning tower gliding in on the other side of the lagoon.

Sally was bringing *Wild Child* into the lagoon, not the more easily accessible docks in the basin. Well, *shit*. Why the hell do that? Did she know how narrow that channel entrance was? Debris from the carved-out lagoon dumped on either side, just below water level? Did she *know* that?

He ran back along the docks, heading for the lagoon, wanting to shout a warning but not quite daring to make himself heard. He didn't know what was going on, maybe she was being pursued, for all he knew she had a good reason for choosing the lagoon, but God in heaven, she was bringing it in without lights. No way she could pick up those buoys without a spotlight.

A small path curved along the limestone breakwater that enclosed the lagoon. Small dock and a couple of floats out there. He put it in high gear, could see the dive boat clearly now, approaching the entrance. At least she was coming in real slow, feeling her way.

Burning in his chest. Blood pounding in his temples. Hell of a stress test, doc, got the old heart maxed out. Pedal to the metal time. Don't think about it, just run, let your feet find their way over the rocks.

Tom was going so fast he very nearly ran off the end of the breakwater. Put on the brakes, skidded on the slick limestone, smooth and chalky underfoot. Waving his arms and leaping up and down. The dive boat was very close now, coming out quite straight into the channel entrance, and he thought he could make out a slim figure up there in the conning tower.

Screw it, he thought, time to get loud. Get her attention, tell her to back it out, come in straighter, that channel was barely wide enough for a boat the size of *Wild Child*.

He was shouting her name when the dive boat touched bottom. Nothing very dramatic, just a slight hesitation, a shuddering in the hull, but Tom knew in that instant the boat had gone aground.

The pitch of the diesels changed abruptly. Sally was putting it in reverse now, backing off, the hull slipping off whatever it had touched down below.

He shouted her name again and this time she heard him. He saw her stand up in the conning tower, wave her arms, acknowledging him. ''This way!'' he bellowed. ''Keep to the starboard side of the buoys!''

She backed out, repositioned herself, and came in hugging the buoy line. Slow and easy, with just enough forward momentum for steering.

Tom got down on the end of the breakwater, leaped aboard as the boat glided by, into the lagoon. Up top, Sally cut the engine. They drifted in, water leaping against the side of the hull, and Sally scrambled down the ladder to meet him.

''Lois,'' she said. He could see her eyes shining in the dark, teary with emotion. ''She's in here. I heard her.''

''Sally, I don't think they'd just—''

''Listen, Tom!'' She grabbed him, pulled him close, touched a finger to his lips.

He listened. And heard the squeak and chatter of a dolphin, the splashing of flukes.

''Okay,'' he said. ''Time to stop sneaking around.''

He climbed up to the helm, switched on the spotlight. A thousand watts of candlepower sweeping the lagoon. Sally, standing on the bow, spotted the pontoons.

''Over there. Check it out.''

Tom nailed it with the spot, and they could both see the dolphin raising her beak through the bars of the floating cage.

The male was so intent on reaching the female that he did not at first notice any of the echo shapes directly in his path. The male's way of ''seeing'' by echo location was, like that of all dolphins, instinctive, automatic. He could, if he chose, focus in on a specific shape, just as the visual eye might choose to focus on a particular object.

Focusing told him the shapes were large and alive.

Shark shapes, swimming in that distinctive, whip-sawing shark pattern.

The male had no fear of sharks. He could outswim any shark in the sea, flee from them if necessary, or turn inside their swimming radius and pierce their vulnerable abdomens with his bony beak. Among dolphins, only the sick or the newborn were vulnerable to shark attack. Sharks understood this, and feared healthy, full-grown dolphins.

The focusing, however, brought with it a stunning surprise: *these shark were singing with the voices of dolphins.* The male dolphin didn't understand their song, but the tone was eerily similar to his own and to the female's. A strange, yet disturbingly familiar distortion of his own voice.

The male flicked his powerful tail flukes and changed direction. He would swim around these strange, singing intruders.

The shark shapes moved, cutting off the dolphin's angle on the lagoon. He veered back, reacting instantly, and a moment later the sharks responded.

The shark shapes were blocking him from the female. This, to the male, was intolerable.

He swam straight for them.

Sally, crouching on the bow, slipped a line through the pontoons and cleated it. Keep the dive boat close to the cage while Tom checked it out. He was in the water right now, skin-diving without scuba gear. You could see him down there, one hand on the cage, the other holding the submersible flashlight. The beams of light flickered through the bars as Lois continued to splash and call out. You couldn't tell if she was happy to see them or frightened half out of her mind. Maybe both.

Even in the dark you could see where Lois had been smashing herself against the enclosure, fresh gouges and marks in her sleek outer skin. The cage

wasn't even big enough for her to turn around in—
what kind of humans were these, who would treat
a fellow creature like this? Sally felt her fear and
anxiety congeal into cold anger. She hated the men
who'd done this.

A splash as Tom surfaced, filled his lungs with air.
''Padlocked!'' he gasped. He kicked around the the
stern, came up the dive ladder.

Sally met him in the cockpit, where he was already pawing through the toolbox. ''What have they
done with Clark?'' she asked.

''No idea. We'll need a hacksaw. Padlocks are
case-hardened steel. A bitch to cut. *Shit!*'' He'd cut
his thumb on a chisel, then, triumphant, held up a
hacksaw.

''I better do it,'' Sally said. She was already stripping off her shorts. ''Look, you're exhausted. I can
handle a hacksaw. You keep a lookout.''

Tom shook his head. He had that stubborn, don't-
mess-with-me look he got sometimes. ''The sharks
can hear her,'' he said.

''What?''

He told her, as briefly as he could, about the xenograft files, the gene splicing of dolphin and mako,
and Lois's role in the procedure. Decided, for the
moment, to leave out the part about finding Dr.
Higgs in the freezer. That, like the dead man himself, could wait until later.

As he talked, Sally kept shaking her head, but in
a crazy way it all made sense.

''That's how they communicate,'' he said. ''And
if they can do that, they can pick up on dolphin
noises, too. I assumed Sealife snatched Lois for more
research, but look at this setup, a cage moored in an
open lagoon. That's not research.''

''What is it, then?''

''Hell, they're using her as bait, Sal. Like a staked
goat.''

Sally reacted by snatching a scuba tank from the rack. She had it flipped up and over and in place on her back almost before Tom could rise from his knees.

He said, "Damn it, no."

"What, a shark wouldn't attack you?"

Now he was right up on her, hooking a bloody finger through the tank strap. "How about this? You can reach the padlock from the top of the cage. You don't have to dive."

"Why didn't you say so?"

"Didn't give me a chance, Sal. Let's work together on this. First thing, I'll crank up the engine—we already know these things are spooked by boat noises, maybe that'll be enough to keep 'em out."

"Sure," Sally said. "Fire up the diesel, why not?"

"Okay. I'll take care of the engine. You work on the padlock, I'll try to free the mooring chains. We get the cage free, we could tow it out of here."

"We could do that, yes." Sally said this over her shoulder, heading for the side of the bow with the hacksaw in hand. At the bow she dropped the tanks, lowered herself to the pontoons. Lois was bumping at the bars right under her feet.

Sally paused just long enough to reach into the cage, stroke the female's beak. "Take it easy, girl. We'll have you out of this thing in a jiffy."

The engine came on, a rumbling comfort. A man-sized splash followed. Sally looked below the cage and saw the beam of the submersible flashlight, Tom in scuba gear, heading for the mooring chains. Go for it, babe.

Sally gripped the hacksaw, reached into the water, and felt around until she found the padlock. Big son of a bitch, and heavy. She'd barely started sawing at it when she heard another splashing sound, this one sustained.

Looking up she saw a small geyser of water jetting

from the side of the dive boat. The bilge pump. She continued to saw at the padlock, keeping an eye on the stream of water. *Stop*, she willed it, *stop*. Could be rainwater shifting around, setting off the pump. But the jet of water continued to pour from the side of the hull. Minute after minute.

Wild Child was leaking.

The mooring chains were anchored on two massive blocks in about twenty feet of water, the deepest part of the lagoon. Big shackles that had been peened over so they wouldn't work loose. Tom set the flashlight on the mooring block, aimed it at the shackle, and set to work with a marlinspike. Prying with all his might. He thought the dolphin might actually be safer in the cage if they could only get it free of the chains and tow it out of the lagoon.

Let Sally do her thing. She was safe enough, hacking away up there. Take her forever to get through that padlock, though, and by then he'd have the cage free to travel. Get the hell out of here.

He set his heels against the mooring block and lifted with all his might, both hands gripping the marlinspike, trying to twist loose the shackle bolt. Heart pounding to beat the band, he could feel the blood pulsing in his ears. Air tasted rusty, but there was plenty of it, a full tank. Mask fogging with his exertion.

His foot slipped, kicked out, knocked the flashlight off the mooring block. Damn. He left the marlinspike where it was, jammed in the shackle, and went to fetch the flashlight.

The beam was pointing in the opposite direction now, picking up the area between mooring blocks. Picking up another, smaller mooring block, one he hadn't noticed before. There was a short chain rising from it.

What the hell?

Tom reached for the flashlight, lifted the beam along the smaller chain. There, suspended a yard or so above the bottom, was what appeared to be a buoyancy tank or buoy, a round metal sphere the size of a big beach ball.

He kicked over, playing the flashlight around and under the metal sphere. Saw the attached radio transponder and knew, finally, what he was looking at. Some sort of underwater mine or explosive device, moored right beneath the dolphin cage.

A bomb. *A goddamn bomb.*

He realized he was hyperventilating, sucking air at a dangerous rate. Forced himself to slow down. A panicked diver was a dead diver. Hart's first rule of survival: Maintain self-control. Second rule: Control your air supply, don't let it control you.

What to do. Surface and warn Sally? Sure, give it a try.

He popped up within a yard of where she was working, sawing feverishly at the padlock. Yanked the respirator from his mouth and said, "Bomb."

"Huh?"

"Explosive device right below us. We should leave. Sooner the better."

Sally gave him a look. Even in the dark you could see it in her eyes. That crazy stubborn streak. "You go," she said. "I can't leave, babe. Not without Lois. I just *can't*. I gave up on her once, I'm not going to do it again."

Tom nodded, mouthed the respirator, dropped back down. Option one was out, not really a surprise if you knew Sally. Leaving option two: If you can't get Sal away from the explosive, you'll have to get the explosive away from Sal.

Made perfect sense, you thought about it like that. Plus the shackle and chain were a hell of a lot smaller, therefore easier to free. So go ahead and do it.

Tom kicked over, retrieved the marlinspike, and set to work on the smaller shackle. Trying not to bump the sphere, never know what might set it off, although he was fairly confident that the radio transponder meant it could be detonated only by radio signal, like the explosive device used for underwater demolition.

Small comfort, really, when you thought about who might be in control of the detonator. He yanked on the shackle bolt, felt it give. Backed it off several turns and was preparing to release the shackle when he became aware that something was different.

The sound in the lagoon was all wrong. Too quiet. The dive-boat engine had stopped. Had Sally shut it down for some reason, or had it simply stalled? Except the diesel *never* stalled, it was reliable as hell.

No time to worry about it now. He had the shackle bolt loose. Twist it and the chain would come free and the sphere would rise, if he let it. Better idea, keep it down here, under his control. Bump hard against the bottom of the cage and it just might go off, radio detonator or no radio detonator.

Tom gripped the small chain just below the sphere and slipped the shackle off with his other hand. His weight slowed the ascent, but the sphere was still going to rise, no matter what he did.

He started kicking like mad, his strong legs powering the fins, pulling the explosive device along with him, away from the cage, away from the boat, away from Sally.

7

Fear Things

THE US HOLD themselves still, spread out at precise intervals, at the limit of where each of the Six can hear the heartbeat of the next, a heartbeat that echoes its own, is, indeed, part of the whole. Six hunting in perfect harmony.

An Other is approaching, closing rapidly. This Other sings very much like the Us, so much so that nothing in their experience tells them how to react. And yet the speed at which this Other approaches, the speed itself means Fear Thing, Danger Thing.

The Us know, by shaping the intruder with their song, that it is smaller than any of the Six. But the speed. The speed is—incomprehensible, therefore dangerous.

To make it more confusing, another, similar song comes from the distance behind them, in the opposite direction. This song, even more familiar, does not move; it remains stationary and is therefore not perceived as a threat.

The Other is coming, faster, faster.

The Us wait, their heartbeats quickening, their bodies alive to the sensation of pressure in the water, their nerves able to detect microscopic particles of blood or the scent of fear.

They hear it now. The sound of the Other moving through the water, the hiss of tail and fluke. The sound of speed. They hear also, at a range of thousands of yards, the Other's heartbeat. And this sound is different, alien, it is not the heartbeat of the Us.

The Us stir. They are uncertain, and yet this distinctive heartbeat racing at them has eliminated some of their confusion—the Other is not part of the Us, despite the familiarity of its song.

And any creature that is not part of the Us is an enemy.

The Us shiver, anticipating action, and each of them feels the shiver of the next. They are all quivering, eager to move, when suddenly the dolphin streaks from the darkness and shoots through them.

Gone in a heartbeat.

As one, the Us turn and follow.

Eat the Fear Thing, they sing. *Eat, eat, eat.*

Wade was being, to his way of thinking, a good little boy. Tagging along behind the chase boat and the trawler, barely making five knots as they all headed back toward Sealife Key. Don't spook the sharks by revving the engines. Don't *chase* the things.

Dr. Speke was right about that. Chasing the things was useless. What they had to do was corner the bastards and blow them to smithereens. That's what Speke *said* he was going to do, but Wade didn't trust the man. Not as far as he could spit into a hurricane. Too crafty and devious. Maybe all he wanted to do was trap the creatures in the precious little lagoon of his, try to control them somehow. Or let a couple survive, just to prove what a hot-shit scientist genius he was.

No way. Wade had already vetoed any possibility of survival. The fuckers were going to die; they were history, one way or another.

Meantime he steered like a good little boy, keeping his place in line. But his fingers kept reaching up to touch the lanyard that was looped around his neck. On the lanyard, poised like a fat, ugly medallion, was an armed Seal grenade.

All he had to do was yank it free, toss it overboard. Five seconds later it would detonate and the shock waves would kill anything underwater, within a hundred yards.

Dolphin, shark, human—Wade didn't give a damn, so long as the maxis died.

Tom's heart felt like an old steel drum. Beaten and hollow and as thin as a sea-worn shell. Booming inside him as he kicked, kicked, kicked. Swimming on the surface now, a one-armed backstroke as he held the chain, dragging the sphere of explosives along behind him. He'd spit out the respirator and was breathing deep, sucking in lungfuls of humid, mangrove-scented air, breathing so hard it hurt.

His head smacked into something hard. He gasped, swallowing a mouthful of seawater, and that made him panic for just a moment, so exhausted he was afraid he might lose it right here, just let himself sink under without bothering to mouth the respirator. He reached out, touched hard rubbery plastic. Shit, a buoy. He'd bumped into one of the channel buoys, a round plastic ball tethered to the bottom. He was outside the breakwater now, on the lee side of the lagoon. Far enough, goddamn it, far enough. *Had* to be far enough, he couldn't possibly swim another yard, towing this heavy son of a bitch.

He wrapped the chain around the buoy, pulled the links of the chain through and knotted it. Let the damn thing blow. The breakwater would protect the lagoon, and if it exploded up on the surface like this, it wouldn't do all that much damage underwater, the shock waves would be deflected. That was why the Sealife fuckers had moored it so deep, for maximum damage, maximum killing power.

Bastards.

Tom took the time to clear his mask. Swimming blind at night, that was nuts. Although no crazier, he supposed than doing a water tango with a ball of dynamite or whatever. Hell, if *that* hadn't stopped his heart, nothing would, right?

He adjusted the mask straps, gobbled the mouthpiece, and inhaled. Compressed air cooled his hot throat, just a tang of rust. Feeling fairly calm, considering, and quite proud of himself, he began to stroke his way back into the lagoon. Get his ass around that breakwater, the sooner the better.

He swam toward the dim lights on the shore of the lagoon. A large, strong human male equipped with an underwater lung and the mechanical advantage of flexible plastic power fins.

Which made him not quite as fast as the slowest fish in the sea.

Sally's hands were aching where she gripped the hacksaw. Left hand bleeding where the blade had slipped and she'd cut open the palm of her hand. Stinging with salt water. Let it hurt later, she was too busy for pain right now.

The cramp made her hand feel like an old claw, barely able to grip the handle. She forced herself to keep going, keep sawing, the blade had eaten deep into the hardened steel. Maybe three-eighths of an inch to go, how long could it take?

Tom out there in the dark. She'd heard him

splashing and grunting, caught a glimpse of the buoylike thing he was towing away. Crazy thing to do, why not just leave it alone, help her free Lois so they could all get away?

She hadn't told Tom about the leak in the boat—he was back under before she'd had the chance. The bilge pump going full blast. Sally didn't want to think about it now, all she could concentrate on was gripping the hacksaw, but she couldn't help but be aware that *Wild Child* was dangerously low in the water, low enough that the engine had cut out. The bilge pump still pissing away though, so maybe it would be okay, maybe the problem would solve itself.

And then, just like that, the blade snapped.

Sally screamed in frustration. Right below her the dolphin chattered, nudging at the backs of her legs. Bumping the bars again, as if to say, Come on, hurry up, let me out of here *now*.

"Be right back, girl. Promise."

That was when she discovered how hard it was to pull herself up onto the bow of the dive boat with a cramp in one hand and a deep cut in the other. Knees like jelly, where had it come from, this sudden weakness? Right, her body drenched with adrenaline for too long, the shakes were spreading.

Sally gripped the safety rail with her bleeding hand, make her way back toward the cockpit, the toolbox. Her mind fixed on the idea of finding a new hacksaw blade there. Had to be one, right? Tom would have seen to that. Good old Tom, Mr. Reliable when it came to tools and equipment—hell, when it came to *everything*.

She didn't at first notice the sluggish way *Wild Child* responded to her weight. Like a heavy drunk shifting in his sleep. Tons of water sloshing in the bilge, a sickening list. For a moment she thought the boat was going to sink right under her feet, just keep on going down as the water shifted inside.

It made her feel ill, sick to the bone to know that she had done this to *Wild Child*, so good to them all these years, but it was just another thing she didn't have the time or energy to think about.

Get a saw blade, that's what she had to concentrate on. Get a blade, free the dolphin. Couldn't think beyond that, it took way too much effort.

The water in the cockpit was ankle-deep. She felt the dread of it then, the inevitability of *Wild Child* sinking. Fairly shallow water here, they'd get her back up okay, but the *damage*, submerging that beautiful, expensive diesel that Tom treated like one of the family.

Don't think about it. Get the blade.

The toolbox was filled with water. She plunged her hands in, fingers clawing to find a blade, and of course she cut herself again, all those sharp tools in the box, and she knew it was impossible now, *never* find a thin little hacksaw blade in there. And dear God, as she crouched, the water was lapping at her butt, rising, she had to *hurry*, dammit.

Her hand closed on something solid. Iron bar. A heavy pry bar that took up most of the length of the box. She was startled by the piercing memory of Tom hunkered down over the engine, grinning as he held the pry bar aloft and saying, *Give me the right lever and I can move the world*, making a joke.

Sally dragged the pry bar out of the box, scattering tools, and splashed her way out of the cockpit. The boat rolled under her, the smallest change shifting a huge amount of water; hell, it was up to her knees now.

With the pry bar in hand, Sally jumped over the side, into the water. Astonished at how *heavy* the damn thing was, it wanted to drag her right to the bottom.

A strong, confident swimmer, she kicked and struggled, fighting her way to the dolphin cage.

Lois right there at the surface, eyeballing her through the bars. Looking surprised—what was this crazy human doing, struggling like that?

Hooking the pry bar on the cage, Sally hauled herself up. Pontoons teetered as she crouched and jammed the pry bar down until it caught on the padlock. She pulled back, yanking with all her weight, heels skidding.

Come on.

For the first time in her life she wished she carried about fifty more pounds, could really get some weight into this. The bar shifted and she grimaced, tugging, tugging. Couldn't see it there, under the black shiny water, but the lock felt like it might be bending. Just a damn smidgen of steel left, it *had* to give.

Under her the dolphin suddenly went nuts, slamming against the bars and crying out. My God, had she hurt Lois somehow? And then Sally heard a splash, the crash of a body slamming into the water, and she looked up and there he was, soaring into the air again, a leap of pure joy.

The male. Clark!

In her surprise Sally slipped and fell backwards, her hip slamming into the pry bar, and that did it, the padlock snapped open. Lying on the pontoon, she reached down into the water, pulled the broken padlock away, and with numb bleeding fingers lifted the latch.

The door blew open under her hands and Lois was free.

8

The Nightmare Alive

THE DOLPHIN SHOT right under Tom, coming out of nowhere and giving him the scare of his life. For just a millisecond he thought that the dolphin was an attacking shark, going for the soft meat of his belly, and then it went by and he recognized the familiar flukes.

Had to be Clark. So both animals were still alive. Amazing. Sally was going to flip out, she'd given up on recovering the male.

Relief gave him new strength and Tom began to kick harder, wanting to get back to the dive boat and Sally as soon as possible.

Something wrong again. Through the blurred dive mask the boat looked *tipped* somehow, the conning tower listing at an impossible angle. Tom shook his head, convinced he was disoriented, out of balance. But when he looked again, *Wild Child* was still listing severely and the relief turned to a clot of ice in his belly.

The boat was sinking.

No, impossible, got to stop it, got to *fix* it somehow. Tom snugged his teeth on the mouthpiece, pressed the mask firmly to his face, and dove. Kicking his way down.

Submerged below the boat he turned over, looked up. Surface of the water silvery dark above him and the underside of the dive boat even darker, a black mess.

He swam along the keel, feeling his way. Thinking, flashlight, where did I leave the flashlight? and then realizing it was right there, clipped to his waist, all he had to do was reach down and grab it.

One hand searching along the keel, skimming the glass-smooth surface for damage, the other trying to aim the flashlight. Not much to see, really, other than the very familiar bottom of a boat that he scrubbed every week, like clockwork. He watched his exhaust bubbles expanding, passing through the light, and *there*—his fingertips encountered something.

A flaw. A deep, jagged scrape in the gel coat. He followed it along, and that's how he found it, a softened depression where the fiberglass had been punched through. He could feel the pressure of water being sucked in. Hell, a hole not much bigger than the palm of his hand, no way was he going to let a little hole sink his beautiful *Wild Child*, drown his perfect diesel engine.

Tom ripped at his ragged T-shirt, pulling a piece of the fabric out from under his tank harness. He'd wedge the cloth into the hole and the pressure should hold it in place. Then get topside and bail like crazy, get the boat into shore somehow, let it founder there, where at least the engine wouldn't be submerged.

That was his plan, conceived in haste while he was upside down underwater, trying to plug a hole with a cotton T-shirt. Convinced it would all work out, that he could save the boat.

Tom didn't know that *Wild Child* was going down, actually sinking, until the keel struck bottom. In that same instant the back of his tank struck, his mouthpiece was jarred loose, and the whole hull shifted over, pressing its great dark weight against him.

Dark. A great weight pressing down, crushing the air from his lungs. He could not move. He could not breathe. The nightmare alive. His heart had stopped beating.

As *Wild Child* rolled over and sank, it took the dolphin cage with it, tied by a line to the bow. The yank up-ended Sally and she fell backwards into the water. She swallowed a lot of water, started choking, and became disoriented.

Blind panic for a moment, not knowing whether she was going up or down, and then something was nudging at her and her arms went out and wrapped themselves around a dolphin and she was being lifted up.

The surface, air. She gulped, filled her lungs.

Lois. Chattering and squeaking, telling her to be more careful.

Sally caught her breath, saw the conning tower canted over at an extreme angle, from where the boat had come to rest on the bottom. Oh God, their beautiful boat, Tom was going to kill her.

Tom. Tom? He should be back by now, giving her hell.

She screamed his name. No response. She began to swim around in circles, looking for the telltale exhaust bubbles, the reassuring sign that he was still down there.

Lois right beside her, as if worried that the frail human might do something foolish. And now there were two dolphins, Clark had joined them, he was speeding around and smashing his flukes, really making a lot of noise.

Like he was angry, ready to attack her. Was this possible?

Sally reached out, grabbed Lois by the dorsal fin, and hung on. Safe enough here, this was a game she and the female often played, carry the human. Sally screamed: "Tom! Tom-meeee!" at the top of her lungs, shouting until she choked, all that splashing from crazy Clark, didn't he understand that now she was looking for *her* mate, just as he'd been searching for Lois? Why didn't he *help*, why was he acting so wild, so panicked?

And then she knew. Knew it instinctively, as if Clark had spoken to her.

They were coming.

The maxis were coming and Clark was trying to warn them.

The Us shoot through the narrow opening, swimming as one. They know this place, know the shape and smell and feel of it. They fed here, grew here, learned to sing here. For almost all of their lives the lagoon was home.

The False Singers are in here now, the Fear Things, and they must be destroyed.

Eat the fear.

Eat the Fear Things.

He could feel the bottom muck oozing through the tank rack and against the backs of his legs as the hull pressed him down, down. A variation on the theme—there had been no muddy bottom in his dream, simply the weight of suffocation.

He wanted to scream but you can't scream underwater and he didn't have enough air to scream anyhow, he'd been exhaling when the mouthpiece was jarred from his mouth.

Go ahead, he thought, breathe the water. That will change the pain and you'll die that much quicker, why prolong the agony? But some stubborn part of him refused to inhale water.

Mouthpiece. Couldn't see a damn thing, can't move, no way to recover the mouthpiece. Drill all divers practiced, recovering the mouthpiece. What did you do? Reach behind your back, find the regulator, follow the hose to the mouthpiece.

He couldn't reach behind his back. Arms were pinned. Well, not quite pinned. He could move his hands a little. He was a bug squashed under a heavy glass, waving his wings.

The other mouthpiece.

That came out of nowhere, although in his head it sounded just a bit like Sally's voice, an echo in his memory. This was true, there was a spare mouthpiece attached to his buoyancy control vest, used to inflate the vest. A standard equipment safety device so that two divers could take air from the same tank.

Lower, near your waist.

Weird, like Sally was there talking to him, had to be his mind playing tricks. This was what happened when you died of oxygen deprivation, apparently. Very interesting. Remember to tell Sally about it, except you can't talk when you're dead.

Find the spare mouthpiece, you big jerk.

Fuck you, sweetheart, I'm dying. But his right hand was groping, trying to bend it enough to get near the vest, you couldn't argue with Sally when she was pissed off and she sure sounded pissed off, giving him a hard time when this situation wasn't his fault, how did he know the goddamn boat was going to try and kill him? Give a guy a break, honey, and let him expire in peace. Tell him it's okay to inhale the nice cool water, stop the burning pain.

His fingers closed on a small plastic thing. A

mouthpiece-feeling thing. Amazing. What would they think of next?

Get it up to your mouth, silly.

Who's a silly? I'm a silly? Don't you realize I practically have to dislocate my shoulder to get my hand up to my mouth in a position like this, a great big boat trying to grind me into a mucky bottom? Huh? Have a little consideration.

New pain, there in the shoulder. As if it didn't already hurt almost everywhere, now you expect me to try and make it worse? Hey, why not, let's really punish Tom for being a jerk, trying to save his boat.

Mouthpiece thing touching his chin. Fingers fishing the hose. Go on, take a bite.

His teeth encountered rubber. Hard to make his mouth work, hard to make anything work when your heart has stopped beating. Been so long since he took a breath he'd forgotten how to do it. Did you say *breathe* and your lungs obeyed, or was there some other trick he'd forgotten?

He inhaled. A couple of ounces of seawater came rushing in with the first lungful of compressed air. He choked and coughed and gagged, but he did not give up on the mouthpiece.

With a little oxygen inside him the darkness backed off and he realized that his heart was beating, *had* to be beating, had never stopped beating, that was in the dream and this wasn't the dream, this was really happening.

The hull was really trying to crush him. He had air now—God what a miracle it was to breathe again, it hurt but it hurt so good. Wouldn't last long, though. Couldn't be much air left in the tank, not after the exertion of freeing the explosive device and towing it out to the breakwater. Few precious minutes to compose his thoughts, and *really* regret the foolishness of trying to save a sinking boat.

Because he still couldn't move.

Wiggle his hands and feet, sure, but he was still pinned like a bug under glass. It didn't matter that his heart was beating. Soon enough, when the air ran out, it would stop.

The first thing Sally noticed was how pretty they looked. The glistening, scimitar curves of the dorsal fins cutting the water, coming into the lagoon. Like skaters on black ice.

Beneath her, Lois shivered, as if uncertain what to do. Clark? Where was the male? After all that warning noise he'd disappeared. Finding a place to hide, probably; he'd always been good at that.

The female was moving with purpose now, her tail pumping, carrying Sally toward the submerged boat. Of course, the conning tower! Get the weak human out of the water.

Sally was surprised at how little strength she had. Was this what fear did, drained your strength away? It was all she could do to wrap one arm around a rail, haul herself up until she was wedged in the tipped-over seat. Legs dangled down, almost touching the water.

If the things wanted her, they could take her. She was like bait on a hook, held just above the water.

Lois circled beneath her, tail flukes thrashing.

Sally screamed her husband's name until her throat was raw, until no sound came out.

It was hopeless. If he was out there in the lagoon the creatures had found him by now. They were whipping around, spray flying, very active. Were they feeding?

It was too horrible to think about.

Then, in the midst of all those big curved fins, a dolphin leaped. Clark. And rising out of the water behind him, a leaping shark. A huge thing, what terrible beauty. It made the dolphin look small in comparison, but the jaws snapping on empty air, unable to connect with the agile dolphin as it crashed back into the water.

The spray hit Sally, it was that close.

Something slapped her heel. A shark fin. She strained to lift her feet higher, but the creature wasn't after her, it was just racing by, the fin rising a yard or more out of the water.

Chasing Lois. Or maybe the female was chasing the shark, they were going so fast and the spray was flying so high she couldn't really see what was happening. Tails and flukes smashing the water, making it boil, and then another dolphin leaped clear of the water, soaring overhead, and this was definitely Lois.

A creature exploded out of the water behind the dolphin and soared over Sally's head. For one, electrifying instant it seemed suspended in midair. Sally could see its entire length, from sleek snout to the notch in the swept-back tail. She saw the silver-slitted eye, the sheathed lid winking down as it twisted in the air, snapping at where Lois had been the instant before.

The splash drenched her, and by the time she could see again the frenzy in the water had moved slightly away from her perch.

Sally felt something slick and oily as she cleared the hair away from her eyes. She lowered her hands and found them covered with a black fluid. Viscous and oily where she rubbed her fingers together. Not black, she realized, but dark red.

There was blood on the water. Lots of blood.

9

Shock Waves

THE CHASE BOAT won the race. A sea turtle race, really, because all three vessels had been coming in slow, keeping engine noise to a minimum. At the last possible moment Speke gunned the throttle, cut in front of the trawler, and took the lead position at the entrance to the breakwater.

Speke killed the engine, cocked an ear. "Hear all that splashing? They're in there, all right."

He left Lucy at the helm and went up on the forward deck with a pair of binoculars. Cursed himself for not thinking of infrared night goggles, really make it look like high noon in there. As it was, he could make out the plumes of water, see glimpses of flukes and dorsal fins. Oh, yes, the maxis were in there and they were raising hell.

He was startled by a dark shape in the binoculars. A form that didn't belong in the lagoon, hadn't been there a few hours ago. Looked like metal struts extending just above the water, what the hell was that thing?

Son of a bitch. He knew. That was a flying bridge or conning tower, tipped way over. There was a sunk boat in there, not far from where he'd moored the dolphin. Not far from the explosive charge.

A bump, rocking the chase boat. The trawler was coming alongside, rafting up. Speke glanced over, saw Mendez inside the lighted wheelhouse, pointing. He'd spotted the sunken boat.

"Doesn't matter!" Speke shouted. "They're in there!"

He hopped down into the cockpit and picked up the detonator. Size and heft of a walkie-talkie, with a short, flexible antenna.

Mendez was shouting something or other. Fuck him.

Speke aimed the detonator antenna at the lagoon, pushed the button sequence that armed the transmitter. Mendez still shouting for him to stop, what a crazy notion *that* was.

Then Lucy Savrin came out of nowhere and actually grabbed his hand. Right in his face, saying, "Robby says there's someone in there!"

Speke wrenched the detonator away. "He's seeing things. Pay no attention."

"But you can't just—"

He turned his back to her. Little bitch in her cute little shorts, what gave her the right to interfere? He'd seen something there, atop the canted conning tower, but he'd had the good sense to look away before he could really focus. Who could say if it was a person? Sorry, officer, it was too dark to tell.

And if there *was* someone in the lagoon they were trespassing. More to the point, anyone out of the water had a pretty good chance of surviving an underwater detonation, probably just get drenched.

Most of the force would be expelled down below, that was the idea.

Didn't matter. No time for a change of plans, they had the maxis where they wanted them and it was time to make them go away.

Lucy was actually grabbing him by the wrists. "You can't do this, don't you get it? You can't!"

Speke glared at her and then something inside him snapped and he kicked her. Lashed out and connected with her kneecap. Lucy made a soft whooping noise and went down, a stunned expression on her face. Trying to say something but no words were coming, she'd had the breath knocked out of her.

Robby Mendez was shouting from the trawler: "Vernon! Jesus Christ, man, put it down! I can see her in there, she's right over the charge. It's a woman and she's moving around, she's alive!"

Speke turned his back on Mendez. Fucker was trying to spook the deal here. Ruin it for everyone, they didn't successfully conclude this phase of the experiment. That Pentagon admiral wouldn't hesitate to pull the plug, get them all fired, banned from the profession.

Dr. Speke tucked the detonator under his arm, grabbed a safety rail, and leaped back up to the forward deck, where he could trigger the thing and no one could stop him.

Boat shoes slapping down on the deck behind him.

"Vern! Don't be crazy. We can shoot the things from here. Block off the channel so they can't get away." Mendez standing there, waving his one good arm. His face pinched and his eyes looking about a thousand years old. Pleading, he looked pitiful and tired.

Speke said, "You don't understand."

He jammed his thumb down on the detonator button.

* * *

The flash lit up the whole lagoon. Sally was so astonished that she didn't even attempt to shield her eyes. It was like someone had snapped a giant strobe light, frozen everything for just that instant. The flash was followed by a deep, air-quivering thud as the shock wave hit.

The force almost blew her out of the conning tower, like a huge hand shoving her backwards. An instant later there was another, smaller thud, and hot orange flames leaping into the sky.

The wave came last of all. A three-foot surge racing outward from the point of impact. She saw it coming, had time to weave her arms and legs into the metal rails of the tower and then it was on her, a wall of water smashing her backwards, pinning her against the rails.

The conning tower started to move.

Tom heard it as a flat noise way off in the distance. A slapping sound, as if something very large had smacked the water. Activities on the surface that didn't really concern him anymore. Running out of air concentrated the mind.

Suddenly he felt lighter, as if the great weight was being lifted away. He was fading, losing feeling as the scuba tank went hollow. But his hands, pressing against the hull, were rising, floating away from him. *The hull was shifting.*

He rolled over, yanking the scuba tank from the muck, and clawed his way along the bottom. Not thinking, just reacting. His legs were so weak that they almost refused to function, as if he was running in deep sand, not making any headway.

He looked up, saw the silvery black surface of the water. His hands tore at his waist, freeing the weight belt, and he began to rise. His strong heart beating fast, but beating, beating.

* * *

The Us were not Six now, they were Five. The Fear Things, small and incomprehensibly fast, had punched their hard beaks into the soft abdomen of one of the Six. Blood poured from the gill slits and the great shiver of death followed almost instantly.

The song of the Us turns into a scream of rage and fear.

Kill the Fear Things. Kill or be killed.

The explosion on the surface of the water does no more than confuse them momentarily. They swirl, all five that remain, snapping and leaping at the Fear Things.

The conning tower arced through the air as the boat shifted, tipping over on the opposite side, and when it came to an abrupt stop Sally was catapulted out of the chair into the water.

Slapped almost immediately by a thrashing tail, she didn't know whether it was a dolphin or a shark, it happened so quickly. Fins all around her, furious wet things bumping at the bottom of her feet. She wanted to scream, but she was all out of screams, she'd used them up.

She swam, wanting to fight her way back to the conning tower, the closest refuge. Found water that was calmer, free of fins and thrashing tails. Go for it, keep stroking, keep swimming, don't think about it.

Something rising under her, coming up fast. Feel the water move. All she could do, curl her toes, take a deep breath.

It exploded from the surface a few yards to her right, coming half out of the water. Gasping, sucking in air like it hadn't breathed in a thousand years.

"Tom!" She swam to him.

* * *

Robby Mendez regained consciousness when the water hit the back of his throat. Instinct made him kick out and helped him keep afloat. He gagged, cleared the salt water from his throat, and took a deep breath.

Boat wreckage all around him, he had no idea what had happened, but the chase boat was in pieces and the pieces were burning. Those big gasoline engines, all that fuel.

The trawler was still there, still intact. It had been pushed up against the breakwater, shoved aground by the force of the explosion. He could see figures scrambling ashore. Was that Lucy, crawling from rock to rock like a child who'd lost her way? He yelled, tried to attract their attention, but nobody seemed to hear him.

The *Squali*, Colson's boat, was still afloat, apparently undamaged. Mendez shouted, splashed, tried to attract Colson's attention. No response.

Alone, he decided, fend for yourself. He tried to clear the water from his eyes and discovered he was bleeding. Must be a scalp wound, he couldn't feel it, couldn't feel much of anything, not even the bite wound on his arm. And yet his arms and legs were functioning, he could move in the water.

Get to shore, fast.

He swam right into the thing in the water. A lumpish, flexible thing. To his horror, it moved, it was alive.

"Ahhhh!" it sputtered. "Ahhhhhhhh!"

Vernon Speke, his eyes white with shock. Barely moving, it was all Speke could do to keep his head above water. His long, spidery arms looked wrong, disjointed. He'd been badly busted up, bones broken.

Robby Mendez didn't know if he had the strength to get himself ashore, let alone a severely injured man. But he didn't think about it, he simply reached out and hooked his good hand around Speke's shirt collar and started to kick, swimming backwards, relying on his legs for propulsion.

"Ahhhhh!" Speke tried to tug himself away. Robby gripped the collar hard, pulled with all his might.

The shirt collar was ripped from his hands. Speke was being yanked under. Mendez, trying to kick out of the way, felt his foot connect with something large and powerful and alive.

"*AHHHHHHHH!*" Vernon Speke flew out of the water, blood foaming from his open mouth. Arms flapping crazily as the maxi thrashed, severing his body at the waist.

The crunch of bones was deafening.

Robby Mendez exploded away in panic, trying to kick himself right out of the water. He never saw the *Squali* until the boat was almost on top of him.

He screamed and flung up his hands, extending them to Wade Colson, who was leaning out, one hand on the wheel.

Wade ignored the outstretched hands and threw the grenade at the thrashing shark. The *Squali* glided right on by, Mendez pawing at the slippery sides and trying to scream, let Colson know he was there.

Robby Mendez never saw the grenade, and when the explosion came, rising from deep underneath to kill him, he thought, for just a single instant, that he was being lifted from the water.

10

Last Rites

IN THIS VERY place, at a time now only dimly remembered, the male dolphin was trained to kill human diver shapes. Again and again the mechanized dummies were towed before him and he was encouraged to strike their soft underbellies with his hard, bony beak. Success was rewarded by plentiful food, failure was punished by mild electrical shocks. And when the male finally rebelled, attacking his trainers instead of the dummies, he had been stunted away from all contact with humans or with other dolphins—except for the female Lois, who responded to his plaintive songs.

Now, in the bloodied waters of the lagoon, the male uses his never-quite-forgotten skills to attack the creatures who threaten the female. The brutal strength and cunning of *Isurus maximus* does not protect them from the superior speed and quickness of the dolphin.

Every inch of the male's body is alive to the resonance of movement in the dark waters. He can feel the maxis moving, anticipate the snap of jaws.

He accelerates, twisting his way through the thrashing tails, and slams his beak into the belly of a shark just as it turns to attack him. His beak pierces flesh, severing cartilage, crushing inner organs.

The male pulls his beak free just as another shark turns, jaws straining to reach the dolphin's tail fluke. Razor-sharp teeth rake his flukes, but he is gone before the jaws snap shut.

As he turns to attack again, the male sings, screaming his angry song. He wants to mute their dolphin-like sounds. Their song is a lie that must be destroyed, as they must be destroyed.

Clark is moving so fast now, his fury is so concentrated that he is no longer aware of his own fear. He writhes, twisting and turning, rolling up and then down, reacting instantly to every movement by the sharks, searching for a position of attack. Relying on instinct and the killing lessons he was taught in this very lagoon.

Strike. Avoid and strike. Keep moving, never pause, even for an instant.

At the same time he is aware that the female dolphin has joined him in song, that she too is feinting at the sharks, confusing them. This kinship gives him strength.

A shark charges out of the darkness, jaws gaping. Clark feints one way, then goes another, confusing the predator. He veers around and down, his fins touching bottom, and then surges suddenly upward. When he perceives a tender, unprotected flank he kicks his tail flukes and smashes his beak into flesh, feels the shark-shudder of a mortal blow.

The dolphin called Clark wrenches himself free of the bleeding flesh, shivers his way through the thrashing confusion of the panicked creatures, and turns to attack again.

He is relentless, unstoppable.

The Us are three.

Two more have been punctured by the sharp dolphin beak and their song has faded. They shiver in their dying throes, eyes unseeing, driving themselves into the bottom, into the eternal dark.

The three surviving maxis spread themselves out in the lagoon, trying to find a way to escape the Fear Things. But as they try to sing to each other, coordinating their defensive maneuvers, the Fear Things sing louder, in the same frequency, making it impossible to communicate or to shape the darkness of the lagoon.

Without their song, the Us are blind. They are running, alone in their blindness, snapping and tearing at whatever comes within reach of their extended jaws, when the shock wave of the underwater explosion slams into them.

The maxi who blindly devoured the Walking Other is itself instantly destroyed, internal organs compressed to jelly.

Thirty yards away another of the maxis floats to the surface, belly up.

Now the Us is one.

In sudden, terrible loneliness it swims in the white heat of fear-maddened rage, no longer trying to escape from the Fear Things.

There is room in its highly developed brain for only one thought: *Kill and die*.

The explosion stuns the male dolphin. As he shudders back to full consciousness, he senses terrible damage at his core, a crushing that makes him feel cold inside. The injury is beyond pain, beyond survival.

He must hurry. He must kill all of the creatures soon, before the icy numbness spreads.

Lois kept pushing at them, shoving them both into the shallow water at the edge of the lagoon. Even the concussion of the last explosion did not deter her. Tom and Sally felt the blast like a hammer blow, making their ears ring, their bones ache.

At some point Tom put his feet down and realized they were in about four feet of water. They could stand up, if need be.

Lois kept nudging, not satisfied.

"Let her," Sally said, sputtering as the flukes splashed them. "She'll be safer in shallow water, too. Maybe we can get her right up on shore. Any sign of Clark out there?"

"I can't see him," Tom said, searching the lagoon for the familiar dolphin fin. "Hope he wasn't too close to that blast."

Dawn was just about to break. The last explosion seemed to blow calm through the lagoon. Only minutes before, the water was alive with thrashing fins and tails and spumes of blood, and now it had gone suddenly still. The only sounds were a few low moans coming from the breakwater, a couple of survivors out there scrambling around on shore.

No birds, Tom was thinking as he slogged backwards, trying to appease the dolphin as he made his way toward shore. The birds were gone from this island, frightened off. And who could blame them?

Beside him Sally was stroking Lois just behind the dorsal fin. Sal was trembling, really starting to get the shakes, and Tom wanted to get her out of the water, wrap a blanket around her. Wrap a blanket around himself, for that matter. He felt like he'd clawed his way out of a damp grave. At the same time he felt strangely buoyant, almost giddy.

The air was still, the long night was nearly over, and they were both alive. No wonder he felt serene.

Sally said, "Do you feel something?"

Before Tom could respond, it exploded out of the water just behind Lois. Huge and terrible as it rose up over them, cutting off the dim light of dawn. A ton of teeth and fear-maddened muscle came crashing down, snapping at the dolphin.

The winglike stub of a lateral fin smashed the top of Tom's head, driving him down into the water. The tail bashed him sideways as the creature turned, trying to fasten its teeth on Lois.

The shark was crazed, there was barely enough water for it to swim in, let alone maneuver for a killing bite. The great, sleek head rose above Sally. The creature lashed down again, ignoring the human, concentrating on the dolphin below.

Lois was trapped under the weight of the shark's body, unable to wriggle away. Sally kept trying to get hold of her flukes, help her.

Tom stood up just in time to get clobbered by the thrashing tail again. As he went under, another creature shot by him.

Dolphin creature, going so fast the water seemed to stream off its body.

Clark slammed into the side of the maxi, just behind the gill slits. His beak was buried deep in shark flesh. Gills spurting blood, the shark arched in a terrible death frenzy, attempting to slam itself against both dolphins.

Sally grabbed a tail fluke and pulled—no idea which dolphin she had in her hands, it didn't matter—and the dolphin came free, slipped out from under the thrashing body of the shark.

Now the death throes were slower, more deliberate. Blood poured from the gills and the jaws. Sally was closest to the thing when it finally rolled over and died, and she thought she heard it scream. A weird, dolphin-like squeal of agony.

The gills quivered once and it was dead.

Out near the entrance of the lagoon Wade Colson was seeing if he could make himself famous. The big sucker that had chomped on Speke had been pretty well destroyed by the blast. The other, floating belly up, looked more or less untouched and this was the creature he wanted to bring into Vaca Cut and hoist up over his dock. Hell of a piece of advertising for a shark killer. Might even get him on TV like Jack Finley.

Hell, Finley hadn't even *killed* one of the things.

Wade tied a loop in a length of rope and slipped it over the tail. Biggest mako he'd ever seen, had to be all of two thousand pounds. Might be a record, he told himself, and then the notion made him smile because he doubted there was a record category for makos killed by grenade.

Record or no record, he hung this monster over the dock, it would make a powerful impression on potential customers. Might even scare a few away, and *that* would be okay, too.

Wade tightened the loop and then wrapped the end of the rope around the drum of a hydraulic winch. The rope tightened, started to wind around the drum, and the tail came up over the transom.

The creature was too big to get into the boat in one go. With the tail up tight to the starboard winch, Wade rigged another rope. Made the loop bigger this time. He was about to lean out over the transom and slip it over the head, winch up that end of the fish, when he thought: *Shit, skipper, you're forgetting something. Can't be too careful.*

Prudent man always gave a big shark one in the head, just to make sure. Wade rummaged through his munitions crate, found his old reliable, a 9mm

Ruger P85. Fifteen in the magazine, but this would only take one shot, he didn't want to spoil the head.

He carried the pistol back to the stern and leaned over, aiming with both hands. Pulled the trigger and pop! saw a small, neat hole appear in the flesh just behind the eye.

The shark woke up.

The bullet to the brain would kill it in another minute or so, but by then it would be too late for Wade Colson. He saw the gills quiver and knew his mistake—the damn thing was still alive—and was trying to back away when the head lunged straight at him.

Rows of teeth closed over his hand and chomped upward, dragging him into the jaws. He slammed up against the fish, wedged tight, his arm and most of his shoulder severed.

Wade found himself looking into the great silver eye of *Isurus maximus*, saw himself reflected there. Did the shark, he wondered, did the shark see it the same way? Itself reflected in a human eye?

He died before he could figure it out.

Sally was with Lois, urging the female to beach herself in the shallowest waters. No way, at that precise moment, to be sure all the maxis were dead. Lois was resisting, she kept twisting out of the water, squealing and bleating, looking for Clark.

It was Tom who found the male.

"Sal? He's over here, right on the beach. I think he's hurt bad."

Clark lay on his side, gasping. A little pink fluid oozed from his blowhole and he was having great difficulty breathing. Tom ran his hands over the dolphin's body, could not find any visible wounds, beyond a few fresh scratches in his tail flukes.

"He must have been a lot closer to the explosion

than we were," Sally said. "Got torn up inside. He's dying."

Lois nudged his tail and then backed off. The female was silent, waiting.

"I think she knows," Sally said. She stood up and stroked Clark gently. They waited with him as his breathing became more labored and shallow. His eyes closed.

There were footsteps behind them. Tom looked up and saw a young woman. Her clothing was seared and torn and she was limping badly. Her eyes were unnaturally bright and her teeth were chattering. On the verge of going into shock, from the look of her.

"M-m-mistake," she managed to say. "Mistake."

They waited for the dolphin to die before they came out of the water to help her.

Twelve Months Later

Tarpon Key

UNDER THE TIN-ROOFED eaves, the writer slumps at his desk. The cursor on the computer screen is blinking, waiting. It has been waiting for quite some time now as the writer searches for his last words. The final sentence that will sum up the entirety of the manuscript that rests, in a neat white stack, on the corner of his desk.

Thomas J. Hart sits there, staring at the screen and sweating bullets. He is not sweating from heat—the air conditioning keeps his little work area quite comfortable, thank you. He is sweating out words, the last words after nine months of almost continual immersion in the world of his first novel. Writing time stolen from a busy life, in the early hours before dive parties gather at the dock, demanding his attention. Time borrowed from warm evenings by the canal. Time given to him as a gift from his wife. And yes, time stolen wherever he can find it.

Regina Rhodes was at first disappointed to learn

that he was attempting a novel, rather than the non-fiction work she had envisioned him writing. Over the months, having read portions of the manuscript, she has come to understand his search for truth in the form of a story.

Her promise is like a light in the window: if he can't find a "proper" publisher, she'll print the book in *Reef Life* in installments or browbeat a mainstream editor into reading the thing, whatever it takes.

It is comforting to have someone like Reggie on his side, but nothing can happen until Tom finds the last few words. He is sitting back in his chair with his eyes closed, his mind stupefyingly blank, when a voice calls his name.

He gets up, throws open the loft window. A kiss of warm tropical air. Sally is standing by the edge of the canal, waving her arms.

"Come on, babe!" she cries, "it's time! She's ready!"

Oh, my God. He kicks on his boat shoes, slides down the ladder from the loft, and hurries outside. Sally rushes forward, gives him a quick hug. He can feel her heart beating, quick with excitement.

"Hurry," she says. "I want you there when it happens."

She turns from him, hurriedly dons her dive gear, and plunges into the canal. The dolphin circles the spot where Sally goes under, raising her beak and chattering. The dolphin appears to be agitated, nervous.

Wild Child is ready at the dock. Refitted, repainted, the engine rebuilt until it purrs like new. Tom throws off the lines and follows the dolphin and Sally out of the canal.

Sunset is less than an hour away and the water and the sky are exactly the same shade of translucent blue. Just a hint of burnt orange bleeding through, and air that smells of salt and palm fronds.

A few hundred yards from shore the dolphin stops swimming and waits for Sally to catch up. Tom kills the engine and drifts. Lois appears to be distressed. Her eyes are huge and she rolls from side to side, showing her flukes. She is both frightened and excited.

The dolphin Lois is about to give birth for the first time. Free-swimming dolphins form pods, swimming together as family units, and when one of them gives birth another female will often act as "aunt," helping to guide the newborn dolphin to the surface, for it must breathe air quickly or drown.

Although Lois has been hunting and feeding on her own for quite a while now, she has not yet bonded with a pod, and Sally is acting as midwife and aunt. Sally has been fretting for days about this, worried that Lois won't let her help, that she will try to do this thing on her own.

The fear is unfounded; Lois wants her there, demands it. After a few minutes of slow circling, the dolphin dives. Sally lifts her hand, waves to Tom, and then follows Lois down.

Tom paces the length of the cockpit, watching the air bubbles. He can see them in the water, the dolphin shape and the Sally shape. Hard, at times, to distinguish one from the other. Both of them turning, rolling, the bubbles blurring their shapes.

It happens very quickly, much faster than he's anticipated. Lois surfaces first, expelling a great spout of mist. The dolphin swims in tight circles, agitated, until Sally's head breaks the surface.

In her arms, writhing and wiggling, is a newborn dolphin. Sally holds it up, making sure the blowhole is clear of the water, and Tom can hear it, a bright whistling sound as the dolphin inhales for the first time.

A moment later the newborn is nursing, taking rich, life-giving nutrients from its mother. And now

Sally leaves mother and child and swims to the boat, her mask up on her forehead, and Tom sees her eyes beaming at him and suddenly he knows that the last line of the book will be this:

The world is strange and full of wonder.